HEAVEN HAS NO RAGE

HEAVEN HAS NO RAGE

A Laurel Highlands Mystery

Liz Milliron

Copyright Page

Heaven Has No Rage
A Laurel Highlands Mystery

First Edition, First Printing | 2019

Level Best Books
www.levelbestbooks.com

Cover & Interior Design: Shawn Reilly Simmons
Author Photo: Erin McClain Studio

This is a work of fiction. Any references to historical events, real people, or real locales are used fictitiously. Other names, characters, places, and incidents are the product of the author's imagination, and any resemblance to actual events or locales or persons, living or dead, is entirely coincidental.

Trade Paperback ISBN: 978-1-947915-12-1
Also Available in e-book

Printed in the United States of America

PRAISE FOR THE LAUREL HIGHLANDS MYSTERIES

"Obsession, betrayal, and greed conspire to create surprising twists and breath-stealing suspense in this riveting page-turner." ~ **Kathy Valenti**, author of the Maggie O'Malley Mystery Series

"With visually descriptive narrative, the author knows how to tell a story with engaging dialogue and an action-filled tale that never let go until the very end. This well-written drama reached a feverish pitch as the story came to its conclusion. I was holding my breath as I watched it play out. Well done. I enjoyed this book and I look forward to more adventures with Jim, Sally and the gang in this terrific series." ~ **Dru Ann Love**, Dru's Book Musings

"Big city crime encroaches on the lush backdrop of Pennsylvania's rustic Laurel Highlands in this tense and gritty debut. Liz Milliron has crafted a tightly written, heart-pounding tale of suspense that will keep you on the edge of your seat from page one until its explosive conclusion." – **Annette Dashofy**, *USA Today* bestselling author of the Zoe Chambers Mystery Series

"Lawyers, guns and money; Root of All Evil is a true page-turner." – **Bruce Robert Coffin**, bestselling author of the Detective Byron Mysteries

THE LAUREL HIGHLANDS MYSTERIES

Root of All Evil (A Laurel Highlands Mystery 1)

Heaven Has No Rage (A Laurel Highlands Mystery 2)

To Paul, who believed in me from the start.

CHAPTER ONE

The wheels of the marked Ford police cruiser crunched on the snow-covered gravel. State Trooper Jim Duncan gazed through the windshield at the snow-globe night. The flakes, big and fluffy, would leave at least two feet of new powder by morning. But they weren't thick enough to obscure the cause of the call. One of the units at the Winding Valley ski resort looked more like a funeral pyre than a faux Swiss chalet.

Don Lassiter, his partner on the midnight shift, opened the driver side door, letting in a blast of frigid air. "You go find out what's happening," he said. "I'll take traffic detail." He hurried off before Duncan could object.

Duncan sighed and tugged on his gloves. Traffic detail. If Lassiter saw four cars over the next six hours, it would be a miracle. Then again, Lassiter was a year away from retirement. He'd earned the easy duty. Also, he'd be freezing his ass off while Duncan stayed warm, or at least warmer, moving around.

He exited the Ford. He'd definitely be warm. A wall of heat pressed against him, even from fifty feet away. The flames licked at the sky and sparks flew in every direction. A thick plume of smoke swirled upward, melting every snowflake that dared get near it and tainting the crisp, dry winter night air. But it wasn't the clean wood smoke scent of the bonfires of his high school days or even from his fireplace at home. This smoke was greasy, heavy with all the chemical odors associated with a burning building. The nearby cabins had wood shingles, white gingerbread trim, and black roofing. Exactly what American vacationers thought a Swiss ski lodge looked like. The quaint exteriors probably contrasted with the luxury interiors. Tourists who came for skiing or winter recreation in the Laurel Highlands didn't want *rustic* in anything but appearance.

Duncan recognized Adam Carlton, the county fire marshal, standing off to the side and walked over. "Anyone in there?" he asked.

Carlton shrugged massive shoulders inside his heavy jacket. "Manager said the cabin is rented." He jerked his thumb in the direction of a dark gray Mercedes. "Fire's going pretty good, but nobody's been seen. As soon as they get it under control, I'll be able to get in and take a look."

The fire crew extinguished the blaze by five o'clock and Carlton started his investigation. The discovery of a charred body necessitated a call to the coroner's office. A few members of the fire crew stayed behind to make sure the scene was securely roped off.

Before he went to interview the manager, Duncan checked in with Carlton. "What's your first impression?" Duncan asked. "Accident or arson?"

"Not an accident. I've seen enough that I'm suspicious. Come take a look."

"I saw the coroner's wagon is already here."

"Yeah, deputy coroner's checking the body out. What's left, that is." Carlton shook his head. They entered the cabin. Duncan gagged at the smell of overcooked human flesh, combined with burnt wood, and the unmistakable whiff of gasoline. He hadn't eaten anything in hours, but the scent of fire destruction and burnt flesh made him want to empty his stomach.

His shoes squelched water from the carpet. There was

enough residual heat in the air that it hadn't frozen despite the sub-zero temps. The wallpaper had peeled away from the combination of flames and water. Furniture showed various levels of burn damage, but the smoke and water ensured everything was destined for the dump. The fire crew had done a thorough job.

Deputy Coroner Tom Burns bent over a charred figure on the floor, a few feet from the bed. He looked up briefly and nodded to Carlton. "I've heard fire pits are the big thing these days. I think this one goes to the extreme, though."

Duncan shook his head. "Knock it off, Burns."

"Why?"

"It's too early for that shit." Duncan moved to the center of the scene.

Burns shook his head. "Aren't you a cranky-pants. Where's your sense of humor, Duncan?"

"I am not cranky," Duncan said.

"Wrong, you're definitely cranky," Carlton said from the corner, where he crouched to examine a particularly black spot.

"I don't like third shift," Duncan said, wiping sweat from his forehead. The air was hotter than a grill, contrasting sharply with the night outside. "My least favorite for a reason. It'll take three days for me to get my sleep schedule back on track."

"You volunteered," Carlton said, still focused on the corner.

True enough. Duncan'd been glad to join with the other singles at the barracks to keep McCloskey on the day shift while he waited for the birth of his first child. Duncan hoped the kid would make an appearance soon.

"Operation Baby-Watch," Burns said and pushed back his glasses.

"Can we just talk about the scene, with a minimum of the usual mordant humor, both out of respect for the victim, and the fact it's oh-dark-thirty and most normal people are rightfully asleep?" Duncan said, taking his own visual inventory of the space. Single room. A queen-sized bed occupied one corner, a small nightstand with a lamp next to it. A sitting area with a charred, overstuffed chair and love seat graced the other side of the twenty-by-twenty-foot space. A kitchenette with a sink, fridge, and microwave was located in the back corner. Duncan assumed the door near the bed led to a bathroom. The thick, waterlogged carpet covered the entire floor, except for soot-streaked hardwood in the kitchenette. Everything one or two people needed for a weekend ski trip.

"Okay, there's an ashtray on the bed, butt next to it." Carlton said, pointing to the heavy glass dish in the middle of the bed. The mattress and box spring were soaked. The tan bed-spread and exposed edges of the mattress were heavily charred, but otherwise intact. "We are supposed to think that the occupant left a lit cigarette on the bedspread, setting the blaze. There are a few problems with that scenario."

"Such as?"

"Night office clerk reported the fire at two-twenty-three," Carlton said, consulting his notes. "For it to be blazing like it was when we showed up, that cigarette would have to have been there hours earlier."

"Maybe he fell asleep."

"Bed's still made. And the victim is on the floor. Even if that was the case, somebody should have smelled something long before the place went up like a Viking funeral pyre."

Duncan noted the heavy damage on the bottom of the mattress. "Looks like it burned up, not down. If the cigarette had started things, it would be opposite."

Carlton nodded. "Observant. That's what I like about you." He pointed at the corner he'd been inspecting. "Heaviest damage is there. Looking at the burn pattern, I think that's the point of origin. A corner away from the bed."

"The firebug started it there and left the ashtray for distraction."

Carlton sighed and knelt to examine the floor. "Why do

people assume we're stupid?"

"Too many idiotic TV shows." Duncan wiped his forehead again. "Accelerant?"

"It's preliminary, but I think gasoline. Very combustible. Starts fast, burns quick." Carlton stood.

Duncan's nose hadn't lied to him. "Million-dollar question." Duncan looked over at Burns. "Dead or alive when the fire started?"

Carlton pointed at the deputy coroner. "Ask him. My job is cause of the fire. But if I were a betting man, which I'm not…"

"Exactly. Why burn the building if you don't have something to hide?"

Carlton stood and zipped his jacket. "Except fire doesn't destroy evidence. All the water and the boots might, though."

"That's why we call you the evidence-destruction crew."

"I'll be in touch once I've got the analysis on the accelerant."

"Thanks." Duncan glanced over where Burns was still working over the charred body. He'd come back to get the scoop, but Carlton's assessment didn't bode well for a natural death.

✳ ✳ ✳

Duncan exited the fire-ravaged building, breathing deeply to rid his nose of the burnt body smell. Snow continued to swirl. He'd gone from the fires of Hell to the top of Mount Everest and swore icicles formed in his nostrils as he inhaled.

The building marked *Office* looked like a larger version of the cabins. Spotting a man in a down jacket by the door, Duncan walked over. "Evening. Well, technically morning. You the manager?"

"That's me." The man had a medium build, a few inches shorter than Duncan. Close-cropped dark hair peeked out from under a newsboy cap. Dark eyes surveyed the scene, the cold enough to lend a blush to his pale brown skin.

"This can't be good for business," Duncan said, taking out his notepad. "What's your name?"

"Maurice Thompson." He sighed. "Not good at all. And we had a promising Valentine's weekend earlier this month. Shit."

"Address and phone number?"

Thompson rattled off an address in Farmington, not far from the resort.

"Were you here when the fire broke out?"

"No." Thompson wiped melted snow from his face. "I'm generally only here during the day. I don't have a night manager. One of my senior staff works overnight in case of emergencies. Gail Woodbury. She's in the office."

"I'll need to talk to her before she leaves. The cabin was rented to whom?"

"Ray Capshaw. I pulled his name and address from the registration." Thompson handed over a sheet of paper. "That's his car over there." He pointed to the Mercedes.

Duncan noted the license plate. "When did he arrive?"

"Earlier today. Well, yesterday. About three-ish? Vicky Hanson, she's the daytime clerk, would know for sure."

"Alone?"

"As far as I know, yes." Thompson stared at the wrecked cabin, flakes of snow dotting his shoulders before disappearing. "Was it an accident?"

"We can't say yet." Duncan made a few more notes. "Did you see Mr. Capshaw after he checked in?"

"Not that I remember. He didn't order room service. He might have left to eat. Or not."

Duncan blew snow from his notes. "I assume he used a credit card to secure the rental."

Thompson pointed at the paper. "Visa. It's in Capshaw's name. There's a copy of his driver's license, too. The signatures all match."

The man had been thinking. "Anybody visit him? Capshaw?"

"I didn't see anyone. Then again, I wasn't paying attention." Thompson stared past the trooper as if not quite comprehending what had happened.

Burns approached. Water from melted snowflakes dotted his glasses. "Trooper Duncan. You have a problem."

Duncan didn't look at his friend, but continued to write. "Be with you in a second, Burns. I think Mr. Thompson has more to worry about."

"You're not listening. You have a problem," Burns said.

Burns's tone of voice, on top of the way he emphasized *you* and *problem*, made Duncan look up into Burns's unnaturally serious face. "You're going to complicate my life, aren't you?"

Burns cracked a grin and slapped him on the shoulder. "How would you know I love you if I didn't?"

Duncan sighed. "Mr. Thompson, would you stick around for a minute please?" he asked. "Tell Ms. Woodbury I need to speak to her. And get me a phone number for Ms. Hanson." An eventful shift kept him on his toes, but the overnight shouldn't be this eventful. He turned to Burns. "Show me."

Burns led him back to the fire scene and the charred body. He crouched down. "Meet John." He wiped water from his eyeglass lenses with his sleeve.

"When did you get glasses?" Duncan asked, his attention momentarily diverted.

"When I was seven." Burns looked up. "Pay attention. Male, extensive burns, but there's enough undamaged skin to tell me he was Caucasian. Age unknown."

"Room is registered to Ray Capshaw, Caucasian, forty-five. From Pittsburgh. Adam Carlton already told me there are problems with the scene."

"And with John."

Great. "If the guy's name is Ray, why are you calling him John?"

"John, as in John Doe. I found no identification on the body. Until I get more than a hotel registration, he's John Doe to me. And he should be to you, too. Don't let the early hour lead you to get sloppy."

"I told you not to be a smart ass. What's the cause of death?"

"Could be smoke inhalation. Won't know until we crack him open. Could be he had a heart attack before the fire started."

Duncan had been on the verge of thinking of breakfast, but the return of the charred barbecue smell banished any desire for food. "I'm not seeing the problem."

"Right here." Burns waved him down.

Duncan crouched and peered at the spot on the victim's throat where Burns pointed.

"That mark, right there." Burns pushed up his glasses. "Gah. I hate wearing these things to work."

Duncan squinted. The skin on the victim's face and neck was severely burned, but where the charred flesh ended he could just make out a red band stretching around his neck. "That looks like—"

"A ligature mark."

"Ligature. Like strangled?" *Arson and murder. Shit.*

Burns nodded and pushed up his glasses again. "Not sure with what, but nothing thin like wire or fishing line. The mark is too wide. Maybe a curtain tieback or a necktie. I'll have a look in better light, but I think it's wrong for an electrical cord." Burns sat back.

"Could he have committed suicide?" *But then who started the fire?*

Burns took off his glasses, removed a paper towel from his pocket, and wiped water off his lenses again. "You can't strangle yourself. And it's not a hanging. Line is straight behind the neck, not in an upwards V. Someone stood behind him and choked him."

So much for suicide. "He was strangled, then someone

set the fire to try and hide it," Duncan said.

Burns blew an invisible speck from his lenses and put the glasses back on. "Or he was choked into unconsciousness, someone started the fire, and he died of smoke inhalation while unconscious. The question is if there is smoke in the lungs or other inhaled debris. I doubt we'll find a fractured hyoid. That would indicate manual strangulation and external signs point to ligature."

"Wouldn't both fracture the bone?"

"No. Pressure from a ligature strangulation is usually even and the hyoid is rarely broken. The point is, before he was barbecued, someone at least choked him into unconsciousness. Which means—"

"Suspicious death, possibly homicide." Duncan rubbed his face. "Why do you do this to me?"

"I don't do anything to you. I'm just here when it happens." Burns nudged Duncan's shoulder. "You could always hand this over to the Criminal Investigation division."

"You know I don't do that. I caught the call." He jerked his thumb toward the door. "Although Lassiter will probably suggest we do just that."

Burns chuckled. "Then blame your sense of responsibility, which sounds like it has 'roid-rage. Not me."

Duncan bit back a retort.

"But don't worry," Burns continued. "Mr. Doe and I will become good friends. I'll get you time, manner, and cause of death."

Duncan stood, the scent of charred flesh finally overpowering. "Better you than me. This reeks."

Burns reached for the body bag. "I've got the easy part."

"How so?"

"I just figure out the science." Burns unzipped the bag. "You've got cleanup duty."

Duncan watched as his friend maneuvered the corpse into the bag. "When is the autopsy?"

"We've got three scheduled for today already. We might

not get to John here until tomorrow, probably around eight or nine. Meaning Monday." Burns zipped the bag.

"Got it."

"You sure? These early morning incidents can confuse the meaning of *tomorrow*."

"Geez, I've got it."

"Be there or be square."

"I'll try. I've been tapped for security for the Ohiopyle Winterfest this afternoon."

"Fun-wow. If you don't make it, call for the preliminary." Burns went for a gurney.

Duncan walked back to Thompson. He still had to interview the night desk clerk and talk to Vicky Hanson. And sleep. And work the festival. Hopefully Lassiter would abandon the deserted traffic detail and pick up some of the interviews.

Third shift could be stultifying and Duncan had hoped for just enough action to keep him from falling asleep. Wasn't there some proverb or curse about getting what you asked for? Next time, he'd ask for the most boring third-shift possible.

CHAPTER TWO

Sally Castle's breath hung before her like a cloud. Monday brought more cold, the county gripped in a late-February freeze. Nobody had sent the memo to the environmental control folks at the Fayette County courthouse. Odds were good the interior of the public defender's office would be frosty as well. She swore they hadn't programmed the heat to kick on until nine. Environmental Control always seemed to forget people worked Monday mornings.

Her watch said eight-thirty, but running behind schedule didn't stop her from brewing a pot of coffee and swinging by the local bakery for a breakfast sandwich. She had to make time for grocery shopping. Fortunately, she didn't have anything on her calendar until ten, when she had to present a plea agreement in court. There would be time to eat breakfast and put the final touches on the paperwork. Maybe review a couple more proposals and make counter-proposals as necessary.

As she hurried through the front door of the courthouse, the crash of boxes made her stop and look left. A wheeled cart was on its side, FedEx packages scattered across the floor. "Benjamin, let me help you," she said, reaching for one near her after setting down her briefcase and switching her coffee cup to her other hand.

The delivery man faced her, arms full of envelopes and boxes. "Thanks, Ms. Castle. Damn snow. I think a rock or something is lodged in the wheels. The cart stopped rolling and...

here's the result." He stacked items on the cart.

"You should invest in a sled," Sally said.

"No kidding." He took the boxes from Sally.

Another courthouse employee jogged over. "Benjy. You mind taking this now? I'm late for an appointment." He held out a box wrapped in at least half a roll of packing tape.

Benjamin accepted the package and scanned it.

"Thanks. You're the man, Benjy. See ya." The employee headed for the stairs, forgoing the elevator.

A scowl replaced Benjamin's professional smile. "My name is Benjamin." He tossed the box onto the cart.

"Maybe he's just trying to be friendly," Sally said and placed the last box on the cart.

"I hate all those nicknames. They make me sound like a little kid. Or a dog. You're the only person who gets it right, Ms. Castle." He laid the scanner on the top box.

Sally started to reply, but a familiar male voice interrupted her. "Sally Castle. My God, is that you?"

Benjamin forgotten, she turned toward the speaker. "Mark. Uh...hi." Talk about a blast from the past. She hadn't seen Mark Framingham since before she'd left Allegheny County, but she remembered their painful dates. "I haven't seen you in ages." Behind her, Benjamin muttered something, but she focused on Mark.

He brushed his bangs from his forehead. He had the same floppy brown hair and boyish face he'd had when they'd dated. "I left Pennsylvania for a while. Moved back from Phoenix about six months ago."

"You left Phoenix for this?" She waved at the falling snow and the icicles adorning the windows.

He chuckled. "Believe it or not, I missed it. What's it been, five years? You still with the DA's office?"

"Public defense," Sally said as she picked up her case and took a sip of her coffee. It had cooled quite a bit, but she could warm it in the office microwave. "You?"

"Still in property law. You know me. I wasn't cut out for

trial work." He didn't offer to relieve her of briefcase, coffee, or sandwich bag. "Say, you busy? We should get together. Catch up. We can talk differences in law practice. I have great pictures from my time in Arizona. The mountains, wow. Very different from here, really breathtaking."

"That would be great, but I can't. I have plea agreements and sentence recommendations to prep. Everybody thinks criminal law is glamorous. If they only knew." And by the time Mark decided on a place to eat, she'd have missed all her afternoon appointments.

"Not everything can be *Law & Order*," Mark said, with a grin. "Come on, half an hour for an old friend? We can get something quick. Maybe a burger. Or Chinese. Or Indian, are there any Indian places around?"

He hadn't changed. A person should be able to come right out and say what he wanted. None of this wishy-washy nonsense. "I really can't. Sorry. Maybe some other time."

"My loss." Mark put his hands in his pockets. "You going to the annual charity dinner? I see they're still holding it."

"Oh, uh, yes. You?"

"Yeah, I figured it would be a good way to reintroduce myself to the legal community. Maybe we can go together."

The lie slipped out. "I already have a date, sorry."

He shrugged. "Then I'll see you there. Later."

"See you." She breathed a sigh of relief as he turned. She didn't want to hurt his feelings. But she also didn't want to go out with him.

Sally didn't linger to watch him walk away. Benjamin had left at some point, so she went to her office, greeting the secretary, Doris, on the way. She pushed aside a niggling guilt. She should have simply told Mark she wasn't interested in having lunch or going to the event with him. But that seemed rude. Much better to let him down easy. Use work and a prior date as an excuse. Even a fictional date.

She sorted through the papers on the surface of her desk when a knock sounded on her door. Bryan Gerrity, her boss, stood in the doorway. "Happy Monday," he said. "Nice week-end?"

"Yeah. Went to Winterfest with my sister. You?"

"Tolerable. You set for the day?"

"Yes, although I see the county's newest assistant district attorney is asking for another meeting on the plea I submitted last week."

"I didn't think it was that complicated a case."

"It's not. And it's a good deal. It seems like after the mess last fall, every plea requires fifteen meetings and three weeks of deliberation." She sipped her coffee.

Bryan shrugged. "They're being cautious. We all got a black eye in that fiasco. Murder, corruption, doesn't get worse."

"I suppose." She set her coffee cup out of harm's way and kept sorting through files. Bryan didn't move and Sally could feel the heavy weight of his gaze. She stopped and stared at him. "Is there anything else? There must be, you wouldn't be standing here otherwise."

"I was just wondering if you were okay. You've pretty much buried yourself in work these last few months. You rarely go out with the gang anymore."

She averted her eyes. "I'm busy, that's all."

"You still seeing that guy, the cop?"

"He's busy, too. After all, it's barely past the holidays." She kept her focus firmly on the paper in front of her. She was busy. And so was Jim Duncan. That's all Bryan needed to hear.

"You call the end of February *barely past*?"

Sally paged through the papers, not even registering the contents.

"You're making excuses. What's wrong?" Bryan sat in the metal and vinyl chair she kept for visitors and leaned forward. "You won't look at me, either. Something's up."

"Nothing's up." She forced herself to look Bryan square in the eye. If she unloaded the turmoil in her heart over Jim and what happened last fall, Bryan, as a guy, would tell her to get over herself. Like it was that easy. "If you hadn't noticed, we're short-staffed. As you said, we all took a hit in that shit storm. I'm still crawling out from under all the cases Colin left behind and they haven't stopped coming. Instead of worrying about my personal life, you'd be better off hiring another assistant defender."

Bryan said nothing, but his raised eyebrows told Sally he didn't buy the argument. At least not all of it. "If you say so. Speaking of hiring, you look at those resumés I gave you?"

"I did." Relieved the conversation had turned back to business, she pulled the resumés from under a pile of folders. "I put them in order of preference. The one on top doesn't have the strongest professional credentials, but I think she has passion. That takes you a long way in this field. If Colin had had more passion—"

"He might not have ended up like he did. Right." Bryan took the papers. "I'll get out of your hair. You need any help convincing the new ADA, holler." He left, shutting the door behind him.

Sally closed her eyes and leaned her head on her desk surface. She'd barely talked to Jim since October. They *were* busy. It *had* been the holidays. Not that she'd made much of an effort to connect. Then again, neither had he. If that didn't send a message about how he felt, Sally wasn't sure what did. Okay, there had been a brief visit on New Year's Eve, but had he come because he wanted to or because he felt bad for her? She didn't know, but one thing was certain. Unlike Mark Framingham, Jim Duncan was anything but wishy-washy when it came to what he wanted.

CHAPTER THREE

On Sunday, before he headed to Winterfest, Duncan called the county coroner's office. They confirmed the autopsy on the fire victim would be later that day. He had planned to attend the autopsy, but his body called it quits. Tomorrow, he'd call Burns tomorrow.

On Monday, after first shift roll call, he saw fellow trooper Aislyn McAllister. "You look like hell, Boss," she said.

"Third shift followed by special security duty will do that." He didn't bother to correct McAllister's use of the word "boss." He'd been her FTO last fall. Despite the fact they were now equals, she persisted in calling him "boss."

"You catch that fire at Winding Valley in the wee hours of Sunday morning?"

"Yep."

"Heard there was a victim."

"There was."

"When's the autopsy?"

"Yesterday. I need to call Burns at the coroner's office for the preliminary report." He downed the rest of his coffee and headed for the pot. He didn't much like barracks brew, but his situation felt desperate.

"Tell Tom I said hi." McAllister sauntered off, sipping from her ever-present bottle of Mountain Dew.

He watched her go. Tom?

A call confirmed Burns was in, but not able to come to the phone. With nothing specific to do, Duncan drove to

Uniontown. He found Burns, this time sans glasses, in the morgue slurping from an oversized fast-food drink cup and listening to music at a volume that set Duncan's teeth rattling.

Catching sight of him, Burns adjusted the speakers. "Where were you yesterday?"

Duncan pointed at the cup. "You know it's eight in the morning, right?"

"You like hot water poured over the burnt and crushed beans of a plant. I like caffeinated sugar water." Burns took another drink. "Differences make the world go 'round."

"Whatever. McAllister says hi."

"Does she now?" Burns winked. "Tell her I say hi right back."

"What am I, Western Union?" Duncan knew Burns had a thing for McAllister from when they'd met last fall. He'd not been under the impression the feeling was mutual. "Something going on between you two?"

"None of your business, Dad," Burns said, setting aside his cup. "Thought you were going to be at the autopsy for Mr. Doe."

"I fell asleep."

"Too old for the all-nighter, huh?"

Duncan ignored the question. "We're still calling him John Doe?"

Burns picked up a folder. "Yup."

"Ray Capshaw rented the cabin. Showed his license and credit card. Confirmation from the receptionist. What more do you want?"

"A positive ID. Build and height are right. Blood types match. No usable fingerprints. We're waiting for dental records to confirm. Until then, he's John Doe."

Ray Capshaw was married. Police in Pittsburgh visited his home, and Mrs. Capshaw insisted her husband was at his hunting cabin near Punxsutawney. The cabin did not have a phone and the area had unreliable cell service. She wasn't alarmed when she didn't hear from him for a few days. Duncan asked troopers out near Punxy to check, but they reported the cabin was completely snowed in. Unless Capshaw was wanted for a major crime, they didn't have the manpower to clear the road.

"What did you find?" Duncan asked.

"I know you don't like the boring parts, so I'll skip those," Burns said, reading. "As I suspected. Larynx was severely bruised, although not crushed, and the hyoid bone not fractured. Significant bruising on the neck, consistent with strangulation with a soft object like a necktie."

"Smoke in the lungs?" Duncan asked, but suspected he knew the answer.

"Negative. He wasn't breathing when the fire started." Burns snapped the folder shut. "Cause of death, asphyxiation by strangulation. Manner of death, homicide by person, or persons, unknown."

"Shit." *Boring shifts, wish for boring shifts.* "The burns?"

"Significant. The arsonist probably splashed accelerant on the body, hoping it would go up with the cabin. But all it did was prevent visual identification. It's harder to burn a body than people think." Burns slurped again from his cup.

Duncan closed his eyes. "Time of death?"

"Fire makes it tricky. Negligible stomach contents, he hadn't eaten recently. Most of the burns were on the front of the body. Based on lividity of the skin on his back, he'd been lying there for maybe two hours?" Burns set aside his folder.

The call came in around two-twenty. Gasoline would start the fire quickly and the building wasn't totally destroyed. That gave him a window between midnight and one. "Could it be less?" he asked Burns.

The younger man thought. "Yeah. Lividity maxes out at eight to twelve hours. This was way less than that."

"In other words—"

"Death within a couple hours of the fire. Probably."

When Duncan interviewed the night clerk at Winding Valley, she said she saw headlights, but hadn't noticed any particular cars. He'd check the CCTV footage from the parking lot. See if anyone pulled up to Ray Capshaw's cabin around midnight. "Thanks. Call me when the dental records come in." He picked up his hat.

"You got it. You'll tell Ace I said hi?"

"Ace? When did you start calling her that?"

Burns gave him a lopsided grin. "Its a nickname I came up with. To be honest, I haven't used it yet. Let me know how it goes."

"Oh no. You first."

"Don't tell me you're afraid of her. You've got more than eight inches and at least fifty pounds on her. If not more."

"No. That nickname is all yours." Ace? Not in a million years. Duncan headed out the door. Maybe Adam Carlton had more information on the fire scene by now.

✳ ✳ ✳

Sally read the first paragraph of the proposed agreement for the fourth time. For the fourth time, it dissolved into black smears on the page. The new ADA, concerned with covering all the bases, turned everything into a quagmire of legalese. Maybe she should ask Bryan to have a chat with the district attorney. Tell him to have his assistants dial back the flowery language.

She squeezed her eyes shut and opened them, trying again to read the proposed sentencing agreement. This time, the intercom buzzed.

"Sally, there's someone here to see you," Doris said.

"Who?" She wasn't expecting a visitor.

"A woman. She says her name is Rhonda Naif and she's an acquaintance of yours."

It took a moment to place the name. Rhonda Naif, formerly Rhonda Jacobs. She'd worked for the Indiana County DA's office before she married. She and Sally struck up a friendship since there weren't many women in prosecution. What was her husband's name? Steve. Sally had been at their wedding. She hadn't seen Rhonda in several years and couldn't think of any reason Rhonda would come to see her now. "Sure, send her back," she said to Doris.

A minute later, Rhonda stood in her doorway. Sally's first thought was that the woman wasn't aging well. Rhonda looked to be in her mid-forties, not mid-thirties. She wore a full-length fur coat and diamond earrings. Perfectly manicured nails on her slender hands and hair a shade of strawberry-blonde that had to come from a salon. Her forehead and the skin around her eyes had the plastic look Sally associated with Botox injections.

"Sally Castle. It's been a long time," Rhonda said. Her voice had not changed, still a silky alto that could lull a jury.

"Rhonda, come in. Have a seat. It only looks ready to collapse, I swear." Sally waved at the chair. "I'd give you a hug, but I'm afraid I'd wreck your coat. Is that mink?" She stood and exchanged an air kiss with the other woman.

"Sable." Rhonda sat, but didn't unfasten the coat and clutched the strap of her Marc Jacobs handbag. Her deep blue eyes betrayed a palpable air of worry.

Steve did something with investments, Sally remembered. Apparently quite successfully. "What's it been, five or six years? How are you?"

"About five," Rhonda said. She hadn't relaxed. "I'm okay. Well, I was until yesterday."

"What happened?" Instinctively, Sally knew Rhonda had no intention of requesting representation. Something else brought her to Uniontown. Strange. Unless they'd moved, the Naifs lived in one of Pittsburgh's more affluent suburbs.

Rhonda bit her lip. "Steve didn't come home."

"Um, okay." Sally stared. Rhonda drove from Pittsburgh to Uniontown to tell someone she hadn't seen in five years her husband hadn't come home? "I don't want to sound insensitive, but why tell me?" Maybe Rhonda didn't have many friends to confide in.

"I should explain." Rhonda ran her fingers over her purse. "Steve went away last week. Ski vacation with the guys. We texted every night and he said he'd be back on Sunday."

"He didn't call?"

"No, but I didn't think anything of it. He said he'd be home and I believed him." Rhonda bit her lip.

"He didn't come home."

"At first I thought he'd hit a bad patch on the Turnpike. Then it got to be seven at night and he still wasn't home. I called his cell, but it went straight to voicemail. I sent a couple texts. No response. It's like he vanished." If Rhonda's forehead skin could move, it would have been wrinkled. The worry in her voice and eyes didn't match the smoothness of her face.

Sally played with her pen. "Did you call the Pittsburgh police?"

"Yes." Rhonda bit off the word. "They took my report and said to call them if Steve came home."

"That's pretty standard. I'm not sure what else you want them to do. Steve is an adult, after all," Sally said. "I know you're worried, but maybe he stayed and didn't tell you, or..." Could be he was shacked up somewhere.

"Steve wouldn't cheat on me," Rhonda said, correctly guessing Sally's thoughts. "We have a good marriage, two kids, and a nice life. There is no reason for him to stray."

The spouse was always the last to know. "All right, say he's missing. Why are you coming to me?"

Rhonda ran her fingers over her purse strap. "I'm afraid he's been in an accident, or something happened to him. You're still in criminal law. Aren't there people you can call to find Steve?"

Rhonda Naif could afford to hire her own investigator. She'd been a prosecutor. She knew how things worked. Sally couldn't help through official channels and Rhonda knew it. Or she should know it. Why drive all the way to Uniontown?

She didn't want people thinking her husband left her. Sally was far enough out of the area that if she nosed around, she wouldn't set off any gossip in Rhonda's social circle. No woman wanted her perfect family life to come under scrutiny. "I'm sorry. If I needed to start an investigation for legal purposes, perhaps I could help. But I'm not a PI nor can I ring one up. If Steve had been in an accident, you would have gotten a phone call. They'd look you up based on his ID or check his cell for emergency contacts." She paused. "You know all this. At least you should."

"What am I supposed to do?" Tears of frustration shone in Rhonda's eyes.

"My advice? Wait and see if Steve comes home. Let the Pittsburgh police do their job. They'll find him." Wherever he is.

Rhonda stood. "I was hoping you'd help me. My mistake." She shouldered her purse.

"Rhonda, it's not that I don't want to help. I just don't see what I can realistically do." Sally stood, too.

"You think he's cheating," the other woman said, her voice icy. "My husband is *not* cheating. He's missing. And I'm going to find him." She stormed from the office.

Sally sat back down. What an absolutely bizarre visit. A woman she hadn't seen in five years comes to ask for help in finding a husband who's been missing a little more than a day? If Rhonda was convinced her husband didn't stray, there were a myriad of better options than coming to ask an assistant public defender for help.

No matter what she said, Rhonda had to suspect infidelity. If she thought Sally could investigate Steve Naif's activities under the radar, stress was making her irrational. The desire to keep the hint of misbehavior from anyone she knew was the only possible explanation for seeking Sally's assistance.

She glanced at the clock. Ten-forty-five. She had fifteen minutes to get to court. Whatever Rhonda Naif's issue, she didn't have time to figure it out.

CHAPTER FOUR

Fire marshal Adam Carlton worked out of the county Emergency Management Agency, located in the county courthouse. Duncan paused by the stairs to the public defender's office. Later. He had things to do. He made his way to Carlton's office, where the receptionist sent him back.

"Hey," he said, entering the cluttered space.

"Figured I'd see you today or tomorrow." Carlton stood and shook Duncan's hand. "You could have called."

"I was in the area. You aren't done yet?" Duncan set his hat on a pile of paper.

"Not quite, but the prelims are finished." Carlton pulled out a sheet of paper and handed it over. "Gasoline. Soaked the carpet under the window. There was also gasoline residue on fabric samples from your victim."

"Pour it on the carpet, splash some on the body, light it, and gone." Duncan scanned the report. "Wouldn't take long."

"The fire would have started immediately." Carlton sat and nibbled at some French fries from a fast food bag on his desk.

"That shit will kill you." Duncan nodded at the fries and passed back the paper. "I'm surprised the sprinkler and alarms didn't go off."

Carlton took the report. "Sprinklers were disabled. Batteries ripped out of the smoke detector. Whoever set the fire didn't want it discovered before it could serve its purpose."

"Destroying the identity of the victim." Duncan set

aside a pile of paper and sat. "If not the body."

"Yep. Even gasoline isn't as hot as a crematorium, though. Anyway, we already know it was Capshaw."

"Coroner is waiting for dental records to confirm. Mrs. Capshaw insists her husband is at his hunting lodge in Punxy. The lodge is snowed in. No one can get in to check and cell service is crap."

"He die of smoke inhalation?"

"Strangled. Dead by the time the fire started."

"Damn." Carlton popped another fry. "Lucky you."

"Yeah, I should play the lottery." Duncan rubbed his forehead. "Best guess. How long before the fire would be noticed?"

Carlton shrugged. "Not that long. An hour? Half an hour? Remember, it was early morning. People were asleep."

"Fire was reported at two-twenty. Coroner says he lay on the floor for maybe two hours before he was found." It worked. A small window, but it worked.

"Killed between midnight and one, take some time to set up the fire, then leave. I can see it."

"Then I want to get CCTV footage from nine to two, just to be sure." Duncan stood. "Call me if anything else comes up."

"You got it. Good luck."

Duncan left. As he walked out, he was seized with the desire for a Reuben at Dex's. He should ask Sally to lunch. Give it a shot, at least. He'd caught sight of her briefly at Winterfest, but she'd turned away too fast for him to make eye contact. Weird. Her entire demeanor toward him had been off kilter since last fall. It had been a big thing to get over, but surely she didn't blame him, right? Maybe she still remembered all those texts he'd ignored, believing those had led to the more-than-unpleasant situation. He wouldn't blame her if she did.

Get over yourself. The only way to find out was to talk to her. He turned toward the stairs.

As far as the fire went, he hoped McCloskey's wife had their baby soon. It would be really hard to conduct a homicide investigation at two in the morning.

❋ ❋ ❋

Sally left her office around noon, intending to grab a quick lunch. The first thing she saw when she reached the top of the stairs was Jim striding through the lobby. She froze.

"Sally, there you are," he said.

She advanced with caution, tugging at her gloves, already snug on her hands. "Hey. I, uh…"

He didn't flash a welcoming grin, his hazel eyes dark and somber. "Something up? You're usually more articulate."

Was he embarrassed to see her? Uncomfortable? It certainly looked that way. "You caught me off guard, that's all." They hadn't talked for months, then she saw him twice in a matter of days? She caught a brief glance of him at Winterfest, but he didn't react when he saw her. No wave of acknowledgement, no greeting. Because he was working, duh.

Which would be a perfect excuse, her voice of insecurity said. He wouldn't have to go out of his way to avoid her, he could claim he hadn't seen her in the crush of people. The very sight of her had to drag up painful memories and she could hardly blame him for wanting to avoid a meeting. She'd been impulsive and foolish, and the results had been…not something to dwell on.

He spun the keys in his hand and looked out the door, beyond which shone a painfully clear and deceptively sunny day. "I was about to grab something at Dex's." He glanced at her. "Care to join me?"

She paused, studying his body language. Ramrod stiff posture, no smile, voice neutral. Ever the gentleman, the invite smacked of something he felt he *should* do out of courtesy. Should she make an excuse, give him a graceful way out? Or would that make her look ungrateful? Everything he'd done, he did it for her, after all.

She cleared her throat. "I'd like that." Did her voice really sound that squeaky?

He stepped back and held out an arm. "After you." Still no answering smile. Possibly he regretted speaking.

Dance, dance, dance.

She tugged her gloves again. "I'll meet you there. That way you don't have to come back. I'm sure you have a busy day." At least he wouldn't have to endure her presence a minute longer than necessary. She'd already caused enough pain, she was sure of it.

He paused, still spinning his keys. "Okay."

Dex's had a full lunch crowd, but they got their usual booth in the back corner, a flash of normal in the sea of her uncertainty. Jim waved Sally into her seat and took the bench facing the door.

Sally shrugged out of her coat, then placed purse and gloves next to her. She glanced at the menu. "Bryan raves about the Sam Smith oatmeal stout." *Keep it light, maybe he'll forget who he's with.*

He answered, voice brusque. "Another time. I don't need to be seen drinking in uniform." He pushed aside his menu without looking at it. A waitress came up to their table and he nodded at Sally to order first.

Okay, maybe not. "Grilled chicken salad and water for me," Sally said, handing over her menu.

A faint grin flitted across Jim's face. "No bacon cheeseburger?"

She recalled the last time they'd been at Dex's, drowning her anxiety in Applewood smoked bacon, cheese, and whiskey. "I'm watching my figure."

"Like that's something you need to worry about," he said. "Reuben and a Coke, please," he said to the waitress, who jotted their orders on her pad and walked away.

Her cheeks turned as hot as if she stood in front of a bonfire. She couldn't figure him out. On one hand, he definitely had the demeanor of someone who wished he was someplace else. On the other…that comment.

They sat in uncomfortable silence until the waitress returned with their drinks. "How are you?" he asked. He lifted his Coke to his lips.

She stalled by taking a drink. "I'm okay. Busy, especially as we're still short-handed."

He played with his silverware, eyes never leaving her face. "I saw you at Winterfest. You didn't say hi."

"You looked like you were working. I didn't want to get in your way."

More silence. He tilted his head. "We've kind of been strangers these last couple of months."

Was that relief in his voice or accusation? "It's okay. Work. Holidays. Craziness. We saw each other New Year's Eve."

"Briefly."

After everything that happened, what could they talk about? He didn't want to relive events. She didn't either. At the same time, she didn't have anyone else to talk to. It wasn't like either of her siblings could relate.

The whole event was the elephant in the room, but if she steered the conversation to the professional, they could both make it through lunch. "I got the weirdest visit earlier." She told him about Rhonda.

Jim furrowed his eyebrows. "If you haven't talked to her in years, why come to you?"

Sally took a sip of water. She should have gotten something hot. "I guess if you're trying to hide the fact that your husband might have strayed, you call a relative stranger."

The waitress arrived with the food, and he paused until she left. "What did you tell her?"

"To file a missing persons report. She said she had, so really there's nothing to do but wait." She lifted a forkful of salad. "It's not like I have a personal relationship with the cops."

"What am I, chopped liver?" He held the bottle of ketchup over his plate.

Brilliant, Sally. On top of everything else, go ahead and insult him. She set down her fork, sure her face was flaming red. "I meant...not like I can just pick up the phone...after all, I'm sure you're busy."

He studied her. "Are you sure you're okay?"

"Why do you ask?"

"You seem...uncomfortable." He picked up his sandwich, gaze fixed on her face.

The buzz of the lunch crowd was loud enough to cover their conversation. No one would hear if she spilled the fears and stress that had bogged her down since October. Except, did he actually want to hear the truth? "I'm fine. Tired. Midwinter blahs."

He took a bite, appraising her. "Did Rhonda tell you anything else? Give any other reason why her husband might be missing?"

Sally didn't know whether to be grateful or disappointed he accepted her weak excuse. The fact he'd let it go so easily, however, was a good indication of how he felt. "She wondered if he'd been in an accident on the way home, but wouldn't someone have contacted her?"

"Either the hospital or the police, yes. Assuming he had a cell phone or a wallet, which he probably did." Jim leaned back and wiped his fingers. "What does Steve do?"

"Something in investments. Considering the fur coat and diamonds Rhonda had on, he's pretty successful, too."

"He receive any threats lately? Problems at work? Disgruntled clients?"

"Not that she mentioned. I didn't ask."

"I still don't see what she wanted you to do."

"She might have thought I had investigative resources she didn't. Ones that wouldn't be public or visible. It makes me think she's worried about something embarrassing."

Jim pushed aside his plate. "But she didn't say anything about those suspicions."

"Nope." A quick glance at the clock told Sally it had

been forty-five minutes. That long? She speared a leaf of lettuce. The salad had been unsatisfying. She should have ordered a burger.

"Then there's something going on we aren't aware of." He glanced at the clock, then leaned back, drumming his fingers as he studied her face.

Counting the minutes until she was done, probably. She cleared her throat. "I should get back, I've got a meeting at one-thirty. Should I bother to offer to pay?"

"When have I ever taken you up on that?" He signaled the waitress, who came over, then handed her the check and a credit card. "I have to get going myself."

Outside the restaurant, the sun still shone, but a few flakes drifted from the blue sky. After the warmth inside, the cold was a punch in the face, worse than Jim's distant attitude. She faced him, fiddling with her purse strap. "Thanks for lunch."

He put on his hat and looked at her, his breath a crystalline cloud, expression unreadable.

"Good luck with whatever you're doing."

They faced each other, like two teenagers ending a first date. Normally she'd give him a kiss on the cheek, but such an intimate gesture felt out of place after their frigid, professional conversation. She cleared her throat. "Well…later, I guess."

He said nothing, merely touched the brim of his hat with his forefinger.

She walked to her car, feeling the weight of his gaze on her back.

* * *

Duncan watched Sally's Camry disappear around the corner. He thought about the look on her face when he'd caught her outside her office. He'd seen that look before. Seen it in any number of people who'd been trying to not be noticed. Fear. Since he'd been the only person in the area, he had to conclude she'd been afraid of him.

Well, no shit. However justified his actions had been during the confrontation with Aaron Trafford, how could she want to spend time with him? He'd told himself he'd make it up to her, apologize the right way, but there had always been something to prevent him. The investigation. The hearing. The holidays. The never-ending crush of work for both of them.

The refusal to accept a ride. Her body language in the booth. The way her gaze flicked to the clock. She couldn't wait to get out of Dex's. Why had she accepted his invite? Because she didn't want to come off as rude, that's why.

He pushed the matter out of his mind and got in his car. Work to the rescue, as always. From the road, he called ahead to request the surveillance footage from the Winding Valley parking lot for the night of the fire. With any luck, he'd be able to see who else had arrived. Who might have met up with Ray Capshaw. Or whoever rented the cabin in Capshaw's name. Burns's refusal to issue a positive ID meant that possibility was open.

He arrived at Winding Valley and went immediately to the front office. Aside from the charred building, the place looked like a winter fairyland: quaint buildings dusted with powdered snow, smoke curling from the chimneys. Colorful flyers advertised special ski rates for guests and a variety of posters for Laurel Highlands events dotted the glass-enclosed board outside the door. Inside, boughs of fir and spruce dressed with seasonal ribbons adorned the reception area. Burned-out building aside, Winding Valley was trying to compete.

He walked up to the desk, rang the bell, and asked for Maurice Thompson. After a minute, the manager appeared.

"Trooper," Thompson said, nodding in greeting.

"Mr. Thompson. Where can I see the video?" There was

no TV in the reception area and Duncan was sure Thompson didn't want visitors seeing it anyway.

"Well...there's a problem with that." Thompson's expression stayed bland, but Duncan didn't miss the sheepish quality in his voice.

"What kind of problem?" The viewer was broken. No problem. Duncan could take the video back to the barracks.

"Seems we had some kind of outage that night. There is no footage. I didn't know until I pulled the recording."

"None at all?"

"The camera was plugged in and had power, but it didn't record. I've sent it for maintenance, but bottom line is I don't have anything for you." Thompson shrugged. "Sorry."

"I'm sorry, too." Inconvenient didn't cover it. Vicky Hanson identified Ray Capshaw from a photograph, but no one else had checked in with him. The overnight clerk, Gail, had not noticed another car. Not one she could describe. Without the video, the event was a black hole. They needed to bulldoze a path to that cabin in Punxy. See if Capshaw was there and ask about Winding Valley.

"Were the units on each side of Mr. Capshaw's rented that night?" Duncan asked.

"I believe so."

"I need names and contact information for those residents, if they've checked out."

"They have. We do mostly weekend rentals. Very few units are occupied during the week," Thompson said, frowning. "But I can't release that information. Privacy concerns."

"Mr. Thompson, I respect that. But this is a felony investigation. Arson and homicide."

"Are you saying this is a murder? Can't you ask Capshaw's widow who he might have met that night?"

"We have not confirmed the identity of the victim," Duncan said. "Talking to Mrs. Capshaw would be premature. And yes, this is a murder. Whoever that body is, he was dead before the fire started. Will you give me the names or not?"

Thompson bit his lip. "I can't. Not without a warrant. My guests would never trust me again."

Duncan settled his hat. "I understand. Then I'll come back when I have one. Good day, Mr. Thompson."

Dirty gray clouds streaked the sky, and the snow fluttered down. Duncan wouldn't be surprised if there was another snowfall overnight, making things perfect for some cross-country skiing with Rizzo or friends. Maybe even Sally. He could find out her thoughts and put the whole issue to bed.

Instead, he'd be getting a judge to approve a warrant to obtain Winding Valley's guest list. Man, did he know how to live or what?

CHAPTER FIVE

O n Tuesday, the phone rang just as Sally headed out for her morning court appearance. She debated letting it go to voicemail, then picked it up. It might be important. "Fayette County Public Defender, Sally Castle speaking."

"He's missing. I know it."

"Rhonda?" Sally blinked. "Calm down and tell me what's going on."

"It's Steve. He still isn't home. What am I supposed to tell my kids?" Rhonda's voice was thick. She'd been crying for a while.

Why is she calling me? Sally immediately rebuked herself. Whatever the reason, Rhonda had called and Sally needed to hear her out, be sympathetic, and help as best she could. "Tell your kids their dad has been delayed. Then call the Pittsburgh Bureau of Police again and ask for an update. You did file a missing persons report, didn't you? That's what you said yesterday."

"I...I called the police, but I didn't file an official report. Can't you call a PI to look for him?"

"No, I can't. Rhonda, you need to trust me. Trust the system." If Steve Naif had been a witness in one of her cases that would be one thing. But this was straight-up police business. "The police have better resources. This is their job. Call them and file the report."

"And if they can't find him? What am I supposed to do then?"

"If that turns out to be the situation, and I'm not saying it will be, call me back. We'll figure out something." What, Sally had no idea. But she'd try.

Rhonda took a shuddering breath. "I...okay, I'll call again. But I'm worried, Sally. Steve's never done this before." Her voice dropped to a whisper. "What if...what if he really did leave?"

"Does he have a reason to?"

Rhonda gulped. "No. No, I...no."

That sounded like a woman trying to convince herself. "Call the police. File the report. One thing at a time." Sally waited until Rhonda agreed and hung up.

She replaced the phone and glanced at her watch. She'd barely make it to court on time. Damn. She was public defense, not missing persons. What the hell was Rhonda thinking?

❃ ❃ ❃

Before heading to the barracks for Tuesday's second shift, Duncan stopped at the county coroner's office to check the fire victim's ID.

Burns set down the phone when he saw Duncan enter. "Your Spidey-sense must have been tingling."

"You know who John Doe is."

"Sort of." Burns reached over and grabbed a folder.

"What do you mean sort of? You've either got an ID or you don't." Duncan needed a name. Without security footage from Winding Valley, he was groping in the dark.

Burns flipped to a page in the folder. "I can tell you who it isn't." He handed the folder to Duncan and tapped the page. "He's not Ray Capshaw."

"Son of a bitch." Duncan scanned the paper. The dental records weren't even close. "Then who the hell is it? Ray Capshaw rented that cabin and that was absolutely his Mercedes."

"Damned if I know." Burns chugged an energy drink. "You get me something to compare, I'll get you an ID. Until then, that's all I can tell you."

Duncan dropped the folder onto the desk. "Great. Just… great." *Good news, Mrs. Capshaw. Your husband isn't dead. Not in the Laurel Highlands. But he might be missing.* It didn't explain why Capshaw's car turned up here, though, instead of his cabin in Punxy, where he was nominally holed up. Duncan wondered if they'd cleared the road to the cabin, so he could ask Mr. Capshaw that exact question.

"Sorry I can't be of more help." Burns slid the folder back into place. "Maybe you can check security film. Find out who might have met up with Capshaw, or at least arrived in his car."

"There is no video. Camera didn't record." He really needed that guest list.

"That sucks. Intentionally?"

Duncan consulted his notes. Thompson said the camera didn't record. Not why. "Good question. I got the impression it malfunctioned, but I'll confirm that." At least his turn on third shift wouldn't be up for a couple days.

"Good luck. I'll keep this guy on ice in the meantime." Burns stood. "Hey, did you tell Ace I said hi?"

"About that." Duncan slipped his notebook in his pocket. "The nickname. The coy friendliness. Something I should know about?"

"I told you, Dad. None of your business."

"I was her FTO. I feel responsible for her."

Burns grinned. "I asked you when I first saw her if she was single. Turns out she is. I've seen her a couple times since then. Still working on winning her over."

"You're persistent. I'll give you that."

"Maybe you should take a lesson." Burns waggled his eyebrows.

"I'll be in touch about our John Doe." Duncan left, Burns's comment bringing the awkward lunch to the forefront of his mind. He suspected the last thing Sally probably wanted from him was persistence. Not in that area.

He shook his head and got into his Jeep to head to the barracks. He had more important things than dating to worry about anyway. Like who the hell the mystery fire victim was. And why Ray Capshaw had checked in to Winding Valley, left his car, then disappeared without a trace.

CHAPTER SIX

Wednesday morning found Sally thinking about the charity dinner on her way to work. She'd fibbed to Mark, therefore, she needed a date. Her first choice would be Jim, but would he want to go with her? That lunch at Dex's had been stiff and awkward. At least for her. And this wasn't a simple lunch. She could always go alone and tell Mark her date had fallen through.

Except if she showed up date-less, and Mark was also on his own, she'd spend all evening trying to tactfully tell him that she wasn't interested. That would put a crimp in the evening. Maybe she would skip the event this year. Plead illness or something.

"Morning, Sally," Doris said. She held out an envelope. "This came for you late yesterday."

"What is it?" Sally took the square envelope. It was postmarked Uniontown, delivered Express Mail.

"I don't know. But it doesn't look like business." Doris turned away to answer the phone.

Sally went to her office, where she sat to study the envelope. It wasn't business-size. More like something for a greeting card, maybe a little smaller. Plain, cream-colored paper with the address printed on a standard mailing label, most likely by a laser printer. The hand-written return address was illegible. The missive had no logos or business marks. Who would send something like this Express?

She slit open the envelope and removed a single, folded

sheet of white paper. The text was Courier, large size, and had also probably come off a laser printer. She read the words, each sentence sending a chill that had nothing to do with the weather inching down her spine.

Don't turn me away, Sally. You're mine. If you think I'm going to let another guy take my place, think again. I will never let you go and that's a promise.

No signature followed, but below the message *Your true amor* was printed in a script-like font. Who the hell could that be? She'd never called anyone her *amor*. She took a deep breath and turned over the note, careful to only hold the edges. Blank.

Holding the note in a tissue, she went to Doris's desk. "You said this came yesterday. Who brought it?"

"Mail carrier. Express delivery."

"Did it require a signature?"

"No. It was just a piece of mail." Doris blinked. "Your face is as red as a tomato. What's wrong?"

Red? It should have been bloodless. "Read this. I'll hold it."

The older woman's mouth hung open as she read. "Holy mackerel. You've got a stalker."

Sally pulled the note back. "One message does not a stalker make. This is the only one?"

"Only one I've seen." Doris pressed her hands together. "Should I call the police?"

Should she? No. Not yet. It had been one letter. With all the handling any physical evidence, like prints, would most likely be long gone. No way anyone would spend money on DNA testing over one note that didn't even make a real threat. "It's a crank. Don't worry." She started toward her office and stopped. "If I get any more special deliveries, don't let the carrier go before I see him. Assuming I'm here. Refuse delivery if I'm not."

"Okay," Doris said. "Are you sure it's nothing?"

"Positive. Thanks, Doris." Sally returned to her office.

In all her years of litigation, she'd never gotten a letter like that. Verbal threats, sure. But not notes. And yet the day after she met a guy she hadn't seen in years, and turned him down, this happened. She'd dated Mark. He'd gone out of state. Six months after he came back, he "ran into" her at the courthouse and now an anonymous note?

Coincidence? She didn't believe in the concept.

She looked at the note again. In terms of threatening letters, it was pretty tame. If this were evidence in a case, she'd be leery. No sense in bothering Bryan or wasting the time of the Uniontown police. Not until she had something more solid. Keep her eyes open, yes. But no cause for alarm. Yet. For the time being, she had real work to do, work that didn't involve some crackpot with a hang-up. She had bigger problems.

Like finding a date for the charity dinner two weeks from Saturday.

* * *

First thing after Wednesday's first-shift roll call, Duncan placed a call to the state police barracks near Punxsutawney. The trooper he talked to didn't know if the road was clear, but he promised to check and send someone to Capshaw's hunting lodge. When he'd left the coroner's office yesterday, Duncan had called Mrs. Capshaw and Ray Capshaw's cell phone. Mrs. Capshaw denied hearing from her husband in the past week and insisted he was at his hunting cabin without cell service. Whether because of that, or something more sinister, every phone call to Capshaw went to voicemail.

Duncan's cell phone rang slightly before noon.

"Trooper Jim Duncan? This is Trevor Polaski, out of Troop C near Punxy."

"I assume you're calling about Ray Capshaw. Road clear? What did you find?"

"We got through. Found a fat lot of nothing," Polaski

said. "No car. Place is dark and no one's been there recently."

"You sure?"

"Positive. The snow is undisturbed and drifted at least five feet deep around the building. Including against the door. There is no sign anything without four legs and a tail has been on the property."

Duncan frowned. New question. Why was Capshaw hiding from his wife? "Thanks."

"You want us to be on the lookout for the car?"

"We have the car. I'd appreciate a call if anyone matching Capshaw's description turns up in your area, though."

"You got it." Polaski hung up.

Duncan was standing in the same spot when Lieutenant Nicols walked by a few minutes later. "You look confused," he said. "What's on your mind?"

"Ray Capshaw." Duncan told the barracks commander about the report from Punxsutawney. "He checked into Winding Valley. We have his license, credit card, and a visual ID. His car was at the scene. He's gone. Vanished. Poof." People didn't go poof.

"What next?" Nicols asked.

"I'm going to check with Capshaw's friends and business associates. Maybe they know something Nora Capshaw doesn't."

"Maybe Capshaw has a reason for hiding from his wife." Nicols shrugged.

"He doesn't have a reason for hiding from the PSP." Duncan sat to look up the address for Capshaw's investment firm.

"Just because you can't find him doesn't mean he's hiding. You're turning into a cynic." Nicols tapped the desk. "Keep me posted."

Duncan grunted in assent as he wrote down the address he wanted. Was he a cynic? Or merely suspicious? After all, what kind of innocent person disappeared from the face of the earth?

* * *

Capshaw & Associates, Ray Capshaw's investment firm, was in the Oakland neighborhood in Pittsburgh. Duncan could have called for information, but he chose to drive up to the city. He had no idea what he was looking for. Being there in person might uncover something a phone call would miss.

The office was a small space on South Craig, not far from St. Paul's Cathedral. Finding parking proved difficult, even for a marked state police car. Avoiding the throngs of college students from Pitt and Carnegie Mellon, as well as the business folk who casually crossed streets regardless of walk signs, added to the challenge.

Pittsburgh air was a lot cleaner than it used to be. But for someone used to the open spaces of Fayette County, it still felt close, smelly, and dirty. Paper, bottles, and other refuse littered the sidewalks. People walked with eyes glued to their smartphones, not looking at their surroundings. Every few minutes an irate driver sounded a horn.

Duncan hated it.

He located the Capshaw & Associates office and entered. "Afternoon," he said. "I'd like to speak to an office manager or an officer of the company."

The receptionist didn't look up. "Mr. Capshaw is on vacation and Mr. Naif isn't here. Would you like to make an appointment?"

"It's important."

She looked up and appeared ready to argue, but stopped at the sight of a uniformed trooper. "I suppose you could talk to Herman, he's the senior investment analyst here today. What is it regarding?"

"The location of Ray Capshaw," he looked at the nameplate, "Melinda. Anyone would be helpful."

Melinda paused, phone in hand. "Mr. Capshaw is at his

hunting cabin in Punxy."

"His car was found at the scene of a fire in the Laurel Highlands. Would he change his plans without telling you?"

Melinda put down the phone. "I read about the fire in the paper. It mentioned a body. Was it Mr. Capshaw?"

"We haven't identified the victim. Are you sure he went to Punxsutawney?"

"That's what he said." She chewed a fingernail. Outside, people hurried up and down the sidewalk, but no one stopped. There didn't appear to be any clients at the modest, but well-furnished office.

Duncan pulled out a notebook. "How long have you worked here?"

"Three and a half years this April."

"What kind of boss is Mr. Capshaw? Is he easy to work for, argumentative?"

"He's nice, I guess. I mean, we don't hang around outside of the office." Melinda shrugged. "But he brought flowers on Administrative Professionals Day last year, always asks after me. Never gives me a hard time if I need to take off for something. So yeah, he's okay. I've worked for worse."

"The last time you saw him, was he upset? Worried? Anything unusual?"

"No. We talked about his vacation. He always takes a week in the winter to go to Punxy, sometimes with friends, sometimes alone." She straightened her desk calendar. "He calls it his hunting lodge, but I don't think they shoot anything, you know?"

"Did he go with anyone this time?"

She frowned. "I don't know. Not anyone from the office. He might have met someone there. He didn't say."

"Did he often vacation with people from work?"

"Mr. Naif. They'd go for guys' weekends, as Mr. Capshaw called them. Discuss business, have a few drinks, that sort of thing." The phone rang and Melinda paused to answer it.

Naif, where had he heard that name? When Melinda

hung up, he asked, "The week before Mr. Capshaw left was business as usual?"

"Yes." The phone rang again. While he waited, Duncan reviewed his notes. No mention of the name Naif. But it was familiar.

After Melinda hung up, Duncan asked, "Are there any other senior partners here? Anyone he might have confided alternate plans to or who might have gone with him?" He wasn't getting the picture of a man with something to hide.

Melinda thought a moment. "Only Mr. Naif. He's Mr. Capshaw's partner. Well, senior associate and Chief Financial Officer. He's not in the office at the moment. I expected him back on Monday, but I guess something came up. Oh, maybe you could speak to Mr. Trenton. He's our controller, but he works from home. He talks to Mr. Capshaw a lot."

"Can you give me Mr. Trenton's address and phone number? And if Mr. Naif comes in, please give him my card and tell him to call me." Duncan handed a business card to Melinda. In return, she wrote Trenton's information on a slip of paper and said she'd be sure to have Mr. Naif call as soon as he came back.

Duncan thanked her and rejoined the crowd of college kids. Once in his car, he started the engine and wove through Oakland traffic, toward the Parkway. He slowed before the Squirrel Hill Tunnel, and got stuck in the first crush of commuter traffic. God, he hated the city.

CHAPTER SEVEN

On the way back to Uniontown, Duncan called Trenton. No answer. His address was in Dunbar, easy to hit on the way back to Uniontown. Melinda said he worked from home. Not home? Or too busy to answer his phone? Duncan would find out.

Barren trees stood on the edge of the yard in front of the house. The only splash of color came from three dormant rhododendron bushes, their leaves curled tightly against the frigid air. No car in the driveway. Plain white drapes hung in the front window, which also displayed a sticker alerting emergency personnel that a dog lived in the house. No toys or evidence of children lay in the yard.

Duncan rang the doorbell. When the dark red door opened, he said, "Afternoon. Are you Bob Trenton? Trooper First Class Duncan."

"I'm Trenton." Contrary to the work-at-home stereotype of pajamas, he dressed in faded jeans, a dark gray fisherman's sweater, and battered slippers. "Is something wrong?" He didn't open the storm door, and kept the interior door closed as much as possible.

"Maybe. I'm looking for your employer, Ray Capshaw." Duncan glanced around, but couldn't see past Trenton into the house. "May I come in? I hate to let all this bitter February air into what I'm sure is a nice, warm home."

Trenton hesitated. "Guess there's no harm." He unlocked the storm door and stepped back.

Duncan entered and stood on the vinyl square inside the door. Snow slid off his shoes. He tried not to read anything into Trenton's reluctance. Anyone with half a brain didn't let police into the house without cause, guilty or not. But Duncan's innate skepticism made him wonder. Occupational hazard.

Trenton waved at a couch. "Have a seat."

The house showed a spare interior. Spartan even. Simple furniture covered in serviceable brown fabric. The walls were mostly devoid of pictures, either photos or paintings. The decor screamed single man. Duncan pushed the door shut.

"Trooper?" Trenton asked. A Golden Retriever in a blue vest, the logo of a service animal organization stamped on it, padded in and Trenton scratched him behind the ears.

"Sorry, habit. Evaluating your surroundings, especially when they're unfamiliar."

"As former military, I understand."

Was there a note of wariness in Trenton's voice? Duncan took out a notepad and pen. "Nice looking animal. I've got a Golden myself."

Trenton glanced at the dog. "This is Nero. He's a seizure dog. I have epilepsy. What can I do for you?"

So much for small talk. "I'm sure you've read about the fire at Winding Valley last week."

"Yes. They found a body. Was it Ray?"

"Why do you ask that?"

A faint grin appeared on Trenton's face. "The newspaper said the authorities found a car registered to Ray Capshaw on the property. Why else would you be here if I didn't know the victim?"

"The fire victim is currently unidentified. Yes, we identified Mr. Capshaw's car. Winding Valley staff confirmed Capshaw reserved and checked into the resort." Duncan uncapped his pen and flipped to a clean sheet. "I spoke to Melinda at your office. She says Mr. Capshaw went to his cabin in Punxsutawney."

"That was his plan, yes."

"Any reason he'd be at a Laurel Highlands resort instead?"

"I can't help you there. Ray doesn't tell me the details of his life."

"What about Steve Naif?"

Trenton's face stilled. "What about him?"

"Would he and Mr. Capshaw have gone away together and not told anyone about it?"

Trenton's eye twitched. "No idea."

Nero cocked his head and whined.

Trenton knew something. That much was clear to Duncan, but hammering him wouldn't yield information. "We have determined the man found inside the building died before the fire started. The fire marshal has listed the cause of the fire as arson. Neither of those facts have been made public yet."

Trenton gripped his upper arms, limbs still tightly crossed.

"Do you know anyone who wanted to harm Mr. Capshaw?"

"Not specifically, but..." Trenton paused, biting his lip. He seemed to come to a decision and continued. "I recently discovered some irregularities in the company accounts. I was paying bills, balancing the books, and things are...off. I wanted to discuss it with Ray. He dodged me a couple times, then told me we'd get together after he returned."

"Define off."

"Not right. The reason I like numbers, Trooper, is they are consistent. Unless you're dealing with theoretical mathematics, two plus two equals four. This was more like two plus two equals negative one. It's not how I expected to see things reported. As I said, it might have been fine. But Ray's refusal to explain made me suspicious. I went to Steve."

Nero rose from where he'd laid down by his owner's feet, still whining. Trenton ignored him.

"What did Mr. Naif say?"

"He was as confused as I was and said he'd talk to Ray. But he never got back to me and I have no idea what happened. Or if they even talked." Trenton rubbed his face. Nero pawed his knee. "Anyway, I didn't have the same questions about other accounts. Only ones managed by Ray. All the others were straight-up normal."

"Mr. Trenton," Duncan looked into the other man's eyes, which almost vibrated in their sockets. "Would it surprise you if I said the victim from the fire was not Ray Capshaw?"

Trenton unfolded his arms and wiped the corner of his mouth. "Then who is it?"

Genuine surprise? Maybe. If Bob Trenton had been involved in the arson, he believed Capshaw was the victim. Or at least he was putting on a good act. "We don't know yet. But no mistake, it's not Ray Capshaw. Think again. Do you know where Mr. Capshaw is? He's not in Punxy."

Trenton rubbed Nero's head. "I...I have no idea."

"No clue why he's hiding?"

Nero barked. Sweat broke out on Trenton's face. He dashed saliva from the corner of his lips. "No. I..." He swallowed. "I'm sorry, Trooper. I have to go lie down. That's Nero's seizure warning. The shock and stress."

Damn. "Can I do something for you?" Duncan hadn't intended to send the man into an epileptic seizure.

"No. I just...excuse me." Trenton, now visibly trembling, lay down on the floor and Nero curled next to him.

Duncan cleared the area around Trenton and waited for the seizure to pass. After, he confirmed the semi-conscious man could breathe and draped a blanket over him. Then Duncan let himself out and locked the door. Trenton had no wedding ring. There'd been no sign of another person in the house. His breathing had been easy and pulse steady. If Trenton lived alone, this couldn't be an uncommon event. Thus the presence of Nero.

As he slid into his car, Duncan stared at the house. Trenton certainly knew more than he was letting on. But about what? Something to do with Naif and Capshaw? Possibly. Yet his reaction to learning the fire victim was not his boss seemed pretty genuine.

The investments statements were "off." How badly? Had Capshaw known? Had Naif? Were they victims of fraud or the perpetrators? It was way too coincidental for both men to be missing. Duncan put the car in gear. He hated coincidences.

He didn't know much about finance, but he did know about crime. The stated chain of events led him down a very specific path. The deceased wasn't Ray Capshaw. But he'd give even odds his John Doe was Steve Naif.

❈ ❈ ❈

Wednesday afternoon, unable to avoid natural curiosity, Sally Googled Steve Naif, finding his address, phone number, and employer. Capshaw & Associates, an investment firm in Pittsburgh. Capshaw. The name rang a bell.

The fire at Winding Valley. Sally pawed through the paper on her desk until she found a copy of the *Uniontown Herald*, which contained a story on the fire at the resort. The unit in question had been rented to Ray Capshaw, his Mercedes parked outside. They found a body inside, but a positive ID hadn't been issued.

What were the odds? The timing worked for sure. She picked up her phone, hesitated for a fraction of a second, then sent Jim a text: *Can you come see me at the courthouse?*

She received his answer less than a minute later. He'd be there shortly. That must mean he was nearby and off duty. He never answered that promptly when he was on the clock. And since she hadn't mentioned a reason, he couldn't know it regarded business. What did the timing mean, if anything?

Snow dusted his campaign hat and water dripped down his state-issue jacket when he arrived. "What's wrong?" he asked, voice abrupt, as he came through her door, gaze darting around her office.

"Nothing. I'm fine. You're working."

"Yes. I do that."

"You don't answer when you're working." At least he usually worked Wednesdays, but stranger things had happened than a guy getting a day off.

He took off the hat, careful not to drip on her desk. "Are you complaining?"

"Not at all. I just didn't expect such a quick response." A tiny part of her hadn't expected any response. She had never been so glad to be wrong.

"You called, I came. Simple as that."

She detected an undercurrent of tension in his voice and his expression gave no hint at his thoughts. Did he resent being summoned? But then why answer? "I had an idea and I wanted to run it by you." He didn't move and she continued. "Remember I told you about Rhonda Naif? She came to see me. Her husband, Steve, was missing."

"That's where I heard the name. Steve Naif who works for the same investment company as Ray Capshaw."

"That's him. According to Rhonda, Steve is still missing. Have you found either of them?"

"No." He scrunched his face and his eyebrows puckered. "Well, I wasn't really looking for Naif. But he might know about Capshaw and he's not at work. The folks at Capshaw & Associates are claiming ignorance about both of them. I'm starting to think they went away together." He glanced at her visitor's chair.

"Please, have a seat." He'd either gotten over the awkwardness or business drove the elephant from the room. Either worked for Sally. "A gay love affair? Definitely something you want to hide from the wife."

Jim moved a pile of books then sat. "That's one possibility."

"Here's another. What if Steve knew why Ray Capshaw

was at that resort? And he's hiding because he knows who's responsible for the fire?" Sally leaned forward and put her arms on her desk.

Jim got up, pushed the door shut, and returned to the chair. "I'm going to tell you something that needs to stay between us. Something we haven't told the press." He paused. "The deceased isn't Ray Capshaw."

Almost like old times. "Who is it?"

"We don't know. Two missing men, though? That's two too many for me." He kept his gaze on her, face seemingly immune to the glare of sun through the window's winter grime.

"Try this," Sally said, thoughts whirling. "What if the body you found is Steve Naif?"

He rubbed his chin and seemed to consider her words.

She ticked off the points on her fingers. "Both men went on vacation around the same time. Both are missing. One allegedly rented a cabin destroyed by fire. But he's not the victim. Ergo…"

He stood. "Can you give me Rhonda Naif's phone number? We'll need her husband's dental records. The fire destroyed physical recognition. Blood type won't be enough." His voice was grim.

Sally scribbled Rhonda's name and contact information. "I still think she's worried that Steve is cheating on her, no matter what she says. That's why she came to me instead of calling an investigator. At least you'll be able to set her straight on that. You know, assuming they aren't having an affair."

"Your spouse was faithful, but he's been murdered. Have a nice day. Yes, much better." His eyebrow quirked as he took the paper. "It'll be good to get an ID, but I'm kind of hoping it's a bust. I need to ask Naif questions. I can't do that if he's burnt to a crisp."

"No problem." Sally hesitated. "Keep me informed?"

"You know the answer. As much as I can." He picked up his hat. He looked around the office, seeming to realize where he was. The air congealed, instantly tense and uncomfortable. "Is that all you wanted to tell me?"

The business over, did he expect her to say something else? He did, his expression gave it away. The pachyderm lumbered back into the tiny space, squeezing out the feeling of camaraderie. She averted her gaze. "That's all. I'll see you later."

He opened the door and paused. "I guess..." For a moment, he appeared on the edge of saying something else, but then he left.

Sally stared at the open door. What just happened? "You called, I came." True, he acted naturally, but as soon as the work part of the conversation ended, they went right back to that uneasy truce. Unless he could deal with her on a professional level, but no further. Yes, that had to be it. Nothing else made sense.

❋ ❋ ❋

As soon as he made the request, Rhonda Naif provided her husband's height, weight, and blood type, which were consistent with the victim's. But A+ blood and general physical characteristics were not an ID. Duncan also obtained Rhonda's permission to have dental records faxed directly to the Fayette County coroner's office.

His shift ended at three, but Duncan drove to the coroner's at five to check on the identification. He found Burns reading a report, the remains of a fast-food meal on his desk. As usual, the music was loud. Burns used two pens as makeshift drumsticks.

"Why am I not surprised?" Burns asked, reaching over to turn down the volume on the speakers.

"Tell me we've got an ID." Duncan ran his hands through his hair. "I think."

"You think?"

"It's confusing. I want a name. On the fence if I want the deceased to be Steve Naif."

"Because he can't answer questions if he's doing his best imitation of charcoal." Burns nodded. "Well, I've got good news and bad news."

"What's the good news?" Duncan needed the information, but he knew what was coming.

"The good news is we have a positive ID for your overcooked murder victim."

"The bad news?" Here it comes.

"We have identified the body as one Steven Michael Naif. Dental records are a spot-on match." Burns turned the monitor of his computer so Duncan could see.

Good news-bad news indeed. He could tell Pittsburgh police, and Rhonda Naif, the missing man had been found. But it didn't get him any closer to finding Ray Capshaw, knowing why Capshaw rented the cabin at Winding Valley, or why he left his car behind. And now he had two new questions. Who wanted to kill Steve Naif? And why?

CHAPTER EIGHT

Sally took Thursday off to answer a call for help from her sister. Noreen dismissed her, with thanks, at noon, which left her with a wide-open afternoon. She changed into her sweats as soon as she got home and contemplated freedom. The frigid weather made it the perfect day to snuggle in her favorite quilt on her sofa, with hot chocolate and a trashy novel in hand.

If only it didn't also sound boring as hell.

She'd resigned herself to being happy with her book, quilt, and hot beverage when there was a knock at the door. She'd left Noreen less than two hours ago, medicated within an inch of her life. Her brother, Jonathan, would have called first. It was Thursday. Jim usually had the day off, but would he pop by unannounced? Hardly.

"Just a minute." She padded over to the door and checked the peephole. Not Jim, not Jonathan.

Mark. Rocking on his heels in the hallway, dust motes swirling in the sunlight coming through the front window. A kid who'd shown up for a date. Or hoping for a date, more likely.

Sally grasped the door handle and paused to get control of her thoughts. Her address and phone number were unlisted. How had Mark found where she lived? She hadn't seen him in years. Now twice in a week? Kind of creepy. Was he stalking her? Except Mark didn't have the backbone to be a stalker. At least he hadn't when she'd last seen him. Nevertheless. First the anonymous note, now he showed up at her door?

Slow down, girl. Jim would remind her finding someone was not particularly hard. She might not be listed in the white pages, but her contact information was registered with state and local legal associations, including the folks who organized and ran the upcoming charity dinner. Mark was a member. He could easily have found it there. If he'd truly returned to the area recently and wanted to get together, it wasn't a stretch to believe he'd look her up.

If only she hadn't called out. Nothing for it except to open the door and be gracious. "Mark. This is a surprise." She only opened the door a couple of inches.

"Hey," Mark said. He wore jeans and what looked like a sweatshirt under a shearling coat, hair a bit mussed and cheeks still pink from the cold. It gave him the air of being younger than he was. A lot younger. "I was in the area. I hope I didn't interrupt anything."

"No. I'm staying in for the afternoon." She waved at her clothing. "What's up? You must have stopped for a reason."

"Oh, yeah. I was thinking we could go to lunch. For old times' sake. Seeing you the other day, well, it brought back memories."

Lord help her. The smart thing would be to tell him "no." If only he didn't remind her of a puppy. A puppy with big brown eyes and floppy hair. "That's really sweet of you. I'm not feeling it today. But thanks."

His eyebrows pulled together. "Is something wrong?"

"Oh, um…" She cast around for an excuse. "I spent the morning at my sister's house. Her kids have strep and they graciously shared it with her. You know, the Petri dish of childhood."

"I hope it's not serious."

"I doubt it. But although I made liberal use of soap, water, and hand sanitizer, I did spend all morning wallowing in germs. I'd hate to get you sick if I picked it up." Behind the door, Sally crossed her fingers, hoping Mark would buy the excuse and leave.

Her conscience stabbed her. *Coward. Just tell him no.*

Her mother's voice answered. *Don't be rude.*

Mark stuffed his hands in his pockets. "I wouldn't mind. Running the risk, that is. I could make you some soup or something."

"Oh, no. I couldn't let you. I'd feel horrible if you caught something from me." The last thing she wanted to do is let him in her apartment where he might get the wrong idea. "No, I'm going to have to pass. Sorry."

"Okay." He paused. Shadows from the winter light transformed him from sweetly harmless to coldly calculating.

It was not a look she'd ever seen before, and it made her feel like her sweats were somehow revealing. "I'll see you in a couple weeks, though." The edge in his eyes disappeared and the shadows softened, leaving Sally to wonder if she'd imagined it.

"The charity dinner. Definitely," he said. "Take care of yourself. Don't want you to get sick and miss anything important." He hunched inside the jacket.

"Thanks," she said again. "Drive safe."

She pushed the door mostly shut, but left enough of a gap to watch as he descended the stairs. As the top of his head vanished, Sally finished closing it. Mark fell into the category of "harmless." Most assuredly harmless. It was weird he'd shown up at the same time she received a strange note. Too much of a coincidence. But he'd been out of state and the letter had a sense of immediacy, a closeness of presence. Unless Mark had installed secret cameras in her office, it didn't make sense for him to be the writer.

* * *

Duncan sat at a desk, staring at the report from the Winding Valley fire. Rhonda Naif had been less than helpful. She'd dissolved into hysterics as soon as she had been notified about her husband's death, insisting no one on the face of the planet would want to kill him. He'd been the perfect husband, father, and business partner.

Except he'd been murdered. Someone in southwestern Pennsylvania didn't think Naif was perfect.

He read over his notes from his interview with Trenton. The controller had questions about the company finances. He'd reported it to Naif. Naif had gone to…who knows. Capshaw, presumably.

Maybe not. Maybe Naif had talked to someone else and that person had killed him to prevent exposure. Killed him and set the fire to make it look like an accident. But why was he in a cabin rented by his partner? Or were the two incidents completely separate?

McAllister came up to his desk, concern on her face and the ever-present bottle of Mountain Dew in her hand. "Aren't you usually off Thursdays?"

"These third shifts have my schedule all screwed up. That baby better make an appearance soon."

She chuckled. "Tell me about it. You look confused, Boss."

"I think I have a right to be."

"Talk. Maybe I can un-confuse you."

Duncan leaned back. McAllister had a sharp mind. She'd shown that during her training. "Ray Capshaw. He's missing. His wife says he went to Punxy. However, he rented a cabin at Winding Valley and his car was left at the scene of the fire at that location."

"You're sure he rented the cabin?"

"Yes." He recapped what he'd learned at Winding Valley.

"Nobody swapped the plates on the car?"

"Same make, model, year, and VIN. Troopers in Punxy checked, place is empty."

"Why go to the trouble of making it look like he was at Winding Valley?"

"Exactly. His wife claims not to know. I also have a statement from one of his employees, Bob Trenton, saying he had questions about the company financials."

McAllister unscrewed the top of her bottle of Mountain Dew. "Go on."

Duncan rubbed his face. "Body at Winding Valley is Steve Naif. Coroner says homicide. Reported missing by his wife this past Monday or thereabouts." A wife who had come to Sally. He made a note to look into that. "He works at Capshaw & Associates. And he's the guy Trenton spoke to about the irregularities."

McAllister's blue eyes narrowed. She sat on the edge of an empty desk, tapping the bottle against her palm. "I can think of one very good reason why a guy makes a reservation in his name, but another man stays. And the wife is clueless." She arched an eyebrow.

Infidelity. Sally said she thought Rhonda suspected her husband was cheating. If Capshaw knew about the affair, it was possible he helped his buddy cover up an illicit overnight tryst. "Capshaw has to go dark to sell the story. But Naif was strangled before the fire was set. Fight with the paramour?"

"Maybe the paramour was married." McAllister took a swig of Dew. "Husband found out, crashed the romantic getaway, killed Naif in the heat of the moment. Or Rhonda Naif found out her husband was playing the field, confronted him, and killed him. In both cases, the arson covers the murder."

Duncan doodled on the paper. It was a solid idea. "If that's the scenario, why is Capshaw still MIA?"

McAllister furrowed her forehead. "Dunno. Especially if it was supposed to be a one-night thing. He have any other properties in Pennsylvania?"

"Not that I can find." An earlier check showed only Capshaw's house in Pittsburgh and the lodge in Punxsutawney. "Doesn't mean he isn't hiding with a friend."

McAllister rolled the bottle and it made a cracking sound. "The other question I have is whether Capshaw was the intended target.”

“What do you mean?”

“It could be that our actor went to that lodge expecting to find Capshaw. He killed Naif to prevent him either talking to the cops or warning his partner. Or the murder and arson are a warning of some kind.”

“Why would Capshaw disappear instead of going to the Pittsburgh police?”

“He’s scared?” She drained the contents of the bottle. “What about the business?”

“The office in Oakland. One rental place near Seven Springs for entertaining clients. Still need to check if anyone’s at that one. Naif only owns his house in Highland Park. At least in this state.”

“What about West Virginia or Maryland? Ohio?”

“I’m looking there next.” Those requests would go to the respective agencies today.

McAllister ticked the points off on her fingers. “To recap: a missing guy, now deceased, whose wife says she doesn’t believe he cheated on her, but maybe he did. A second missing guy who was presumed dead but might not be, an arson, and a suspicious accountant.”

Duncan held out his hands in acquiescence.

She paused. “Yeah, that’s all I got.”

He sat up, chair creaking. “Thanks.” He stood and walked toward the vending machines.

“No charge.” She followed. “It’s three-thirty. Shouldn’t you be clocking out?”

He glanced at the clock. “I suppose.” With his schedule upended, he’d canceled all his usual plans for the day. “You doing anything?”

McAllister shrugged. “Not especially. Why?”

“See if you can find anyone associated with Capshaw who might have real estate ties. You know, who leased or sold the office in Oakland or who the Capshaws used to buy their house.” He put on his jacket and zipped it.

"Someone who maybe arranged for other real estate not associated with Capshaw's name or business that could be a hiding place?" She pitched her bottle into the trash. "You got it, Boss."

He started for the exit, then faced her. "Are you ever going to stop calling me that?"

"You were my FTO."

"I was one of your FTOs."

"Yeah, but you were my favorite." She grinned. "Face it. You'll always be the boss."

He shook his head. "See you tomorrow."

In the Jeep, he blasted the heater, hoping it would take the edge off the chill that grew as the sun dropped toward the horizon. If there was anything to be found, McAllister would find it. Another trooper might have found her obvious affection suggestive. Duncan was pretty sure McAllister's romantic feelings were otherwise engaged.

He headed home to Rizzo and a beer. A free Thursday night, maybe he should give Sally a call. She'd been acting funny for months. Closed off, wary. The reality of his job proved to be too much and the distance was her way of letting him down easy.

That or she didn't want to be with a man who couldn't be there for her.

✻ ✻ ✻

Sally sat in her car, staring at the lights in the house in front of her. Smoke curled from the chimney and the tangy scent of wood smoke reached through the falling evening twilight. Jim had a wood-burning fireplace, perfect for a night like tonight.

Before she'd left Uniontown, coming out to see him felt like the most natural thing in the world. But now, sitting in her rapidly-cooling car as the sun fled the sky in a fiery red-orange glow, she wasn't as sure. If she'd miscalculated, and he didn't want to see her outside of a professional capacity, what would he do when he opened the door? Throw her out? Slam the door in her face? No, he wouldn't do that. Well, not slam, but he'd have no problem telling her to leave. Politely.

She got out of the car and crunched her way to the front door. Her steps slowed as she reached the porch. She could still turn around. Leave before she was noticed. Maintain her dignity. She turned, intending to go back to her car.

Light and warmth surrounded her as the door opened.

"Sally? I thought I heard an engine," Jim said. "What are you doing here?"

Too late. She faced him. "I shouldn't have bothered you. You're eating." Along with heat, the tantalizing smell of beef and gravy reached her. Not only had she arrived unasked, she'd interrupted his dinner. Fantastic.

"I just sat down. It's only stew from the slow cooker, but you're welcome to have some." He paused. "Seriously, come in. It's too damn cold to hang out in my front yard."

He sounded puzzled, but nothing more. Over what? That she'd come at all, that it was a weeknight?

Noreen's voice. *Stop overcomplicating things*.

What was the saying? How do you eat an elephant? One bite at a time. Sally gave in, mounted the porch steps, and stepped into the blissful warmth of the house. She no sooner entered when Jim's dog, Rizzo, swarmed her, his Golden Retriever tail threatening to knock anything in its vicinity to the ground.

Jim closed the door behind her. "How'd you know I wasn't working? I'd hate for you to have driven almost two hours round trip for nothing."

She rubbed Rizzo's head. "You don't work Thursdays."

He blinked, apparently taken by surprise by her answer. "Give me your coat. You hungry?"

He sounded and acted awfully normal, pleased, even. Could be the elephant would be easier to eat than she thought. She handed him her bright pink Columbia jacket. "I'm starved.

A bowl of chicken soup for lunch is not enough for a cold day. I don't want to impose though."

He hung the jacket on a peg by the door, his expression still one of confusion. "I'll be right back." He disappeared into the kitchen.

She took off her boots. He bought new furniture, all warm browns and reds. A man's room. No more traces of his ex. What did it mean that he did it immediately after last fall? Anything? Nothing?

She busied herself with Rizzo, who was all too happy to accept all the attention she wanted to give.

"Here you go." Jim returned and was holding a tray. "Eat in front of the fire?"

They sat on the floor by the fireplace, bowls of stew and slices of sourdough bread in hand. Sally declined a beer, opting for Coke in the absence of red wine. Rizzo sat beside them, on the alert for handouts. They didn't talk, but the silence was one of companionship, not an awkward lack of words. No trace of the elephant.

"You good?" he asked, nodding toward Sally's bowl.

"Yeah. You make a mean beef stew for a single guy." She mopped up some gravy with the bread.

"That's a horrible stereotype, you know." He set down his bowl and Rizzo began licking it. "So, um, why'd you come? Because of the body at Winding Valley?"

He thought it was work. Not like he'd encouraged anything else lately. "Yeah, did you get a positive ID?"

"Last night. Steve Naif."

"Poor Rhonda." She picked apart her bread. "Any idea why he was at that resort?"

"Not sure." He stretched, nudging Rizzo with his foot. "But Capshaw knew his partner was there." He told her about his conversation with Aislyn McAllister.

"What about Naif's car?" Sally asked.

"Capshaw could have driven it away to maintain the fiction." He rubbed his foot against the dog. "Could Rhonda strangle a man?"

Sally tilted her head. "If she was angry enough. Rhonda's no stick figure." She pushed her bowl aside and Rizzo attacked it. "But it would mean her visit to me was a sham."

"It happens. Playing the distraught wife, thinking that will divert attention."

She leaned back on her forearms. "Did Bob Trenton give any details of these suspicious finances?" Her foot rubbed against Jim's thigh as she stretched, soaking up the warmth.

He tensed. "Only that he had questions and was going to talk to Naif about them." He inched away.

His reaction cast a chill over her. "Steve Naif confronted his partner and was killed." She sat up, and pulled her arms and legs in, determined not to touch Jim again, even accidentally. It clearly made him uncomfortable. "What about Trenton? Are you sure he isn't involved? Maybe he met up with his boss, they argued, and he killed Naif."

"Trenton doesn't drive." He told her about the epilepsy.

"He doesn't have a driver's license. That's not the same as not driving," Sally said.

"Well, it's a mess. I've got McAllister looking for other property connections. Maybe Capshaw bought property on the sly under another name and he's hiding there. He has to be somewhere. We'll find him." He stood and brushed crumbs from his sweats, threw another log on the fire, and picked up the bowls to return them to the kitchen.

Sally remained sitting cross-legged on the floor. Rizzo flopped beside her, head in her lap as she rubbed his ears. At least the dog still liked her.

Duncan returned, resumed his seat, and leaned against the couch. "He'll never move. Not with you lavishing attention like that."

"He's a good boy. This makes up for the fact I can't have pets in my apartment." Rizzo yawned and she scratched under his chin.

"Sally, I'm not sure why you came over tonight, but—"

His cell phone jangled and he snatched it from the table, glancing at the caller ID. "Oh damn. I have to answer this. Just a sec." He flipped open the old phone. "Hey, sweetheart. I'm sorry, I forgot. I have a visitor. Give me a minute, will you?" He looked up. "Sally, I—wait, where are you going?"

She jumped up, startling Rizzo who stared at her with a hurt expression in his soft brown eyes. "I've gotta go. I shouldn't have come." She jammed her feet into her boots, grabbed her jacket, and was out the door while her fingers fumbled with the zipper.

"Sally, hold on. It's not what you think."

"No, it's cool. I've taken up too much of your time." She took a huge step from the porch straight to the ground and heard a gasp behind her. He must have come out without shoes or socks on. Why was he chasing her?

She heard words behind her, Jim trying to explain. He didn't need to. It all made sense now. Throwing the Camry in reverse, she gunned it, snow flying as she pulled out of his driveway.

She yanked a wad of tissues from her center console. He'd moved on. Perfectly natural. He could have told her, kept her from making a fool out of herself. Unless he couldn't figure out how to explain and thought if she found out through a fortuitous conversation it'd hurt less. Kind of like the way you ripped off a band-aid. It hurt like hell for a bit, then faded.

A new woman explained everything. The way he distanced himself, how even an accidental touch made him uncomfortable. He didn't want a relationship tainted with the memories of last fall.

But he could have told her.

CHAPTER NINE

Thick gray clouds had rolled in by Friday morning, bringing the threat of more snow. If Sally had a job that allowed telecommuting, she wouldn't have left her apartment. But all she could hope for was that the worst of the weather would hold off until after she got home.

What in the world had she been thinking, going to Jim's like that? In the midst of an ugly-cry last night, she forced herself to examine his behavior, looking for clues. He'd definitely used the word sweetheart on the phone. Her imagination didn't supply the flinch at her touch, the cold professionalism of his demeanor over the past months. She tried to respond in kind, figuring that's what he wanted from her, a business-only relationship. One moment of weakness and she might have ruined even that.

The office was quiet, the whir of her computer fan sounded like helicopter blades. Bryan gave her another case, a woman accused of stabbing her abusive boyfriend. Sally followed up on the plea agreements from last week and sipped her third cup of coffee, familiarizing herself with the new file, when Doris buzzed her on the intercom.

"You have a delivery."

She did? "Who's it from?"

"It's flowers. No name except the florist," Doris said. "There might be a card inside. You want to come get it or should I bring it to you?"

Who would be sending her flowers? Hopefully it wasn't

Mark. That would be his style, though. Send an expensive bouquet of flowers in an attempt to win her acceptance of his invitation. "I'll be out to get them." She needed the break.

She reached the front desk and saw the long, white box sealed with packing tape. Didn't they seal flower boxes with ribbon? Maybe you had to ask for special packaging. She examined the label. It displayed the name and address of a Uniontown florist, along with her name and the courthouse address. "Who delivered them?"

Doris spread her hands. "No idea. I signed from both DHL and FedEx this morning."

"You didn't pay attention?"

"Both Benjy and the DHL guy were here with a jumble of stuff. I didn't notice the details."

"He prefers to be called Benjamin." Sally ran her hand over the white cardboard. A long box, the kind that was filled with roses in the movies. Who on earth had sent her flowers? Too late for Valentine's, too early for her birthday.

"Open it." Doris handed her a pair of scissors to cut the thick tape around the box. "I've got a vase if you need one."

One end of the box was heavier than the other. Maybe the ends of the flowers were capped with those plastic things filled with water. Sally snipped through the tape, removed the lid, and looked inside. They were deep pink roses. She lifted them out, feeling her fingers brush something fuzzy. She looked down, screamed, and dropped the box.

Nestled in the green tissue paper was the body of a dead rat. The naked tail curled around the stems of the bouquet, the beady black eyes staring. She took a step backward, her heart in her throat. Eww. She touched a dead rat. It took a few moments for the next question to surface. Who put a rat in the flowers?

Doris bent to pick up the box, but yelped and jumped as the body of the rodent rolled onto the floor. "Oh my God. What kind of sicko sent you that?"

"I have no idea." Sally's voice cracked on the last word.

She bit her lip, waiting to get control over her voice before she spoke again. "I can't even think of a name." But she should spend some time on the subject, because the police would certainly ask the same question. Now was definitely time to call the cops.

"There's a card." Doris reached for it.

"Don't touch it." Sally grabbed the other woman's hand. Through her shock, her brain was churning. The rat had not been placed in the box at the florist. She was pretty sure of that. The police might be able to get fingerprints off the card.

Using a tissue from Doris's desk, Sally removed the card from the box. It wasn't handwritten. It had been run off a printer, same as the note. She checked the back, but it was blank.

"What does it say?" Doris asked.

Sally looked at the front and read:

Roses are red, violets are blue.
This rat's heart is slain and mine is too.
The rat and pink roses I'm sending your way
in thanks for the gifts that you've sent me, but hey.
A token of my admiration, it's true.
But I won't give up hope. I'm coming for you.

Doris squeaked. "That's messed up. Bad poetry, but messed up. I'm calling the police. First the note in your office. Now this? Someone's got it in for you." She picked up the phone and dialed.

Sally didn't try to stop her and she dimly heard Doris speaking, presumably talking to the county dispatcher. She laid the card back in the box. That's why it had been sealed with tape, not a ribbon. Someone had opened it, put in the rat and card, then sealed it up again. She checked the label. It had come via FedEx. Maybe tampered with while the truck was at another stop.

Once again her thoughts flashed to Mark. The coincidences piled up. The encounter at the courthouse. The note. The visit to her apartment. Now this. Four in a row. She shivered.

Aside from Mark, who else would harbor such animosity? Because if anything said "I'm pissed" it was a dead rat in a bunch of flowers.

✻   ✻   ✻

Duncan pulled his cruiser into a spot outside the courthouse. Snow frosted the gray stone like sugar icing. The dull, muted light matched his mood. The call from Doris, the secretary in the public defender's office, troubled him. Flowers and a rat? What the hell?

A uniformed Uniontown officer tramped down the stairs as Duncan approached the building. "Did you handle the call at the public defender's office?" he asked.

"I did." The officer, Clemens, was a little older than Duncan, thinning red hair cut close and touched with gray at the sides. "I'm not sure why you're here."

"I'm a friend of the woman who received the flowers. What happened?"

Clemens consulted his notes. "Ms. Castle received a delivery. No name. Some crackpot put the body of a dead rat and this note inside. Might be able to get prints. Ms. Castle said she used a tissue to pick it up." Clemens handed over an evidence bag containing a simple white card.

Duncan read it through the plastic, a swarm of emotions going through his head. Anger, fear, disgust. Sally didn't have any psychotic ex-boyfriends. Not that he knew of. A rat and roses spoke of affection and anger. A past case? Someone who didn't think she'd done a good job? Most of her cases were plea bargains. She hadn't been to trial lately. He handed the bag back. "You talk to the florist yet?"

"That's my next stop. According to the label on the box,

FedEx made the delivery."

"You talk to the delivery man? Or woman?"

"Man. Not yet. Got a call in to find out his route or have him call me. Maybe he noticed someone at the truck."

"Or the FedEx guy is our actor."

"I asked about that. Ms. Castle doesn't think that's likely. She has no personal connection with the guy outside work. No dates, no romance, nothing."

Duncan stared at the building. Sally was a pretty sharp judge of character. Wouldn't be the first one-sided obsession, though. Uniontown might be content to wait until this guy called them. Duncan would get a name and hunt him down. "Ms. Castle still inside?"

"Yeah. Said something about how she hoped she could get her nerves back before some meeting this afternoon." Clemens shook his head. "My wife would be a wreck. She'd probably need a double-shot of Jim Beam to steady herself after a surprise like that."

Duncan grunted, headed inside, and down to the public defender's office.

Sally sat in a plain chair near one of the front area desks. Her hands were clasped around a steaming mug of dark liquid. She looked up and blinked. "Why are you here?"

"I called him," Doris said. "I figured you wouldn't, stubborn as you are."

"You shouldn't have," Sally said, shaking her head. "Trooper Duncan has better things to do with his day."

Was she serious? He watched emotions flit across her face until it landed on...embarrassment? He removed his hat and set it on the counter in front of the desks. "I want to make one thing clear. I always have time for you, no matter what."

She looked up, embarrassment replaced with sheepish gratitude. "Thanks, but it's not that big of a deal. Honestly."

"I'll be the judge of that." He pulled over another chair and sat. "Are you okay?"

Sally chuckled, a weak sound. "I think so. I'm not physically hurt. Opening a box of flowers and finding a dead rodent with a vaguely threatening note was quite a surprise."

"I read it." He looked at her. Her face was pale and there was a flicker of unease in her deep-green eyes. It had been more than a surprise, but Sally had survived worse. "Any idea who might have sent something like that?" Or maybe the unease had to do with him. He pushed the thought aside.

She shook her head. "Officer Clemens asked the same thing. I can't think of anyone who'd have it in for me this badly."

"At least you gave the first note to Clemens," Doris said.

Sally scowled.

Duncan focused on the older woman. "There was a first one?"

Sally remained silent and Doris answered. "It was a note card, no name. Something about how she was his and he'd never let her go."

"Doris, be quiet," Sally said.

How very typical of Sally. She wouldn't be intimidated by an anonymous letter, but she should have said something. Anonymous threats had a way of escalating. Last fall she would have called him in a heartbeat. This time, he found out from Doris. It stung, but he pushed on. "You said you gave that note to Clemens?" he asked.

"Yes. But it's going to be useless. I know it." Sally sipped her drink.

"What about the envelope?" Doris asked. "Can't they get DNA from that?"

Duncan remained focused on Sally as he answered. "They can, if they run it."

"What do you mean?" Doris sputtered.

"One, DNA testing is pricey," Duncan said. "Two, there has to be a match in the system. Three, the state lab has a six-month backlog. We can catch the guy by the time they get to that envelope."

A spot of color appeared high on Sally's cheeks. "Let's

not get ridiculous. Jim, I appreciate your concern, but Doris shouldn't have bothered you."

Why did she keep insisting on that? He leaned forward, voice firm. "I'll say it again, this is not a bother." He laid his hand on her arm.

The self-conscious look returned and she bit her lip.

"Clemens said you thought the notes, both of them, sounded personal. Why?"

Her shoulders twitched. "I don't know. Just a feeling. Whatever that's worth."

"It's worth a lot." He shot a look at Doris, but the secretary's face was blank. No help there. "Any candidates?"

Sally shook her head and sipped. "Not really. The guys I've dated, the relationships sort of faded."

"Okay. What about someone from your time as a prosecutor in Allegheny County?"

"You've got to be kidding. I think I was at one, maybe two trials during that time. Real trials with juries. I can't possibly keep track of all the plea bargains I presented. You know the system. And I did press conferences. If some whack-a-doodle got a bee in his bonnet, I'd never know. But that's hardly personal."

"Not to you, but maybe to one of them. Tell me about the trials. Men? Women?"

Sally's forehead creased. "One man, one woman. These notes feel like men. The guy was…Enrico Serrano. I don't remember the exact charge. And yeah, he was pretty angry when he was convicted. He was planning on getting an alibi from his girlfriend and she recanted on the stand."

"He still in prison?"

"I have no idea."

"I'll find out." Duncan could find out if Serrano was still incarcerated pretty easily. He stood. "I want the name of your FedEx guy, too."

"Benjamin? You can't think—"

"I don't think anything. But maybe Benjamin saw something that will help."

Sally set down her mug and caught his jacket. "I appreciate this, I really do, but Uniontown has this note thing under control. You don't have to waste your time."

"Didn't I tell you once before you could never waste my time?" He put his hat back on. "I don't like it when my friends are threatened. Doris," he looked at the older woman, "call me if any more threatening messages cross your desk. Don't let her open any unexpected packages. Even if she recognizes the sender. Call the Uniontown police, then call me. Immediately."

Doris nodded, her face drawn.

Sally stood. "You've got an arsonist, a murderer, and a missing guy to find. You don't need to add this to your workload."

"I dealt with just as much, if not more, last fall. This is cake." He nodded to both women and left.

Back in the car, he counted to ten before he drove off. If Sally thought he'd walk away from this, well, she didn't know him as well as she thought she did.

* * *

Sally watched Jim disappear up the stairs. Then she turned to Doris. "Why did you call him?"

Doris's chin jutted in defiance. "Because I knew you wouldn't, for whatever stupid reason you came up with."

"He's busy."

"I'm sure he is, but if you can't tell that man will never be too busy for you, then you need your eyes examined. Maybe your head, too." Doris huffed and snatched the empty coffee mug from Sally's hands. "I don't know what is wrong with you, but you need to get over it. You've been moping and skittish about him since October. Have you even talked about it?"

Sally stared at the scuffed floor. "He doesn't want to."

"Have you tried?"

Sally shook her head.

"Then you don't really know, do you? Don't you think you should find out?" Doris tossed her head and stomped off to the kitchen.

Sally clasped her hands, intensely interested in her cuticles. She should, she knew that. Except every time she was around Jim, he acted distant and hesitant. He never brought up the confrontation. Didn't that mean she shouldn't either? The only reason he could have to be reluctant was that he held her responsible, yes?

But he'd come today. Without question. And he definitely appeared indignant it was Doris who had called, not Sally.

Just what the hell did it all mean?

CHAPTER TEN

The FedEx distribution facility provided Benjamin Kardys's delivery route, but it was Saturday before Duncan had the opportunity to chase him down. He'd been deliberately vague when the FedEx manager asked why the state police needed the information. Hopefully it wouldn't blow up in Duncan's face.

He pulled his cruiser behind the FedEx truck at the curb and studied Kardys. Hard to assess him through the layers of cold-weather clothing. He looked slight of build and on the young side. For this type of crime, it didn't matter. "Are you Benjamin Kardys?" Duncan asked, exiting the car.

Kardys looked over. "Uh, yeah."

"Got a few questions for you."

Kardys held a couple packages and an electronic tablet. "Uh, sure," he said, cheeks apple red. "Mind if I make this delivery first?"

Duncan waved at the building front. He waited by the truck until Kardys returned a few minutes later. "Are you the regular delivery person for the county courthouse?" Duncan asked.

Kardys nodded. "Fairly regular. Why?"

"You made a delivery to the public defender's office yesterday. What was it?"

Kardys hesitated, frowned, then tapped a few things on his tablet. "Couple of boxes and three envelopes. What is this about?"

"I'm interested in a delivery to Sally Castle," Duncan said. "A flower box."

"FedEx handles a lot of the local florist deliveries."

"This particular one didn't have a name beyond the florist. Any way you can tell from your records who the actual sender was?" Probably not, but it was worth a shot.

Kardys's eyes narrowed, gloved hands clutching his tablet. "No. I'm sorry, Trooper," he said. "Even if I could, I wouldn't tell you without a warrant. You might have more luck with the florist, but I bet they'll want a warrant as well. Unless there was a problem with the delivery, I can't help you."

Duncan hesitated. Kardys was right. Without a court order, Duncan wasn't getting anything more than what was on the box. Which was nothing. That order could have been placed locally or from out of town. In any case, he was shit out of luck. The Uniontown boys would have to take care of following that angle. He tried another tack. "Do you know Ms. Castle? Someone sent an unwanted gift to her. It was hidden in the flower box."

Despite the cold, Kardys's cheeks paled. "Sure. Nice lady. Always says hi, asks how I'm doing. Something was inside the flowers? What?" A note of wariness entered his voice.

Duncan studied the man's face. "Body of a dead rodent."

Kardys paled further, accentuating the apple-red of his cheeks and nose. A smattering of freckles dotted his face. "Gosh, that's awful. Who would do that?"

"That's what we're trying to find out." Duncan looked at the truck. "Maybe you saw something near your van yesterday?"

Kardys shook his head. "Not especially. Not that I would."

Duncan waited for an explanation.

"See, with a delivery like this, it's not so bad." Kardys gestured at the store front. "Single delivery point, lots of windows. But a place like the courthouse is different. I have to go to lots of different offices and not all of them have a view of the truck. Most of them don't, in fact. Someone could be loitering and I'd never know."

Duncan glanced at the blue and green markings on the vehicle. "How secure is the truck?"

"I lock it, but you know thieves." Kardys shifted and clutched his tablet like a life raft. "Who would want to steal anything? You'd have to know what was in each package."

True. "Did you tamper with Ms. Castle's delivery?" Duncan asked. Such point-blank questions rarely worked, but maybe if he caught Kardys off balance, the man would let something slip.

"Me?" Kardys's tenor voice shot up an octave. "I would never...Ms. Castle has never been anything but kind to me. She's like that to everyone. I'd never—"

"Relax. I have to ask." Duncan wasn't swayed by the protest, but he recognized a futile line of questioning when he heard it. "What about someone else? Someone you've seen hanging around the courthouse during your deliveries? Someone who talked to Ms. Castle recently?"

The panic in Kardys's eyes faded a bit. "Not really," he said. "Not unless...no wait, there was a guy."

Again, Duncan waited. Silence was often more effective than questions.

"A couple days ago, maybe," Kardys continued. "He was inside the courthouse and spoke to Ms. Castle. She looked surprised to see him. Not a good sort of surprised, either."

"What did this guy look like?"

"White, maybe mid-thirties." Kardys frowned in thought. "Light brown hair. Maybe dark blond. I wasn't close enough to see his eyes. Dressed in a suit and overcoat. He acted like he knew Ms. Castle."

Duncan filed away the description, which was general enough to be useless. "Did you hear what they talked about?"

"Not after they said hello." Kardys's grip on the tablet relaxed.

"Then how do you know Ms. Castle wasn't happy?"

Kardys shrugged. "Her body language. She got kind of tense. Crossed her arms. And her voice sounded careful. I couldn't hear the words, but I think he was harassing her. She shook him off, I think. I went up in the elevator before I saw him leave."

Duncan held out a business card. "If you see him again, or notice anyone unusual, give me a call. Or if you remember anything else. Even if it doesn't seem important."

"Sure, sure." Kardys took the card. Reluctantly? Or was he slow because of the awkwardness of handling small objects with thick gloves? "Like I said. Ms. Castle is a real nice lady. I'd hate to think someone was troubling her. Was it just a rat or something else?"

Duncan had shared enough. "I can't say. Again, thanks and give me a call." He nodded his goodbye and got back into the cruiser.

While the car warmed up, he studied Kardys. The man looked at the card, pocketed it, and drove away. There'd been something odd in his mannerisms. He couldn't remember anyone hanging around his truck, yet he gave a description of a guy from a distance. He was young. Did he have a crush on a woman who was good to him and got shook up when she was threatened? Maybe. Or was it more than that? Except Sally described the notes as personal. Kardys didn't appear to fit the bill. Sure, he made regular deliveries, but he'd be more likely to interact with Doris, not Sally.

Duncan put the car in gear. His next task was to follow up with the one name Sally remembered from her prosecutorial career. Enrico Serrano. Might be a little hard to justify, but he would figure out a reason. Later.

* * *

Sally slept in Saturday morning. After some easy morning

yoga, she faced a day empty of appointments. Glorious, had it not been the second such day of the last three. Way too much free time.

After yoga, she checked the weather. Sunny, with no snow in the forecast, but temperatures in the teens discouraged a run. Yet the confines of her apartment felt like a prison. She had to get out. A quick drive to the local coffee shop, pick up a Pittsburgh paper, and come home. Perfect.

The coffee shop turned out to be a vanilla, cinnamon, sugar, and coffee-scented haven. Sally splurged on a venti caramel macchiato and a sugar-speckled apple-cinnamon muffin. While she waited, she chatted with the barista.

She also thought about Jim. How he'd showed up yesterday in response to Doris's phone call. His insistence on taking a hand in this stupid anonymous note business. Yes, he'd been carefully polite. Then again, he'd been on duty and Doris stood right there. The situation called for a certain amount of decorum.

But he'd come.

Fifteen minutes later, after she'd devoured the muffin and half her coffee, Sally wrapped her scarf around her neck and strolled back to her car. The sun winked at her from behind the clouds. Cold it may be, but the clear blue sky made it hard to worry about stalkers or getting a date to this charity dinner. Or anything, really.

As she approached her car, something white fluttered in the brisk wind, held in place on the windshield by her wipers. "Damn, I thought you could park here," she muttered. In fact, she had parked in that lot before, multiple times. She'd paid her parking, was she over? She checked her phone. No, she still had five minutes left.

A flyer, she decided. But a very small one if that was the case. She reached her car and extended her hand to the sheet. And froze.

Not a flyer. When the wind died and the sheet lay flat on the glass, she could see it was another anonymous note.

Sally almost dropped her coffee as she whipped her head from side to side, looking for whoever had left it. But the street was empty save for a few dead leaves scratching their way down the street and some birds who decided to brave the southwestern Pennsylvania cold. No people.

She set the cup on the roof of the car, pulled out her phone, and dialed.

Jim answered after two rings. "Sally, what's up?"

She swallowed. "I'm at a parking lot in Uniontown." She gave the cross streets. "I need you."

"I'm on my way."

The distance, the awkwardness, it all disappeared in a flash. Faced with yet another unwanted missive, one name leaped to the front of her brain and she'd called Jim practically on reflex.

She wasn't sure how much later, but a marked state police cruiser with lights flashing pulled up beside her and Jim got out. She pointed at the note on her windshield.

He snapped on a pair of nitrile gloves before he removed it from underneath the wiper. "Have you touched it?"

"No," she said, voice creaky. "I assumed...is it a flyer? I hope I didn't freak out and call you for nothing."

Jim read the sheet, face set and grim. "Nope." He held it out so she could read.

Don't you get it? she read. *The flowers—my admiration. The rat—your betrayal. Can I make myself more clear? You are mine, even if you don't know it. We are destined for each other. I **will** make you see that. Eventually.*

Same plain paper, same Courier type from a laser printer. She trembled and not because of the cold.

Jim got a plastic bag from his car, dropped the note inside, and sealed it. Then he took her hand. "Come on. Let's go where it's warm and talk."

They went back to the coffee shop and sat at a back table, where Jim could see the front door. He took out a pen and notebook. "Tell me what happened."

She spoke, stuttering at first, but the words came easier as she spoke. Her voice sounded flat and monotone to her ears. "I don't understand. Who is doing this?"

Jim leaned across the table. "I am going to ask you again, are you sure you can't think of anyone who would do this? Past boyfriend, someone who might have thought a relationship was more significant than you did?"

The macchiato had turned ice cold a while ago, but Sally still clutched the cup. "I don't…I don't date much, Jim. You know that." She met his calm, hazel eyes, which were filled with concern. How had she ever thought they'd be otherwise? "I don't even remember the last time I went out with a guy on a real date."

He laid down the pen. "When I talked to Kardys earlier, the FedEx delivery guy, he mentioned seeing you with a man. Said you seemed cautious."

Sally blinked. Who? "Wait, you mean Mark?"

"If that's the only man you've met with at the court-house recently, aside from me, must be. Who is he?"

"He's a fellow attorney. We went on two, maybe three dates years ago. He wasn't my type. Too indecisive. Three dates does not a relationship make."

Jim laid a hand over hers. "To you, no. To him?"

She couldn't help it, she laughed. "Mark is not the type to do this. He couldn't even make up his mind where to go for dinner when we went out. He might trail after me, but he'd do his begging up front. At least I'm pretty sure he would."

Jim's expression betrayed his skepticism. "Has he tried to contact you again?"

"He came to my apartment, but…I don't…I just don't see him doing this. I really don't." She could tell Jim thought she was being naive, but seriously. Mark? No way. "He only re-cently came back to the area. If he'd been as hung up as you think, wouldn't he have done this ages ago?"

"Maybe you're right. Mark have a last name?"

"Framingham."

He jotted that down, then closed the notebook.

"Are you going to look him up?"

"Maybe. First you're going to call the Uniontown police, make a report, and hand over this latest note. Then I'm going to take you home, where you're going to lock your door and stay inside."

"Sure thing." She didn't admit it, but that sounded like a pretty good plan to her.

CHAPTER ELEVEN

After leaving Sally at her place with strict instructions not to open the door for anyone, Duncan drove north to Pittsburgh to visit Rhonda Naif. He worked until three today. He'd spend his Saturday shift following up on the Naif homicide. He had all day tomorrow to locate Enrico Serrano and do some digging on Mark Framingham. Sally might dismiss him as a suspect, but Duncan wasn't willing to do so. Not yet.

He arrived at the Naif residence in Highland Park and pulled into the driveway behind a Lexus SUV. He studied the brick exterior. Stained glass panels above the front windows. Small front yard, not atypical for Pittsburgh. The bushes sagging under the snow would be green and flowering come spring, adding a splash of color to the stately red facade. The house cost some money. Add in the expensive car and either Naif made a good living or he lived beyond his means. If the latter, and there had been shenanigans at Capshaw & Associates, what were the chances Naif had been involved?

Duncan walked up the short sidewalk and onto the porch. He pressed the doorbell next to a dark wood door with an ornate glass insert. He didn't like doors with glass in the middle. Too much of a security risk. But it looked nice. He heard the booming barks of what sounded like a large dog.

The door opened to reveal a woman with a shapely figure and red-blonde hair. She struggled with a giant black dog. "Come in, Officer. Rufus won't bite. He sounds more threatening than he is." She hauled the dog back. Or tried to.

Duncan opened the storm door and stepped into the foyer. Lots of dark wood, hardwood floors covered with expensive-looking area rugs, lamps with crystals hanging off the shades. A couple of family portraits hung on the wall and coats hung from a row of pegs near the door. All high-end. "Trooper First Class Jim Duncan, ma'am." He touched his hat.

"You found Steve's body. Rufus, down!" She lost control of the dog, who lunged for the newcomer.

Duncan stepped back, but Rufus reared, placed his front legs on Duncan's shoulders, and proceeded to lick his face, slobber flying everywhere. It took no small amount of effort to wrestle the dog down.

"Rufus! Stop! I am so sorry." Rhonda grasped the dog's leather collar with both hands and heaved. "Damn it. Rufus, back off. Come into the sitting room. He's not allowed on the furniture so it'll be easier to talk."

Duncan wiped his face with a pocket handkerchief. Hazard of the job. Run-ins with dogs. He rubbed Rufus's head then pushed him aside.

"Would you mind taking off your shoes?" Rhonda asked, pausing. "The hardwoods don't do well with melting snow."

But they did okay with giant mastiffs? "I can't, sorry."

"Oh, just…stomp hard. It's warmer in the sitting room." Rhonda led the way to a large room with a mix of modern furniture and antiques.

He sat on the leather sofa. Rufus butted his head against Duncan's leg the second he settled in. "Mrs. Naif, please accept my condolences on the death of your husband."

"Thank you." She clapped her hands and Rufus trotted over to his mistress. "You didn't come all this way for that. Did you?"

"No, ma'am." He removed his pen and notebook, and studied Rhonda Naif's abnormally calm face. Like she couldn't frown properly or show emotion. Why? Was she upset about her husband? Sally told him Rhonda had been distressed. "I understand your husband was away last week."

"Yes. He and some friends routinely go away on skiing trips. They were at Nemacolin." She stared at her hands. "I don't ski."

"Did he always go to Nemacolin?"

"They switched it up. There were five of them. They always got a big cabin and split the cost." She twisted her rings.

"Did he ever mention Winding Valley?" The resort offered ski packages, but the cabin where Naif had been found was not big enough for a group of five.

"Not to me." Rhonda continued to twist her engagement ring. "Every once in a while, one of the guys would suggest a new place. But they tended to stick to the big ones. Because of the size of the group, I guess."

Duncan watched her face. The skin was taut, but her eyes were somber and dark. "Your husband was strangled before the fire started. Do you have any idea who might have held a grudge against him?"

"Steve got along with everybody for the most part. Well, he got snarky with the next-door neighbor a couple weeks ago. The guy blew out his driveway and sent all the snow over to our place. But I hardly think that's worth killing over."

"You'd be surprised." Sometimes it was the small things. "What about work?"

"No. Although…"

He waited. "Although what?"

"Steve was tense lately. He blamed work stuff, nothing he couldn't handle. I assumed there were some troubling investments. The markets are always volatile somewhere. Clients don't always understand that."

Troubling investments or troubling reports from his company controller? Either way, Steve Naif didn't confide in his wife. "Can you think of any reason he would have been at Winding Valley?"

"Not unless someone suggested trying it as a new location." Rhonda stopped fiddling with her rings and stroked the dog.

What was wrong with her face? "I hate to ask, but is there any possibility—"

"That Steve was meeting another woman? No." Rhonda's face didn't move, but her eyes turned hard. "We had a happy marriage. Yes, couples argue. You're not wearing a wedding band, so you might not understand, but it happens. But it doesn't mean Steve would look for companionship elsewhere."

Duncan flexed his left hand. He knew all about marital strife. "What about threatening letters? Anything in your husband's personal life?"

"No. Nothing has happened that would make me think Steve's life was in danger."

"I see." Duncan paused. "What about you?"

"Me?" Her eyes, a deep blue, widened.

"Is there anything related to you that might lead someone to bear a grudge against your husband? Any old lovers? People who wanted to be lovers? Someone who viewed your husband as a barrier?" The Naifs' life looked perfect on the outside, but Duncan knew that could be misleading.

"No one like that. I haven't looked at another man since Steve and I got married."

"What about other men looking at you?"

"A woman with two kids? Are you kidding?"

Kids, not a problem. Plastic face…Botox. Had to be. Which prompted another question. Why was she using Botox? For her husband or to catch the eye of another man? He didn't say any of that. "Is there anyone you can think of, maybe someone at work? Anyone who your husband might have been unhappy with?"

She bit her lip. "There was that tacky guy."

"What guy?"

"His name was Mike, no Mark. Mark Framingham. He's a new attorney. I think he helped with real estate deals or something."

The guy who used to date Sally. "What about him?"

"Steve came home one night seriously annoyed. With this guy and Ray, actually. Ray had been trying to get some vacation spots or something, places they could take high-end investors. Steve thought it was a giant waste of time and company money. A nice dinner, tickets to a show or a game is plenty. The firm has season tickets for the Penguins."

"Is this something your husband would normally have a say in?"

"As the senior partner, absolutely. He'd already given his opinion. He was pretty pissed that he'd been ignored. I think he told Mark to cancel any deals, but Mark refused on Ray's authority. Steve said something like maybe they needed a new real estate attorney, one who would take directions."

Resulting in a significant loss of fees and money. "What else?"

"I'm sorry. I really can't think of anything. Steve was a laid-back guy. He made a point of trying to get along with everyone. Sometimes I wished he'd be a little less pleasant."

Duncan made notes. Botox could explain the lack of facial expression. Alternatively, maybe Rhonda only played the grieving widow. She was a little too calm for his liking.

When he didn't continue, Rhonda spoke. "Do you have any idea who could have done this?"

"The investigation is still in the early stages. We're compiling information, but we'll be in touch if there's anything we need from you." He stood.

Rhonda followed suit. "Do you think you'll find who killed Steve?"

"I hope so. Here's my business card. Call me if you remember anything you think might be helpful. No need to come to the door. I can show myself out." He put his hat back on, touched the brim, and left Rhonda Naif in the sitting room, twirling his card in her fingers, her face expressionless but a worried light in her eyes.

Out in his car, Duncan reviewed his notes. Rhonda Naif hadn't supplied anything particularly valuable, except for Mark Framingham. Sally didn't think he had the stones to be a stalker, but he might be fine with a spot of embezzlement. Or maybe even murder.

* * *

After Jim left, shortly after noon on Saturday, Sally puttered around her apartment, more than happy to follow his instructions to stay put. Notes at the office were bad enough. Right on her car? How had the writer known where to find her? Unless he'd seen her at the coffee shop and taken advantage of the situation. Or followed her. She shivered at the thought.

Sally tried to remember what had been around when she arrived. A couple of people, bundled up against the cold, all of whom walked with the air of those desperate to reach their destinations quickly and get somewhere warmer. Lots of parked cars, most of the windows too dirty or snow-covered to see inside, but who would loiter in a parked car when it was fifteen degrees out? A white panel van, probably making local deliveries.

She sighed and made a mental note to work on her situational awareness. She decided to watch a movie when a knock on the door stopped her in her tracks. Jim warned her not to open her door. At least she could check and see who it was. She crept over and peered through the peephole.

Mark stood in the hallway, slapping a pair of thick gloves against his leg. Again? She had the perfect out, though. Jim's instructions were explicit. Do not open the door for anyone.

Sarah Marie Castle, her mother's voice chided. *Do not be rude.*

Mom always liked Mark. He was good looking, he flattered her, and he was another lawyer. Never mind what her youngest daughter thought. Louise Castle had given match-making her best shot once she'd met Mark and Sally didn't think her mother had ever quite managed to get over it when Sally ended things.

Mark knocked a second time. "Sally? Are you in there? I saw your car downstairs."

Damn it. Okay, she'd open the door, but not let him in. She opened the door and stood in the gap. "Mark. I didn't expect to see you."

"I heard about your unwelcome admirer so I came to check on you." He made a move toward her, but stopped when the door didn't budge. "I have an old college buddy in the Uniontown police department. I had to come into town for business and stopped to see him. I asked what he'd been up to. He mentioned crazy stalkers and lawyers, and said there had been some uproar in the public defender's office. I was worried."

Jim would not approve, but cops gossiped. They might try to keep it vague to non-cops, but anybody with half a brain cell could usually decipher the veiled references. Mark knew where she worked. "There are other attorneys in the office. How'd you know it was me?"

He cracked a grin. "Okay, I wasn't positive, but I figured it was a great reason to come by."

Double damn.

"Any idea who's behind it?" He tilted his head. "Uh, I showered this morning. You can let me in."

No, no I can't. "I'm really tired, Mark. I was on my way to take a nap when you knocked." She yawned to sell the story. "As to who it might be, the police are still investigating." She paused. It still seemed ludicrous that Mark could be responsible, but what the hell? "When did you say you came back to Pittsburgh?"

"Six months ago. I was homesick for Pennsylvania winters. Also, the gun culture out there is crazy."

"This is southwestern Pennsylvania. We have our own

gun culture."

"Yeah, but it's different. Around here it's big for hunting or sport shooting. Out there it's different. Guns just aren't my thing."

Might be the truth, might be fiction. Sally said nothing.

"Besides, I've always said there are better ways to get what you want than shooting someone."

She'd been on the brink of relenting, but just like that, he went back to creepy. "Well, thanks for stopping. I'd ask you in, really, but I am beat. I'd probably fall asleep mid-sentence and what kind of hostess would I be if I did that?"

"If you're sure." He bit his lip. "Hey, about the charity dinner. Are you certain you don't want to go with me? I mean, we'll both be there. Seems silly not to go together." The words came out in a rush.

Such a rush that Sally suspected it was the real reason for the visit. Stalking, yes, but of a different kind. "Mark, I'm sorry. I told you I've got a date. Backing out on him at this point would be rude." There it was. She had to issue the invitation now, come hell or high water. Jim had seemed concerned enough about her earlier, maybe he'd even say yes.

Mark smiled, but his disappointment shone through. "Lucky guy. I guess we'll see each other there?"

"Absolutely. Thanks for stopping. I'll see you at the dinner." Hopefully the last statement would cut off any more surprise visits.

He looked like he wanted to say something, but stopped. Then he nodded. "Take care. See you." He tugged on the gloves and left.

Sally pushed the door shut and turned the knob for the deadbolt. If Jim did say no, there was no way in hell she was going to that dinner.

CHAPTER TWELVE

After Duncan checked in with the fire marshal in Uniontown regarding the Winding Valley incident, he swung back to stop at Sally's on the way out of the city. Slush and large chunks of icy mess from passing cars filled the streets. Thick clouds obscured the sky. There'd be more snow that night. With any luck, it wouldn't roll through until after he was home.

Duncan saw Sally's Camry parked in its usual spot and spotted a light in the window of her apartment. She'd stayed home. Good. The last thing she needed to be doing if someone was after her was to go out by herself after dark. He headed for the second floor and knocked on the door. Despite the peephole, she didn't open it immediately.

"Who is it?" Sally's voice sounded through the door.

"It's Jim," he said. "Come to see how you are."

The deadbolt slid back. She opened the door just enough to let him see that she wore an oversized hoodie and her trademark black yoga pants. The ones that showed off her legs to perfection. Blue toenail polish this time. He felt a surge of regret that he was on duty.

"Seems to be the day for men stopping by to check on me," she said, leaning on the doorframe.

"Who else?" Why did that make him slightly jealous? He and Sally weren't a couple. She could see other guys.

"Mark stopped by this afternoon." She shrugged, and the sweatshirt slipped, revealing a bit of shoulder. She wasn't wearing a t-shirt underneath, just a bra. Typical lounging around at home clothes or did it mean she was getting comfortable around him again?

"You opened the door for him? What did I tell you?"

"I know him and I didn't want to be rude. Besides, I didn't let him into the apartment or anything."

Thank God for small favors. "I don't like how he shows up and you start getting threats, Sally."

Her cheeks turned pink. "Well, they aren't really threats, just…uncomfortable messages."

He raised an eyebrow.

"Okay, they are vaguely threatening. Look, I understand and I'm not dismissing your concern. But I don't get the stalker vibe from Mark. Just the guy-who-wants-a-date vibe." She pulled open the door. "I'm being rude. Come in."

He stepped inside. Five minutes. "I can't stay long, I'm on duty. But I wanted to stop again before I went back out on patrol."

She flashed a faint smile. "I'm glad you did. Jim, about Thursday. I want to apologize. I guess I'm…a little off these days. You are perfectly free to date whomever you please."

Date? Oh, the phone call. "If you're referring to the call that made you bolt like a spooked buck, that was my niece. She's five and lives in Seattle. Thursday was her birthday and I promised to call her. But then her parents surprised her with a party at some pizza and games place, and she was afraid I'd be asleep when they got home because of the time difference. That's why she called me."

Sally flushed again and dropped her gaze. "Oh. I guess I should have listened to you, huh?"

The prospect of getting back in a solitary cruiser had never been less appealing. "Yes. You are the only woman I talk to on a regular basis. Outside of work and family, that is."

She bit her lip, but said nothing.

"On another note, Framingham. He does real estate law. Guess who one of his clients is?"

Her eyebrows furrowed. "No clue."

"Capshaw & Associates."

She beckoned him into the living room and took a seat on the couch. "That's where Steve Naif worked, right? And the guy who nominally rented the ski cabin that burned."

He adjusted his duty belt and sat, hat in hand. "Yes. Framingham ever involved in anything you'd consider shady? Maybe threaten anyone over a bad deal or something?"

"Mark?" She laughed. "You've got to be kidding. Mark is so deferential he'd never get around to arguing. He'd be too busy asking if it was okay with you that he was angry. That's why it didn't work."

"Between you two you mean?"

"Yes. He'd ask me to dinner and say we were going for Indian. But then he be all, 'unless you want Chinese, or steak, or Italian. Or maybe you'd just like a pizza, or...' You know. Completely incapable of deciding and sticking to it. Drove me nuts. It's one of the reasons I can't see him behind these anonymous notes. If they were filled with waffle, sure, but poetry? No way. I much prefer your style."

"You do?" He had a style? And she liked it?

"I mean," she stammered, "you can make up your mind. You want a Reuben, you suggest Dex's. It's not a fifteen-minute decision-making process where you ask my opinion every thirty seconds."

He could see that. "Framingham brokered some deals for Capshaw & Associates. I wondered if there was a possibility any of those deals had been rocky."

"I very much doubt it. Mark is not a rocky deal guy." She crossed her arms, opened her mouth as if to say something, and then closed it again.

Something was on her mind. Something she was hesitant to bring up. But she seemed more at ease than last Thursday, too. "Any more anonymous notes?"

"Not since this morning. I've been trying to come up with more names, but I can't." She nibbled her thumbnail, a stray wisp of brown hair floating across her face.

"Well, keep trying. I hear what you're saying about Framingham. I would never tell you not to trust your gut, but don't trust it beyond reason, okay?" He tilted his head. "You look like you want to ask me something else."

"Oh it's not important. I'm sure you've got to get going. I'll ask you later." She tried for a casual tone and completely failed, like a witness at a crime scene.

He stood. "Keep your door locked and report any new notes." He studied her face, the gentle curve of her jawline. It had almost certainly been more than five minutes. When she didn't speak, he tugged on his gloves and zipped his jacket higher. "I've gotta go. Stay warm."

"I will. 'Night."

Duncan returned to the cruiser and headed back to the barracks. The chill seeped in, barely kept at bay by the blast of the car heater. Sally might dismiss Framingham as a suspect, but Duncan wanted to do some checking, and not only because of Sally's mystery correspondent. Had Framingham really left the state? And what had he been doing since his return? It was his turn on third shift Sunday, but McAllister would help him out.

As he drove down Route 40 he watched the snowflakes dance in the beams of the oncoming headlights. His mind turned to Sally. Up until tonight, his presence made her nervous, he was certain of that. Although they'd had a normal conversation, she continued to hold something back. What? More importantly, would she tell him or would he have to drag it out of her?

CHAPTER THIRTEEN

Despite not being on duty Sunday, Duncan headed over to the tech division. The computer whizzes there had cracked Naif's laptop yesterday. They'd sent a summary of the findings, which included some suspicious emails.

When he arrived and entered, all kinds of computers in various states of assembly greeted him. "I'm looking for Kevin Allston," he said to the guy working on a machine. "Following up on a laptop."

"I'm Allston." The man, heavyset with a pierced ear, shaggy hair, and a goatee, stood up. The top of his head barely came to Duncan's chin. "Over here."

Duncan followed the overweight tech to a table where Naif's black laptop was open and running. "Most of the files are junk. A few letters, business-related, a couple of spreadsheets with numbers. I've sent those to be looked at by accounting. The columns add up, but hey, isn't that always the case?"

"Anything in the browser history, cookies, email? Your summary mentioned suspicious correspondence."

"Nada on the browser. Some news sites. Financial industry news, the NASDAQ, New York Stock Exchange, some trading sites. You said the guy was an investor, so that all made sense."

Duncan sat on a nearby desk that was covered with half-assembled electronics.

"Email is a different story." Allston handed Duncan a pile of paper, then brought up the list on a monitor. "Hard as hell to delete email, you know. Nothing ever really gets deleted from the internet."

"Thank God."

"All of these," Allston pointed at a list on the screen, "are things that are theoretically no longer in existence, but we were able to recover them. Some of it is spam, but I think the ones you're holding will pique your interest."

Duncan read. One from Bob Trenton to Steve Naif, subject line "financials." Trenton wrote about some questions he had. He strongly suggested Mr. Naif call or visit him to discuss and clarify.

Presumably Naif had made the trip. A week later, there was a series of emails between Naif and Capshaw. Naif relayed his concerns and Capshaw dismissed them. The tone of Naif's emails grew heated. These were valuable clients. They needed to look into the accounts. Again, Capshaw blew off the concerns.

As Duncan continued to read, he saw Naif wouldn't let it go. He'd done additional research. Maybe they needed an outside audit. Capshaw responded saying Naif was overreacting and he, Capshaw, had the situation in hand. Nothing to worry about. Naif wasn't buying it. "We need to meet," Naif's last email said. "Clear this up and answer these questions. We could be facing an SEC audit if we aren't careful."

Capshaw seemed to acquiesce. "Next Saturday. I'll come back early and we'll talk."

Duncan checked the date on the email. The fire where they'd found the body assumed to be Ray Capshaw, and subsequently identified as Steve Naif, occurred in the early hours of Sunday morning. The date of the meeting would have been the Saturday afternoon before the fire. "Nothing after this?" he asked Allston.

"Nope. Naif's Out of Office was on, set for that entire week. Nothing came through the laptop. If he had a smartphone, he might have read emails there and deleted them. We can pull them from the server, if the warrant covers that."

"It should. If it doesn't, let me know." He held up the paper. "That stuff is all printed here?"

"Yup. If you've got the phone, that'll be faster than trolling the server."

They hadn't recovered a phone from the fire scene. Perhaps it was in Naif's car. Something else they also hadn't found. Yet. "Start with the server. I'll keep you posted."

"You got it." Allston sat down at another computer.

Duncan left with his sheaf of emails. It was time to pay another visit to Bob Trenton.

*   *   *

Fifteen minutes later, Duncan pulled into Trenton's driveway. The man might not drive, but that didn't stop him from keeping the driveway and the walk leading to the front door clear. Trenton wasn't a hermit. The mailbox stood at the foot of the driveway, facing the street. What man, or dog, wanted to slog through two, three feet or more of snow? Okay, the dog might not mind. Rizzo wouldn't.

The sun's reflection off the snow made Duncan glad he'd worn sunglasses. As the temperatures plunged, the snow changed from a soft powder to an icy grit that sparkled like diamonds.

As before, the house looked quiet when Duncan pulled up. No movement could be seen at the windows. The light filtering through a thin layer of hazy gray clouds showed off fresh footsteps in the snow. They went up the drive to the door and back. A box sat on the small porch. The prints indicated a shoe or boot with a heavy sole. Most likely the mailman.

Nero barked from the backyard. The bark ended with a high-pitched whine. Golden Retrievers had a lot of fur, but the temperature hovered at twenty degrees. The bark sounded frantic. The dog thought it was high time to go inside. Why hadn't Trenton let him in?

Duncan picked up the box and knocked. "Mr. Trenton, Trooper Duncan from the state police. You in there?"

No answer.

As he waited, Duncan became aware of a scent. It didn't take long to recognize it. Natural gas. He checked the front of the house, but didn't see a gas meter. For the smell to be noticeable outside, the buildup had to be high. If Trenton were home it was possible he'd passed out. And even if he wasn't there, the house could be in danger of exploding.

Duncan pulled out his cell phone and dialed 911. "I need an ambulance and a fire crew to 3457 Morrell Road, Dunbar. And the gas company. Gas leak with possible injuries."

"Fire, ambulance, and police units are on their way," said the dispatcher.

If Trenton could possibly be inside, Duncan wasn't inclined to wait. The man would not leave home without his seizure dog. Nero hadn't run to the front. He must be tethered. First things first. Get Trenton to safety. Then worry about the dog.

He went to his Jeep, pulled a heavy flashlight from the back, and surveyed the house's windows. Picking one that would be easy to enter, he smashed the glass, using the handle of the flashlight to clear the pane. The rush of gas was nauseating. Inhaling as much air as his lungs would hold, he slithered through the window.

The window led into the living room. Trenton was sprawled on the floor, an ugly purple bruise on his temple. Duncan lifted the inert man in a fireman's carry and brought him outside. He pulled a spare blanket from the Jeep, spread it, laid Trenton down, and felt for a pulse. Slow, but it was there.

He hurried to the backyard. Nero strained against a cable lead. As soon as Duncan unclipped him, he rushed to the door. Familiar with how hard it was to contain an over-enthusiastic Golden Retriever, he grabbed Nero's collar and hauled him to the front. As soon as Nero saw his unconscious owner, he broke free and ran to his side.

In the brisk air, Trenton came around, blinking with sluggish reflexes. "What...who—" He struggled to get up.

Duncan held him down, the sound of sirens cutting the air. "Stay put. Ambulance is on its way. Gas leak."

"Nero?" Trenton's voice was a whisper. The dog whined and lay down next to his owner, snuggling close.

Duncan picked up Trenton's hand and placed it on the dog's shaggy coat. "Right here. He's fine. You relax."

Ambulance and fire crews arrived almost at the same time. Just behind them, a state police cruiser came up and McAllister got out. "What happened?"

Duncan waved at the house. "Gas leak."

While the fire crew attended to the house and assumed leak, EMTs treated Trenton and Duncan gave McAllister his statement. After several minutes, the head of the fire crew exited the house. Duncan stopped him. "Jim Duncan," he said by way of introduction. "I called this in. You find the leak?"

The fireman nodded. "Del Cavanaugh. One of my guys said gas was on at the stove, but no flame. Nothing on the stove. The owner must have forgotten to turn it off. We're inspecting the rest of the house to be sure."

Or someone had turned it on after bashing Trenton over the head. There was that bruise. Or he'd fallen, overcome by the fumes, and hit his head. But on what? He'd been in the middle of the living room with nothing around to explain the mark.

McAllister pocketed her notebook. "Why were you out here? You should be sleeping."

"I got the report on Naif's laptop earlier. Wanted to talk to Trenton." Duncan filled her in, continuing to review in his head. He'd unlocked the door on his way out. But not a deadbolt. He made a note to check. He turned back to Cavanaugh. "Are your guys out?"

"Yeah, we shut off the gas and opened the windows. When the guy from the gas company gets here he'll check for a leak." Cavanaugh grinned. "We tried not to make too much of a mess of your crime scene, if that's what it is."

McAllister removed a roll of crime scene tape from her trunk and worked on stringing it around the house. Duncan would accompany her on a walk through as soon as it was safe to breathe. "Let me know when you're done," he said.

He headed over to the EMTs, who were loading Trenton into the back of the ambulance on a gurney, oxygen mask in place. Trenton's eyes were closed. "He okay?" Duncan asked.

The EMT nodded. "Lucky you came along. He'd be gone if he'd spent much more time breathing that in."

"You taking the dog?"

"Nah. Someone else's department." The EMT shut the bay door. "As for your victim, call Uniontown General to see when he'll be available for questioning. I'm sure you'll want to talk to him."

"Will do."

Duncan called the vet number on Nero's license to arrange for someone to pick up the dog. Once he got the all-clear, Duncan snapped on some gloves he kept in the back of his Jeep and inspected the front of the house.

McAllister returned from her tape duty. "Anything?"

"Aside from the footprints, no." The footprints he'd noted earlier were completely obliterated by the rushed exit from the house and the arrival of the fire crew. Mail was in the box. He went inside and McAllister followed. The package he'd picked up and dropped outside the door was from an on-line retailer and delivered by the US Post Office. That could tally with the tracks he'd seen.

A gas company rep came to check the lines. "No leak," Cavanaugh said, finding Duncan in the kitchen. "It was the stove."

"But you didn't find anything on the stove."

"Nope. Maybe he turned on the gas and got interrupted?"

"But why didn't it ignite then?" Not only were pots and

pans missing, Duncan didn't see anything that might have been headed for the stove. Who turned on the gas when they weren't ready to cook, then walked away to answer the door if the flame didn't catch? No one, that's who.

He headed back to the living room where McAllister inspected the front door. "No deadbolt, but there is a security chain. It was unbroken. No way to tell where the attack happened, inside or out. An unbroken chain means the actor could have locked the door upon exiting the house."

In the middle of the day, few people were around. They'd canvas the neighbors in a bit. "Can I borrow your fingerprint kit?"

McAllister nodded. Duncan fetched the kit and dusted the stove and front door for prints. He lifted a few of them. One or two might even be good enough for a match. He went to find Cavanaugh, still looking over the appliances in the kitchen. "Which burner was on?" Duncan asked.

Cavanaugh pointed. "The high-powered one, front right." He left.

Duncan looked around. McAllister joined him. "What are you thinking?"

"Running through possibilities. Why leave the gas on with no pot?"

"He forgot to turn it off?"

"With no flame? Could be Nero alerted Trenton to a seizure before he really got started." Would Trenton have thought to turn off the stove if that were the case? But Nero had been outside, probably put there by his owner to do doggy business. That wasn't it. And it didn't answer the nagging question. Why turn on the gas before prepping a pot and contents, and why leave it running with no flame? He shared his thoughts with McAllister.

"Yeah, definitely something not right. Let's look in the living room again."

They checked around for anything that might have been used to hit Trenton and cause that bruise. A marble paperweight sat on the mantle of the fireplace. No fire tools. Duncan dusted the paperweight and lifted a single set of prints. "Let's check the rest of the house while we're here."

The other rooms proved as sparse as the living room. No pictures, few keepsakes. In Trenton's office, Duncan found a folded American flag in a wood-and-glass holder with an engraved plate that said *In Recognition of Service 2008-2014*. A photo of Trenton in Army fatigues and a tan beret posing with three other soldiers stood next to it.

McAllister held up a box. "Boss, what's this?" She handed it to him.

It was made of mahogany with a glass top. Inside was a medal, a golden star with an inset silver star hanging from a red, white, and blue ribbon. A silver plate on the outside read *Operation Enduring Freedom, 17 November 2012, US Army Rangers*.

He handed it back. "Looks like some kind of service award."

Aside from that, they found nothing. A few dog toys. A half-full bowl of kibble in the kitchen. Trenton's desk was immaculate, not a paper out of place. McAllister fired up the computer. "Password-protected."

They left. McAllister made sure the door locked and placed the bright yellow crime scene tape over the door, while Duncan scrounged a piece of plywood from the garage to cover the broken window. Depending on what Trenton said, he'd be back. Because while he wasn't positive, his instincts told him this hadn't been an accident.

CHAPTER FOURTEEN

On Monday, Sally arrived at work determined to locate Enrico Serrano. She'd spent most of Sunday night pummeling her brain for names. But Serrano floated to the top of the list. It had been an actual trial. He'd not been happy with the verdict. Not with his girlfriend and not with the female prosecutor he thought bullied said girlfriend into recanting.

The notes had a definite tone of possessiveness. It didn't fit with a disgruntled convict. But if Sally had learned anything, it was not to make assumptions.

Once upon a time, she'd have needed help in her task. But now everything was online. She hit up VINE, a website that tracked the custody status of accused criminals and case information. A few clicks and she had information on Enrico Serrano. He was supposed to have been paroled this month, but he'd gotten credit for good behavior and had been let out in January.

As a defender, Sally approved. As a former prosecutor she ground her teeth. Jails were full. If the system could parole someone, it only made sense to do it. Except he didn't serve his full sentence, yet another man who got a pass when the crime involved abusing a woman.

Still, it did mean that Serrano was on the outside, able to find Sally. The site listed Serrano's current address as Duquesne, a working-class Pittsburgh neighborhood. Next, she checked all the official records. Since his release, Serrano had been clean, a model parolee. He'd made every check-in like clockwork and got a job through the parole system doing maintenance. He hadn't done so much as jaywalk or throw a cigarette butt on the ground.

Sally made a note of the location. Duquesne was closer to Pittsburgh than Uniontown, but if Serrano had access to a car, or a friend with a car, the trip would be easy. She wouldn't be hard to find, either. The Fayette County website listed all employees of the county, including the public defender's office. It would be a little trickier for Serrano to find her home address, but it wasn't impossible. For all she knew, he could have followed her home one night.

She closed her web browser. It wasn't unheard of for felons to get hung up on prosecutors. And this case roused some animosity. Serrano's then-girlfriend alibied him to the police, then recanted on the stand. Serrano thought the prosecution, Sally in particular, had pressured her.

But it still felt wrong. Waiting five years for revenge on a lawyer he barely knew didn't make sense. Far more logical to go after the duplicitous girlfriend who'd turned on him and he'd be more likely to feel possessive of her.

She made a note to find Serrano's girlfriend. She couldn't shake the feeling this was more of a personal motive than a professional one, but Jim's admonition not to dismiss anything until she had proof rang in her ears.

Enrico Serrano was free and he could have sent the notes, the flowers, and the rat. Hopefully that's all this was, a felon with a chip on his shoulder, laboring under some kind of fantasy. Someone the police could deal with easily. Because the alternative was too scary to contemplate.

❋ ❋ ❋

It was Duncan's turn on third-shift Monday night to Tuesday morning, which left little opportunity to check into Framingham. But McAllister was more than happy to help her former FTO with his research.

He was shoveling his front walk early Monday afternoon when McAllister pulled in. "Hey." He jammed the shovel into a bank next to the walk. "You could have called."

"I was driving. This way I can give you this in person." She waved a stack of paper.

"Come in. It's frigging cold out here." He heard her behind him, stamping her feet to shed the snow as he opened the front door. "Don't worry about the drips. I'm not that fancy."

Rizzo came running out of the back of the house and jumped up, putting his paws on McAllister's shoulders. Then he snuffled her hair. "Hi bud," she said, pushing him down. "I guess this is Rizzo."

"That's right. You didn't meet him the last time you were here." The dog had been at the vet's when McAllister had responded to the break-in at his house last fall. "Get down, doofus." He pulled Rizzo away and looked at McAllister. "You don't drink coffee. Tea or hot chocolate?"

"I'm fine." She sat on the couch he'd bought to replace the flowered monstrosity Tish left behind, laid her hat next to her, and unclipped a sheaf of printouts. Rizzo tried to do his best imitation of a lap-dog. "Get down. Mark Framingham."

"Hold that thought." He hurried to the kitchen, poured himself a cup of coffee and came back, pen and pad in hand. He sat in the armchair across from the couch. "Go."

"No priors," she said, shuffling the papers. "Not even a speeding ticket. He's worked for the same law firm for the past six years. He did transfer to their office in Phoenix for a while, but he returned to Pittsburgh six months ago."

Then Framingham's story was solid. But it didn't mean he hadn't nursed a broken heart the whole time. Maybe the return put him in a position to do something about it.

"The firm specializes in corporate litigation, including real estate. No complaints against him and no record with the state ethics board. The entire firm is squeaky clean."

"But Capshaw & Associates isn't their only client." Duncan took a sip of coffee, feeling the warmth thaw his frozen core.

"Obviously I couldn't get the firm's entire client list, but I assume that's true. One of the things they do is rental or purchase agreements when companies want to obtain new properties. Framingham is listed on their staff as a real estate specialist."

"What else?" He set aside the pad and pen as McAllister started handing over papers.

"He lives in Avalon, on the Ohio near Pittsburgh. I looked up the house and records with the county assessor's office. It doesn't look like a place that's out of reach for a single guy who happens to be a lawyer. Framingham drives a BMW. Not new, not ancient. He has an E-ZPass. Lots of trips on the Turnpike recently. He enters in Monroeville, exits near Uniontown. Then back."

"What do you mean by lots?" He scanned the sheet. "Two, five, ten, more?"

"I counted four round trips in the last two weeks. You said he's been to visit Ms. Castle. That might explain it. Or he might have business. It just seems like a lot of time driving between Pittsburgh and Uniontown. That's what, an hour and a half one way?"

"Three hours a trip times four. Fair amount of driving." One of the trips was right before the fire. That put him in the area at the time of Naif's death and the arson. "Anything else interesting?"

"Not really. I ran a standard credit check. It's decent. He's got money in the bank, but not enough to make me suspicious. He could be hiding it, but that would require warrants and stuff."

"We don't have cause. Nothing in his work history sets off alarms?"

"Nope. Some of the additional information you requested for Steve Naif came in, too." McAllister nodded at the paper since she was busy rubbing Rizzo behind the ears. "It's at the bottom of the stack. Naif didn't have any complaints or criminal activity personally, but check the history."

"He had an investment business on his own." It went bottom-up seven years ago. That's when he'd joined Capshaw.

McAllister let go of Rizzo, who whined, and pulled out her notebook. "Naif had a partner. There's a bit of bad blood over the business failing."

"Really?"

"Oh, yes. The partner, Andy Whitehall, was emphatic. He believed then, and believes now, that Naif's reckless investment strategy led to their demise. Basically, Naif targeted high-risk/high-yield bonds. Junk bonds. Mr. Whitehall lost quite a bit of his own money and had to go back to working for Federated Investors. He said, and I quote, I'd have gladly wrung the bastard's neck, end quote."

"Naif was strangled before the fire." Duncan looked at his former trainee. "Nice job."

She put her notebook away. "I asked Whitehall if he still felt that way."

"And?"

"He said as long as he didn't see Naif he was fine. But if they ever met, he'd still like to wring the bastard's neck."

"I think we need to find where Mr. Whitehall was the night Naif died." Duncan set aside the stack.

"I didn't ask about an alibi. Figured you'd want to handle that. But I can, seeing as you're probably on your way to bed soon. Whitehall said he was on his way out of town for this week. Some family thing in Virginia. He'll be back next Monday." She stood and zipped her jacket. "I'd better get on the road. Let me know if you want anything else. When's McCloskey's wife due?"

"Not soon enough." Duncan walked her to the front door. "If you find anything on Whitehall, let me know. Otherwise, I'll call him in a week."

"Will do." She tugged on her gloves and patted Rizzo on

the head. "Later, Boss."

He shut the door behind her, returned to the living room, and sat down next to Rizzo, sipping the last of his coffee as he re-read the material from McAllister. He definitely wanted to talk to Andy Whitehall.

CHAPTER FIFTEEN

Mid-afternoon Monday, Sally sat at her desk and turned the cream-colored invitation over in her hands. The annual Southwestern PA Legal Association charity fundraiser. She didn't mind going. The money went to legal services for lower-income families, including abused women. Definitely a worthy cause. And dinner at the Le Mont, with a fantastic view of downtown Pittsburgh, was nothing to sneeze at.

But to be brutally honest, she didn't want to go alone. For one, she simply didn't feel like it. Two, Mark would be there. He'd bother her. After all the drama with the anonymous notes and her stalker, she wasn't up to playing polite-but-not-interested for the umpteenth time. If she went, she wanted peace and quiet. A nice glass of wine. Not to be followed all night.

Three, she told Mark she had a date. If she turned up solo after that, he definitely wouldn't leave her alone, especially if he thought she'd been ditched. Going with Mark was not an option. She'd have to backtrack on her previous statement and it would be encouragement she didn't want to give.

Attention and admiration were cool. What woman didn't like that? But Sally wanted a strong, capable partner. A man who knew what he wanted and could get it, while at the same time being respectful and kind. If he happened to have hazel eyes with flecks of gold, strong hands, good shoulders, and a nice ass, so much the better.

She looked at the invitation again. There was only one guy she wanted to go to this dinner with. But would he feel the same? True, he'd been friendly enough in their past couple of conversations and his concern over these notes touched her. But responding in a crisis, having a lunch or dinner, or stopping by her apartment was not the same as being with her for an entire evening.

Only one way to find out. She reached for the phone and paused. It would be soul-crushing to hear Jim make excuses. He'd be polite. He always was. But it would still be hard to hear.

It might be easier to hear a rejection in person. Then again, maybe he'd surprise her and say yes.

❄ ❄ ❄

The sun had barely set when Sally arrived in Confluence. In the twilight, she could see snow drifted against Jim's house, but the driveway was clear. And the front walk. Same with Marge's drive and walk next door. Jim's work, almost certainly. It would be his style, taking care of others. Wasn't that one of the reasons she was attracted to him?

Rizzo, alerted to her arrival, strained against his lead in the backyard, barking for all he was worth. His yellow fur was speckled with snow and more flew through the air as he jumped around.

Sally trudged down the drive and rubbed his ears. "Hey, silly," she said. "Yes, yes. Good to see you too."

"There you are. I heard the noise and recognized the car." Jim had come up behind her, footsteps muffled in the snow. He was wearing a thick flannel shirt, but his uniform pants and boots. The last bit of setting sun shone off his hair. His nose and cheeks were red and his hands were inside the pockets of the shirt. "How'd you know I'd be home?"

"Marge," she said. Jim's neighbor often helped with

Rizzo and thought her divorced friend had been alone too long, so she was a willing informant for Sally.

He stamped his feet. "What brings you to Confluence? More notes?"

"No, thank God. You're not wearing a coat. Coming home from a shift or getting ready to go out?" She nodded at him. *You're stalling, Sally.*

"I'm on graveyard tonight. Another fifteen minutes and I'd be napping. Unclip doofus, and we'll go in the back."

Sally obliged and followed him through the back door. Inside, Rizzo shook himself, sending bits of snow flying everywhere. After a quick trip to the water dish, he ran back to Sally and butted his head against her legs.

"Coffee, hot chocolate, something stronger?"

"Coffee would be great, but don't brew anything special. I don't want to keep you from your sleep. You're going to need it." Rizzo nudged her, whining for attention. "All right, let me sit down." She dropped into a kitchen chair and busied herself paying attention to the dog.

"There's about one cup left. He's such an attention hog." Jim filled a mug and set it in front of her. "At least when you're around. Me, he hardly pays attention to."

"I don't think that's true." She sipped the coffee. "I didn't know I was so cold. Thanks."

"No charge. What's up? You said no new missives from your secret admirer. Not that I'm unhappy to see you. But it's a long drive from Uniontown." He pulled out a chair and sat across from her, hazel eyes unreadable.

"I felt like coming." She sipped again. "I want, no, I need to ask a favor."

* * *

He waited. What favor? Maybe this was what he sensed she'd been hesitant to ask before.

"I was wondering…if you'd be willing to come with me to my annual charity dinner."

Was she asking him out? Not quite what he expected. He lifted an eyebrow. "You can't go alone?"

She shifted her gaze to the coffee. "I can and have. This year, I don't want to go solo." She wrapped her fingers around the mug. "And I kind of said I had a date."

Ah. "You're trying to avoid someone, huh? Ex-boyfriend who won't go away, but you want to let him down easy?" Like Mark Framingham. Maybe she suspected him after all.

Her voice turned defensive. "What makes you think that?"

He chuckled. "You lied about being with someone at this shindig. Okay. You're not the type of woman who normally worries about being alone. The person you're concerned about can't be a woman. You wouldn't care about appearing dateless in front of another woman. A man, but not merely a colleague. Someone where there's history. But if it was just a failed relationship, you wouldn't have a problem brushing him off."

She mumbled under her breath.

"He's a nice guy. You like him. Not in a romantic way. You don't want to cut his ego. Showing up with a guest gives you a graceful reason to refuse his advances." He leaned back and crossed his arms.

Her faced turned redder with every word. "I hate you."

He laughed. He'd been right. "You do not. Come on, Sally. We can both read witnesses too well to play games. It's Framingham. Am I right?"

"You suck." She busied herself with Rizzo. Probably so she didn't have to meet his eyes. "I told you before Mark and I didn't have a great romantic history. He wants to resume things. I don't. And he won't take the hint." Face still tilted down, she lifted her eyes to look at him.

"You're using me? I'm offended." But he grinned to let her know he was amused, not mad.

"Oh hush. Then there's the whole anonymous note thing. I don't think he's the culprit, but if he is..."

"You don't want to be around him." She'd asked him on a date. A real date, not hey, do you want to grab a Reuben? Yeah, it was so she didn't have to be alone in front of her ex, but still. She'd asked him. Maybe she'd gotten over whatever hang-up she had about last fall. Their last couple of conversations felt remarkably normal.

"Anyway, yes, I told Mark I had a date and naturally I thought of you when I said it. I suppose that is using you." She chewed her lip. "You don't want to go. I understand. I'll have to deal with the consequences. He can't monopolize me all night."

"Want me to take that?" He pointed to her mug and she nodded. "When is it, where, and what's the dress code?"

She looked up at him with a look that could only be described as incredulous. Did she think he'd say no? Clearly, she did. "A week from this Saturday at the Le Mont in Pittsburgh. Not black tie, but not casual."

It would require some schedule juggling, but no way he would pass this up. "If I pick you up at your place around five is that enough time to get there?"

"It should be." She gaped at him, blushing a bit. "I think cocktails start at six, dinner at seven."

"Then I'll pick you up between five and five-thirty. I have a suit around here somewhere. Haven't worn it in years, but it should be good enough." He picked up the mug. "Don't mean to rush you out, but I want to take a quick nap before my shift. Call me if the plan changes."

Sally blinked. "Just like that, you'll go? Why?"

He sobered. "Sally, this is not complicated, not for me. You need a friend at your back. Happy to oblige. And who can turn down dinner at the Le Mont?" He leaned on the table, lines creasing his forehead as he studied her. Beyond all expectations, the universe was giving him a chance to make up for failing her. It wouldn't even be a hardship. "Besides, I was going to ask you to talk to Framingham. This way I get to do it myself. You might say I'm using you as much as you are me."

A smile spread across her face. "Great, then it's a date. I mean, not a date-date. It's settled and a date in the sense that —"

He leaned over and patted her shoulder. "Relax, Counselor. I know what you meant." While she appeared to have gotten over whatever bothered her these past months, he still wanted to know what it was. This dinner could tease it out. If nothing else, he would finally get a night with conversation that didn't revolve around mayhem and murder.

CHAPTER SIXTEEN

Sally arrived at the office on Friday determined to accomplish one thing: find everything she could about Enrico Serrano. Tuesday, Wednesday, and Thursday had brought the perfect storm of work, leaving her barely enough time to go to the bathroom between meetings. Fortunately, nothing had arrived by mail, FedEx, DHL, or had been stuck to her windshield, to distract her. It also meant no forward progress, a fact that chafed at her natural inclination to always be moving. But one couldn't always have one's way. Jim called daily to check on her, but her reports were always blessedly boring and he hung up sounding relieved.

Serrano wasn't her only suspect in this anonymous note business, but he would be the easiest to cross off the list. The craziness of the past three days ought to result in a quiet day, with nothing new scheduled to start until Monday. She could have been an eager beaver and gotten a head start on next week's work. Normally that's what she'd do. At that moment, all she wanted to do was find out about Serrano.

Locating information about the trial was relatively easy. A quick phone call to a friend who could pull the old trial records in the Allegheny County court system. Sally's memory supplied the rest.

Serrano had held up a beer distributor in Mt. Lebanon. He refused a plea agreement, insisting that his girlfriend, Janice Carruthers, would corroborate his alibi. In her initial statements to police she had. On the stand, she recanted. Asked why she changed her story, Janice's answer had been simple. She caught Serrano with another woman. Hell hath no fury and all that.

Less public information existed after Serrano was incarcerated, but Sally got in touch with an old acquaintance from her prosecution days. A man who still worked for Allegheny County Corrections at the county jail. After swearing the conversation was off the record, he told her Serrano had been a model prisoner. He never caused a problem and rarely mouthed off to the guards. "Did you ever hear him talk about the prosecution from his trial?" Sally asked.

Not a word, the corrections officer said. Serrano had been plenty angry at his girlfriend, but he'd never been heard to mention Sally, by role or by name.

Which didn't mean that he hadn't said anything. Just that he hadn't been overheard.

Then after his release, the details matched what she already knew. Serrano moved to Duquesne, registered with the parole board, and acted the perfect parolee.

It didn't make sense. Would a man feel enough resentment after five years in jail to hunt down and stalk the co-prosecutor at his trial? It sounded ludicrous. But, as Sally was forced to admit, stranger things had happened.

Maybe she should take a trip to Pittsburgh tomorrow and visit Serrano. She nixed the idea immediately. One, she had zero legal reason to visit, and would probably get into all sorts of ethics trouble. Two, if Serrano was the stalker, seeing him on his home turf would be beyond stupid. She'd always relied on her self-defense training as a fallback, but she learned last October the training wasn't perfect.

With a sigh, Sally closed her computer browser. She found almost nothing useful. Nothing the police wouldn't be investigating. She had cases to defend, pleas to arrange. Real work to do. So far, the so-called "threats" amounted to a few notes. While the presence of a dead rat had been unnerving, it wasn't dangerous. She'd be much better off leaving it to the authorities, who were equipped to handle this sort of thing.

However. Sally went back to the case history to find the name of Serrano's girlfriend. Surely there wasn't any harm in talking to Janice Carruthers. Maybe she'd heard from her old boyfriend and knew something that could be passed on to the police. Like the cops wouldn't think to talk to her. But it was something. Something safe to do. Janice Carruthers wouldn't shoot her. Probably.

CHAPTER SEVENTEEN

Saturday morning, Sally stared at Janice Carruthers's information. A simple internet search was enough to give Sally an address in Mount Oliver, a borough south of Pittsburgh that resisted being sucked into the city proper, but relied on its urban neighbor for a lot of services. No phone number listed. Before she left work last night, she also ran a criminal background check. Nothing beyond a few old charges for marijuana possession, small potatoes. That had not surprised her. Five years ago, the defense would not have called a woman with any sort of serious criminal record as a witness. Janice's record was clean since then.

Sally could wait until Monday and do a little more digging to really crawl over the details of Janice's life. But if she waited to do additional research, she wouldn't be able to drive to Pittsburgh until next weekend. That Saturday was dinner with Jim. She didn't feel like doing work on the day of her big date.

He'd said yes. She didn't even need to convince him. The thought simultaneously elated and confused her. Elated, because she knew he wouldn't have said yes unless he truly wanted to go. He wasn't the type to do otherwise. Unless you appealed to his duty as a trooper or a human being, and she hadn't done that. At least she didn't think she had. But at the same time, if he wanted to go and didn't mind being in her company, why had he been tip-toeing around her these past months?

Focus, she needed to focus on the task at hand. If Janice flipped on her boyfriend at trial, surely that meant there was no love lost between them. A visit to find out if she'd seen Serrano lately couldn't hurt.

What made up her mind was the prospect of spending all day in her apartment, fretting and wondering. She called Reen to see if her sister was free, but no dice. Nan was booked for some work thing. Sally would go. She called Aislyn, on the off chance she could provide some backup, but the young trooper couldn't go with her. Jim usually worked Saturdays, there was little point in calling him.

No. Sitting at home, maybe getting another anonymous note, wasn't an attractive option. She'd drive to Pittsburgh, see if Janice would be open to talking. To provide a little security, she sent a text to both Jim and Aislyn, informing them of her intention. At least this way they could check on her and if she turned up missing, they'd know where to start looking.

She grabbed her keys. On the way to her car, she checked her mailbox. Nothing. A voice behind her made her stop.

"Hey, Ms. Castle. You live here?" Benjamin said. He was muffled up against the cold, earflaps on his hat tied securely, arms full of boxes.

"Benjamin. What are you doing here? This isn't your usual route, is it?"

"Nah. The guy who has this Saturday route is sick. He thinks it's food poisoning." Benjamin checked the boxes in his arms. "They asked me to fill in. Nothing for you. You going out?"

"Yeah, I have an errand to run." It was inexplicable, but she wasn't inclined to share information. His reason for being there was plausible, but Benjamin just happened to fill in on a route that included her apartment building? Jim had warned her to be aware of anything out of the ordinary. At the same time, Benjamin? It was hard to see the boyish delivery man as anything other than what he was. She shouldn't be paranoid. Uniontown wasn't as big as New York City, it wasn't even as big as Pittsburgh. There couldn't be that many FedEx routes, which increased the likelihood she'd see him outside the courthouse. Still, she made a mental note to mention the meeting to Jim. "Stay warm out there. See you Monday."

He grinned. "See you."

She left and headed west on the Turnpike. Janice's address in Mt. Oliver was a modest house on a tiny lot. A blue Ford Focus that looked as if it had seen more than a few Pennsylvania winters parked half on, half off the curb. A few teens walked down the street in their wannabe urban gangster dress, an old man with a cane hobbled down the other side of the street. Also in Pittsburgh fashion, the road crews, most likely supplied under contract from the city, had plowed snow around many of the parked cars. Sally noticed some lawn chairs marked empty spots. In the city, you didn't want to lose your parking space. Especially not in the winter.

Sally picked her way around a few chunks of snow and patches of ice. Handmade snowflakes graced the windows of Janice's house, interspersed with some pink and red hearts. Did she have a child? Yes, a little girl. In fact, the child was Serrano's if Sally remembered correctly.

She looked for a doorbell, finally spotting a worn button at the side of the front door. She pushed it and heard the metallic ring inside. What if the Focus belonged to a neighbor and Janice wasn't home? Sally would have driven all the way to Pittsburgh for nothing. But she could leave a note or a business card in the door. Maybe Janice would call her. She pushed the bell again.

"Hold on. I'm coming." The door opened. "Yeah, yeah. I ain't signing your petition and I ain't buying anything. If that's what you want, get out."

The last time Sally saw Janice Carruthers, she'd been dressed in a tight skirt and cropped top, wore too much makeup and had platinum hair extensions. There was only a faint resemblance to the woman who stood before her now. The Janice of five years ago looked like a street girl. The woman in the doorway, dressed in blue jeans and a sweatshirt, little makeup on a flawless face and neatly braided hair, looked like a working, single mom. Which was probably what she was.

"Do I know you?" Janice's voice snapped Sally back to the present.

"Yes and no. My name is Sally Castle. I'm an assistant public defender for Fayette County." Sally started to extend her hand, but Janice hadn't opened the outer storm door, so she pulled it back.

Janice's brows scrunched together. "But I know you from somewhere else, don't I? Least you sorta look familiar."

Sally swallowed. "Five years ago, I worked for the Allegheny County district attorney. I was one of the ADA's on the prosecutorial team for your then-boyfriend, Enrico Serrano."

Janice struck a pose, hip jutting, hand on the doorframe. "I don't know what that asshole has done this time, but I ain't got nothing to do with it."

Sally stamped on the front step. "I'm looking for him as a possible connection to a few anonymous notes over the past few weeks. I've learned that Enrico was paroled. I'm wondering what you can tell me about him since he got out. If anything."

Janice paused, looking her visitor up and down. Then she opened the door. "Come in. Damn cold out here." She turned away.

It wasn't quite the response Sally expected, but she wasn't going to pass up the opportunity. She stepped into the house.

Sally didn't have expectations, but the plain, clean interior of the home didn't surprise her given how Janice had changed. A few child's toys littered the floor, kid-sized boots lined up by the door. A girl, her face framed by a mass of braids adorned with colorful beads, wandered out of a side room. "Who's that, Mama?" She pointed at Sally, brown eyes solemn.

"A friend, sweetie. Go back to watching TV." The little

girl returned to her program and Janice beckoned Sally to follow her. "I wish shows these days were more like *Dora the Explorer* or something. Least that way she'd be learning." They entered a kitchen with worn linoleum and a small table between two chairs. Old cabinets hung over laminate countertops and the furniture looked like it had seen a lot of owners, but everything gleamed, not a dirty dish in sight. "Have a seat. Something to drink? Don't have coffee made, but I got water, milk, and Coke."

"No, thank you." Sally sat and unbuttoned her coat. Now she was here, she didn't know what to say.

"Rico been threatening you or someone else?" The other woman sat, leaning a chin on her hand, fingers showing nails neatly trimmed and manicured. Not the three-inch talons she had at the trial.

"Me." The admission might win over Janice, make her more likely to talk. "I'm not sure it's him, though. I've gotten a few notes, including one in a box of flowers with a dead rat. That one was written in bad poetry."

"Flowers and poetry don't sound like Rico. The dead rat though. That sounds like him." Janice sat back and crossed her arms.

"Ms. Carruthers—"

"Janice."

"Janice." Sally stopped to think. "I have no specific information linking the note-writer to Enrico's trial. However, it does sound like the writer has known me, or known of me, for a while. Naturally one of the suspect pools I'm considering is past cases, both as a defense attorney and a prosecutor. Enrico's name floated to the top of my list. I gather the two of you aren't on the best of terms, but has he tried to contact you since he was paroled?"

"No. I got a different address and a new cell phone number. After that mess, I don't wanna hear from him. 'Spose he don't wanna talk to me, either."

"You were supposed to be his alibi." Sally paused again.

"Do you mind telling me what happened? You surprised even the prosecution with your testimony."

Janice tilted her head. "I was a hot mess back then. Single, kid, no job, no education. After, I went to community college. Got myself a job as a medical transcriptionist. Enough to pay for the house and send Leonora to a good school."

Sally said nothing, mostly because there didn't seem to be anything to say.

"Leonora, she's his daughter. Rico's. That's why I was gonna be his alibi. He said he'd get the money so we could move to a better place, maybe get married. Then he was gonna try and get a job."

"What happened?"

"I went over to his place one day after taking Leonora to the doctor. Found him in bed with a girl from up the street." Janice's lip curled. "He tried to say it was all a mistake. I don't need that shit. If it had just been me, I would've disappeared, left for my mom's in Morgantown. But I had a baby. What kind of man does that to the mother of his kid? I got on the stand and said I lied. I'd get slapped for making a false statement, but at least that SOB would go to jail."

That's why Janice recanted. Revenge. Simple motive, simple action. "That's why he hasn't talked to you since he got out?"

Janice shrugged. "He called a few times from jail. Or tried to. Left messages saying he was sorry, but he never asked about Leonora. I didn't answer. A few of them got nasty, at the end, but I got a concealed-carry. He comes after me, his ass is toast."

Considering her stalker, maybe Sally should get a permit. She tried to imagine Jim's reaction when she asked for his help getting one. "You said he turned nasty. Threatening? Do you think Enrico would follow through on those threats?"

"I doubt it. He's a weasel. But you're asking me if I think he would threaten you. Ain't you?" Janice raised one eyebrow. "Hell yes. Rico, he got anger issues. First few times he called, he was sure he'd been screwed by the system, by me, by God. Me, he got over. But if you're asking if I think it's possible he coulda sent those notes?"

Sally waited. Janice zeroed in on exactly what she was asking, even if she hadn't said it.

"Yeah, he could do it. Anonymous notes, that'd be his style. All flash and bang. No action." Janice shrugged again. "Like I said, poetry ain't his thing, but he could get someone to do it. The rat, yeah, that's him. Man's got a chip on his shoulder. Ain't no doubt about that."

The answer Sally had half-expected. That didn't keep her from shivering at the matter of fact tone of Janice's voice. Maybe Sally should seriously consider that concealed-carry thing.

❊   ❊   ❊

Sally returned home, head buzzing. As she drove, she again ran over every name she could remember. No, that was the only one that fit.

Unless the note writer was sending her on a wild goose chase.

Dusk had settled in when she pulled up to her apartment building. Fluffy white flakes, like bits of pillow stuffing, floated from the sky. This time next week, she'd be getting dressed up for a much-anticipated date with Jim. She probably should have gone cross-country skiing this afternoon, not up to see Janice. If nothing else, she'd be less stressed. She could have found someone to go with her. Instead she'd allowed her letter-writing fan to rob her of some quality time outdoors.

In the foyer, she checked her mailbox and pulled out a few items. A quick glance told her it was mostly junk mail. Copies of the Saturday paper lay in a pile on the floor. She hadn't bothered to get one that morning. She grabbed a newspaper and her mail, and headed upstairs.

Once inside her apartment, she locked the deadbolt, threw her keys in the basket, hung up her coat, and lined up her boots on the mat. She'd left a light on in the living room and the kitchen. All things considered, she most certainly didn't want to come home to a dark apartment. The window overlooking the fire escape was still locked, the quilt she'd bought last summer on a trip through Amish country still folded neatly at the end of the couch. The room looked exactly as she'd left it, not a pillow or picture frame out of place.

She changed into her favorite yoga pants and grabbed the paper and the mail. She bent and picked up an envelope that had fallen and landed on the floor. Then she made her cocoa and curled up on the couch, quilt draped over her. She sorted through the post. Bill, bill, junk mail, bill. Then she froze.

The envelope she'd picked up, thinking it had fallen out of the collected post. It looked just like the other anonymous notes.

She wanted to scream and fling the envelope across the room. That wouldn't solve anything. Maybe it was just a note from the building manager. But what were the odds of that? She retrieved a knife from the kitchen to open it, then picked up the envelope with a tissue. Her fingers shook as she did. No poetry this time. Only simple lines.

You still don't understand. We are meant for each other. I will not go away.

Good thing she'd set the hot chocolate down on the end table, or it would be all over the floor. She scrambled in her purse for her cell phone, bringing up Jim's contact information.

It rang twice. "Hey there. Hope you're not calling to cancel next weekend. I'm looking forward to it," he said.

Her voice froze in her throat and she couldn't speak.

He must have heard something, or her silence made him switch to his professional tone, the one designed to coax a frightened victim or witness into speaking. "What's wrong? Talk to me."

That's what he does. The thought from the rational part of her brain broke through the panic. "A note. I thought it fell out of my mail, but it must have been pushed under the door." She choked the words out around the lump in her throat. "He found my apartment, Jim. He found my home." Hot tears prickled and she wiped them away. This was no time for crying.

His voice took a controlled, commanding tone. "Call 911. Don't touch the note any more than you already have. Lock your door. I'll be there as soon as I can." He waited. "Tell me you've heard me and you understand."

She took a shaky breath. "I…I understand. Please hurry." The polite part of her wanted to tell him not to make the trip. The emotional part said to hell with polite.

"I will. Make that call." He hung up.

She bit her lip as she dialed, and gave her information to the EOC dispatcher, who promised to get an officer to her. She hung up and wrapped the quilt around her. The temperature in the apartment felt like it had plummeted twenty degrees. Her stalker found her home. Did that mean he knew her? Or had he followed her from the office? Had Mark stopped again? Or what about Benjamin? He'd been there this morning. Maybe he wasn't as innocent as he seemed after all.

CHAPTER EIGHTEEN

Duncan glanced at the Jeep's speedometer. The needle hovered at eighty-five. Thankfully, he'd worked first shift today, so he was able to respond to Sally's late-afternoon call. He had never in thirteen and a half years used his badge to get out of a speeding ticket. If he got pulled over now, that would change.

Every day that week, when he knew she was at work and when he figured she'd gotten home, he'd called for news. Nothing, nothing, nothing. Until today. Whoever the writer was, he had a lot to pay for.

There had been no mistaking the panic in Sally's voice when she called. Receiving anonymous notes at the office when you worked in a public job was one thing. Getting them in your home? Completely different.

She said he'd found her. Had they identified the culprit? He'd been so busy investigating his arson-homicide-missing person case, he hadn't done much since talking to the FedEx guy. Damn it. Even if Uniontown hadn't told him a suspect was in custody, and no reason they would, Sally might have. No, Sally would have. Period. Yes, she'd been holding back lately, but she wouldn't on this.

She probably didn't know. And that freaked her out the most. She didn't like not knowing. Not being in control.

There was no sign of a Uniontown black-and-white when he arrived, but Sally's Camry resided in its usual spot. He looked up. Every light in her apartment had to be on, since every window shone like a beacon. Good.

He glanced around and saw no one. A layer of fresh snow covered the dirty piles from previous storms. The cars parked along the street all had chunks of brownish-black slush hanging from them, tires streaked white with the residue of road salt. No strangers lurked, no shadows hung back, watching Sally's building. The creep didn't appear to be hanging around her apartment.

Yet.

He trotted up the stairs, footsteps echoing in the empty hall. After a quick look around, he knocked on Sally's door. "It's Jim," he said.

The bolt shot back and the door opened to reveal Sally, dressed in yoga pants and a hooded sweatshirt, her hair tied back in a messy knot. For once, he realized the sight didn't provoke suggestive thoughts. Then again, he did find the marble rolling pin in her hand rather distracting.

"What took you so long?" she asked, stepping back to let him in.

"The Jeep isn't a performance racing car. I was speeding as it was," he said. "What's with the rolling pin?"

"I don't have anything else. I didn't want to answer the door and find a surprise."

He unzipped his jacket, shrugged out of it, and hung it on a peg by the door. "You have to be able to swing the weapon fast enough that your opponent can't evade. That thing looks too heavy to be effective."

"It's all I've got. I don't have a gun." She went into the kitchen to replace the rolling pin. "Maybe I should change that. Janice Carruthers said she has a concealed-carry permit."

Holy shit. "I don't think you have to jump to a gun."

"Why not? Don't stalkers usually escalate? Why be unprepared?"

"Because deciding to carry is serious. It requires a complete change of lifestyle." This was fear talking. If Sally had been on a gun range even once in her life, he'd be stunned.

She went to the living room, sat, and wrapped a colorful quilt around her, shrinking into the folds. "I don't like being vulnerable."

He sat next to her. "Did you call the police?"

"Yes."

"And?"

"The officer took the latest note to compare to the others. He told me the same things you did. Lock my door. Don't open it without checking. Stay out of unfamiliar areas alone. Report any more mail or phone calls." She rubbed her forehead.

"They get prints off the other notes?" He rested his forearms on his knees.

She shook her head. "Yes, but nothing useful. Mine, Doris's, several blurry sets, probably from postal workers. It's winter. Whoever wrote the letters probably wore gloves." She let out a breath deep enough to make her shudder. "When I saw Janice, she said she hasn't heard from Serrano, but the anonymous threats would be right up his alley." She closed her eyes. "If it's even him."

"I got your text on that. I don't like the fact that you went alone, but at least you told McAllister and me before you did." Duncan looked at her. She was pale. A couple of tears leaked out from under her eyelids. He'd never seen her cry.

"I don't have proof. Mark could have come by. Oh, and Benjamin was here today."

"The FedEx guy?"

"Yeah. I've never seen him outside the courthouse and suddenly he was here, making a delivery."

Duncan frowned. "Did you ask him about it?"

"Yeah. He said he was covering for a sick coworker. Which is perfectly reasonable and plausible. God, I'm turning into a paranoid freak. Next thing you know, I'll be suspecting you."

"Very funny. Under the circumstances, you're not being paranoid, you're concerned. And you should be." He paused.

"What do your instincts tell you?"

"My instincts?" She laughed, sounding a little hysterical. Manic laughter gave way to sobbing. "I don't…I can't…oh, God."

He didn't even think. He pulled her close and held her, feeling her tears soak the front of his Henley shirt. He let her cry, patting her back and feeling awkward. He wanted to kiss away her tears, tell her everything would be all right. That he wouldn't let anything happen to her. Let her exhaust herself in his arms and put her to bed.

Eventually, Sally pulled away. Her cheeks were streaked with tears, but she must have not been wearing makeup because he didn't see any traces of it on her or his shirt. "I'm sorry," she said. "I didn't mean to fall apart. You didn't sign up to be my emotional safety net."

"What are friends for?" He wanted to brush the hair off her face, but he didn't. Touching her might lead to a kiss, which might lead to…things they might regret. She was overwrought, emotional. What kind of sleaze-ball took advantage of that? His mother would be horrified, his father livid. They'd raised their son to be better. "Listen to me. We will figure this out. Find out who's sending these crappy notes. I promise."

"Don't you folks in law enforcement stay away from saying things like that?" She smiled, but her eyes told a different story. She clung to his words like a lifeline. Which was exactly why police officers never made those promises. They were too hard to keep.

"We do. I'm saying it anyway. How about a cup of tea or something?"

"That would be great. Chamomile. In the cupboard." She pulled the quilt back around her, a child lost in her parents' bed covers.

"Coming right up." He stood and went to the kitchen, found the chamomile, and used the one-cup machine to brew it. He worked second shift tomorrow. He'd find time, make time, to go to Pittsburgh and talk to someone at the prison.

Then he'd find Enrico Serrano.

Yeah, technically it wasn't his job. But he'd be damned if he'd let Sally down on this one.

* * *

The first call Duncan made Sunday morning was to the Uniontown police department. Proprieties had to be observed. But he learned precious little. There were no usable prints on the envelopes. The one with postage had been delivered regular US mail with generic stamps. It was postmarked locally, and had been processed by the main post office. That meant it could have been dropped in any one of over a dozen curbside mailboxes, or even left in the sender's box for the postal worker. All of the notes and envelopes had been printed on a standard Hewlett-Packard laser printer. Available in every office in America and more than a few homes.

The level of threat didn't justify the expense of DNA testing. That news made Duncan grind his teeth, but he understood. With money at a premium in most departments, unless the threat was severe tests were cost-prohibitive. Even if the target happened to be a county attorney.

The notes effectively proved a dead end.

The Uniontown police did not object to Duncan visiting Allegheny County in a quest for more information. Departments could be territorial, but as a smallish city force with limited resources, why turn down a fellow law enforcement official who was willing to work on his free time? Enrico Serrano might be a long shot, but he could legally learn more about a parolee than he could about a private citizen without a conviction record. Anybody could do a Google search on Mark Framingham. But the information Duncan wanted would not come from that kind of investigation.

Kardys was interesting. Sally didn't consider him a threat and his story about filling in for a coworker could easily be verified with FedEx. The first time Duncan questioned Kardys, his actions and words didn't raise any red flags. But Duncan would confirm the "filling in for a co-worker" statement once he'd completed his trip to Pittsburgh.

His second call went to Roland Cartwright, a buddy of his who worked at the Allegheny County jail. They'd gone to college together and saw each other occasionally at alumni events. Cartwright had been moderately surprised at the phone call, but agreed to help. "Don't remember much trouble from Serrano," he said, "but yeah, I'm working Sunday. Come up and I'll get you time with his former cellmate."

In a blaze of deceptive February sunshine, Duncan made the drive to Pittsburgh. His shift started at three and he wore his uniform, intending to go straight to the barracks. The downside was that the subject might be intimidated and clam up. A risk worth taking, in Duncan's mind.

He arrived at the jail and asked for Cartwright. After he checked his duty weapon, he followed Cartwright to a medium-sized room. A two-way window, nothing on the walls, harsh lights, and austere metal furniture. A room for interrogations, not conferences. "You'll be talking to Henry Jones," Cartwright said. "He was Serrano's cell mate for the last three years of his incarceration."

"Before that?" Duncan debated putting his hat on the table and decided to leave it on.

Cartwright consulted the folder in his hands. "Before Jones, Serrano shared space with a guy named Declan Hartnell. He's out."

"Parole?"

"Time served. You can check with the Pittsburgh cops to try and find him. Then again you state guys can do that yourselves." Cartwright set the folder on the table. "I'll have Jones brought in."

Sweat trickled down Duncan's back and he unzipped his jacket. His duty belt felt unbalanced without the weight of the Sig and extra magazines, but the rules said no firearms in a prison interview. He was sure someone, somewhere, watched the whole show.

Eventually, Cartwright ushered in a tall man. Duncan automatically assessed his subject. His hair was cut so close it might as well be shaved off. One ear showed evidence of piercing, although he didn't wear an earring. Dark-brown eyes looked out of an intelligent face.

"Trooper First Class Jim Duncan, Dr. Henry Jones," said Cartwright. He led the prisoner to the table, watched him sit, then secured him. "Dr. Jones, Trooper Duncan has a few questions regarding your former cell mate. We'd be much obliged if you'd answer." Cartwright looked at his friend. "You know the drill. Buzz when you're done." He left the room.

"Dr. Jones, thank you for meeting with me," Duncan said. He removed pen and notepad from his pocket.

"Did I have a choice?" Jones's measured, educated voice lacked the cadence of a street criminal.

"Yes and no." Jones didn't necessarily have a choice in the meeting, but he would have a choice in what he said. "As Mr. Cartwright said, I'm seeking information about a former cell mate of yours, Enrico Serrano."

"What about him?" Jones laid his clasped hands on the table.

"You shared a cell for three years, before Mr. Serrano's parole."

Jones inclined his head.

"Did he ever talk about the prosecution at his trial or his girlfriend? Complain, make any threats?"

"Quite frequently." Jones smiled. "His girlfriend was supposed to corroborate his alibi and she recanted on the stand, if I remember correctly. She received most of the verbal abuse."

"What about the prosecution?"

"You mean did he threaten them?"

Duncan nodded.

"Not in so many words," Jones said, spreading his hands.

"But he believed his girlfriend had been pressured by the prosecution prior to her testimony. 'Bitches always stick together,' he said."

"Bitches referring to one of the prosecutors?" That had to be Sally. The lead ADA had been a man.

"I would assume so." Jones shrugged. "I didn't pay him a lot of attention when he ranted. Some men can't accept they've been caught. The putative girlfriend never visited him, so they couldn't have been close."

Jones acted very cooperative. Maybe too cooperative. Why? "Did he ever mention the female prosecutor by name, or say he planned to contact her after his release?"

"Not that I remember," Jones said, refolding his hands. "He once told me 'some day I'll teach the ho what for,' but I assumed he meant his girlfriend. I suppose he could have been speaking about the prosecutor."

Duncan looked at his notes. The possibility was there. Faint, but there. Perhaps Serrano hadn't solidified his plans until after his parole. "Can you think of anything else, anything threatening that Mr. Serrano said or did, specifically related to the woman assistant district attorney at his trial?"

"No, I cannot." Jones's eyes were unreadable.

"If you do, I would appreciate it if you'd pass the information to Mr. Cartwright. He can contact me," Duncan said, putting away his pad and pen. He paused. "Thank you for your time. You've been most helpful. May I ask why?" The answer would either lend weight to the information or flag the visit as a waste of time.

Jones flashed another brilliant white smile, this one tinged with malice. "Enrico Serrano was a sneak and a thief. He bullied other prisoners, trying to get them to give up the little comforts they had. Soaps, chocolate, things like that. He tried to steal from me. Once."

The man's voice remained pleasant, but the undertone sent a chill down Duncan's spine. "You're a very accomplished man, Dr. Jones. What are you doing in here? If you don't mind telling me, of course."

"Not at all. I was a professor at CMU. Chemistry. I ran stolen materials from the lab to support my drug operation. I got caught when one of my sellers tried to rip me off." Jones paused. "I cut off the fingers on his left hand at the first knuckle, but failed to intimidate him enough to prevent him testifying against me. In retrospect, I should have killed him."

A chemistry professor with a doctorate. That explained the speech. And a man who didn't like being cheated. No honor among thieves. Duncan pushed the buzzer.

Cartwright appeared to escort Jones back out of the room, then returned. "Get what you need?" he asked.

"Sort of. I owe you one." Duncan retrieved his weapon and left the jail, stepping out onto a salt-streaked sidewalk. He'd gotten Serrano's address from the parole board, his PO assuring the trooper that Serrano had thus far been a perfect parolee. Before Duncan drove off, he re-read his notes from the conversation with Dr. Jones.

His cell phone rang. It was the hospital, letting him know Trenton finally felt well enough for an interview. He arranged to visit later that afternoon, then headed for Serrano's home. Time to find out if jailhouse talk translated into real-world actions.

CHAPTER NINETEEN

Serrano's address turned out to be a ratty building in Duquesne, a neighborhood that had seen better days. Duncan supposed that it had been filled with working-class families at the height of the steel-boom. Now it was filled with dilapidated houses, junk cars, and garbage.

He stepped around an overturned trash can to approach Serrano's door. After a second knock, a male voice floated through the door. "What the hell you want?"

Not as cultured as his cellmate. Watching the interaction between Dr. Jones, the former CMU professor, and Serrano, a street thug, must have been interesting. "Mr. Serrano, Trooper First Class Jim Duncan from the state police. I need to speak with you."

As a parolee, Serrano didn't have a choice. He opened the door and squinted, looking up at his visitor. "What do the state police want with me? Where's your badge?"

Serrano's face was deep brown, his pockmarked skin and dark beady eyes giving him a ratty look. His hair tufted around his ears, one of which bore a gold hoop earring. A large tattoo that looked religious with a Spanish caption was on his right shoulder, visible under the grayish-white tank-style undershirt that stretched over a hairy chest. The dirt-streaked jeans were worn and had to predate his incarceration. Despite the cold, he didn't wear shoes or socks.

Duncan held up his ID. "Mind if I come in? It's not that warm out here."

"Hell no. I gotta talk to you. Not make you dinner. Nobody gonna freeze. What do you want?" Serrano pulled the door close to his body, cutting off any view of the inside of the house.

He must have been busted by a plain-view search. Only experience, or intimate knowledge of the Fourth Amendment, lead to that reaction. Pity. No beating around the bush with this one. "Mr. Serrano, while you were in prison, you made uncomplimentary comments about your former girlfriend and an ADA from your trial."

"What of it?"

"Why?" Duncan thought he knew why, but it would be good to hear Serrano say it.

"Janice was my girl. She had my back. Until that bitch lawyer pressured her." Serrano hawked and spat, hopefully into an unseen container on the floor.

Sally had told Duncan about her conversation with Janice Carruthers. Serrano would blame someone. Machismo at its finest. Sleeping with another woman had nothing to do with it. "Why would an ADA have done that?"

"Man, I don't know. Somebody reports a Hispanic guy robbed them, so the police grab the first guy with a Spanish name they find and the DA sends his ass to jail. Gotta make the numbers good or some such shit." Serrano's eyes narrowed and he gripped the door harder.

"Have you been in contact with anyone from your trial? Tried to find either of the prosecutors?"

Serrano shrugged. "Why would I do that?"

"Curiosity, maybe. Did you?" Duncan looked at him. "Remember, I can call your parole officer."

A wily light came into Serrano's eyes. "Yeah. Looked the lawyer bitch up online. Like you said. Curiosity. She went to Fayette County, I think. Defense. Maybe got wise to a new racket. Pressure people into testifying the other way."

"You're very sure she's the reason your girlfriend changed her testimony."

"Janice and I were tight. She had my baby. Why else would she turn on me?" Serrano hawked and spat again.

"She caught you with another woman." Duncan didn't wait for a response. "Do you own a computer or a laser printer?"

Serrano sputtered. "Yeah, like I got money for that. Because people are lining up to hire a felon. Got a whole home office set up with a leather chair and everything." Bitterness dripped from his words.

"Maybe you go to the library."

"Ain't got a library card. Don't read no damn books."

Duncan decided to try a blunt question. "Have you sent anonymous letters to Ms. Castle?"

Serrano laughed. "Not me, man. But hey, gotta give style points. Serves the bitch right if someone's pressuring her for a change." His eyes narrowed again. "You done?"

Was he? Duncan thought. He could stand on this ice-cold porch step for the next three hours. He could call Serrano's PO and get a search warrant. But his instinct told him none of it would result in different answers. Serrano would have time to dispose of, or explain away, any evidence. No, if Serrano was the mysterious stalker, they'd have to find him another way. "That's all. You'll be getting a call, or visit, from the Uniontown police. Maybe through your PO. Hopefully the story you tell them will match what you've told me. Have a nice afternoon."

Duncan touched his hat and walked away. He could feel Serrano's glare on his back as he went, hot and angry. Then he heard the door slam.

Inside the Jeep, Duncan assessed his information. The trip hadn't yielded much. Serrano was angry and vindictive. But if he blamed anyone, why had he chosen Sally? Why not harass Janice Carruthers? Unless he had. He looked at the clock. One in the afternoon. Time to make it to roll call, but not enough time to talk to the ex-girlfriend. Damn. Because if Serrano had harassed his ex, that upped the odds he was Sally's stalker. Calling Pittsburgh would be a waste of time. If Carruthers had filed a complaint, Serrano wouldn't be at home. He'd be back in jail.

He looked at the clock again. No way he had enough time for a real conversation with Carruthers.

* * *

Duncan arrived at the hospital around five o'clock to interview Trenton. He lay in bed, eyes closed, when Duncan entered the room. Seven days had allowed the bruise on Trenton's forehead to turn an ugly shade of purple tinged with green. The raised lump was visible.

Whoever clocked him hadn't been messing around. A whole week, though, before he agreed to speak with authorities. Quite a time. It made Duncan wonder. He cleared his throat. "Mr. Trenton? Trooper Duncan from the PSP."

Trenton blinked his eyes open. "Hello. I understand I have you to thank for saving me from an explosive situation."

"I'm glad I was able to pull you out before it got messy. I'm afraid I had to trash your front window to do it."

"Windows can be replaced." Trenton waved a hand. A shadow crossed his face. "Where's Nero?"

"I called your vet for a temporary kennel."

Trenton closed his eyes and breathed a sigh. "At least I kept him safe."

Odd choice of words. "Excuse me?"

"At least he was safe."

"That's not what you said."

"It's what I meant. My head…" Trenton waved a hand.

Duncan eyed the man in the bed. "Between the concussion, the gas fumes, and your refusal to talk to us, I've put this off. We really do need to go over what happened. Before you forget any details, if you haven't already."

Trenton opened his eyes again. "I'm fine. I don't remember much as it is, though. Haven't from the beginning."

"Let's start with the basics." Duncan flipped to a clean sheet in his notebook. "You were at home that day. Alone or did you have a visitor?"

"Alone. I don't go out much. I expected you after lunch." Trenton's forehead puckered as he thought back. "Because of the cold, I decided to heat some chili for lunch."

"We didn't find the chili. Or a pot."

"I didn't get that far. Someone knocked at the door. I expected a package delivery that day. Figured it was the postal guy, knocking to let me know he'd delivered the box. He does that."

"The gas was on."

"It's like I said. I don't remember doing that. Short-term memory loss from the head injury, I guess."

Duncan made a note to check the statement with Burns. "You didn't sign for the box?"

"No signature required. I often do that because if I'm in the middle of work, I don't like to be interrupted." He shrugged. "I'm home every day, so it's not like someone is going to steal it. The delivery guy knocks to let me know he's left the package and I pick it up at my leisure. It was, oh, five minutes between when he knocked and when I went out. Give or take."

Duncan made a note. "Do you keep the security chain on when you're at home?"

"Always." Trenton smoothed the covers. "I looked out the peephole, saw the box, and opened the door."

"Did you see a truck or the delivery person?"

"No. I didn't look closely."

Duncan recalled the encased flag and medal. Trenton spoke previously about a military background. He looked out the peephole, but didn't pause and check his surroundings again when he exited the house? Duncan found that hard to believe. "Then what?"

Trenton stared at the wall, a spot just over Duncan's left

shoulder. "I opened the storm door and bent to pick up the box. Something hit me on the head. After that, nothing. He must have dragged me inside if that's where you found me."

"You didn't see who hit you?"

A sheen of sweat glistened on his upper lip. "No. I was focused on the box."

Duncan visualized the front of Trenton's house. Two large bushes flanked the door. It was possible someone had hidden behind them. But the front of Trenton's head bore the injury. If someone struck him from behind, why would the lump be on his forehead? "Where was Nero during all this?"

"Out back. I put him there so he'd—" Trenton broke off. "So he could go to the bathroom."

"You let Nero out, turned the stove on, but didn't light it, then went to retrieve a package?" No way.

Trenton shifted in his bed, still refusing to look straight at Duncan. "I'm not an idiot. I might have put the pot with the chili on to start warming, but I certainly wouldn't leave the gas on with no flame."

"But it was. On, that is."

"The person who hit me must have done that."

Duncan reviewed his notes. The story sounded all wrong. Why wouldn't Trenton look him in the eye? "Any idea who would want to do this to you? Anybody you argued with? Old lovers, unhappy neighbors?"

"No. I've been thinking and it must be related to my questions about Capshaw & Associates. Have you found Ray yet?"

"We have not." Duncan closed the notebook. "You're sure you didn't see anyone else that morning? Someone who stopped by earlier or called you?"

Trenton's hands tightened on the covers and he glanced at Duncan before resuming his study of the wall. "No. You were the only person I expected. Was the security chain on?"

"No."

"Then the assailant must have hit me, dragged me back

inside, turned on the gas, and left. Footprints?"

"One set. We'll be looking into that." It would have been easy to follow the booted prints. "You have my card if you remember anything else. Hope you feel better."

Trenton closed his eyes again.

Duncan left. In the car, he thought over the statement. The hospital had given him pictures of Trenton's injury. Duncan didn't have a medical degree, but he'd seen enough. He'd bet money that the blow had come from the front, not behind. The concussion might be the cause of the subpar answers, stress due to fatigue and memory loss. Could be why Trenton claimed not to have seen his assailant. More likely he lied. The question was why. Was he protecting someone or was he afraid? Badgering a man in a hospital bed wouldn't result in answers. And it might get the PSP hit with a harassment charge.

Burns in the coroner's office could confirm his suspicions. Duncan sighed as he put the cruiser in gear. Why did people always lie? It made things much more complicated. Duncan hated complicated.

❊ ❊ ❊

Duncan walked into the coroner's office to find Burns sitting with a finger in his eye.

"What the hell are you doing?" Duncan flinched and closed his eyes. "Whatever it is, stop."

Burns chuckled. "It's called removing your contacts. Hold on."

Duncan risked a glance. Burns had removed the lens and screwed on the cap to a case. Then he put on a pair of black glasses that looked cheap, but probably weren't. "How blind are you?" Duncan asked.

"Pretty damn blind." Burns put away the lens case and contact solution. "You've seen bodies in all states. I have never seen you jump like that. What gives?"

"Eyes. Specifically things in eyes. Ugh."

"Then movies where the eyes are taped open and needles are closing in on the eyeball—"

"Stop it!"

Burns clapped his hands. "Oh man, I could have fun with this."

"You know, I can leave." Duncan half-turned to the door.

"Sorry. The Man of Stone has a weakness. Like kryptonite for Superman." Burns reached to turn down the volume on a desktop wireless speaker. "What's up?"

"You told me once you have a medical degree."

"Degree, yes. License, no."

Duncan held out the photo of Trenton's head injury. "Could that be self-inflicted?"

Burns held out the picture, standing to put it next to Duncan's head. "In my professional opinion, no. Not unless the guy head-butted a rock."

"You sure?"

"Pretty much." Burns set down the photo. "To get that angle, I'd have to hit myself with considerable force and not straight on. More like this." He pantomimed striking himself in the face at an angle. "Awkward. Not to mention it would take some serious stones to hit yourself that hard."

"Okay. Assailant to the side or behind?"

Burns mimed striking Duncan. "Frontish. Maybe slightly to the side, but the bruise is here, right above the eye." He touched Duncan's forehead. "You don't get that from a blow from behind."

"Then, in your opinion, the assailant had to be in view of his victim." Duncan's instincts hadn't failed him. Trenton lied.

Burns sat. "Yeah, I'd think. Let me guess. Your victim says he was clocked from behind."

"And he didn't see anything."

"Bull-shit," Burns said in a sing-song voice.

"Next question. He has a concussion. Would that cause loss of consciousness and memory?" Duncan slipped the photo back in his pocket. Memory loss was the only plausible explanation for the weak story. Even then he'd expect Trenton to be unsure, not positive he'd been struck from behind.

"That is entirely possible. I told you last summer, head injuries are funny. The baseball guy, remember?"

"Johnny Pearce."

"The cranium is pretty hard. It's less about force and more about angle. Can you get the brain to bounce off the inside of the skull? You've hit your head, right?"

"Yes. A couple times hard enough to raise a lump." Duncan narrowed his eyes. "What are you implying?"

"Nothing." Burns spread his hands and suppressed a grin. "Just that you're still breathing. Ever had a concussion?"

"Not that I know of."

"Exactly. Not every blow results in traumatic brain injury. But one sign of a concussion is loss of consciousness and short-term memory. Classic symptoms." Burns picked up a pen and tapped his desk. "This have anything to do with the Naif homicide?"

"Maybe. The concussion patient is Bob Trenton. Accountant at Naif's company. An unknown actor attacked him in his house and Trenton is currently in Uniontown General. Says he was unconscious and his attacker turned on the gas for his stove, then left."

Burns crossed his arms. "You don't believe him."

"I'm suspicious. Especially given what you just told me."

"Uh oh. The Man of Stone is on the warpath." Burns grinned. "Let's hope no eyes are involved."

Duncan shook his head. "Smart ass."

CHAPTER TWENTY

On Monday, Sally sat in her office, staring blankly at the casework in front of her. The mail came without another anonymous note. She couldn't focus, thinking about the one at her apartment over the weekend. She could brush off threats at work because there were other people around. Threats at home? She lived alone. Maybe she should look into the gun permit, despite Jim's caution. How complicated could carrying be?

The jangle of her cell phone jolted her out of her reverie. The caller ID read Steve Naif. That meant Rhonda. What did she want? She swiped the phone to answer. "Rhonda. What can I do for you?"

"I need your advice."

"On?"

"I was going through Steve's stuff. Finally. The police still have his computer and work files, but I needed to tackle the crap." Rhonda stopped. When Sally didn't reply, Rhonda continued. "I found something in the bottom of his sock drawer. An envelope."

"Rhonda, I have to ask, why are you calling me? I wish I could be of more help to you, but I don't see how I can."

"They found Steve in a resort hotel. Where he wasn't supposed to be." Rhonda choked back a sob. "I want the police to find his killer, but I don't want them to find out the reason he went there in the first place was to meet some woman." She broke down.

Sally rubbed her temple. "Whatever reason Steve had for being at that resort, woman or not, the police are going to find out. That's the simple truth. Do you think Steve cheated on you? You've been pretty adamant until now."

"No. I know they say the spouse is always the last to know, but honestly. I don't believe he was having an affair." Rhonda's voice regained some composure.

"Then you need to trust that and not be afraid of what the cops might discover. Now. What did you find?"

"Printed emails. I recognize the sender. They're from a former business partner, the guy Steve worked with before he joined Ray." Rhonda paused. "They aren't nice. I always knew the business failure never sat well with Andy. He quit a good job at Federated to strike out on his own."

"What was the business?"

"Investments, naturally. Steve and Andy had just gotten started when the housing bubble burst in 2008. It was a bad time. Andy wound up going back to the corporate world. I knew it hadn't been pretty. Steve had been fairly upset. But I never expected this."

"I'm guessing Andy was angrier than you realized."

"Steve never told me. No wonder Andy's wife stopped returning my calls." Rhonda's anguish came over the phone loud and clear. "Sally, the emails blame Steve. He wanted to make an investment in mortgage stocks. Andy thought it was too risky. He lost a lot of money. Personal money. And…"

Again, Sally had to prompt. "And what?"

"The last email says 'You'd better hope I never see you somewhere outside a crowd, you bastard. Because I'll gladly kill you for screwing things up like this.' And now Steve's dead. What should I do?"

"You know what to do." Rhonda might worry that the investigation would expose a potential infidelity, but murder overruled those concerns. "You need to call the police," Sally said. "Turn over the emails. You said you found them in Steve's sock drawer?"

"Yes." Rhonda sniffled.

"Someone in Pittsburgh Police dropped the ball on that one." Assuming Jim called in help with the search. He wouldn't have skipped the drawer. "You have Trooper Duncan's card, right?"

Rhonda muttered in assent.

"Call him. Tell him what happened. He'll tell you where to send the emails." Sally opened a desk drawer and looked for a packet of Advil.

"And then?"

Sally snapped. "I don't know. I'm not a cop. I—" She took a deep breath. "Sorry. I shouldn't have said that. Just call the trooper, okay? Please. I understand you're trying to keep Steve's name from being smeared, but I know him and he won't publicize anything that isn't relevant." Probably.

Rhonda's voice turned hesitant. "Sally, are you okay? You sound a little wound up. I would hate to think I'm bothering you at a bad time. I never did defense, but I know what a nut-house county prosecution can be."

For a split-second Sally was tempted to unburden herself, but she stopped. Rhonda had her own stress. "It's nothing important. Not compared to what you're going through."

"If you insist. Bye." Rhonda hung up.

She didn't push too hard on that, did she? Sally sighed. A dull ache throbbed behind her right eye. She needed an Advil. Maybe a whiskey. Her stalker hadn't made any physical threats, so yeah, not as important as a murdered husband. Hopefully it would stay that way.

✳ ✳ ✳

Before heading to roll call Monday, Duncan stopped at the post office. The mail carrier for Trenton's route had not seen anyone the day of the attack. The carrier did remember the snow leading up to the house had been untouched. That meant whoever ambushed Trenton came after eleven-thirty and before Duncan arrived. Plenty of time to pounce on the housebound accountant, set up the gas, and leave, all while following the carrier's footsteps to avoid creating a second set.

If that's what had happened. Convenient it had all gone down while Nero was in the backyard.

Next, he placed a call to FedEx. Yes, Kardys had been assigned to cover a route for an absent employee. Out of curiosity, Duncan asked if they'd ever received complaints about Kardys.

"None," the supervisor said. "He's a great employee. Works hard, shows up on time, very customer service oriented. He passed all our checks. Wish we had more like him."

Kardys's statement held water. The fact he'd been in Sally's building was just what it seemed, coincidence. They did happen, as much as Duncan hated to admit it.

"You look cranky," McAllister said, approaching his desk as he reviewed his notes.

"We've talked about this. I don't get cranky. It's frustration."

"Whatever you say, Boss." She shrugged. "I have some news for you."

He looked up. "What kind of news?"

"Mark Framingham specializes in real estate."

"You told me that already. As well as the fact that Capshaw & Associates is one of the firm's clients."

"Framingham drew up the lease for their current location in Pittsburgh. His signature is on the contract, as well as Steve Naif's and Ray Capshaw's." She handed over a piece of paper.

"They knew each other. At least by sight." He reviewed the lease agreement for the property in Oakland.

"I bet they knew each other more than by sight." She looked at another sheet before passing it to him. "Turns out, Ray Capshaw did a lot of business with this legal firm. Framingham executed the purchase of several properties, including two resort-style locations in Fayette County. They are owned by Capshaw & Associates as business locales. Places to wine and dine potential clients. Maybe even vacation spots for staff."

Duncan scanned the list. In addition to the two in Fayette, there was one in Allegheny County, one in Westmoreland, and one in Jefferson. "Are we checking these out? If Capshaw owns them—"

"He might be hiding there." McAllister nodded. "I called the barracks closest to the ones in Allegheny, Westmoreland, and Jefferson counties. That one," she pointed, "is Capshaw's hunting lodge. He wasn't there before. Doesn't mean he's not there now."

God bless McAllister. "While we wait, let's dig deeper on Mark Framingham. I know we did a basic search. See if Framingham owns any other property in the area. And let's get an official interview with him scheduled."

"You got it." She turned to leave.

"While you're at it, run Bob Trenton." He handed her a slip of paper with Trenton's name and the Dunbar address on it. "Same thing, background, property, criminal. And let's get his phone records."

"Isn't he the guy you were supposed to meet with? The one whose house got turned into a natural gas well?" She took the paper.

"He claims he didn't see anything, and didn't receive any visitors or phone calls that day. Says the only trouble spot in his life was the financial questions at work." Duncan stood.

McAllister arched an eyebrow.

"He tried, but he couldn't quite hide the tells when we talked earlier. He saw, or talked to, someone that day. His injury couldn't have happened the way he says it did. I want to know why he's lying to me." Duncan grabbed his coffee mug. Normally he avoided the substandard barracks brew, but at least it was hot and caffeinated.

"What about Capshaw?"

"Still looking for him."

McAllister shook her head. "Any word from Ms. Castle?" She followed him to the break room.

"Not after the weekend. But we're going to Pittsburgh on Saturday. Not only will I be able to look into this note-writing mess, I'll be able to talk to Framingham in a less official setting. Maybe it'll make him open up."

"A date?" Her voiced took on a playful note. "You didn't tell me about this."

"You don't tell me about your dates with Tom Burns, either." He left her standing by the coffee pot, looking a little flustered. She wanted to tease him, huh? Well, two could play that game.

CHAPTER TWENTY-ONE

B y mid-morning Tuesday, Duncan wished someone else had responded to the fire call at Winding Valley. Or that his demon of personal responsibility would take a vacation. Either way, he'd never have heard of Bob Trenton. Never had to bust through the guy's front window. He could enjoy life as a simple patrol cop.

He'd re-interviewed the staff at Capshaw & Associates in Pittsburgh. What did they know about Bob Trenton? Precious little. Trenton rarely came to the office and worked mainly from his Fayette County home. They seldom saw him, a few had never seen him. When they talked to him on the phone, he sounded like a nice man. "Although now you ask, he did argue with Mr. Naif last month," Melinda, the receptionist, said.

"You didn't mention this when we talked before," Duncan said, trying to keep a professional tone.

"I forgot. Sorry." The shrug was audible in her voice.

Inconvenient, but not unheard of. "What was the argument about?"

"I'm not sure. They were on the phone, so I didn't hear much of anything."

"How do you know the call came from Mr. Trenton? Or that they argued?"

"I put it through." Again, there was an audible shrug in her voice. "Mr. Naif said something about how the paperwork would be examined and if he found any evidence of financial mismanagement, he'd look into it."

"I'm confused. You just said you didn't hear anything."

"I didn't hear Mr. Trenton. I took Mr. Naif a cup of coffee and heard some of his half of the conversation. He sounded annoyed and I assumed they must have argued. He shooed me out of his office pretty fast, too. He didn't usually act that rudely."

Trenton said he turned over his suspicions to Naif. Perhaps Capshaw did not believe him. Or Naif had been angry at the senior partner for missing the boat. Or maybe Trenton nagged, wanting action where Naif tried to tread cautiously. "Is there anything else? Anything at all?"

"No, I swear. That's it."

Duncan said goodbye and hung up the phone. He'd taken a break from interviewing other guests at Winding Valley to go back to Capshaw & Associates. So far his interviews at the resort had come up empty, but there were a few names left on the list. Maybe McAllister could help him finish.

As if summoned by thought, McAllister walked up. "Hey, Boss."

"Tell me something helpful." He leaned back and rubbed his face.

"Well, remember Andy Whitehall?"

Duncan thought for a moment. "Steve Naif's original investment partner. The one who blamed Naif for the firm's collapse and had to go back to the corporate world?"

"That's him. He's out of the picture. He was at a hockey game that night with a bunch of friends. I confirmed it. However, it seems unhappy customers are Steve Naif's stock in trade. One of the junior advisers at Capshaw & Associates had one of those 'now that I think about it' moments."

"It's going around. So did the receptionist."

She rolled her eyes. "Anyway, the firm had a disgruntled investor recently. Morgan Donovan. Naif was this guy's advisor."

"How disgruntled was Mr. Donovan?"

"Very." McAllister consulted her notepad. "Seems Donovan made a big investment in junk bonds or something like that. Lost it all. According to the adviser, Donovan threatened Naif with an SEC audit."

Duncan leaned forward. "How did Naif respond?"

"That investments were risky, especially those kind. Donovan replied he didn't care. He'd see both Capshaw and Naif wrecked. That was the word used by the adviser." She put the notepad away.

"I'm no money management genius, but isn't that pretty much the case with those kinds of things? Subprime, junk bonds, all that nonsense?"

"Yes, but there are limits. My source didn't have all the gory details, but it appears Mr. Donovan thought Capshaw & Associates, and Naif in particular, played fast and loose with the rules. Standard disclaimers warn you that you may lose money, but when you believe your tanking investment is caused by unsavory practices on the part of your money manager, I guess you call in the big guns, aka the feds." McAllister put away her notes. "I figured Donovan as a solid suspect. One problem."

"What?"

"He was on a cruise at the time of Naif's murder. I've got it from him, his wife, credit card statements, and the cruise line." She sat on the desk.

"But it's a pattern. At least two of Naif's former clients were unhappy with his investment strategy. That means there are probably more, one of whom may have gone beyond making threats." He tapped the desktop. "Keep digging."

"Will do."

"One more thing. I need some help with the guest list from Winding Valley."

"Already divvied up the names with Porter and started working on it. Figured you could use a hand. Nobody remembers seeing a car other than Capshaw's. A few actually saw Capshaw. Or at least someone who matches his description."

"Then he definitely was there?"

"Maybe. A few folks are out of town. The couple who rented the cabin right next door is in San Diego. Thawing out, I guess."

"Keep me posted." Duncan stood and stretched.

She got up and turned to go. Then she stopped, faced him, and said, "One other thing. Rhonda Naif called. She found some emails in her husband's sock drawer. They're from his old business partner and are pretty nasty. At least according to her. I had her turn them in to Pittsburgh police and they're being sent down. I know he has an alibi, but figured you'd want to look at them anyway."

"Thanks." He gritted his teeth. He should have done the search himself. Saved the frustration.

McAllister left for real this time and Duncan headed toward the bathroom. Once again, the possibilities were piling up. Just once, he'd like to work a straight-forward incident.

The desk officer stuck his head into the squad room. "Duncan. Someone here to see you. Says it's urgent."

Duncan gave the officer a flat stare. "I've gotta use the can. Can't he talk to someone else?"

"He asked for you specifically."

Who could possibly be so important? "Did he give a name?"

"Yeah." The officer consulted a slip of paper in his hand. "Says his name is Ray Capshaw."

❋ ❋ ❋

A less experienced investigator would have rushed to question Capshaw. Duncan took his time. He asked the desk officer to escort the visitor to a conference room and get him settled. Then he took care of business and assembled a list of questions. Starting with "where the hell have you been for the last two weeks?" Worded differently.

He entered the room to find Capshaw lounging in a

metal chair, a cup of black coffee in front of him. "Mr. Capshaw. Sorry for the delay." He closed the door and gestured toward the cup. "How's the coffee?"

"Tolerable, thanks," Capshaw said, voice a lazy drawl. "As for the delay, the police are busy people."

Duncan pulled out a chair and sat. "How'd you know I was looking for you?"

Capshaw sipped. "I called my wife and the office. Both gave me your name and said you were in Uniontown. I'm on my way back to Pittsburgh. I figured I'd stop instead of making you drive to see me."

"I appreciate it." Duncan studied the man across from him. Capshaw looked extremely relaxed, sipping coffee as though he visited the police every other day. "Where have you been? Your wife said you were in Punxsutawney. But when I asked troopers in the area to check, your cabin was empty."

"Sorry about that." Capshaw flicked an imaginary bit of lint from his jeans. "Change of plans. I was on my way to the lodge when an old friend called. He asked me to stay with him for a couple of weeks and I agreed. Our return got delayed by a snowstorm. Didn't dig out until early this morning."

"You didn't tell your wife?"

"She knew I'd be gone. The cell coverage isn't good in Punxy. It's not any better at my friend's house. I didn't see the difference." Capshaw sipped, his slate gray eyes cool and expressionless.

Duncan assessed the man in front of him. There had been significant snowfall in the central part of the state. Capshaw's jeans, Merrell hiking boots, and a thick flannel shirt under a heavy-duty North Face jacket suited the weather. His narrow jaw showed a hint of stubble. But he had the soft hands of an office worker.

"You were with a friend. That doesn't tell me where."

"Frostburg."

Frostburg wasn't far from Punxy. "I'll need a name and contact information for verification. You understand, I'm sure. You've been there all this time?" Duncan said.

"From two weeks ago last Thursday until this morning. I left right after I checked into Winding Valley for Steve." Capshaw smiled. "I stayed in Frostburg longer than expected, but my wife is used to me changing plans on the fly."

Duncan watched him as he took another sip of coffee. "Two weeks is a long time. I'm surprised you didn't try to contact your wife."

"As I said, she was already expecting me to be off the grid." Capshaw shrugged, a smooth gesture suited to a man used to getting his own way. "My friend's cabin doesn't have Wi-Fi. In addition to the nonexistent cell coverage. The perfect getaway."

Or the perfect cover story. But getting "off the grid" was the new chic, especially for the constantly connected. While the story of being in a dead cell coverage area smacked of convenience, it was also possible. After all, Confluence had spotty service right in town.

A friend, Capshaw said. A woman? If that was the case, why not stay at Winding Valley and let her make the reservation. More comfortable than a cabin in Frostburg without Wi-Fi. "I want to back up. Before you went off the grid, you booked a room at the Winding Valley ski resort," Duncan said.

"I did." Capshaw did not offer any further details.

"A room, cabin really, that burned down the night of your alleged check in."

"Did it? I wasn't there."

"Your car was."

"Yes." He sipped and again did not elaborate.

"How did you get to Frostburg?"

"I rented an SUV, the one I'm driving now. Better traction for the trip."

"From where?"

"A car rental place, where else?"

The games irked Duncan, but he held it in. Blowing his top would not be helpful. "We found the body of your business partner, Steve Naif, in the burned-out building."

"They told me when I called the office. Dreadful accident. Poor Steve. Poor Rhonda."

Too smooth. *He's hiding something.* Duncan pushed on. "Yes. Especially since we've determined Mr. Naif was murdered prior to the fire."

That got a reaction. Capshaw's gray eyes widened, with a flicker of panic, and the hand holding the cup shook the tiniest bit before he set it down. "Murdered? How can you possibly tell? Melinda said the body was burned beyond recognition."

"The same way we determined it wasn't you, as we originally assumed from the rental agreement," Duncan said. He paused. "We did an autopsy. Standard procedure. The coroner determined that Mr. Naif stopped breathing before the fire."

"Ah." A shadow passed over Capshaw's face, but disappeared as he adjusted his jacket. "How clever."

"Mr. Capshaw," Duncan leaned in, "your name is on the paperwork at Winding Valley. Your car was in the lot. Yet Mr. Naif is the victim. Tell me, why did you make the reservation when Mr. Naif turned out to be the guest?" No way for Capshaw to wriggle out without looking even more suspicious than he already did.

"I was afraid this would come out." Capshaw picked up the coffee cup and set it back down. "It's a bit awkward."

"Try me." Duncan's gaze bored into Capshaw's eyes.

Capshaw licked his lips and played with the cup. "Yes. I rented the room. Steve needed a meeting place. For an assignation."

"He was having an affair."

"He wanted to keep it a secret from Rhonda. He kept it from everyone except me. He told his wife he was going away. I rented the cabin using my name. I left my car to keep up the story and drove Steve's to another one of the company's properties. Then I rented the SUV for my own trip." Capshaw looked up. An observer might have thought he looked right at

Duncan, but Capshaw's gaze fixed on a spot ever so slightly to the left.

"Favor to a friend," Duncan said. "Which property?"

"Excuse me?"

"Where you left the car. Which property?"

"Oh, another one we have in the Laurel Highlands."

"I'll need the address. Do you know the name of the woman?"

"I knew of her existence, not her name or where she lived." Capshaw hurriedly downed the rest of the coffee.

Leaving only Capshaw's word this woman even existed. To date, none of the other Winding Valley staff or guests reported seeing a woman or another car. But he could always go back with more detailed questions. "Then what happened?"

"You already know." Relaxed once more, Capshaw looked up. "I went to my friend's. This woman and Steve must have argued, she killed him, and set fire to the cabin in an attempt to hide her crime. Or her husband showed up. Same results."

"If you didn't know her name, how do know she was married?"

"I'm guessing."

Capshaw's behavior was too erratic to ring true. "Then other people at the cabin—"

Capshaw sat straight up. "What about them?"

Ah ha. There was someone else. Capshaw? Or another actor? "I'm referring to the other guests at the resort. Are you thinking of someone specific?"

"I misunderstood. That's all." Capshaw relaxed. "Believe me. If I'd known how it would end, I wouldn't have left Steve alone. I considered him a good friend and an excellent partner."

Duncan looked at his notes. Capshaw was way too polished, except for the minuscule shock when Duncan told him about Naif's murder. That had been real. And the alarm when Duncan mentioned other people. But he didn't have enough information to trap Capshaw in a corner. Not beyond what he'd already shared. Damn it.

"Is there anything else? I'm not sure how much more I can tell you." Capshaw glanced at his TAG Heuer watch. "I should get on the road. I told my wife I'd be home for dinner."

There was more. A lot more. But Duncan didn't have the questions to make Capshaw admit it. "As I said I just need the name and contact information for your friend. And the address for where you left Mr. Naif's car." He pushed his notepad to Capshaw, who wrote briskly. "It's been a rough month for your employees. Someone attacked Bob Trenton last week."

The pen clattered from Capshaw's fingers. "Bob? He's practically a recluse. Who would want to hurt him?" Real fear and shock registered in Capshaw's eyes.

Unless Duncan imagined things, the attack on Trenton alarmed Capshaw more than his partner's murder. Why? "We're still looking into it, but the person was pretty serious. The attacker turned on the stove to create a natural gas build-up before they left." Duncan stood and retrieved his notepad, at the same time passing Capshaw a business card. "Call if you think of anything. I'll send the desk officer to show you out."

As he left the conference room, Duncan's last vision was of Capshaw studying not the business card, but the wall. His eyes had gone back to an unreadable gray.

Duncan returned to his desk to call Capshaw's friend, a man, for corroboration. As sure as Duncan knew when the fish in the Middle Yough gorge were biting, he knew Ray Capshaw hadn't been honest.

CHAPTER TWENTY-TWO

"McAllister." Duncan scanned the room for her. Once again, he had more questions than answers.

She hurried over. "Yes, Boss?"

"What's the status on the background check for Trenton and the interview with Framingham?"

She went to another desk and returned with a sheaf of papers. "Bob Trenton. No criminal history. Good credit. Current on the mortgage. No driver's license, but he does own a car. At least there is a car registered in his name."

No license, but a car. Odd. Then again, maybe not. Maybe he couldn't bear to part with the car as a last symbol of independence. Or he kept it for use by people who drove him around. "What else?"

"He's boring. His bills get paid on time. He has worked for Capshaw for four years." She shrugged.

"What about his military service?"

"How'd you know about that?"

"Stuff I saw in his house. The flag and the medal. He was an Army Ranger."

She nodded. "I couldn't get military records without more paperwork. He was in the Army from 2008 to 2014. Honorably discharged. Like I said, he's boring. But…" She tilted her head. "There is one thing."

"What?" If McAllister noticed something, there was something to be noticed.

"He makes cash deposits into his bank account. The deposits aren't huge, around a thousand bucks. Every few weeks, but not on a regular monthly date." She pointed at a line item on one of Trenton's bank statements.

Another thing to ask Trenton. "Is that all?"

"Pretty much. If he's up to something, he's flying way under the radar." She unscrewed the cap to a Mountain Dew bottle and took a swig.

"What about the analysis of Capshaw & Associates?" Duncan flipped through the papers.

"Still going." She swirled the bottle of soda.

Duncan set down the paper. "And Framingham?"

"He's being difficult." Her voice was grim. "I've called. Left messages. He always returns them when I'm not available. It's a never-ending game of phone tag. I asked Pittsburgh police to send someone to interview him. They always just miss him, both home and work. It could be coincidence, but this guy I trained with passed on a real distrust of coincidences."

He rubbed his chin. "I'll catch Framingham later this week or I'll pigeon-hole him Saturday night. Meanwhile, if you get a chance, check this property and see if Naif's car is there, will you?" He handed her the address from Capshaw.

"Sure thing. What are you going to do now? Go home? Drag your suit out of storage? Even if you're just going to this thing as friends, you should look nice. Unless you intend to go in uniform."

"Don't be a smart ass." Duncan picked up his hat and jacket. "Yes, I'm going home. But not before I talk to Mr. Trenton. I hate it when people lie to me."

* * *

Tuesday afternoon, Sally returned from lunch with a slight spring in her step. True, it was still ridiculously cold, although the sky was a dazzling blue. Such low temperatures usually didn't have her skipping. But it had been a few days without another note or threatening delivery. Perhaps whoever it was had gotten bored.

At the end of the week, she and Jim would be at the Le Mont. While the room would be full of other lawyers, chances are at least some of the conversation would be about something other than dead bodies.

Benjamin was stacking the day's delivery on Doris's desk when she entered. She started to greet him, but was interrupted by her cell phone. "This is Sally."

"Sally, hi. It's Mark. How's it going?"

He still had her cell phone number? Geez. "Going fine, thanks. How about you?"

"Fine." There was a beat of silence and Sally could almost picture the hopeful light in his eyes. "Are you sure about Saturday night?"

Sally closed her eyes, did a quick count to ten, then opened them. "I'm quite sure."

"Okay, cards on the table. I know it's been a few years. I hoped we might be able to give it another shot."

"Mark, look. You're starting to border on creepy. You and I didn't have a spark back then. There is no reason to think now would be any different."

"You didn't give it enough time to find a spark." His voice held hurt and accusation.

Sparks don't need time. That's why they were called sparks. "Mark, I'm sorry. I'm at the office and someone is waiting. Bye." She clicked off after hearing his muttered "goodbye" and sighed.

"Problem?" Benjamin asked.

She'd forgotten he was standing there. "Not really."

"Sounds like a problem to me." Benjamin scanned his packages and handed her the tablet. "Since Doris isn't here, could you sign for these? Who was on the phone? Sounded like a guy you'd rather avoid."

Sally signed. "Something like that."

"This about that dinner Saturday?"

How did he know about that? Unless he'd been standing around when she and Mark talked about it when they first met at the courthouse. Had they talked about it? She couldn't remember. God, this whole mess made her almost certifiable. "Yes."

"Do you have to go?" Benjamin's eyes lit up. "Say, what if you went with me? That way, you'd have an excuse not to talk to him."

"I already have a date. But it's nice of you to offer to bail me out."

The light died. "Oh. Just a thought." He took back the tablet. "A date, huh? Anyone I know?"

"I very much doubt it." Sally turned as the door opened to admit Doris. The older woman arched an eyebrow, but said nothing. "I've got some work to do. Stay warm."

Benjamin left and Sally went to her office. She thought about his offer, the eagerness in his voice. Like her junior year in high school when that freshman guy asked her to homecoming, knowing she and her then-boyfriend had just split. Well-intentioned, but not an offer she'd ever accept.

Mark, however, was a different story. The annoying thing wasn't that he had asked her out, but he wouldn't stop. He'd shown up at her office, her apartment, and now called her cell phone. It had been years. The Mark she remembered didn't seem dedicated enough to be stalker material. Time could change people, though. She shivered, an involuntary reflex that had nothing to do with the chill. Thank God she'd worked up the nerve to ask Jim because she definitely didn't want to go to the Le Mont alone.

* * *

It had been fairly easy to learn Trenton had been discharged from Uniontown General on Monday. Duncan decided to wait until Tuesday to confront him. Let him feel a little settled and maybe he'd open up. The lights shone through the windows when Duncan pulled into Trenton's driveway. Plywood still covered the broken one. He crunched up the front walkway and rang the bell. After a short delay, the door opened to reveal Trenton in sweats and fleece-lined slippers. "Evening, Mr. Trenton. Figured I'd stop by. See how you were doing."

"I'm fine, thanks. But the state police don't stop by to check up on you." Trenton gave a tight grin. "What do you want, Trooper?"

Duncan held up his hands. "I have a few additional questions. May I come in?"

Trenton hesitated, then pushed the door open. "Are you on duty?"

Duncan stepped inside, tapping the snow from his boots. "Just got off," he said. "Mine is not a nine-to-five job. Much like being in the Army."

Trenton turned, a scowl stamped on his face. "How'd you know I was in the Army?"

"I saw the flag, the picture, and the medal when I pulled you out last week."

"You searched my house?"

"We needed to make sure there were no leaks or hazards."

"Who authorized that?"

Duncan took in the stiff posture, wrinkled forehead, and hard-eyed stare of the man in front of him. Nobody liked having their things searched, but this felt extreme. "Your house was a crime scene. Someone assaulted you. It is likely that person left the gas running to kill you." He paused. "You want to find out, correct?"

Trenton stood a pace from Duncan, effectively blocking access to the house. Nero was nowhere in sight. "We talked in the hospital. I don't see what more you want."

Duncan considered his options. He could play sympathetic or hard-ass. Considering that Trenton had deliberately lied and showed no inclination to change his mind, Duncan chose the latter approach. "I want to know why you're lying to me."

The hard light in Trenton's eyes turned hostile. "Who said I was lying?"

"No person. But the facts say you are." Duncan paused, but Trenton showed no sign of cracking, so he continued. "Your injuries are not consistent with your story. You claim you didn't see your attacker. Yet that blow could not have come from behind and I have medical evidence that proves it."

Trenton narrowed his eyes and crossed his arms.

"Also, we ran a background check on you."

"Why?"

"Standard procedure. You make cash deposits on a frequent, yet irregular, basis to your bank account. Where does the money come from?"

"My sister. She helps me out. Sends cash because she knows it's hard for me to get to the bank to cash checks."

More lies. Duncan decided to call Trenton on it. "Most banks provide for mobile deposit of checks. I think it would be harder to get to the bank or an ATM to deposit cash." No response. "Mr. Trenton, why do you continue to lie? You're either protecting someone or you're scared. If it's the latter, I can probably help you. But these constant untruths don't make you look good."

Trenton gripped his biceps. "Get out of my house."

Not exactly the response Duncan expected, but not a complete surprise. Especially if fear was not Trenton's motivation. "Mr. Trenton—"

"I said get out. Now. Before I call my lawyer." Trenton's voice sounded deadly calm, but he trembled. Fear, anger, stress. Any one of the three or any combination could explain it.

Duncan wanted to stay. Unfortunately, he had no cause. Trenton's request ended the conversation, at least for now.

"I'm sorry you feel that way," Duncan said. He gave it one more shot. "If someone is threatening you, we can help."

Trenton pointed at the door. He didn't say anything, but the message was clear. He no longer welcomed Duncan's presence.

Recognizing defeat, Duncan left. After he closed the door, he heard the rattle of the chain and click of the lock. Back in his cruiser, he stared at the house. Why the animosity? He saw only two possibilities. Extreme fear or involvement, either as a co-conspirator or the ringleader. But if Trenton was afraid, who would he be afraid of? And if he was involved, how deep did it go?

CHAPTER TWENTY-THREE

Duncan filed the request for Trenton's military records Wednesday morning. Knowing that process would take some time, he called Framingham. No answer. He continued to call throughout his shift. And continued to not reach his target. "I'm very sorry, Trooper Duncan," the secretary at Framingham's law firm said. "The entire firm is in an all-day meeting. But if you want to leave a message, I'll make sure he gets it."

Duncan had already left multiple messages and said so. "It is important he call me back as soon as possible." He gave the woman his cell number and the barracks number.

McAllister had checked the address where Capshaw claimed to have stashed Naif's car. Not only was the car not there, there was no evidence the place had been used in weeks. More lies. Where was the damn car? He debated the value of calling Capshaw to challenge the statement, but decided to hold off until he had more ammunition for his argument.

As of Thursday, there'd been no return call from Framingham. People didn't, or shouldn't, brush off messages from the police. Unless Framingham had something to hide. Duncan took out his frustration on the snow piled up on his driveway, debating the wisdom of driving north with every pile of fluffy white powder he tossed. February had crossed to March a week ago, and winter showed no signs of letting up.

McAllister pulled in as he was finishing up. "I wondered if I'd find you here or if you'd driven to Pittsburgh to hunt down Mark Framingham."

Duncan didn't comment. She knew him well.

Reading his silence, she grinned. "Total asshole. He's either telling his office secretary to say he's not available, or he's the busiest damn real estate lawyer in Pittsburgh."

"He's dodging us," Duncan said, voice flat. "It's pissing me off. If I can't get him by Saturday, I'm coming down on him like a ton of bricks at this dinner. Discretely."

"Because a ton of bricks is discrete." McAllister stamped her feet. "You asked me to look at properties he owns. He's got the house in Avalon. Looks like a nice place from the internet pictures. Nothing too fancy."

"That all?"

"Why else would I be here?" McAllister snorted. "Framingham's got a vacation home in Ligonier. That's your hometown, isn't it?" She held out a computer printout.

He took the paper from her. He recognized the address as being on the outer edge of Ligonier Township, where the houses gave way to the woods. "We should go out there and look around." He gestured toward his house. "You want to go inside?"

"I can't stay." McAllister pulled out her notebook, breath frosting on the air. "I already visited the place for a plain-view search. House is deserted. However, the garbage men haven't been by and there are bags of trash in the cans. The driveway has been plowed, but I can tell a car parked there. And recently. Evidence of a fresh oil leak."

"Nice work." Not for the first time, he thanked the universe for his former trainee.

She preened. "I also talked to the neighbors. They don't live real close, but close enough to see a car not that long ago. And they've seen lights and smoke from the chimney."

People noticed things in a small town like Ligonier. "Framingham's car?"

"They couldn't tell," McAllister said. "It was night. All they can say is a dark-colored sedan."

"They never saw Framingham? What about Capshaw?"

McAllister shook her head. "No one. Framingham's not overly neighborly, so they didn't think anything of it. But someone has been in and out of the house over the last couple of weeks."

"Anybody there now?"

McAllister shrugged. "They haven't seen anyone. Garage door wasn't open and I didn't see a car in the driveway. I'd love to have pushed my nose against the front window of the house, but I figured that would be bad."

Definitely a no-no. "Maybe I shouldn't wait until Saturday to talk to Framingham. I could drive to Pittsburgh today."

McAllister's expression sobered. "You can't go, Boss. It's your day off. You have no compelling reason to drive up there. Lieutenant Nicols finds out, you'll hear about it. You already push the boundaries, insisting on doing your own investigations. Don't cross the line."

He had to admit she was right. The barracks commander gave Duncan a lot of latitude and it would be stupid to abuse it. "Damn it." He jabbed the shovel into a snowbank. Saturday. He'd see Mark Framingham at the charity dinner. And uniform or no, Framingham would find it hard to duck out of the conversation.

* * *

Sally's desk phone rang just as she flicked off her desk lamp and prepared to leave on Thursday. "Sally Castle."

"Ms. Castle, this is Detective Kronebusch from the Uniontown police department. I'm calling to check in with you."

She glanced at the clock. Almost five. "I'm well, Detective, thanks for calling."

"Any new unwanted communications we should know about?"

"Not since the last one, what, Sunday?"

"Good, good." Kronebusch paused and the sound of rustling paper came over the line. "I also wanted to let you know we got a partial print off the flower box delivered to your office. Not a great match, but something."

Sally set down her things. A bubble of hope bloomed in her chest. "Match to whom?"

"Do you know a Benjamin Kardys?"

The bubble burst. "Yes. He's the regular FedEx delivery person for the courthouse."

"Oh." From the tone of his voice, Kronebusch had been hopeful, too. "Then it's not surprising his prints are on the box."

"Not in the slightest." Sally fought to keep chagrin out of her voice. "Especially since the box was delivered via FedEx. And even if it wasn't, he might have moved the box, or touched it when he made his delivery."

Kronebusch paused. "Have you considered the possibility he sent the flowers?"

Sally laughed. "Yes, and I don't think it's him. He's a nice young man whose work happens to bring him to my place of employment. Besides, I received the last note at my apartment. He doesn't even know where I live." Sally sobered a bit. That wasn't true. She'd seen Benjamin that day. But he didn't deliver there regularly. In fact, didn't he say he was subbing and been surprised to see her?

Yup, she'd become certifiably paranoid. She realized she'd missed part of Kronebusch's response. "I'm sorry, could you repeat that."

He coughed. "Just saying we're still looking and to stay on your guard. We'll be in touch."

Sally thanked him and hung up. So much for Jim's hope they'd catch this guy quickly.

CHAPTER TWENTY-FOUR

T he report from accounting came late Friday morning as Duncan headed out for lunch. Instead, he hit the sandwich vending machine for a roast beef on wheat, a bag of potato chips, and settled in to read.

He skipped the columns of numbers and pages of detail. There had to be a summary. Not surprisingly, it was on the second-to-last page. He read, chewing slowly.

McAllister walked by, a fast-food bag and cup in her hands. "Whatcha looking at?"

"Financial report from Capshaw & Associates." He smashed up the wrapper for his sandwich and tossed it in the garbage, then opened the bag of chips.

"Anything interesting?" She set down her lunch and picked up the paper.

"You have an accounting background, take a look. According to this, Trenton's suspicions had merit. Someone was siphoning money off the investments received."

"Equity retirement account," she read, lines creasing her forehead. "What the hell is an equity retirement account?"

"A completely generic term." He dumped chips into his mouth, chewed, and swallowed. "It's not a 401K or a Roth. And it's not a Federal retirement account."

"Nice hiding place for stolen money." She handed back the papers. "You think Naif knew and that's why he was killed?"

"I told you last fall. Money and sex. The oldest motives

around." He popped the top on a can of Coke. "Trenton said he talked to Naif about his questions. The manager on the funds where the money went missing is Ray Capshaw. Possible that Naif did his own audit, confronted Capshaw, and yes, got himself killed."

McAllister continued to rifle through papers. "That's probably true if Capshaw is the advisor for the source funds and the destination. But this is weird." She pointed at a column. "That's a series of payments to Trenton, unless I'm misreading something."

"You're not." He took a sip from the Coke. Money from a guilt-ridden sister. More like money under the table from his employer. "Bob Trenton has a lot of cash coming in."

"He have an explanation?" She sipped from her cup and munched a couple of fries.

"Claimed he didn't. Last time we talked, I confronted him on the implausibility of his story the day of the incident at his home." He related the encounter with Trenton.

"He threatened a lawsuit?" McAllister asked.

"Not in so many words, but that was the general message." He pitched the empty Coke can into the recyclable bin, then gathered up the report papers.

"Huh." She wiped her fingers and tossed her trash after his. "A reaction like that makes me think he's in on the scam."

He stretched. "Or scared, but of whom? Ray Capshaw? Trenton used to be an Army Ranger. He could probably break Capshaw in two with his pinky finger. Figuratively speaking."

"You going to question him again?"

"He's made it pretty clear my presence is not wanted for informal chats. Unless I dig up something concrete today to justify bringing him in for questioning, I'd be wasting my time. I'm off tomorrow."

"Off on a Saturday? Who'd you bribe for that?"

"I switched off with Porter. Nicols okayed it." He could feel the heat moving from the back of his neck to his face.

"That's right. You have a date."

"It's not a date."

"Oh puh-leeze." She poked his shoulder. "Why can't you admit it? You may be...what did you call it, accompanying her, but a rose by any other name and all that."

Why didn't he want to call it what it was? Sally pretty much said, "Would you?" and he'd agreed. A fancy dinner. In Pittsburgh. Sure, it was a professional association charity gig, but the atmosphere would be social. Whether he was anything more than a safe escort for Sally was yet to be determined.

"Are you listening to me?" McAllister rapped on the desk.

"Sorry, thinking about the investigation. What'd you say?" He looked at her.

The blue eyes twinkled with a mischievous light. "Sure you were."

He didn't like the knowing smirk on her face.

"I only said it's been a while. Don't forget women like chocolates and flowers, especially on a first date." She glanced at her watch. "Gotta run. Good luck." She walked off, giving him one last knowing look.

She left before he could respond, but her giggle echoed across the empty room. A date. What was he, fifteen? Except what else did you call it when two people went out together, even to a professional event?

* * *

Sally left the office at noon on Friday and saw Benjamin on the way out. "Have a good weekend," she said, shrugging into her coat.

"You're cutting out early. Court date on a Friday?" he asked, scanning the packages on Doris's desk.

"For a change, Friday afternoon's schedule is for pleasure, not business," she said.

"Oh right. Your dinner thing." Benjamin flipped the tablet in his hands. "Who's the lucky guy?"

"Friend of mine. No one you know. See you Monday." She noticed the disappointment on his face and thought again of that high school freshman. Surely Benjamin didn't think her friendliness was anything more than common courtesy toward someone she saw every day.

She put all thoughts of him out of her head. She had an outfit to plan. A manicure, facial, and massage would wash away the week's tension and put her in the mood for tomorrow.

Unless Jim had second thoughts. She pulled out her cell, looked up his contact, and almost tapped call. He said he would go. He wouldn't back out. Not the night before.

She should call him to confirm the details. Or would that sound needy and hovering on her part, like Mark incessantly calling her?

She dithered all the way home. Finally, as she opened the door to her apartment, she tapped the icon to call Jim's cell.

"Hey, Sally. What's up?" he asked, answering on the second ring.

In a corner of her mind, she realized he hadn't missed a call or a text since last fall, always answering or returning messages within minutes. If she'd thought about it seriously, she might have wondered why, but in her current frame of mind she let it slide. "Nothing much. Just calling about tomorrow."

"Event get canceled? Hope not. I picked up my suit from the cleaners last night."

"Oh, nothing like that." She slipped out of her coat. "I wanted to make sure we were on the same page."

"I told you. I'll be at your place between five and five-thirty. I think I can find my way to Pittsburgh."

She sighed, sinking onto her couch. Relief rushed through her, calming the butterflies she hadn't noticed until they were gone. "I knew that."

"Uh-huh." She could hear the grin in his voice. "I'm looking forward to it. See you tomorrow."

She ended the call and tossed aside her phone. *Stop being a ninny.* This wasn't high school, each person new to the scene. They were adults. If Jim had any reservations, he'd have told her.

She went to her closet and surveyed her clothes. She needed something that would impress him. Not yoga pants.

She fingered a deep red satin shirt with trumpet sleeves. She'd have to introduce Mark to Jim. The prospect of doing that almost made up for having to see Mark in the first place.

❋ ❋ ❋

Since Duncan was stalemated for the time being with Trenton, he decided to stay late and check on the status of the military records request. Service records weren't confidential, but there'd been forms to fill out. After all, paperwork made the world go around.

Although the woman at the National Archives, where the information was stored, acted friendly, she was also pretty firm. "It's only been two business days, Trooper."

"It's for a murder investigation. I marked the request urgent and your website says you get to those within two days."

"I understand, but the site does say try. We've been hit by budget cuts, same as any other federal agency."

He might as well argue with a wall. He thanked her and hung up. Then he looked at the clock. Four-thirty. He still had to vacuum the Jeep.

McAllister's voice sounded from beside him. "You look like you bit a lemon."

He looked up. "Silly me for thinking the federal government might work quickly."

She pulled over a chair. "Ever the optimist."

"Where'd you run off to earlier?"

"I had business in Uniontown."

"Couldn't have taken much time. You weren't gone for much more than a couple hours. Do I need to know about this business?"

She grinned. "Some of it. I was checking into all those properties purchased by Capshaw & Associates for entertaining clients. Guess what I found?"

"What?" If McAllister had an annoying trait, it was her need to be clever.

"Most of them have been sold. Almost all of them within a year of purchase. In some cases, less than six months." She sat backwards on the chair, resting her chin on her arms laid across the chair back.

"Bought and sold within a year?"

"Or less." McAllister nodded, fingers drumming the back of the chair. "And for significantly more than the purchase price."

Duncan blinked. Why buy a house and sell it within a few months? Not for a legal reason. He shared his thoughts with McAllister.

"I can think of one. They do it on TV all the time. All those flip this house shows," she said.

"To make money. Except in this case, they have the money. Dirty, but they have it." McAllister certainly had other things to do, but he appreciated the sounding board.

"What better way to clean dirty cash than a legitimate property sale," McAllister said.

"Steal from the funds," Duncan said, leaning back. "Put some of it in bogus accounts and use the rest to buy property."

"Then sell the property within the year, realize a profit, and turn your dirty cash into shiny, legitimate income." Her fingers beat a rhythm on the chair.

"Nice scheme if you can make it work." Did Trenton know about the real estate scam? He might, if he was in on the action. Or was that what scared him? Someone threatened him in exchange for his silence. Or he'd been bribed and previously felt safe. But when Naif turned up murdered, Trenton feared for his own skin.

"Indeed. Know what else I found?" She stood and stretched, her back making cracking sounds that shouldn't come from someone her age.

"Don't be dramatic. What?" But Duncan thought he might know.

"The attorney who handled all the transactions? Who would have gotten a fee as a result? Mark Framingham." She tapped the side of her nose.

Another thing to talk about with Framingham tomorrow night. "Thanks for the assist. I owe you one."

"Any time, Boss. Not like I've got anything better to do." She glanced at the clock. "Enjoy your interrogation tomorrow. Or date. Pick your term." She sauntered away.

Another glance at the clock told him it was almost five. Time to wrap up. He'd continue tomorrow tonight. He squashed a pang of guilt at using Sally's event to further his investigation. She wouldn't mind. Not if she knew it was important. Hopefully.

CHAPTER TWENTY-FIVE

Saturday, while Duncan ironed a shirt, he ran over the list of questions he wanted to ask Mark Framingham. He did it again while he tied the ruby-red tie and slipped on the charcoal-gray suit jacket. He hadn't worn either in years. Not since his divorce. It felt weird to be putting on a tie that wasn't the black uniform clip-on and to be dressed up without the weight of his duty belt. He hoped Framingham answered his questions and didn't say anything that made it necessary to pull out a set of cuffs. Deep-down, he almost wanted Framingham to no-show. He rather liked the prospect of a nice dinner with an attractive woman.

Outside Sally's apartment, he realized he should have borrowed a nicer car. He loved his Jeep, but for this particular occasion, he wished he had a fancier vehicle. At least he'd cleaned the interior and vacuumed up the dog hair.

He clutched the single, fiery orange rose and combed his hair with his fingers. Was orange okay? Red seemed too forward. White or pink weren't vibrant enough. He paused. What if Sally didn't like roses? Or she was allergic to flowers? Did women even expect flowers on dates these days? McAllister said flowers and chocolates. His father would have been mortified at his son showing up for a night out without a gift.

Dating sucked.

Steeling his nerves, he went to Sally's apartment and knocked. Whatever control he had on his nerves evaporated when she opened the door. "Wow," he said. "You look…"

Fantastic. Beautiful. Amazing. A multitude of adjectives ran through his head, each sounding corny and trite. The red satin blouse clung in all the right places. The neckline was deep enough to hint at what was below. The black skirt ended in a ruffle that set off her waist and legs perfectly. It showed off her hips as well as the yoga pants did. But the shortness of the skirt displayed her calves the way the pants didn't. Did they have to go to Pittsburgh?

The sound of snapping fingers brought him out of his trance. "Eyes forward, Trooper," she said, but her voice held mirth, not anger.

"I'm sorry. I didn't...I'm not that guy. You look great." Lame. He held out the rose. "Brought something for you."

"It's beautiful. Your lascivious look is forgiven," she said with a laugh. She took the flower. "Come in. I just need to put on my necklace and some shoes."

He stepped inside, grateful he'd sent his suit to the cleaners, re-ironed the shirt, and spit-shined his wingtips. He wouldn't look under-dressed standing next to Sally when they walked into the Le Mont.

"Dad told me to always bring a lady something. Especially on a first date," he said. "Unless you don't think of this as...I mean, you did say...oh hell."

She smiled and set the rose on the hall table. "Be right back."

He unbuttoned his overcoat. The list of questions he'd been keeping near the forefront of his mind slid to the back. *Focus.* The purpose of the night was only half pleasure after all.

Sally reappeared, a pair of gold high-heels on her feet and a pearl necklace in her hand. "Would you help me with this? It's giving me fits." She handed over the necklace and turned, gathering her hair to expose her neck.

The scent of her perfume hit him. Nice, not cloying. Duncan swallowed. He hoped the effects of his thoughts, which were not what his father would call appropriate, weren't obvious at the front of his slacks. "All set," he said, fastening the clasp.

"Thanks." She let her hair fall and faced him.

Far from helping him keep his eyes up, the pendant drew his gaze to the neckline of the blouse and the curve of her breasts. He coughed to clear his throat. "You ready?"

"Just let me put on some lipstick and grab my coat. Oh, and get a vase for that rose." She went into the bathroom.

"I'll get it." He found the vase in a kitchen cabinet, put some water in it, and dropped in the rose. "I'll get your coat, too." He removed a cashmere overcoat from the closet and held it out when she returned, lips an inviting, kissable shade of red. "Allow me."

"Why, thank you, sir." She slid her arms into the coat, pulled out her hair, and grabbed a small, black purse. "You out front?"

"Uh huh." He held the door, pulling it shut. "Sorry I don't have anything fancier than the Jeep."

She laughed and locked the deadbolt. "Don't worry about it. As long as it doesn't break down on the Turnpike, we're good. Mind if we listen to some jazz while we drive?"

"Passenger controls the radio," Duncan said, allowing her to precede him down the stairs. Another tantalizing whiff of perfume teased him as she walked past. He adjusted his slacks.

Framingham. Whatever the distractions, he needed to remember to talk to Mark Framingham.

It was going to be a hell of a drive.

❄ ❄ ❄

Sally stood outside the Le Mont, ignoring the frigid air, while Jim parked the Jeep. He let her out near the front door, citing the slushy parking lot. The drive up had been pleasant. He'd seemed a bit awkward and tense at first, but mindless talk about the Pirates' off-season moves, Rizzo, and how to best cook a steak took the pressure off. He relaxed by the time they got to Pittsburgh. Almost like old times.

She didn't expect the rose, but it didn't surprise her either. And that suit. Sally fanned herself. He looked good in anything, uniform, sweats, jeans and t-shirt, but she'd felt like Rizzo, tongue hanging out, when she opened the door. The coat and slacks fit like they'd been tailor made for him, the shirt was so dazzling white it made her eyes hurt, and the deep red tie set it all off perfectly. The sight of him, holding that rose, almost made her chuck the Le Mont out the window in favor of pizza at her place.

She had picked the tulip skirt and red satin blouse with the plunging neckline and trumpet sleeves carefully, thinking both set off her best features, and hoping to make an impression he couldn't brush aside. It had worked. Hard to miss the appreciative gleam in his eye.

"All set?" Jim walked up, picking his way around the heaps of slush. His cheeks were pink from the stiff breeze on Mount Washington.

"Whenever you are."

"Then let's get out of the cold." He offered his arm. "Do me a favor. When you introduce me, don't mention I'm a cop."

She paused. "Why not?"

"Because people get tense when the first thing out of your mouth is 'Hi, I'm Jim and I'm a police officer.' I like to wait until someone's at ease before I spring that on them."

"Except when your goal is to make him tense." She took his arm.

He smiled. "Precisely."

Inside, they handed their coats to the young man at the coat check, and the maître'd led them to the main dining area. After Sally gave him her name he said, "Table six. This way."

They followed him through the room until he stopped at their table. "Welcome and enjoy your evening." He bowed and left.

Jim unbuttoned his jacket and scanned the room, a faint

frown on this face.

"What's wrong?" Sally asked.

"The table's in the middle of the room."

"Is that a problem?"

He looked at her and the frown cleared. "Occupational hazard. I don't like having my back exposed."

"Really?"

"I like to see what's coming at me. You've never noticed I always sit facing a room?"

Come to think of it, he did. Sally had never thought twice about it, but it made perfect sense. "I can ask them to move us."

"I'll manage." He gave the room another look. "Tell me again. What is this?"

"Annual charity event for the Southwestern PA Legal Association." She paused, waiting for the stereotypical joke about lawyers and charity being an oxymoron, but it didn't come. She continued, "Money raised goes to legal services for abused women and lower income clients."

"Good cause. Want a drink?"

"Sure."

"Be right back."

While she waited, she exchanged greetings with a couple of other people, attorneys she'd met in the DA's office while in Pittsburgh, as well as people she knew from elsewhere.

Jim returned five minutes later, a glass of red wine in one hand and a cut-glass tumbler of something amber in the other. "Your merlot. It's from Australia. The bartender gushed about it, but most of what he said went over my head."

She sipped. "It's perfect. I'm surprised you don't have a beer." Maybe they hadn't talked much over the past months, but he'd remembered her favorite wine.

"I don't like what they have."

"You're such a snob." Sally chuckled. "What are you drinking?"

"Bushmill's." Jim sipped his whiskey. He started to say something, then his eyes narrowed. "On your six."

"On my what? Oh." Six o'clock. Right behind her. It could only be one person.

"Sally Castle. You get more beautiful every time I see you." Mark looked like he might go for a kiss on the cheek, but Sally cut him off with a handshake. He stepped back and noticed Jim, a quiet but commanding, figure sipping his whiskey. "Who's this? Friend of yours, I presume."

"Mark, this is Jim Duncan. Jim, Mark Framingham."

The men shook hands, and Sally swore Mark winced. "Duncan," Mark said, flexing his hand. "That name sounds familiar."

"I've been leaving messages for you."

"The cop." Mark took another step backward. "You going to interrogate me now?"

"I'm here for a nice dinner with a friend," Jim said, taking another sip of whiskey.

Mark faced Sally. "You didn't tell me your date was a cop." His eyes narrowed and his nostrils flared a little.

"There was never a reason to mention it," she said. "Why would it matter?"

Mark didn't say anything, his gaze flicking back and forth from Sally to Jim. Sweat had beaded at his hairline. "It wouldn't. Normally."

Normally? He didn't elaborate and Sally didn't press the issue. But the city could power PPG Place with the electricity between the two men. "You with anyone tonight?"

"Unfortunately, no," Mark said.

"Too bad." Thank God for Jim. "What table are you at?"

"Fifteen." Mark pointed across the room. "I think they stuck all the dateless bachelors in the corner." He shot another look at Jim. "I'll leave you two alone. Enjoy your night."

"Maybe we can talk later. Since we're both here. Stop playing phone tag," Jim said.

"Right. Later." Mark hurried off.

"What was that about?" she asked the minute Mark was out of hearing.

"I told you I wanted to talk to him." Jim took another sip of whiskey. "I can see why he's not your type."

"Why?"

"Too soft." He sipped again. "His grip is weak. Dad always told me you can tell almost everything you need to know about a person from their handshake."

She swirled her wine. "You know questioning him here is not precisely legal." She'd have a fit if Mark were her client.

"He's free to not talk to me." Jim shot her a sideways glance. "You know the rules. Miranda and the right to counsel only applies if I take him into custody. That's not in the plan. Just two guys talking."

She shook her head. He never stopped working. Neither did she. "One thing jumped out at me already," she said.

He arched an eyebrow. "Learning I was a cop made him nervous. Really nervous. See, my strategy is working already. If he's that edgy, he might let something slip." He started to take another sip of whiskey, then lowered the glass as he noticed someone at the door. "Son of a…you've got to be kidding me."

"What? Who'd you see?" She craned her neck around, then took note of the couple who'd just entered. The guy, she didn't know, but she damn sure recognized the blonde on his arm. "Oh shit."

Tish Duncan, the woman who had walked out of Jim's life seemingly without a second thought, had just entered the Le Mont.

CHAPTER TWENTY-SIX

Sally floated on cloud nine. There'd been no talk of bodies, crime, or ex-wives all night. She should have known it wouldn't last.

After the dessert plates had been cleared and coffee served, Jim stood. "Be back in a minute." His gaze flickered in Tish's direction.

"Where are you going?" Sally lifted her cup and paused. Would Jim's absence prompt Mark to glom onto her? God, please say no.

He patted her shoulder. "I have to use the men's room."

"Oh. Okay." The knot that had started to build in her shoulders relaxed. "Looks like they're clearing the dance floor."

He glanced over. "I'm not much of a dancer." He squeezed her hand, lingering for a second. "I swear. I'll be right back." He threaded his way through the crowd, heading for the restroom. She watched him as he went. Too bad it was too early to leave.

Someone sat down in his empty chair moments later. Sally, too absorbed in her thoughts and her coffee, didn't pay attention until the person spoke. "Tish Duncan. I'm Jim's ex-wife. I guess you're his date."

Sally glanced over. Tish was trying to look polished and glamorous with her platinum blonde hair, booth-generated tan, and designer dress. Instead, she looked a bit plastic. "We're here as friends."

"Ah. Friends."

"No need to go all air quotes. Can I help you with something?" She studied Tish over the rim of her coffee cup.

Finally, Tish spoke. "Please don't tell me you've fallen for the Boy Scout act."

"What are you talking about?"

"Let me guess. He showed up with flowers. Or chocolate. Something."

Sally didn't move or speak.

"He lives behind an emotional wall. He can't communicate worth a damn," Tish said. She glanced in the direction of the men's room. A malicious note came into her voice and her perfect lips twisted in a scowl. "You've seen it. I can tell. Tell me, has he pushed you away yet?"

Sally's thought flashed to the past months. *Don't let yourself be baited, Sally.* "You're a tad bitter, aren't you?" Sally set down her cup.

"Bitter? Me? Damn right, I'm bitter." Tish leaned back and crossed her arms. "He's done it to you, hasn't he? The I'm busy-can't talk-later routine. It's just the beginning. He'll let you only so close."

"I don't believe that."

"Believe it." Tish stood. "Something will happen and he'll use that as an excuse. It's just a matter of time. But something tells me it's happened already." She gave Sally a final pat and sashayed away.

Hands trembling, Sally set down her cup. Trembling with fear or anger? Both? Was Tish right? After all, she'd been married to Jim, known him since high school. Had October been the excuse Jim hoped for all along? He wasn't mad at Sally, but he wanted to move on. But then why come tonight?

Sally glanced around. He was still missing in action. And so, she noticed, was Mark.

* * *

The need to use the bathroom had been half pretext. Duncan spied Framingham heading in that direction and decided to take advantage. Duncan entered the restroom to see Framingham at a urinal, muttering to himself.

He looked up at the sound of footsteps. "What the hell are you doing here?"

"The same thing you are, I'd expect."

"Now you plan to arrest me while I'm in the bathroom? This is harassment."

Duncan moved to the urinal. "I'm escorting a friend to a social function. You're the one throwing around words like arrest and interrogation. One might think you've got something to hide." Proximity made Framingham nervous and talky. If Duncan played it right, Framingham would let something slip without ever being asked a question.

"I don't have anything to hide," he said, trying to scoff but the waver in his voice ruined the effect. "Ray, Bob, and I are engaged in perfectly legal activities. It's no crime to buy and sell property."

Duncan made no response.

"Steve Naif's presence in that cabin was unfortunate. Bob—"

Not quite there. Framingham was still in control enough to stop talking. Duncan zipped up and stepped over to the sinks. "Being murdered is more than unfortunate I think."

Framingham's skin paled. He also zipped his trousers and washed his hands.

"I've gotta wonder why Mr. Naif was at Winding Valley in the first place." Duncan shot a glance at Framingham. One look at his face and Duncan knew. Mark Framingham was a man with a secret.

"No idea." Framingham shuffled his feet. He made no attempt to leave, despite a clear path to the door. Amateur. He was so desperate to prove he wasn't lying, he was sticking around when he should beat a retreat. "Getaway with his wife? Steve and Rhonda were a fabulous couple. Maybe they wanted some time to themselves without kids."

"I've been told Mr. Naif was having an affair." Duncan turned on the tap.

"Who…who told you that?"

"The man who rented the cabin. Ray Capshaw." Duncan shook the water from his hands and faced Framingham. "Mr. Framingham, I've seen a lot of guilty witnesses. Come clean to me now. It'll be a lot better for you in the long run."

"I'm not guilty of anything." Framingham snapped, but his voice held a familiar undercurrent. Fear. "I repeat. Buying and selling property is legal. Even if the holding time is a bit on the short side. What happens to the proceeds isn't your concern."

"I didn't ask about real estate sales."

Framingham stared, but his stance said he felt under pressure. "Is this conversation over?"

"Door's right there," Duncan said, keeping his voice mild. Framingham admitted the timing of the sales was un-usual. Why buy and sell rapidly? Duncan probably wasn't going to get that answer in the men's restroom of the Le Mont. "I never said you had to stick around and talk to me. Enjoy the rest of your evening."

Framingham turned to go.

"Oh, by the way," Duncan said as though a thought had just occurred to him, "I understand you have history with Sally."

Framingham halted. "Yes. What of it?"

"She's gotten some pretty unwelcome notes and gifts lately."

"Your point?"

"The person sending them seems to know her pretty well. Like they also have history." Duncan watched Framing-ham's posture. No reaction. No stiffness.

Framingham turned. The fear had slipped from his face. Now he looked incredulous. "Wait, you think I sent those? I would never…I asked her to come with me tonight. We dated.

I'd love to give it another try, sure. You think that sounds like a guy who'd send, what did you call them, unwelcome notes? Not exactly the way to a woman's heart."

The reaction Duncan saw was either a masterful performance or not that of a stalker. Or Framingham sent the notes and truly didn't believe his behavior was creepy at the least, criminal at the extreme. "I didn't say that. But know this. Sally Castle is a friend of mine. I don't like my friends being harassed. You think I'm being annoying about the games at Capshaw & Associates?" Framingham sputtered and Duncan held up a hand. "You don't want to see me if I find out you're behind Sally's problems."

Framingham's face colored a deep red. "Sally Castle is one of the finest women I have ever met and I would never disgrace her with that kind of attention. As far as Capshaw & Associates, you think they're playing games? I dare you to prove I'm one of the players." He turned and stormed out of the bathroom, letting the door bang behind him.

Duncan stood for a minute in thought. That dare sounded too much like taunting.

CHAPTER TWENTY-SEVEN

Sally asked for a second cup of coffee, black, and wished they could leave. Earlier, she'd hoped they could spin out the evening after they left the Le Mont. After talking to Tish, Sally only wanted to go home.

Jim appeared and held out his hand. "Let's dance."

"I thought you said you weren't much of a dancer." Sally set down her cup and stood, Jim's hand under her elbow.

"I'm not, but if I don't dance with you he will." Jim nodded toward Mark, who was making his way through the tables. "My duty roster tonight has one official entry. Pest control. I don't intend to fall down on the job."

"And you want to talk to Mark."

"I said official entry. Anything else is gravy." He led her to the dance floor.

Sally would have preferred that he dance out of a sense of desire. But once his hand was on her waist, she didn't much care. They swayed in silence for a few moments, then she said, "That was a long trip to the bathroom. For a guy."

"I had the conversation you referred to," Jim said, pulling his gaze from the room to look at her. "The one with Framingham. Some of it even concerned you."

So much for an evening without talk of crime. "What did he say?"

"He's up to something at Capshaw & Associates. And I still think he could be your secret admirer." He looked at her and his smile faded. "What's wrong?"

"Tish talked to me. She said—"

His expression turned stony. "I can only imagine."

Mark's voice prevented Sally from asking the question on her lips. "Mind if I cut in?" He hovered next to them, hand outstretched as though he took yes as the given answer. "As friends. Hey, I'm here alone. I'd like to catch up on what's happened with you since I left."

Jim stopped, but didn't release Sally. He shot her a quizzical look, but she forced a smile. "Sure. Jim doesn't mind." She squeezed his hand to let him know she was fine.

"I'll see you back at the table." Jim handed her off to Mark, but he didn't smile.

Mark didn't notice, too focused on Sally. They moved to the middle of the floor, Mark's grip cold and clammy. Within thirty seconds, he stepped on her foot, something he didn't even apologize for.

She kept a smile on her face. "I hear you had a chance to talk to Jim."

"He's a nosy son-of-a-bitch."

"He's a cop."

"He thinks he's so smart. If he thinks he's a better game-player than Bob Trenton, he's wrong." Mark looked at her and some of the anger in his face faded. "I've half a mind to file a harassment complaint."

"I'm quite sure it wasn't harassment," she said. "Jim is a good friend and a good cop. He'd never do anything that broke the law." Depending on how angry he was, he might brush up against the line, but he wouldn't cross it.

"Well, whatever." Mark gripped her hand tighter. "You do look like life has treated you well, Sally."

"I've done okay."

"Seeing you, well, it makes me think I might have made a mistake all those years ago. Giving up. Leaving town. Makes me wish we could try again."

She could read the wistfulness in his expression and hear the regret in his voice. None of it changed her mind.

"Mark, that really is flattering."

"And it doesn't matter, does it?"

"I'm afraid not." The music ended and she tugged her hands free. "You're a nice guy. I told you before the chemistry wasn't there and I don't think anything has changed. I'd be wrong to let you think otherwise. Enjoy the rest of your evening." She walked away, leaving him on the dance floor. Her conscience pricked a little, but it was the right thing to do. She didn't feel any attraction and pretending she did would be worse than cutting it off now.

She looked around for Jim. Whatever the clock said, it was time to go.

❊ ❊ ❊

Duncan didn't need to be persuaded it was past time to leave. He'd completed his task. One look at Sally's face and he knew she was done. The talk with Tish seemed to have dampened Sally's spirits, though, and rare insight into female psychology said this might be his best chance to find out what nagged at her. He suggested they get a quiet drink before heading home.

They bypassed the noisy places crowded with twenty-somethings and ended in up a quieter bar that offered a good selection of beer, wine, and tapas. Sally asked for another merlot, Duncan a Sam Smith oatmeal stout draft, and they got a plate of finger food to share. When the waiter deposited the plate, she stared at it. "What we need is a sleeve or three of Thin Mints."

"I'm sorry?"

"The cookies. I read it online. Best pairing for Thin Mints are red wine and dark beer. After tonight, I could really use the chocolate rush."

"Because of Tish? Ignore her. She's obviously still angry, although she has no right to be. I'm sorry you had to deal with her on your own."

She shook her head. "Mark let something slip when we were dancing." She related the comment about Trenton.

"Trenton, huh?" Duncan studied one of the appetizers before popping it in his mouth. "I was thinking Capshaw was the linchpin. It's his company. But maybe not." Well, they'd gotten through dinner without shop talk.

They ate without speaking for a couple of minutes. Sally picked at the food and barely touched her wine. She'd put up a barrier, the same one he'd sensed around her these last months He waited, feeling her slip further away with every passing minute. Finally, he pushed aside his beer glass and leaned on the table. "Sally. This isn't normally my thing. Generally, I wait for people to confide in me because I don't think they like to be pushed."

She averted her gaze.

"Something is bothering you. Something big and it has to do with me." He reached out and grasped her hand. "If you don't tell me, I can't fix it. Please. What's wrong?"

Tears glistened on her lower eyelid and she dashed them away with the back of her hand. She took a deep, shuddery breath and covered her face with her hands, palms pressed against her eyes. "Do you hate me?" she asked, voice cracking. "I know you hate me. I hate myself some days."

The glass of wine perched dangerously close to the edge of the table and he moved it aside. Whatever he expected, it wasn't this. His first instinct was to dismiss the idea as ridiculous, but he sensed that wasn't the right response. When he spoke, his voice was slow and cautious. "I don't understand. Why would I hate you?"

"Last fall. I was...God, stupid." She pressed her palms tighter to her face. "That's what I was. How can you not hate me?"

A punch to the gut couldn't stun him more. "I don't hate you."

She huffed and turned her face away.

He reached out and gently tugged her chin so she had to

look at him. "All this time. My God, why didn't you say something?"

She sniffed. "I was afraid," she said, voice barely audible. "Afraid you didn't want to see me anymore, but you were too polite to say it."

"You know me better than to believe that." His brain buzzed, barely able to process her words. "Who did you talk to last fall? After everything settled down?"

Her response came as a whisper. "No one."

A second gut punch. "No one? Didn't Gerrity tell you to, didn't he make you?"

"He…" She wiped her nose and shot him a guilty look. "He suggested it, but I blew him off. After all, I didn't…and you didn't want to talk about it. At least I didn't think so. You… every time we talked you sounded cautious, distant even."

Talk about letting her down. *Nice going, you idiot.* "I thought it was what you wanted. To put it all behind you. I thought…hell, I figured you saw a therapist or something. I did."

She looked up, doubtful. "You? Talked to a shrink?"

"I didn't have a choice. Turned out to be a good thing." He rubbed his chin. "Here I thought maybe your doc told you to cut me loose and you were trying to be graceful about it."

Indignation replaced doubt. "Why the hell would I do that?"

"I said I had your back. When you needed me, I wasn't there." He brushed her cheek with his thumb. "I am such a jerk. I let you down twice, then and now."

She leaned her cheek against his hand. "I forgive you."

The skin of her face was warm and soft. "I've got the card from the guy I talked to. I want you to call him. Something that big is as traumatic for a witness as the parties involved." He kissed her forehead. "And promise me you will never, ever, keep something like this from me again."

She wiped her eyes. "Promise."

CHAPTER TWENTY-EIGHT

Sally slept in Sunday. When she woke, it was almost noon, far later than she ever slept. Even on a weekend. Snow fell thick outside her window, fat flakes that piled up with alarming rapidity on the windowsill. Not a day that encouraged her to go out, but a perfect one for introspection.

She sat on the couch, wrapped in her fleece bathrobe, and leached warmth from the cup of mint-flavored hot chocolate in her hand, her thick Amish quilt piled on her lap. While she savored the velvety cocoa, she thought. Her relationship with Jim took a big step forward last night. Not just because he came with her to the charity dinner. She remembered the warmth of his hand on hers, the concern in his eyes, more than the concern of a friend.

As promised, Jim had texted that morning, sending the number of the therapist with an additional message. "Call him. Please. And I'm sorry I didn't see you were hurting earlier."

God, she loved him. The realization took her a moment to process. Found him attractive, yes. Wanted to spend time with him, absolutely. Wanted to rip his clothes off, sure. But love? Yes. She understood the pain she caused him was infinitely worse than anything she felt for herself. And wasn't that the definition of love?

She stared at the falling snow, warm mug in hand. Knowing she and Jim were on solid ground re-energized her. She knew the Uniontown police were looking for this stalker, same as Jim. Her turn to get more active and stop letting other people take care of her.

She set down the mug, and picked up a pen and paper. But before she got further than drawing some columns and writing headings, the jangle of the telephone startled her. "Hello?"

"Sally. It's Nan. What's shaking?"

"Nothing. What's up with you?"

"Closed a big account. Celebratory dinner is on. You, me, a couple girls from the office. Five o'clock. Dex's. You in?"

Sally looked out her window. It was the second weekend in March, but spring was taking its time and the snow didn't inspire her to want to go out. "Thanks, but I'm bushed. Next time."

"Aw, don't be like that. This is exactly what you need to forget your problems. An evening out with friends. I'll even pick you up if you don't want to drive in this weather."

All Sally wanted to do was stay home, but Nan had the "I'm not taking no for an answer" tone in her voice. "Fine. I can drive myself, not a problem. See you there."

"Ta."

Sally hung up. She'd never felt less like going out with the girls. But what else was she going to do? Sit at home and fret?

No. She stood up, quilt falling to the ground. A glance at the clock told her it was almost two. Plenty of time for a shower and to get dressed. Her mother had not raised any victims. Sally was damn sure she wasn't going to be one. Not anymore.

❋ ❋ ❋

Instead of being home Sunday afternoon, playing with Rizzo or following up on his re-established relationship with Sally, Duncan worked, payment for being off on Saturday. But he didn't regret making the schedule swap. He'd lost track of how many times he'd let Sally down, but no more. He texted her with the therapist's number that morning and promised himself he wouldn't merely assume she'd made an appointment. If he had to drive her there, he'd do it. She deserved that from him.

Funny, he hadn't felt this strongly about the welfare of another person, especially a woman, since Tish. He might not have felt this way about Tish, which probably went a long way toward explaining why his marriage had fallen apart.

An interesting train of thought, and one he should spend some time on, but he had work to do first. He started running background checks on Capshaw as soon as he got out of roll call. While that was in the works, he set about finding everything he could about Bob Trenton. Still no word from the National Archives, but it was Sunday. The feds didn't work weekends. He'd have to rely on his own resources.

McAllister found him sifting through sheets of paper around four. "Whatcha doing?"

"Reading some background info on Trenton."

She perched on the edge of an empty desk and drank from her ever-present bottle of Mountain Dew. "Anything interesting?"

"He won the Silver Star. That must be the medal I saw in his house."

"That sounds like it's a big deal."

"It is." Duncan highlighted the information on the background report. "It's the third-highest medal for valor there is. Exactly what he earned it for isn't here. That'll probably have to wait until I get the official records. If I ever get them."

"He's a war hero." She tapped the bottle against her hand. "How big is his pension?"

"Doesn't look like he gets one."

"That's weird. If he's such a hero, why no pension?" A speculative gleam came into her eye. "But since he doesn't... those cash payments. You call the sister about them?"

"I talked to her earlier. Her answer was kind of weird." Duncan rubbed his chin. "Said she helps her brother, but stopped short of confirming she sent cash."

"Oh, that's not fishy at all. There's nothing illegal about it, why not say so?" McAllister frowned. "He definitely gets the payments and that begs the question. Where are they coming from?"

"Add that to the fact he's an Army Ranger. They have very specialized skill sets. He'd be more than capable of strangling a man, and probably knows exactly how to do it."

"Always the same. Follow the money. We find that, we'll know why Trenton would have motive."

He pointed at the papers she was holding. "What's that?"

"Preliminary background on Ray Capshaw." She handed it over. "No criminal history. Finance degree from the University of Pittsburgh. Married, no kids. House in Squirrel Hill. Good credit, mortgage up to date, property taxes current. Car paid for."

Duncan took the paper and began reading. "Professional problems?"

"No, but somewhere in there," she pointed, "are a couple of records of investor complaints. Nothing came of it. No fines or slaps on the wrist. Just people who weren't very happy with the performance of their portfolios."

"The stock market is a rich man's gamble." Duncan flipped through the paper.

"Yes, but these complaints were a little more specific." McAllister took another sip of Dew. "Not just oh my investment lost money, but allegations of impropriety, money invested where it wasn't supposed to be, shady funds, that sort of thing. I didn't find any official complaints, though."

"I think it's time to have another conversation with Mr. Capshaw."

She emptied her bottle. "Get anything from Framingham last night?"

"Not really. He's another one who puts my back up." Something else to do, more detailed background on Framingham, including interviewing people at Capshaw & Associates specifically about the firm's relationship with him.

"You don't like him because he annoyed your girlfriend. And you think he's a candidate for stalker-hood."

That got his attention. "I don't like that he won't leave Ms. Castle alone, yes. And yes, he's my top suspect for all the anonymous crap. But please stop calling her my girlfriend. 'Cause she's not."

"Only because you won't let her be. She'd go out with you in a New York second." She added some eyebrow-waggling to her grin.

"Just like Burns would go out with you in the same amount of time." He was rewarded by McAllister's blush.

"Let me know if you need any help," she said. She pushed herself off the desk and zipped her jacket.

"Will do." Duncan looked for Capshaw's contact information and picked up the phone. The man had not been very forthcoming the last time they talked. Now that Duncan had new ammunition, perhaps he could change that.

"Mr. Capshaw. Trooper First Class Jim Duncan," he said when Capshaw answered.

"I remember. What can I do for you, Trooper?"

"I have a few questions I want to ask you regarding some allegations that have come to light."

There was a beat of silence. "Allegations regarding what?"

"Capshaw & Associates. Some complaints about investments made, as well as the potential involvement of Steve Naif and Bob Trenton. And Mark Framingham."

"Trenton is an accountant. He's not involved in the investments. Framingham is a real estate lawyer who has handled some deals. I fail to see how they relate to Steve's death. Why would you be interested in business deals? I thought Steve was killed as a result of his affair."

Was Duncan imagining it, or was there a note of defensive panic in Capshaw's voice? "That's one possibility. We are still investigating. Which means I need to understand if there is a motive stemming from your company's business dealings. And who might be involved from that end."

"Trenton and Framingham?"

"Trust me. My questions are relevant. It would be better if we could talk in person. But if you insist, we can talk now." It would be timely, but the telephone would rob Duncan of the opportunity to study Capshaw's face and body language. Beggars couldn't always be choosers.

"No, I…I'm on my way out," Capshaw said, stuttering.

Nope, not Duncan's imagination. The notion of talking to the police made Capshaw nervous. "Then perhaps we can talk tomorrow?"

Silence on the other end of the line.

"Mr. Capshaw. You can speak to me voluntarily or I can make it official. It's your call, but we do need to talk." Duncan shifted the phone. Why the resistance to meeting?

When Capshaw replied, his voice changed. Where there'd been a clear sound of reluctance, now he sounded… resigned? Hard to tell, but the panic had faded. "Perhaps we should hash things out. You'll have to come to me. My house at twelve-thirty. I'm sure you have the address." He ended the call without saying goodbye.

"I'll see you then," Duncan said to the dead connection. Maybe Capshaw and Naif hadn't been on good terms. Capshaw's tone said he thought Trenton and Framingham were a waste of time. But what changed to make Capshaw go from unwilling to accepting, however reluctant? And so quickly? Almost like he'd come to a decision he rather wouldn't have made.

Whatever. None of that mattered at the moment. Duncan would make sure to be early for his meeting in Squirrel Hill tomorrow. Capshaw had some explaining to do.

CHAPTER TWENTY-NINE

Sally returned home about quarter to eleven. She'd been right. Nan was in a partying mood, so it must have been a big account. She'd ordered pitcher after pitcher of margaritas, but Sally abstained, sticking to Coke for most of the night. Her excuse was that she had to drive. But while she'd laughed at Nan's stories and seemed to go along with the crowd, her brain never stopped trying to work out the identity of her unwelcome correspondent.

The snow piled in thick drifts around the building, but thankfully someone had taken the time to clear the front walk and steps. Sally wore sturdy boots, but she didn't much feel like trudging a path through the snow, especially this late at night. She stamped her feet in the front lobby, not wanting to track any more snow inside than necessary.

"Stupid winter, stupid groundhog," she said under her breath as she went upstairs. A lump of snow lodged inside her boot, probably when she'd stepped around the fresh pile of dog doo on the sidewalk into the deepest drift. She pulled her keys out of her coat pocket and sorted through them to find her door keys. Once inside, she'd get a cup of hot chocolate and warm slippers. The snow in her boot mostly melted on the way upstairs, but that only meant her foot was now cold and wet. Which made her grouchy. A perfect metaphor for her current mood.

As she started to unlock her door, she noticed an addition to the cream-painted metal. Suddenly, her foot wasn't the only part of her that was cold and not from the weather.

Written across her door, in dull red spray paint, was one word: *WHORE*. Written in all capital letters, outline shaky, either because the hand holding the paint can trembled as it grasped the can or the inaccuracy of writing in spray paint. One thought forced its way through the blossoming panic. Whoever sent the letters knew where she worked, knew where she lived, and wasn't afraid to come right up to her door.

She looked around, but no one stood in the hallway. Whoever had defaced the door was gone. She gulped, breath coming faster. Being alone didn't make her feel any safer.

The rational part of her brain told her to call the police. Surprised she could hold the phone, she pulled it out of her pocket and dialed 911. When the operator answered, she said, "My name is Sally Castle, 64 West Main Street, apartment D. I'm not sure, but someone might be in my apartment. There's graffiti on my door."

"Is the door open?"

"It isn't standing open. I don't know if it's unlocked." Had she felt the lock open when she turned the key? She couldn't remember. "I mean, I noticed the graffiti when I'd already turned my key. It's unlocked now, but I don't know if it was when I got here." She forced herself to breathe, willing her voice to remain steady. But all her instincts screamed at her to run.

"Don't touch the door any more than you have. I'll dispatch an officer immediately. Don't hang up," the operator said.

Sally nodded, not caring that the woman couldn't see her. She wouldn't hang up. There was no guarantee the vandal had really left. The silence of the apartment building turned ominous, no longer the welcome of home. After a minute, the operator assured her that a Uniontown patrol officer was en route.

Police would be good. She'd feel a lot safer with a uniformed officer. She considered calling Jim, he'd mentioned swapping his days around. She had no idea if he was still on duty. Knowing the situation, he'd take her call, but what if he couldn't come? What good would it do to worry him further?

She didn't want to loiter in the hallway, but waiting outside in the frigid night didn't appeal to her either. If someone appeared, she could pound on a neighbor's door or scream.

A personal connection. That made sense. But now she wasn't just looking for someone with a personal connection, but probably someone local. And that narrowed the list of suspects quite a bit.

* * *

Duncan parked at the barracks, but had not yet killed the engine when the car's radio crackled. "Possible home invasion. 64 West Main Street, Uniontown. Officer please respond."

His hand froze on the ignition key. That was Sally's apartment building.

He checked the dashboard clock. Ten fifty-seven. No way he could justify taking a patrol car into Uniontown at this hour, not for a city home invasion. But if he was lucky, he could get in and back on the road in less than five minutes.

"Pinsky, I need a favor," he said to the desk officer inside. "I just heard a call from the EOC about a home invasion in Uniontown. It's at a friend's place. Is there any way you can see fit to—"

"Toss me the keys. You got any paperwork?" Pinsky held up a hand.

"Nothing's happened in the last six hours and my earlier stuff is done. I owe you one." Duncan tossed the keys and handed over his shift reports, then headed out to his Jeep.

He made the trip in record time, arriving by eleven-thirty. A Uniontown black-and-white, lights flashing, parked outside. Maybe the victim wasn't Sally. The EOC hadn't mentioned a unit number. Perhaps he should have called first. But as he mounted the stairs without seeing an officer or a tenant, his throat tightened. Sally had a second-floor apartment. Hopefully nobody would be there, either.

No such luck. The Uniontown officer stood outside Sally's door, which appeared to be closed. Sally's back was to him as she gave her statement.

"I got home, I don't know. Ten-thirty? Quarter to eleven? I'm not exactly sure. I saw this and called 911. It wasn't here when I left, but I've been out for a few hours." Her voice wobbled with emotion, but she wasn't crying. She wouldn't.

"Did anyone—" The officer looked up as Duncan came up the stairs. "I didn't call for assistance, especially from the staties. Thanks, but I don't need—"

Sally spun. "Jim! My door." She crashed into him, squeezing so hard he thought a rib would snap. Then she burst into tears, shoulders shaking.

"I'm not here in an official capacity, Officer…Edmonds," Duncan said, noting the young man's name tag. "Ms. Castle is a friend of mine. My shift had just ended when I heard the call from county EOC. What happened?" For the second time in two weeks, he held Sally while her body shook. He opened his jacket so the zipper wouldn't cut her face, and rubbed her back. The growing wet patch on his chest told him she was crying hard, despite her relative quiet. Having had his own house torn apart, he knew exactly what emotions coursed through her at this moment.

"Do I know you?" Edmonds asked, frowning. "Wait, you're the guy who showed up at the Rafferty homicide last fall."

"That's me."

"You follow trouble or does it follow you?"

"A little of both, I guess. What happened?"

Edmonds consulted his notebook. "Ms. Castle said she left to have dinner with friends around four-thirty. She didn't see anyone when she exited the building, either other tenants or strangers. She returned home between ten-thirty and quarter to eleven. Somebody had done that." He waved.

Duncan took a few steps to better position himself. Sally moved with him as she didn't seem willing to let go of her death grip. Red letters reflected the hallway light with a dull sheen. A buzzing sound clouded his hearing and he forced it away. He needed to stay professional. "What'd the actor use?"

"Judging from the scent, I'm guessing spray paint," Edmonds said. "She didn't touch the door, beyond unlocking it. At least she thinks she unlocked it, she can't quite remember. She hasn't been inside yet. I've already cleared the unit. I just about finished the statement and was going to walk her through when you arrived."

"You notice anything when you went through the place?" Duncan nodded at the door.

"Deadbolt was still engaged. Ms. Castle said she always uses it when she leaves."

"Which makes it less likely someone actually got in, but who knows." Sally continued to shake, face still buried in Duncan's shirt. It normally would have been awkward, holding her this long, but all he could think about was calming her down. He shut his own emotions away. He needed to take care of Sally. Make sure she was safe. There'd be time for anger later. "What do you need from me?"

Edmonds hesitated, looking at Sally. "Ms. Castle needs to walk through and confirm that nothing has been touched or is missing. Then I'll check with the neighbors, search the back..."

Duncan understood the unspoken request. This would go faster if he helped, off-duty or not. "Want me to take her on the walk-through?"

"If you don't mind." Relief crossed Edmonds' face. "She was reasonably calm until you arrived. Doesn't seem to be the case now."

"I'm a friendly face," Duncan said. "I'll handle it."

"I'll go out back and see what I can find. You need gloves?"

"Got a pair in my belt. Let me know if you find anything."

"Will do." Edmonds jogged down the stairs.

Sally's sobs quieted and she stopped shaking, but didn't release Duncan's shirt. He held her, rubbing the small of her back. He should say something, but "it's okay" and "it'll be all right" sounded inadequate. It wasn't okay, and while it would be all right eventually, it wasn't at the moment. He wouldn't insult her with platitudes and "I hope you have a better night" implied he would leave.

Hell no.

After a while, she sniffed and pushed away. Crying left her face red and blotchy, and he could see circles on her cheek from the buttons on his shirt. Her nose ran, her eyes puffy and bloodshot. "I'm starting to make a habit of crying on your clothes." She shuddered.

"Why didn't you call me?" He handed her the handkerchief he always carried.

She blew her nose. "Because you might have been busy. Or too far away. Or something."

"Didn't we talk about this? I am never too busy for you. Especially not under the current circumstances."

"I would have had to call the Uniontown police anyway."

She'd been held at gunpoint and found a coworker who'd been shot through the head. She'd get through this. He waited for her to recover.

"I think I wrecked your shirt."

Duncan looked down at the wet patch, which was streaked with black and purple. Her eye makeup. "You don't use the waterproof stuff, huh?"

She hiccupped and gave a weak laugh.

"Don't worry. I'll figure out a way to wash it out. You tell me when you're ready to do this."

She took a deep breath. "No time like the present." She reached for the door.

"Wait." Duncan pulled on a pair of nitrile gloves. "In case there are prints on the knob. Other than yours."

"Right." She sniffed and wiped her nose again. "You go first, I guess."

Inside, a single low-wattage lamp shone in the living room, along with the light under the range hood in the kitchen. He felt for the main switch and flicked it up. "You leave those lights on?" He beckoned Sally to follow him.

"Yes." Inside, she took another deep breath. Her shoulders looked a lot more relaxed, but she twisted the handkerchief. "Especially at night. I don't like coming home to a dark apartment."

"Smart. We'll go room by room. You see anything out of place, point and I'll take care of it. If there has been someone inside—"

"We don't want to mess up any prints. Got it."

The kitchen looked pristine, only a few dirty plates stacked in the sink. The living room also looked untouched, a quilt folded over the back of the couch. He tried the window. "Locked. You do that?"

"At night and when I'm not home, yes. I want more than a screen between me and the world when I sleep. And I wouldn't open the window in the cold anyway."

Nothing had been disturbed in the bathroom or the hall closet. Sally had turned the spare bedroom into an office. The books on the shelves stood in neat lines. A black laptop was on the desk, lid closed.

"Password-protected. I change the password every three months," she said. "I don't give it to anyone."

"Let's check it anyway." She gave him the password and he unlocked the machine. But there was nothing immediately visible and a quick check revealed no new files or electronic notes.

The bedroom appeared excruciatingly neat, bed made, dresser-top contents in military straight position. "Valuables?" Duncan asked.

"Some jewelry," Sally said. "It's in a metal lockbox under the bed. I keep some cash in an envelope in my underwear drawer."

Duncan looked under the bed. The lockbox was still there. When Sally gave him the combination to open it, he recognized the pearl pieces she wore Saturday, nestled safely in their respective boxes. He replaced the lockbox and opened the underwear drawer.

"You're not going to look through my underthings, are you?" Red stained her cheeks and she bit her lip.

"Think of it like being at the doctor's," Duncan said. "He sees you as a patient, not as a naked woman. Same thing here."

He said the words, but they sounded hollow to his ears. Bras and panties in matching colors, some silky, some lacy. He tried his best not to think of Sally wearing any of it, but he couldn't help a few stray thoughts. Luckily, his back was to her and she couldn't see his face.

A plain, white envelope lay at the bottom of the drawer. "Fifty in cash, five tens?" She nodded. "All there. It's looking like the graffiti was the whole of it. No breaking and entering." He shut the drawer as Sally breathed a sigh. Relief that no one had entered her apartment or relief that Duncan wasn't pawing through her underwear?

"Are they going to fingerprint the entire apartment?"

"I doubt it." He stood. "No sign of entry. Nothing missing. I wouldn't if it were me. Edmonds will probably dust the outside of the door, though. Unless you want the place dusted."

"Are you kidding? That stuff leaves a mess. I don't want to clean that."

They went back into the hallway. Edmonds appeared on the stairs, a large evidence bag in hand. "Krylon spray paint, dark red. And a pair of rubber gloves with red stains. Probably the paint used for the graffiti. The gloves mean there's likely not much in the way of prints on the can. Maybe we can pull some from inside the gloves. I'll dust the outside in case our actor slipped up. Anything missing?"

Sally shook her head, but Duncan responded. "No. The side window is locked. You'd have to be Spider-Man to get in the back windows. No access from the fire escape or a balcony that way."

"Good enough. The couple in 1B came out to see what the flashing lights were about." Edmonds checked his notebook. "They didn't see anything suspicious when they went to dinner around five. They saw a delivery guy with a lot of boxes earlier at some point, but can't remember when. And all they can give me in the way of description is that he wasn't from UPS because he wasn't wearing brown."

Sally gave what might have been a weak laugh or a choked gasp and buried her hands in her face.

Duncan understood her reaction. People loved to claim they remembered everything. In reality, eyewitness statements were notoriously unreliable. "Anything else?"

"Not yet. I'm going to knock on the rest of the doors, check if anyone saw anything. Then I'll get out of your hair. If we find usable prints, I'll be in touch." Edmonds looked from her to Duncan.

Sally rubbed her face, then looked at the young officer. "Let me save you some time. The tenant in C on this floor isn't home. They went to Disney World. I know, because they asked me to collect their mail for them while they're gone. The tenant in B works nights. The tenant in A is off on a ski weekend with his buddies."

"Thanks for the tips. I'd say enjoy the rest of your night, but I don't think that'll be possible. I hope it's at least quiet." Edmonds nodded at them and left.

CHAPTER THIRTY

Sally slumped back on her couch as the post-adrenaline crash swept over her. Her determination not to act the hysterical woman crumbled as soon as Jim appeared, one of the reasons she hadn't called him. What had she been thinking? He would hear the call from the county-wide emergency dispatch once it went out. Once that happened, dragons wouldn't be able to keep him away.

Oh well. There were worse people to go to pieces in front of. Truth be told, she preferred walking through her apartment with Jim. If young Officer Edmonds had to rummage through her underwear drawer, she'd have died of embarrassment.

Jim shot the deadbolt, took off his hat and jacket, and unbuttoned his shirt. "Nice guy, Officer Edmonds," he said. He removed his shoes. "Can I get you anything? Cup of tea, glass of wine?"

"Aren't you going home?"

He paused, hand on his tie. "I wasn't planning on it. But if you prefer to be alone, I understand."

"No." The word rushed out and she clasped her arms around her body. Seeing him half out of uniform might have been more distracting except for the circumstances. "I don't want to be here at all, actually. If it wasn't the middle of the night, I'd ask you to take me to a hotel." She shivered.

He unclipped his ties and threw the makeup stained uniform blouse over the back of a chair. Then he stepped over and rubbed her shoulders, his hands warm even through her shirt. "I could find a place if that's what you really want."

"No, because I also don't want to go outside. *Catch-22*, isn't it?" She paused. "Oh shit. What about Rizzo?"

"I called Marge on my way here. She's used to bailing me out. He's fine." He brushed hair out of her face. "Listen, go put on your pajamas. How about that drink?"

"Chamomile tea. It's in the cupboard over the machine. No sugar."

"I remember. You sure you don't want something stronger?"

"No, just tea. It'll relax me better than anything else."

"Okay." His gaze searched her face. "Get changed."

She went to the bedroom, and pulled out her yoga pants and a sleep shirt. She ran a hand through her hair and inspected her face. Most of the blotchiness had disappeared, but blood-shot, slightly swollen eyes stared back at her from the mirror.

She had lived on her own since law school and never had a second thought about her safety. Every time her mother brought it up, she scoffed. Remembering the one meeting be-tween her mother and Jim, Sally smiled. Mom had not been in love with the idea of her daughter being with a cop. Sally wondered what Mom would think of the idea after tonight's events.

By the time she'd returned to the living room, a mug of hot tea waited on the coffee table. Jim had grabbed pillows and blankets from the closet. She thought she saw a gleam in his eyes at the sight of the pants, but a second later it was gone.

He handed her the tea. "You hanging in there?"

She accepted the mug and sat in an armchair. "I'm okay, I guess. Thanks for coming. And staying. I'd be wedging kitchen chairs under the doorknob if you hadn't."

"Wild horses couldn't keep me away. I still haven't en-tirely forgiven you for not calling in the first place. Didn't you know the worst way for a first-responder to hear about a friend is over the airwaves?" He didn't sit, but stood watching her. Taking in her body language, no doubt. Looking for signs of a breakdown.

She gripped the mug, ignoring the burning sensation in her hands. "He's escalating, Jim." Her voice cracked and she fought to regain her control. "That concealed-carry is looking awfully good right now."

He knelt in front of her and lifted her chin to force her to look at him. "I told you before. That's a big decision. If you think through the implications, you might change your mind." He rested his other hand on her knee. "I can see you're scared. Don't let fear lead you into a rash decision."

She studied him over the edge of her mug. As a lawyer, she'd learned to read body language as well as a cop. It was essential when questioning a witness on the stand or a client in her office. Right now, Jim's whole body practically vibrated with tension.

She finished the tea while he made up the couch. She set the empty mug on the table. "You sure you're okay to sleep there? It's not the best bed and you're still half dressed."

He picked up the empty mug. "I've slept in far less comfortable spots and wearing a lot more clothing. I'll be fine." He took the mug to the kitchen. When he came back, he noticed her staring at the couch and frowned. "What's wrong?"

"I…" She bit her lip. "I don't want to sleep alone." In the quiet apartment, her voice was small. A child afraid of the bogeyman.

Jim glanced from the couch to her bedroom. He exhaled a slow breath. "I think we'll both fit here. It'll be tight, but we can do it."

"I've got a king-sized bed, you know."

"I'm not sleeping in your bed. I don't think it would be… wise." He glanced at her. "And I'd be too far from the door."

"But you're okay with both of us on the couch."

He sucked in his breath and held it for a moment before

saying, "It's a mental thing. I'd prefer if you'd go to your bed so I can concentrate." He waved at the door. "But you don't want to be alone, which means you won't sleep. That means you're likely to get up and talk, which will distract me even more. We'll make do on the couch. Both of us dressed. Well, mostly."

This time she didn't miss his gaze, which fixed on her yoga pants. He wasn't comfortable with the arrangement, but he would humor her. "I don't have anywhere to lock up your gun."

"I don't want it locked up." He removed the weapon from the holster and set it on the end table. "I want it where I can reach it. Just in case."

She'd been in the process of getting up, but his words froze her in place. "You think he'll come back?" Like this night could get any worse.

"I believe in being prepared." He pulled her over to the couch. They laid down and he tugged a blanket over them.

It was a tight fit and Sally could feel the stiffness of his body behind her. "You have enough room?"

"I'm fine." His voice was rough, but he rested his arm on her hip. "You?"

The warmth of the blanket and Jim's body, coupled with emotional exhaustion now the crisis was over, brought almost instant sleepiness. The effects of the chamomile helped, too. "Peachy," she mumbled. Sleep overcame her. If he responded, she didn't hear it.

❊ ❊ ❊

Duncan wasn't sure what woke him up, noise or instinct. But his eyelids popped open. By the luminous dial of his watch, he could tell it was a little after three.

Sally twitched in his arms, and he knew she'd woken too. He laid a finger over her lips. Outside, he thought he heard footfalls and saw the shadow of feet at the crack under the door.

Moving as quietly as possible, he pushed Sally aside and rose, picking up his Sig. He crept to the door and eased back the deadbolt.

Not quietly enough. The sound of the lock alerted whoever lurked outside and Duncan heard feet thunder down the stairs. "Stay here," he said in his best command voice. Hopefully Sally would listen.

He ran after the intruder. Judging by the thud, he, or she, vaulted the stairs about halfway down. Duncan resisted the temptation to follow suit and stuck to the stairs. This was no time to land wrong and twist, or break, an ankle. That wouldn't do anyone any good.

He reached the front sidewalk in time to see a figure wearing a hooded sweatshirt sprint away under the streetlights. The only vehicle in sight was a gray compact with what might be an off-colored quarter-panel parked about twenty-five yards away. "Police. Stop!"

The figure continued to run. Duncan didn't pursue. Not in socks and a T-shirt. Snow soaked through the wool, chilling his feet. Now that he wasn't running, he became aware of the bite of the night air on his bare arms. Time to get inside before hypothermia set in.

He returned to Sally's apartment, relieved to find her on the couch clutching the blanket. She hadn't moved.

"Did you catch him?" Her voice trembled.

"No." He relocked the deadbolt and sat to peel off his wet socks. He rubbed some warmth into his feet. "Didn't get a good look, either. Man, or woman, wearing a hoodie. In shape though, because he made good time running away."

"You didn't chase him?"

"I'm not dressed for foot pursuit in early March." He sat next to her on the couch.

"Your feet. Here." She picked up one foot and rubbed, her hands like fire against the ice of his skin. "How's that feel?"

Did she not know? "Fine," he managed to say. Sally certainly didn't mean the gesture to be erotic. She wanted to be kind. Unfortunately, his natural instincts went a bit farther. Exactly what he hoped wouldn't happen. He should have listened to his head and sent her to bed. Maybe she'd still be asleep. Then again, maybe not.

Sally finished with the right foot and moved on to the left. He needed to stop her before things got totally out of control. But he couldn't. Her touch felt too good. He laid a hand on her shoulder, feeling her heat through the thin fabric of her shirt. His feet had warmed, but he didn't tell her. "Whoever it was, he knows there's an armed police officer in your apartment. I doubt he'll be back."

She stopped the motion, but held his foot and bit her lip. "Are you okay?"

"Yeah." At least physically. "I wasn't outside long enough to get frostbite." He pulled his foot out of her hand and put it on the floor. "You?"

She nodded, eyes wide. Her face pale, she leaned toward him.

Their lips met. Hers were warm and soft, just like he remembered. Their first kiss had been a diversion. A nice diversion, but a tactic. Not like this. His left hand rested perfectly on the curve of her hip. With the right, he cupped the back of her head, fingers buried in the soft silk of her hair. All he could smell was the scent of her. The soft flannel of the nightshirt moved, and his fingers brushed the warm skin of her side.

The bite of her nails on his arm shocked him back to his senses. He broke away and stood.

She paused, her hands in midair. "What's wrong?"

"Nothing." He drew a ragged breath, logic forcing its way to the top through the sea of emotions and hormones running through his body. Damn. "Go back to sleep. In your bed. I don't think we should get too close right now." Damn, damn, damn.

Disappointment warred with hurt on her face. "What do you mean?"

"I can't...you...trust me. It's for the best. This..." He breathed deeply again. "It's not right."

She would have kept going. And, oh God, did he want to keep going, too. But he couldn't, wouldn't, do it. He never should have let her lay down on with him in the first place.

Sometimes having a conscience was a real pain in the ass.

"Go to bed," he said again. He tried to sound gentle, but the look on Sally's face let him know he hadn't quite managed it. "Please. I don't think whoever it was will be back. I'll stay just in case. But you need to go back to sleep and by yourself. If you can. Go on."

"Okay." Her eyes shone in the dim light. She stopped halfway to the bedroom and turned. "Will you be here in the morning?"

"I'll stay as long as I can. Good night."

"Night."

Sally trudged off to bed and Duncan heard the door shut. Not a slam, but a gentle close. He laid back on the couch and stared at the ceiling. His body still ached and the part of him that wanted to continue with Sally grumbled.

He punched the pillow. Damn conscience. Definitely a pain in the ass.

CHAPTER THIRTY-ONE

Sally didn't wake until nine-thirty Monday morning. When she went out to the living room, Jim was gone.

She expected that, even though she'd hoped to be wrong. He had to be somewhere at noon. He couldn't go back on duty with a makeup-streaked shirt. Hour drive to Confluence, change, then time to be wherever he needed to be. On top of that, he'd need to take care of Rizzo. He'd said he'd stay as long as he could and she believed him. She just hadn't gotten up early enough to talk things over.

She hadn't meant to kiss him. Not like that. But once they started it felt right. Yes, part of it had been an animal need to feel safe. But it was more. She wouldn't have kissed Officer Edmonds.

She knew, deep down, Jim had been right to stop before events got out of hand. She had been overwrought and not thinking. Seeking comfort from whatever, or whoever, was there.

Still. He'd pushed her away and left while she was asleep. She wanted to love him and he pulled a disappearing act.

Just like Tish said.

She shook herself. That was insecurity talking and she'd given that up, right?

First things first. She needed to call the office. It was late, they had to be frantic. The blinking light on her machine attracted her attention. When she played the message, it was

Bryan. "Heard about your incident last night. The cops came early this morning. I am so, so sorry. I know you're stubborn, but take at least Monday morning off. Please. If you want to take the afternoon, call. Be safe." Bless Bryan. Normally Sally wouldn't let something like graffiti derail her work, but this time she was glad to take advantage of his kindness.

She picked up some stray newspapers from the coffee table. On top was a note. She recognized the handwriting before she saw the signature. *Sally, sorry had to leave. Didn't want to wake you. I'll be back later to check on things. Jim* He didn't leave without any word after all.

In the kitchen, a bowl of cereal sat on the counter and the percolator stood ready to pour forth her morning coffee. She pushed the button to start the brew cycle, got out the milk, and paused. The kitchen looked different. It gleamed.

He'd cleaned the kitchen and he'd done it all without a sound. A quick check told her he'd emptied the dishwasher. Her dirty dishes from last night sat in there, along with another bowl. The sink sparkled and the stainless-steel fridge shone.

After breakfast, she decided to check her door before she called the landlord. Maybe she could scrub it and not have to have it repainted or replaced.

The graffiti was no more. Or almost. Only a faint trace remained. How had he removed the paint? Better question, when? Surely not last night. The intruder and the interrupted romantic post-lude occurred around three o'clock. He had to have gone back to bed. Hadn't he?

She shut the door resolving to ask when he returned. In the meantime, she had time on her hands. Time to think about the heightening severity of her situation. Whoever was behind this knew where she worked, where she lived. She thought about the graffiti. *Whore.* Instinctively, she knew a man was behind this latest incident, not that she'd ever considered a woman as the culprit in the first place. A woman would use different language. Different methods. The use of the word "whore" led Sally to believe the spray-paint artist also knew about her relationship with Jim, such as it was. Maybe the person assumed there was a lot more to things than simple friendship. Which was true and not true, all at the same time. No sex was involved.

But if Jim hadn't pulled away last night, there might have been.

She poured herself a second cup of coffee and sat on the couch with her list. Serrano. He'd been paroled, she knew that. But really, to drive all the way from Pittsburgh to Uniontown to scrawl graffiti on the door of a woman he'd seen five years ago? If anything, the graffiti made things even more personal than they'd been. No, it wasn't Serrano.

One by one, she drew a line through all the names. Paul, the guy from the DA's office in Pittsburgh. They'd never had the same moment free. Jake, who she'd met when she first moved to Uniontown. The one who couldn't handle dating a defense attorney, much less someone in public defense. Evan, the guy who admitted three dates in he was probably gay, but dating women just to be sure. None of these breakups had enough vitriol. And none of them had contacted her in at least six months. Except one. Mark Framingham.

He'd been very polite at the charity dinner. Wistful about what could have been, sure. But it seemed like he realized it just wasn't going to happen. Yes, he'd been squirrelly around Jim, which meant he felt guilty about something. But gut instinct said it had more to do with Capshaw & Associates than stalking an old girlfriend.

She tossed aside the list, classifying it a waste of time. Jim said he would come by to check up on her, probably before whatever he had to do at noon. Maybe he had some ideas. She'd ask him.

Right after she gave him a piece of her mind about last night.

* * *

Duncan knocked on Sally's door around ten-thirty. Next to him, Rizzo barked. "Quiet you. You aren't supposed to be here."

A few seconds later, the door opened to show Sally drawn up to her full height and clearly ready to launch into a speech. At the sight of Rizzo, confusion replaced the look of righteous indignation on her face. "Uh, what are you doing?"

"I told you I'd be back. Knew you'd be home because I heard Gerrity's message. Didn't you find my note?"

"Yes, but…get in before someone sees you and calls the landlord." She held open the door.

Jim tugged Rizzo's leash and they entered. The minute they crossed the threshold and Jim let go of the leash, Rizzo jumped up on Sally, tail beating against the hall table. "Thought you could use some company."

Rizzo licked her hands and she ran them through the dog's silky fur. "There's a no-pets policy in this building." Her obvious pleasure at Rizzo's presence and lack of conviction in her voice belied her words.

He'd been right to bring the dog. Rizzo would make this much easier. "Then lucky for you he's not a pet. Just a friend for the day. An early warning system."

"I don't think he poses much of a threat." She giggled as the Golden wiggled furiously, alternating joyous barks with licking her. "Unless you expect him to lick an intruder to death."

"I don't expect him to do anything except bark. From the other side of that door, a bad guy isn't going to know the difference between Rizzo and a Rottweiler. It's the noise that counts, not the bite." He checked his watch. Still plenty of time to get to Pittsburgh.

Sally gave Rizzo a final pat and stood. "We need to talk about last night."

"I figured you'd say that." He had carefully prepared what he'd say. Seeing the accusation in those green eyes almost made him forget it.

"Why did you push me away?"

"I didn't—"

"And why did you leave before I got up?"

"I had to take care of Rizzo and get ready for work." She still wore the yoga pants. And the slightly-too-big sweatshirt that kept slipping off her shoulder. He took a deep breath. Remember the arguments. "I didn't push you away."

"Like hell you didn't." Anger crept into her voice.

"Well, I didn't mean to. Not like that. Physically, yes, but not emotionally." Shit. Could he make a bigger mess of things? He saw it in Sally's face. He tried again. "Sally, you have no idea how hard that was. Believe me. But I couldn't let you continue. Let myself continue."

Rizzo leaned against her and she rubbed his ears, probably without thinking. "Why not?"

He played with the keys in his hands. "You were emotional last night. Looking for safety and comfort. I was there. It's totally understandable. As I said, not like I didn't want it to happen."

"I knew what I was doing. It wasn't all emotion." Some of the anger had gone out of her voice, but not all. Maybe because she continued to scratch Rizzo behind the ears.

He made a note to thank the dog. "I know. But I couldn't let you go on. It would have felt wrong to me. As though I took advantage of you in a moment of weakness and I can't do that."

She huffed, but didn't stop staring at him. Her expression, hard and stony at first, relaxed. Whether at his words or because of the canine therapy? Didn't matter.

"You can blame my dad. It's how I was brought up. You don't use a woman's moment of weakness to your own benefit." He took half a step forward.

She didn't step away. Bonus. "I don't like it." Her words sounded a bit petulant. She shook her head, almost as if she recognized the same thing and found it distasteful.

"I'm not asking you to like it. I'm not even asking you to understand it. It's the way I am and I'm asking you to accept it. For now." He waited for a response. He'd anticipated this discussion and it hadn't gone as smoothly as it had in his mind when he planned his response. But Sally didn't throw him out, so he must have said something right. "I have to go. I can't be late for this and it's going to take at least an hour to drive to Pittsburgh. We can talk more later, I promise." He should have made the meeting with Capshaw for later in the day.

"Work comes first, huh?"

"Right now, yes. But you understand that." Why couldn't he stop fiddling with his keys? He wanted to touch her shoulder, assure her somehow. But he knew if he touched her, he could forget making it to Capshaw's in time. Hell, he might not even make it to the barracks in time for roll call.

"Fine." She blew out a breath that ruffled the strands of hair on her forehead. "I guess I wouldn't want you to be any other way. You're coming back for Rizzo, I assume."

He inwardly sighed with relief. "Yeah, but not until late because I'm on second shift. I brought food and his bowls. Table scraps are fine, but not directly from the table, please. Doofus has enough bad habits as it is. Like his owner."

A faint smile appeared on her face as she took the bag. "None I can't live with. Should be a routine day, right?"

Wait, did she mean his habits or the dog's? "I hope so. At least after I see Ray Capshaw. I hope he can shed some light on this mess." Duncan adjusted his hat. "Enjoy your company for the night. Anybody gives you grief over having a dog, have him call me. Until I get here, check the door first if anybody knocks. If Doofus there goes berserk—"

"I'll call 9 1 1. Got it. Stay safe."

"You, too." He glanced at Rizzo. "I'd say goodbye to him, but he looks pretty comfortable. See you later." He flashed a smile and left, closing the door behind him. Oh, the temptation to chuck it and spend the next couple of hours cuddled up on the couch with Sally. She wouldn't mind. Not in the slightest. Honestly, neither would he. But duty called.

* * *

As Duncan drove to Pittsburgh, he replayed the conversation with Sally in his head. He knew he'd done the right thing. Sally might say she'd have no regrets. It wasn't only the possibility of an ill-advised one-night stand that stopped him, though. What about the impact to their friendship? Did she take that into account? Sex changed everything. At least she'd heard him out. She didn't like his words, but she accepted them, or at least seemed to.

That was important. More important than the immediate gratification sex would bring. Duncan could be honest enough to acknowledge it would be gratification. It had been a long time, too long, since he connected with a woman the way he did with Sally. She had to know the words had been as hard for him to say as they had been for her to hear.

Duncan shook his head to clear it. Maybe his relationship with Sally would get to that intimate stage. Last night had not been the time. Meanwhile, he was on the way to interview a guy about squirrelly finances and murder. He needed to be on the ball when he met Ray Capshaw.

A little over an hour later he pulled up to the Capshaw home, an elegant Tudor on Aylesboro Avenue. He was ten minutes early. Luckily, Capshaw had a driveway. In Squirrel Hill the properties were a bit more generously sized than some neighborhoods. Even more luck, the drive had plenty of space for the state Ford. A woman dressed in a furry black North Face jacket got out of a deep red Lincoln Navigator ahead of him. In the garage, Duncan could see Capshaw's Mercedes.

"Can I help you, Officer?" the woman asked, as she pulled several bags out of the Navigator.

"I'm here to see Ray Capshaw. Are you his wife?"

"Yes, I'm Nora Capshaw. Ray's inside. I know he has a

meeting at one-thirty, but the car's still here." Nora extracted another bag from the Navigator and tried to bump the door shut with her hip.

"Let me." He pushed it shut. "Can I carry something for you?"

"I've got it," she said, blowing long, dark hair from her face. "The front should be open since Ray is home. Come in."

Once inside, she dropped the bags in the hallway and put her keys in a silver bowl. "Ray? There's a state police officer here to see you. He says you're expecting him."

No answer. Duncan stamped snow from his shoes and listened. Nothing. No music, no footfalls, no sign of life.

"Ray? Where are you?" Nora Capshaw took off her boots and started down the hallway. "Maybe he's got headphones on. He's usually in the den. This way." She beckoned.

Warning bells honed from years on the job went off in Duncan's head. "Mrs. Capshaw? I think I should go first." He placed his hand on his sidearm. He didn't need to draw it yet, but a tingling sensation in his brain told him to be ready.

"That's okay. Ray's probably right in the den." She opened a door. "Ray—" She screamed.

Duncan stepped to her side, ready to catch her if she fainted or keep her from entering the room. Whatever was inside, she didn't need to mess up the scene.

Through the open door, he saw a wall full of floor-to-ceiling bookshelves lined with multi-colored volumes. A large leather armchair filled the corner in front of a brass stand lamp that bathed the room in a gentle glow. A heavy, dark wood sideboard littered with books and picture frames stood against the far wall. A loveseat that matched the arm chair faced it. An elegant Oriental rug in a deep blue and wine-red pattern covered the hardwood floor.

And in the middle of the rug, a gold silk tie around his throat, eyes staring and face bluish, lay a very dead Ray Capshaw.

CHAPTER THIRTY-TWO

The visit hadn't gone quite as Duncan planned. Around him, lights flashed from a photographer who snapped dozens of shots, and CSI techs examined the room. A woman from the Allegheny County Medical Examiner worked over Capshaw's body. It felt weird to be at a murder scene and not see Tom Burns. Duncan hadn't been at the scene of a dead body without the young deputy coroner in a while. He now fully understood what Burns's quippy humor did to lighten the mood.

Duncan called 911 immediately after removing Mrs. Capshaw from the den. He closed the door and supplied her with fresh black coffee, simultaneously attending to a distressed widow and making sure the scene stayed as pristine as possible. Officers from the Pittsburgh Bureau of Police showed up, followed by two homicide detectives. One of them took Mrs. Capshaw aside for questioning, the other conferred with the ME and CS techs. A PSP trooper could wait.

But not for too long. He wrote up some notes in the kitchen while he waited. The second detective returned after about fifteen minutes. "Chris Polencarz." The city detective stood a good eight inches shorter than Duncan, and was probably in her mid to late thirties, with short dark hair and dark eyes. "Thanks for taking care of the scene. Widows are unpredictable."

"I know how important it is to keep things tidy." He nodded in the general direction of the den. "Strangulation?"

"They won't say, but it'd be a hell of a coincidence for Capshaw to have a heart attack while someone loops a tie around his throat, if you get my drift." She lifted an eyebrow.

Humor, the common ingredient of death scene investigation everywhere. "His tie?" Duncan asked.

"According to his wife, yes."

Unlikely Capshaw would let someone else take his tie off. While he'd waited, Duncan examined the door. No forced entry. Whoever it was, Capshaw had known him or her. Had he been getting ready to go out or did he take the tie off after coming home? Nora Capshaw mentioned her husband had a meeting early that afternoon. With whom and about what? More questions to answer.

Then there was Capshaw's apparent resignation regarding the meeting with Duncan. Had he planned to talk to the trooper and come clean with an accomplice afterward? Had the accomplice gotten here first and taken steps to keep Capshaw quiet?

"Mind telling me what you were doing here?" Polencarz pulled a pen and notepad out of her pocket.

Duncan shook his head to bring himself back to the moment. "I had an appointment with Mr. Capshaw to discuss a murder I'm investigating, as well as potential financial irregularities at his investment firm."

"How's Capshaw connected to the homicide?"

"The victim is his business partner. Who was also strangled with a soft fabric, like a necktie. Mr. Capshaw rented the resort cabin where the victim was found. It was subsequently torched."

Polencarz raised an eyebrow. "Steve Naif. The Laurel Highlands arson-homicide."

"Yes. We confirmed Capshaw was at the scene and he rented the cabin," Duncan said, glad he'd removed his jacket. All the lights and people added to the house's temperature. "Don't know if he killed Naif. But I also have information there may have been mismanagement at the investment firm." He brought the detective up to speed on Trenton's suspicions.

"When did you make the appointment with Capshaw?"

"Yesterday. He said as long as I arrived promptly, he'd talk to me."

"He was okay with that?"

"Not at first." Duncan related his conclusions that Capshaw had reversed course. Maybe because of some internal decision.

Polencarz chewed her pen. "Huh. You got here a little before noon?"

"Saw Mrs. Capshaw outside, followed her in, she found her husband here. House was quiet. She didn't mention any-thing looked to be out of place."

"No forced entry. I assume the door was locked?"

Duncan thought back. "No. Mrs. Capshaw said it was open since her husband was home."

"That means anyone could have waltzed in." The de-tective scribbled a note. "You didn't see anyone outside?"

"Only Mrs. Capshaw. Not even the mail carrier. It's cold, middle of the day. People are at work."

Polencarz slipped the notepad back into her jacket. "Suffice to say, you're not going to get any information out of Mr. Capshaw."

"I figured that out for myself, thanks."

She grinned. "My partner's going to ask for permis-sion to search the house. You're welcome to tag along. Need gloves?"

"Got some." He removed the nitrile gloves from his belt. Searching would take longer than an interview, but maybe he'd learn something.

Polencarz's partner, a black man named Jendoff, fin-ished talking to Mrs. Capshaw and met them in the hallway. After making introductions and obtaining Mrs. Capshaw's consent, Polencarz started the search of the downstairs. Jend-off went up. Since Duncan was mainly interested in business information, he stayed with Polencarz.

Capshaw's office occupied a room in the back of the house, another Oriental rug on the floor, more leather and dark wood furniture scattered around. Someone had expensive taste in decorating. Duncan looked under the rug, noting the quality. Not a knock off. This stuff was worth a year's PSP salary. Not out of reach for a successful investment broker. Also well within the budget of a successful man who skimmed off the top. Maybe Capshaw had elected to spend his share of the loot.

A laptop sat on the desk. "No password," Polencarz said, clicking over to the mail application. "Idiot. Spam, stock market notices, something from a Squirrel Hill homeowners' group about parking. I don't see anything personal or business-related. Wait, here are some trading instructions."

"Anything to or from Steve Naif, Bob Trenton, or Mark Framingham?" Duncan asked as he flipped through a pile of mail on the side table. Some junk mail, some envelopes from professional organizations. Nothing that looked personal.

She clicked around. "Email exchange from Framingham about some condo in the Laurel Highlands. Email from Trenton about end-of-quarter reporting. Nothing to or from Naif."

"They were business partners and didn't exchange email?" Duncan set down the mail and joined Polencarz.

"Not that he kept around. Deleted folder is empty. I'll have the techs see what they can dig out." She clicked over to the browser. "Stock sites, social media, real estate listings for Fayette County."

That tallied with what Duncan already knew of Capshaw & Associates' real estate deals. "Anything on social media?"

"Not recently. It'll take time to sift through it. Look at all the pictures." Polencarz bagged and tagged the laptop. "You find anything?"

"Very little." Duncan had gone through the drawers of the side table, but found only standard financial overviews from mutual fund companies. "Doesn't look like he kept business papers at home."

"We'll be searching the work office, too. I'm assuming you searched Naif's, but we'll go through it again. We find anything, we'll call you." Polencarz grabbed a few things from the desk and bagged them. "You headed back to Fayette?"

"Yeah." Duncan shrugged. "Same here. I'll call if anything turns up. Good luck."

"You, too." Polencarz nodded her goodbye and Duncan left.

Outside in the Ford, he stared at the house. Naif strangled with something soft, like a tie. Capshaw murdered the same way. What were the odds that the two murders were unrelated? He put the car in reverse and backed out. In his experience, pretty damn slim.

* * *

Since Bryan offered, Sally decided to take Monday afternoon off. Unfortunately that left her with a lot of time on her hands. And, as her grandmother would say, idle hands were the devil's tools. Idle minds, too. She needed something to take her thoughts off Jim. Off last night, the sight of him in a simple white T-shirt, or this morning in a pressed uniform. Thinking about her stalker ought to do the trick.

Of all the names on her original list of suspects, only Mark remained. A few factors argued for him as the culprit. One, he was local. Two, he'd been in Fayette County recently. He'd come to visit both her work and her home, so he knew where to find her. While he'd seemed to have moved on, or at least grudgingly accepted the fact she had when she danced with him, who really knew? She scoured his professional social media. He hadn't lied. He left Pennsylvania for Phoenix and returned six months ago. On the one hand, she found it hard to believe he'd nursed a flame for her all those years and the first thing he'd done upon his return was look up an old girlfriend. On the other hand, perhaps that first encounter had been accidental and seeing her had given him ideas.

When she returned to the office tomorrow, she'd have more resources to check criminal records. Maybe see if she could request E-ZPass history to find out if he'd been in Uniontown on the relevant dates. Perhaps she could even check information in Arizona or get Jim to help her with that.

She studied the paper. A thought skittered into place. The couple in 1B said they'd seen a delivery guy. Benjamin delivered packages that one time to her apartment and he'd seen her. He regularly delivered to the courthouse. Knowing where she worked was a no-brainer.

She wrote his name on her list and thought. Benjamin? They'd never more than exchanged greetings over boxes. She saw him once a day, sometimes not even that. Many times the delivery happened when she had a court appearance or a meeting, so they wouldn't see or talk to each other for days. Yes, she was always polite. But her mother had taught her to be that way with everyone she met, especially the often-overlooked service industry workers. He had offered to take her to the charity dinner, though.

A quick search showed her precious little for Benjamin Kardys. No address, no phone number, no social media. Again, she'd be at work tomorrow with more extensive resources than Google. But would it be worth her time?

Making up her mind, she scribbled a fat line through Benjamin's name. The delivery man met a couple of the qualifications, namely knowing where she worked and lived. But he failed the most important one, a close personal connection. You didn't forge that with a casual "hello" two or three times a week.

Mark's act at the Le Mont had been good. But that's all it had been, an act. Starting tomorrow, she'd dismantle that act piece by piece.

❋ ❋ ❋

It was close to midnight when Duncan parked in front of Sally's apartment building. After the long shift the temptation to go straight home had been strong. Rizzo wouldn't mind an overnight stay. But Sally would almost certainly return to work tomorrow, if she hadn't that afternoon. The Golden Retriever could not spend the entire day at her place. And he wanted to see Sally more than he wanted sleep. At least sleep in his own bed.

As Duncan climbed the stairs, he wondered if Sally would be wearing those damn yoga pants. Reaching the door, he knocked.

Barking greeted him. He heard a shushing sound, then Sally said, "Who's there?"

"Jim. Come to get the doofus."

He heard the rattle of a deadbolt and the door opened. Sally did not wear yoga pants. No, this time she had on tight black leggings and a sweater. Not one that left much to the imagination, either.

"Come on in."

Didn't the woman own baggy sweats? Then again, his mind could easily provide a visual, so sweats wouldn't help. He stepped inside. "You checked the peephole first, right?"

"Yes, sir." She closed the door and re-engaged the deadbolt. Rizzo took one look at his owner and trotted back to the living room.

"Glad to see you too, buddy." Duncan shook his head.

Sally gathered her hair, using the elastic on her wrist to fasten it into a knot. "We had a good day. I took him for a couple walks. The folks in 1B saw him, but they're dog lovers, so our secret's safe." She frowned. "You look exhausted. Can I get you a cup of coffee? It's a long drive back to Confluence."

"No, thanks." He picked up the leash from the hall table and whistled. Rizzo didn't budge at first, but eventually came back, plunking down just out of reach. "Get over here." Rizzo tilted his head, tongue lolling out in a canine grin.

"Get anything from Capshaw?"

"Not really."

"He changed his mind about talking?"

"No." He glanced at Sally, who looked confused. "He's dead. I have no idea if he changed his mind, but he sure couldn't tell me anything by the time I arrived." He slapped his leg. "Rizzo, I said get over here."

Rizzo laid down, but otherwise didn't move.

"Well that…sucks." Sally crossed her arms. "Does that put you back to square one?"

"Almost, but not quite. Depends on what Pittsburgh's forensics folks pull out of the house." He focused on Rizzo, a great excuse not to see Sally, the creamy skin of her chest, the tantalizing curve of her hips. He'd planned to walk in, get his dog, and leave. So much for that.

"By the way, I owe you an apology."

That got his attention away from Rizzo. "For what?"

"I didn't thank you this morning. For cleaning up." She gave a rueful laugh. "I was too busy being offended, I guess."

"Oh." Don't take a step. Do not step toward her. He repeated the words in his head. If he moved any closer, his already overstressed willpower might break. "Least I could do."

"You must have been up half the night."

"I couldn't sleep. A bit wound up after…everything." And do not look at her legs. Focus on the eyes.

She took a step forward. "I spent some of the day thinking and you were right about last night. I don't like it, but I do understand."

"Do you? Or do you think I'm batshit crazy and you're saying that to humor me." He could see Rizzo, out of the corner of his eye. He sat up again, his head turning as each human spoke. Duncan sometimes thought the dog understood English. This was one of them.

"No, I really do understand. I'm disappointed, don't get me wrong. But I get it." She took another step closer.

Her eyes shone in the light, deep green. She probably felt warm and soft, too. Perfect for cozying up after a shift. "Sally, what happened last night, well what almost happened...I'm not saying it will or won't. Someday. But if it does, I want it to be the right time. I'm glad you understand, even if the timing isn't what you'd prefer."

She didn't say anything.

"Even though we aren't going there, yet, I was wondering if..." He coughed. Why was this so hard? "Maybe we could go out for dinner, or drinks, or...something. Sometime."

"I'd like that." She hesitated a moment, then hugged him.

After a moment, he wrapped his arms around her and stroked the silk of her hair. He kissed the top of her head. If only he didn't have an hour drive. If only he could report for roll call tomorrow morning wearing the same uniform.

All the while, he saw Rizzo continue to watch them, tongue still out, tail wagging. Oh yeah, the dog knew exactly what was going on.

CHAPTER THIRTY-THREE

Sally returned to the office Tuesday and looked up the contact information for Stan McDermott. Stan had been the ADA she'd worked with most frequently. He had a good memory and a sharp mind. If his health hadn't been so bad, he'd probably be DA in Allegheny County by now. And Sally might still be in prosecution. But Stan had moved to Albuquerque. Drier air. She waited until she was less likely to wake him because of the time difference, but he didn't answer the phone. He was probably on the golf course, so she left a message. Fortunately, she had enough work to keep her from thinking about the stalker—or Jim. At least too much. He'd touched base that morning via phone, just to make sure she was okay and she'd heard the rumble of voices in the background. He worked first shift that day, which meant he'd be out of touch for the next eight hours unless there was an emergency.

She kind of hoped there'd be one, but Tuesday passed quietly. She missed Rizzo's companionship last night. Maybe she should change to a pet-friendly apartment. She missed Jim even more. He called again after his shift ended and asked if she wanted company. Stupidly, she'd said she was fine and wanted to spend a quiet night by herself.

Idiot.

Stan called her back early Wednesday afternoon. But he offered nothing. Not a new suspect, not new information, nothing.

That left one man standing. Mark. She hadn't seen him since the night at the Le Mont. Did that mean he'd finally taken the hint and backed off? That act he'd put on when they danced, that he understood they were over, did he mean it? Or was he just plotting his next move?

* * *

After what transpired Sunday night, and the resulting conversation Monday, Duncan hesitated a little about putting himself in Sally's company. He talked a good game, but if he saw her in an outfit like the sweater and leggings again he might lose it. When he touched base with her by phone later that day, she sounded equally hesitant. Best let the emotions cool down a bit.

He spent his Tuesday attempting to track down more guests from Winding Valley. He interviewed several by phone, all of whom reported seeing Capshaw's car, but not the man himself. He left a message for the last couple, who had still not returned from their trip, asking them to call as soon as they arrived home.

When he walked into the barracks Wednesday afternoon around two, Pinsky, at the desk, stopped him. "You've got an interview in conference room three," the officer said.

Duncan blinked. He didn't set up an interview. "Who?"

"Mr. and Mrs. Kevin Shaughnessy."

Shaughnessy. The previously out-of-town couple. "Why didn't they call?"

"They said they did. When they didn't hear from you, they called the barracks. You didn't get their message?"

Duncan checked his phone. No record of incoming calls, no messages. "Nope. Maybe they dialed the wrong number."

"Maybe. How old is that thing again? Maybe you should get it replaced."

"Look, I like my dumb phone. I don't butt dial people.

No one will hack it to get my photos."

"Like you have any photos worth hacking." The main line rang and Pinsky put his hand on the receiver. "Conference room three."

Duncan let Nicols know he might be late to roll call, then went to the conference room and assessed his interviewees. The Shaughnessys looked to be in their mid-50s. They appeared relaxed, water bottles at hand. The woman had tastefully styled silver hair and wore a fur overcoat. She tapped short, but perfectly manicured, nails against her bottle. Her face looked good for fifty. Only a few crow's feet and laugh lines. Her husband had black hair mixed generously with silver. His blue-green eyes crinkled at the corners, his skin Irish fair. The black overcoat looked almost new. Both had tans that looked completely out of place for winter in southwestern Pennsylvania, but lacked the orange tone of spray or booth. The Shaughnessys had money. Probably traveled a good bit. No wonder they'd been hard to track down.

"Mr. and Mrs. Shaughnessy. Trooper First Class Duncan. Thanks for coming down. I apologize for missing your call."

"Understandable. Please, Kevin and Diane." Shaughnessy looked over as Duncan took a seat across from them. "We heard about the fire when we got home. Terrible."

"I'll try not to take up too much of your time. I'm sure you want to get back to Pittsburgh especially if you've been traveling."

"We're on our way to Nemacolin," Diane Shaughnessy said. "Wedding weekend for a friend's daughter."

"Then I really won't keep you." Duncan flipped open his notebook. "You stayed at Winding Valley in February, the weekend after Valentine's Day, is that right?"

Shaughnessy nodded. "Yes. We had the cabin next to the one that burned. As next door as they get, you understand. Far enough that we weren't evacuated that night, close enough to see comings and goings."

"The comings and goings are what I'm interested in.

Did you see the occupant of the other cabin arrive?" Duncan looked between the couple.

"Not arrive. We saw the car when we returned from dinner," Diane said, "a dark gray Mercedes."

Duncan checked his notes and pushed over the page with Capshaw's license plate. "Do you remember if that was the plate number?"

Diane thought, but only for a moment. "Yes. The numbers are our wedding anniversary, 0423. I think I even said something to Kevin."

Her husband nodded.

"Did you see this man at the cabin?" Duncan showed them Capshaw's photograph.

Both Shaughnessys looked at the picture. "No, not him," Shaughnessy said. "Just the other one."

"What other one?" This was the first Duncan heard of another person at the Winding Valley fire site. "This the guy?" He showed them Naif's picture.

Diane Shaughnessy shook her head. "No. The man we saw had a dog. A beautiful Golden Retriever. He must have arrived with someone else, because we saw him take his dog out for a walk, but we didn't see a car."

"A Golden Retriever. Are you absolutely sure?" It was too much for Duncan to believe. He pushed over Trenton's photo. "How about this one?"

Diane studied the photo. "I don't know. I only saw his back, it could be him. But I'm sure about the dog. It was gorgeous. Wearing some type of vest. I gathered it was a service dog. That's why I didn't call the front desk," Diane said. "It had a very regal name, didn't it Kevin?"

"Oh yes." Kevin Shaughnessy smiled. "Nero, like the Roman emperor."

Duncan gripped his pen so tightly it almost hurt his fingers. Why had Bob Trenton been at Winding Valley? More important: why hadn't he said so?

＊ ＊ ＊

After the Shaughnessys left, Duncan headed to a desk to compile a fresh list of questions. The witness statement put Trenton and his dog on the scene of two felonies. This time, the questioning would be more formal than dropping by. And if that meant involving lawyers, so be it.

McAllister walked over holding a stack of printouts, a highlighter, and a bottle of Mountain Dew. "Hey, Boss. Got a second?" she asked.

He looked up. "For you, I've got lots of seconds. What do you need?"

Her cheeks turned pink. "Shucks. I'm flattered, but you're a touch old for me. And won't that make Ms. Castle a little jealous?" Then she laughed. "Relax, I'm teasing. I was looking over the reports from Capshaw & Associates. Comparing them to Trenton's and Framingham's bank records."

"Why are you looking at the bank records for my homicide?"

"Because if I tell Corporal Sheffield I'm helping you with a murder investigation, he can't turn me into his errand girl."

Duncan glanced around, but no one was near. "Lower your voice," he said, pitching his own low. Returning to normal volume, he said, "I assume you found something I didn't."

"Maybe. Trenton claimed those cash payments came from his sister, right?"

"Yep. Although his sister was a little wishy-washy when I asked for confirmation."

"Grand." She slapped the papers down. "Then explain why those cash deposits match, to the penny, these payments from C&A to Trenton." She pointed at the highlighted rows.

Duncan scanned the rows. Son of a bitch. "How did I miss this?"

"Did you have these?" She held up a stack of papers.

"Probably not, since they came in late yesterday. Additional financial information from C&A. Without these, you'd never see the connection."

He looked at them. "That makes me feel moderately better. Although I still don't understand why you picked them up instead of calling me. More work for you."

She ignored the last and continued. "Then there's Framingham." She pulled out another page, also highlighted. "Why is C&A making payments to him?"

"Commission on the real estate sales?"

"Those would go through his employer. Not him personally." She tapped the page.

"Aw, f—"

"Relax, Boss." McAllister nudged him. "Tommy-boy and I were up until three in the morning cross-referencing five sets of paper. And remember. You didn't have the ultimate connection. We did."

"You did this with Burns?"

She froze. "Shit, was I not supposed to show him this?"

"No, that's fine. I'm just wondering what Tom Burns was doing at your place at three a.m." Duncan downed the cold remainder of his coffee. "Or what you were doing at his. Either way. Don't tell me all you did was look at financials."

McAllister did not reply, but her face turned beet red.

"Anyway, you said five sets of paper," Duncan continued, setting aside his mug. "This is only three."

"These are the tax returns for Trenton and Framingham." She handed over another sheaf of paper, face still shining like a beacon. "Look at what's missing. Never mind. I'll tell you."

"The payments we just discussed." Duncan set down the paper without even looking at them. If McAllister said it, he believed it. "You have a summary of this?"

She handed him a sheet with a flourish. "Figured you'd want it."

He took it and scanned. "Good work. Especially since

you didn't have to do it."

She looked down.

He cocked an eyebrow. "And thank Burns for me when you see him next."

"What makes you think I'm seeing him again? I mean again after—"

He didn't bother to suppress the laugh. "You were together until the early hours of the morning. And I don't think you got together to go over financial reports."

McAllister didn't answer. Verbally. The brick red color of her neck was answer enough.

CHAPTER THIRTY-FOUR

Doris came into Sally's office early Thursday morning. "Uniontown PD to see you. Should I send him back?"

"Please." Sally closed the case file in front of her. If Uniontown officers were visiting, they had to have some kind of information.

Officer Edmonds walked into her office. "Morning, Ms. Castle."

"Officer Edmonds." She waved at the metal and vinyl chair. "You have something for me, I hope?"

"Yes, ma'am. Detective Ostrovsky, who is coordinating the investigation, asked me to come see you." Edmonds pulled out a written sheet of paper. He'd probably brought it to make sure he covered all the facts.

"About what?"

"I didn't find any useful prints from your apartment," he said. "Nothing on the door. Prints were all over the paint can, but anything we could use didn't have a match in AFIS."

"You found gloves with the can, right?" Sally asked. After Edmonds nodded, she continued. "Then I'm not surprised. What you found on the knob were probably mine and everybody else who's visited me in the past month. No prints from the gloves?"

"No, ma'am. The prints inside the gloves were unusable. The only others we found on any item related to our investigation belonged to Benjamin Kardys, who you identified as the regular delivery person for the courthouse."

"The box." Sally twirled her pen. Damn it. But the gloves had been a long shot to start with. "Wait, why did you get a match for Benjamin?"

"We found an arrest from three years ago, a misdemeanor shoplifting charge. He received community service and time served as a result of a plea bargain."

"Oh." He'd stolen something of low value. Big deal. Young men did a lot of stupid things. "What'd he steal?"

"I didn't write that down, but I think it was from some kind of candy shop." He paused. "We did run DNA on the envelopes."

"How'd you manage to justify that?"

"We didn't." Edmonds cracked the first smile he had since he entered. "Detective Ostrovsky got a call. I suspect it was from your PSP friend. Anyway, right after that call, the detective said that seeing as you were a county lawyer and all, we should push for the DNA."

Jim had leaned on the Uniontown force. No surprise, not after the graffiti incident and the late-night visitor. But it showed how seriously he took the whole situation. In the past, he'd been adamant about respecting the niceties when it came to jurisdiction and not throwing around his weight as a PSP trooper. Apparently that went right out the door when it came to her. That made him sexier in her eyes than the sight of him in a suit or uniform.

Thankfully, Edmonds didn't seem to have noticed her daydreaming because he continued. "Unfortunately, there's no DNA on the glue."

"The envelopes weren't licked."

"No, ma'am."

Anybody could use a wet sponge and that opened up an entire world of possibilities. Endless, as a matter of fact. Any number of people who might have crossed her path at any time in her career.

"We are continuing to investigate," Edmonds said in response to her silence. "Have you received any threats since

Sunday?"

"No. But I have been thinking and I've come up with one person you should look into. Mark Framingham. He's an attorney in Pittsburgh."

"Thank you. We'll do that." He stood and moved to the door. "Hang in there. We haven't given up. If you receive any other letters or threats, please call."

"I will. Thank you, Officer."

Edmonds nodded and left the office. Sally leaned back in her chair. It had to be Mark. Had to be. And he would slip up eventually. Preferably before things got any more serious than they already were.

❋ ❋ ❋

That afternoon, Sally grabbed her coat and belted it while she headed out the door. A typical mid-March thaw turned the weather gray and drizzly, making her wish for clean, crisp, snow. Doris was at her desk, reading. "I'm going for lunch," she said. "Should I bring you anything?" She undid the Velcro clasp of her umbrella.

Doris looked up from her magazine. "I'm good. Weight Watchers."

"Twelfth time's the charm?"

"Something like that." Doris threw aside the magazine. "Wait, you're going out?"

"I have to eat. I'm not the one trying to lose a few pounds."

"Can't you order in? Maybe I should go with you, just in case."

"That would leave the office unmanned and Bryan wouldn't appreciate that. Besides, I refuse to have my life dictated to me by some lunatic." Sally shook out her umbrella. "I'll be back by one."

"I don't like it. Your friend wouldn't, either."

"No, he probably wouldn't. But he can't accompany me everywhere, either." Oh, if only he could. "I'll be in sight of other people. I'll be careful. I promise. But if I don't get out of this office I'm going to scream."

"If you aren't back promptly at one, I'm calling the cops."

Doris would do exactly that. Sally would grab something to take back to the office and avoid any problems. It wouldn't be as freeing as lunch at Dex's, but she also wouldn't be that pathetic woman eating by herself. Bonus, she'd be less of a target.

She stopped at a fast-food sandwich place full of people. Nice and safe. As she watched the employee make her sub, she heard Mark's voice behind her.

"We keep running into each other," he said, hair damp from the mist. "It's destiny."

"What are you doing here?" Sally clenched her hand inside her pocket. A public space, she'd picked the sub shop because it was fairly crowded. Mark wouldn't try anything here. *Stop being so paranoid.* He'd mentioned he had business in Fayette County. Uniontown wasn't so big that it was impossible they'd run across each other.

"I had a meeting in Dunbar," he said, studying the board. "After that, I had some forms to file with the county. Decided to grab something for the road and bam, I run into you." He shot her a lopsided grin. "What, you think I'm stalking you?"

He joked, but Sally didn't find it funny. "Are you?"

The grin faded. "I wouldn't do that, Sally. I told that state cop the same thing."

Then he knew about the stalker situation. And found it funny enough to josh around. Asshole. "Yet I keep seeing you." She tried to stay calm, but a note of belligerence crept into her voice. And fear. Mark might not notice it, but she did. Which made her more belligerent. "You seem to be completing a lot of deals in Fayette County lately. Maybe spending the night?"

He placed his order and turned to her. "What the hell are

you getting at? You don't honestly think—"

"Someone left graffiti on my door last Sunday night." She grabbed her lunch and held the bag in front of her like a shield. "And someone, most likely the same someone, came back very early Monday morning. Jim chased him off."

"Not me." Mark paid for his order and faced her. "If you don't believe me, go ahead and check my E-ZPass records. In fact, I'll give you the names and phone numbers of some people who will tell you I never left Pittsburgh Sunday. I went to the bar, watched a basketball game, and drank beer."

Like she'd accept an alibi from anyone who might be Mark's friend. Because that would be totally reliable. Did he think she was stupid? The police most likely did check, but they wouldn't accept the information at face value, either.

He took his bag. "Look, Sally. I told you at the Le Mont. I thought it would be cool to hang out with you again. You don't. I get it. You shouldn't flatter yourself so much."

Exactly what he'd say if it was him. Her grip on the bag tightened.

Mark glanced at his watch. "Look, sorry about the stalker business. But I'm not your man. Gotta go." He turned up the collar on his overcoat and headed out.

Once he was out of sight, Sally took a long, steadying breath. He was smart, that was certain. Anybody in the shop who heard him would swear he was completely over her. Except she knew better. Mark might fool all these people, but he couldn't fool her. Or the police. Not for much longer.

CHAPTER THIRTY-FIVE

Dusk was setting Thursday afternoon as Duncan laid another log on the fire, the flames driving a damp chill out of the air. The weather folks called for another snow storm this weekend. The snow would bring lots of weekend skiers to the area. And lots of accidents Saturday night. But news the McCloskey baby had finally made an appearance meant Duncan would be back to his normal Saturday three-to-eleven shift. Hopefully that meant he could avoid the worst of the wrecks.

He had scheduled a meeting with Trenton and his lawyer for tomorrow. It'd be nice to get some answers before the weekend. Trenton's presence at Winding Valley put a new spin on things. Naif's car was still MIA. It hadn't been at Capshaw's. He wouldn't have taken it home if he was an accomplice in murder. He'd ditch it somewhere. Also, if Capshaw had been the main threat, maybe Trenton would open up. Or not.

Duncan's cell phone rang as he was ladling chili into a bowl. McAllister. She wouldn't call on his day off unless it was important. "Whatcha got?" he asked when he answered.

"Get over to Framingham's vacation place."

"I'm off duty. You know this. Why me and not someone else?"

"It relates to the Naif-Capshaw mess. I'll fill you in when you get here. How long?"

"An hour, give or take since I'll be in my Jeep, without lights and siren. Maybe more. What's so important that I have to drive to Ligonier?"

"Hurry. See you when you get here." She clicked off.

What had her worked up? He stared at the bowl of chili. The spicy aroma almost convinced him to stay home. Almost, but not quite. McAllister wouldn't have called if she hadn't found something big.

A little more than an hour later, he pulled into Framingham's driveway. McAllister paced by the garage, oblivious to the chilly damp. "What's so damn important that you dragged me away from my dinner?" he asked. "This place is dark and locked up tighter than a drum. Nothing to see."

"I called Judge Calloway to approve a request for a search warrant over the phone." McAllister's phone rang. "That's her. Hold on a sec."

Duncan stamped his feet. The snow had melted some earlier, but now that the sun had set it had grown cold. And wet. An uncomfortable combination when he had the benefit of state-issued cold weather gear, which he didn't at the moment. He thought of his fire and chili back home.

"Got it. Porter's going to bring a copy. Come to the garage," she said, hanging up.

"Care to tell me what we're looking for?" He wanted to be home, sitting in front of the fire with Rizzo, prepping for his interview with Trenton tomorrow. Not standing in Mark Framingham's driveway in Ligonier.

"Steve Naif's car," McAllister said. She heaved on the garage door.

"Excuse me?" He walked over to help her lift the door. It appeared to be on an automatic opener, but those could be forced open.

"Neighbor reported seeing a car the night of the fire." She pulled some more, bracing her feet.

"Lift with your legs," Duncan told her. "Did they see the plate?"

"No, but Naif drove a dark red Cadillac CTS, right? Neighbor-lady said she saw a dark red, sporty Cadillac. Come on, help me out here. You're not an old guy."

Together, they wrestled the door open. Inside a ruby-red Cadillac CTS shone even in the dull gray light. The license plate frame bore the name of a luxury car dealer in Pittsburgh. "Go run the plate," Duncan said. But it sure looked like the description of Naif's car.

McAllister jogged back to her patrol car and returned no more than two minutes later. "It's Naif's."

"What the hell is Steve Naif's car doing in Mark Framingham's garage?"

"No clue. But either Framingham is the one who drove Naif's car away from Winding Valley or Ray Capshaw never went to Punxy." She straightened from inspecting a tool bench at the back of the garage.

"Or Trenton drove it over here. We haven't put Framingham at the fire scene, but both Capshaw and Trenton were there according to witnesses."

"But this is Framingham's house. His name is on the deed. I bet anything the three of them, Trenton, Capshaw, and Framingham, were involved in something illegal, Naif cottoned on to it, and they silenced him."

"No bet," Duncan said. "You have pictures of Capshaw and Trenton?"

She nodded.

"Go show them to the neighbors. I'll wait here and keep looking. We'll search the house together."

McAllister retrieved the pictures from her car and left.

Duncan grabbed a pair of nitrile gloves from the box of extra supplies he kept in the Jeep. Aside from the car, the garage held nothing of interest. He shone a light inside the Cadillac, but it looked clean. Not even a fast-food bag. They'd have to jimmy the locks to get it open and he didn't have the time or the tools for that. It would wait until they towed the car to a state police garage.

McAllister returned. "No go on Trenton. A maybe on Capshaw. Neighbors saw a man driving the Cadillac pull in the night of the fire. They can't swear it was Capshaw, but the wife says it's a definite possibility. The guy didn't talk to them, but he did yell at their kid when his basketball hit the car. Warrant here yet?"

"No," Duncan said. "Shouldn't take Porter too much longer. How specific did you get?"

"Specific enough that we can look into just about every crevice in this place."

Porter finally arrived, handed over the warrant, and drove away after wishing them luck. The back door had a standard lock that proved easy to get around. The inside of the house, however, yielded almost nothing. No dirty linens in the hamper. Canned and boxed foodstuffs filled the cabinets in the kitchen. The dishwasher held a full load of clean dishes. Whoever had been there had not left behind hairbrushes, saliva, or other sources of DNA. "Let's dust this place for prints," Duncan said. "If the person who drove the car stayed in the house, he couldn't have worn gloves the whole time. I'm sure there's something he forgot to wipe down."

"Right. I'll get the stuff," said McAllister, who had been examining a framed picture she found in a drawer. She handed it to Duncan. "Look at this. Side's torn off. Ex-girlfriend?"

Duncan studied it, then took the photo out of the frame, the edge neatly, but clearly, torn. It showed Framingham, arm around someone, broad smile on his face. He could make out a woman's arm, the edge of a skirt, and a leg. "Bad breakup? His arm is around her, but she's not touching him. This looks like it was taken outside a Pittsburgh restaurant. Maybe a wandering photographer. You gonna get that fingerprint kit?" He set down the frame.

"On it." She looked around the room. "What happens if we do find Ray Capshaw's fingerprints in this house? He's dead."

"Yes, but Mark Framingham isn't. Neither is Bob Trenton." Regardless of the fingerprint results, Duncan planned to have another talk with Framingham. He had already set the interview with Trenton. And this time, neither man was going to foist the police off with half answers.

❄ ❄ ❄

Thursday night, Sally went out for drinks with a few of the other attorneys from the courthouse. All women, some from the DA's office, they'd banded together despite being on opposite sides of the aisle during court proceedings. One, Glenda Evans, stayed to wait while Sally prepared to leave. She had told them about her stalker and they immediately rallied around her.

"Sally, you coming?" Glenda asked.

"Just putting on my coat and leaving a tip." Sally put aside her glass, still about a third of the way full of merlot. What a pity to waste decent wine. But she had a bottle at home. As Glenda tapped her foot, Sally dug around for tip money and her keys when a familiar figure stopped at the table. "Benjamin. What are you doing here?" Her hand closed around the keys.

"Same thing you are, I expect." He held up a bottle of beer. "A bit early to say it's the end of the week, but I met up with a couple friends."

Benjamin appeared to be alone. "Where are they?" She looked around.

"They had to run. Most of them have to be up early tomorrow." He sipped the beer. "That your glass?" He pointed at the merlot.

"Yeah. Couldn't finish it before my friends left. One is waiting for me now—"

"Why don't you stay with me and polish it off? I'll walk you out."

"I really shouldn't. It's been a long day."

"Please? There's nothing sadder than a single guy drinking on his own. Five minutes, tops."

Sally's instincts told her to leave. Her manners, ingrained by her mother, told her to stay. He'd asked nicely. She didn't want to appear rude, especially when it seemed like everybody else in the courthouse treated Benjamin like an errand boy. Most important, he wasn't Mark.

Five minutes wouldn't hurt. What could happen in such a short time? "I guess. Let me tell my friend what's going on." She walked over to Glenda.

"You ready?" Glenda asked.

"I'm going to wait a few minutes for Benjamin to finish his beer. You go."

Glenda looked over at Benjamin. "Is that smart with everything that's going on?"

Sally shrugged. "Benjamin is a Teddy bear. If it were Mark Framingham, that'd be different."

"If you're sure." Glenda clearly had other ideas. "On the one hand, he's the FedEx delivery guy, and there's no reason for him to single you out of the dozens of other women in the courthouse. But still…"

"I'm positive. Go home. I appreciate the concern, but I'll be fine.."

Glenda gave Sally a quick hug. "All right. But if you smell trouble, run. Promise me."

"I promise." Sally made a shooing motion. "See you around."

Glenda left and Sally returned to the table where Benjamin nursed his beer. "Okay, five minutes, that's all. I'm going to have to leave after that. I have be up early tomorrow morning."

"No problem." He glanced at the window. "They say it'll snow later. Hard to imagine since it rained earlier."

"I guess." She glanced outside. "It's the time of year for it. Winter isn't done with us yet. March weather turns on a dime in this area."

"Hope it doesn't make tomorrow's deliveries difficult." He took a drink. "That truck isn't the best thing in the snow.

You want a fresh glass of wine?"

"No, this is good. I shouldn't have another since I'm driving."

They seemed to have exhausted all conversation and a lot of time remained of that five minutes. Sally swore someone had bumped up the thermostat because the air felt stuffier than earlier and it got worse by the second. She hadn't had much to drink, but the heat must have exaggerated the effects of the alcohol because things around her swam in and out of focus.

All the while, Benjamin chattered on, seemingly oblivious to everything.

"Benjamin, I'm sorry, but—" She squeezed her eyes shut against another attack of dizziness. "I need to go. I don't mean to run out on you, but my head doesn't feel so great."

Benjamin set down his bottle. "Are you okay? Need a lift home?"

Sally shook her head, a move she immediately regretted since it set the interior of the bar tilting like a bad amusement park attraction. "No. I'm sure it's just the heat. A nice fresh blast of cold air should help. I'll drive with the windows down." She must have gotten the bug that was going around the courthouse. She hadn't felt the effects earlier, though. Strange, but the wine could magnify those symptoms, too. "I'll see you."

"Be careful."

Sally grabbed her purse and staggered to the door. Talk about a rapid onset illness. She'd felt perfectly fine all evening and *wham*! out of nowhere she could barely stand. Her head toggled between busting at the seams and hopelessly muzzy.

The night air slapped her face, but it didn't help clear out the cotton wool. Her eyes wouldn't focus, the streetlights misty balls of light in a world that looked like an old TV with bad reception. The forecasted snow had started. She could tell not because she could make out the flakes, but she felt little drops of cold water as they landed on her face and melted.

Where did she park? And where were her keys? Coat pocket. She fumbled to reach in, but kept missing the opening. She slipped on the sidewalk and would have fallen if a pair of strong hands hadn't caught her. Before she could make out her rescuer's face, everything faded to black.

CHAPTER THIRTY-SIX

Friday morning after roll call, Duncan sat at a desk to prepare for his interview with Trenton. He'd called Sally the previous afternoon, but didn't connect with her. When he'd called her office number, Doris told him Sally said something about drinks with some of the other women from the courthouse. He wasn't surprised to miss her under those circumstances. As long as she hung out with other people.

He wished he had more details about Trenton's military record. But you couldn't rush the feds. It seemed implausible that a man with such distinguished service would stoop to crime. Especially murder.

McAllister walked over holding a manila envelope and her bottle of Mountain Dew. "You look troubled."

"Trying to get my ducks in a row for when Trenton comes in. I wish I had his service records. I get the feeling they're important." Duncan pushed aside his notes. "What's that?" He pointed at the envelope.

"Trenton's records." McAllister handed over the packet. "Ask and ye shall receive."

"About damn time," he said. He slit the envelope and read the document.

"Anything interesting?" She took a gulp of soda.

At least the records provided him with a reason to delay going outside. Yesterday's rain turned into one of the typical late-winter storms Laurel Highlands residents were familiar with. There'd probably be six inches of snow on the ground by the time he clocked out at three. "Six years of service. He was on active duty when he was separated. Final rank, first lieutenant."

"Basic."

"Commissioned an officer through Officer Training School after college." He ran his finger down the report. "There's the Silver Star. All time spent as a Ranger. No courts martial, honorable discharge for medical reasons. The epilepsy, I bet."

"His pension must be good."

"He doesn't get one."

"Come again?"

Duncan re-read the discharge information. "He only served six years. Service members aren't eligible for a pension until after twenty."

"But you said it was a medical discharge. Not his fault."

"Doesn't matter, I guess. No twenty years, no pension."

"Might make a man bitter." She swigged from her bottle.

"Bitter enough to justify a touch of theft?"

"And if someone threatened that…"

"He'd take care of the threat. Just like he was trained to do." Duncan flipped a sheet. "That's his total service. Six years Special Forces. That makes his statement doubly incredible."

"Why?"

"Trenton said he came out of his house. Saw the box. Went to pick it up and got hit on the head. Did not see his attacker."

"Sounds plausible to me."

Duncan pulled the picture of Trenton's injury out of the file. "Tom Burns confirmed the blow could not have come from behind. The attacker would have been in front of Trenton. Maybe a little off to the side, but mostly in front. It's not self-inflicted, either."

She studied the photo. "Trenton was focused on the box."

Duncan put down the picture. "How long have you been on the job?"

"Six months."

"What's the first thing you do when entering new surroundings?"

She blinked. "A quick check of the area."

He pointed at her. "You've been doing this for six months. And the first thing, the *first thing*, you do is an unconscious scan of the area. Are there any risks? I bet you do it when exiting the barracks."

She snorted. "After that sniper picked off those two troopers out east? Hell yes."

"Bob Trenton was in the military for six *years*. A friggin' Army Ranger." Duncan slapped the desk. "Don't tell me he doesn't do the exact same damn thing."

"Fine. What about this." She swirled the bottle, thinking. "He's focused on his package. Actor is off to the side. Quick motion, he hits Trenton on the head, drags him inside. Could work."

He shook his head. "Nope. Follow me." He led her to a conference room and positioned her inside. "You're Trenton. The box is here on your porch." He indicated a spot on the floor. "Exit the room. Don't look anywhere but this spot." He moved so he was standing to the side of the open door.

McAllister walked out. He jumped and mimed a blow. She blocked him with little effort. "Damn," she said, eyes wide.

"You saw me."

"Peripheral vision. I mean, if I hadn't known it was you, I wouldn't have immediately recognized you. But I saw the movement." She took a step back. "Damn."

"Exactly." He walked back to the desk, McAllister following.

"When is Trenton coming in?"

Duncan glanced at the clock. "One. Five hours from now."

"You think he'll talk?" McAllister asked.

"Yes. His attorney will be present. But he won't be able to stop himself." Most people couldn't.

Bob Trenton was hiding information. Information that could implicate him in two murders. Duncan had to hope the presence of his lawyer wouldn't be enough to shut Trenton up entirely.

✻ ✻ ✻

While he waited for Trenton, Duncan went into a conference room with a set of colored dry erase markers. He set his phone on the table. Then he proceeded to map out the facts of the case, each color-coded by category.

McAllister found him a little before eleven examining his handiwork. "Colored markers again?" She sat at the table.

"I told you last fall. It helps me think. Order out of chaos." He tapped a marker against his chin.

McAllister studied the board. "The three of them were in it together," she said. "Capshaw, Naif, and Framingham."

"Or Capshaw, Trenton, and Framingham."

"Not Naif?"

Duncan jerked his head. "We have emails from Naif to Capshaw, arguing. Over what? Most likely scenario is Naif got wind of the scheme, either independently or through Trenton. I don't see Naif as a collaborator."

"Why would Trenton turn himself in?"

"I don't think he would. Unless he felt he'd been shafted and turned on his co-conspirators. But I think it more likely Naif was smart enough to know that something was up, even if he didn't know exactly what."

"Naif challenged Capshaw and got himself killed? Capshaw's story of renting the cabin under his name to facilitate Naif's infidelity is bunk. He did it to lure Naif away, maybe saying they needed to talk alone. Then...bam." McAllister stood and walked to the board. "We know Capshaw was there."

"Don't forget the Shaughnessys say they saw a man with a Golden Retriever named Nero at Winding Valley the night of the fire. How many guys have Goldens named Nero?"

"Trenton was onsite, too. His story about getting suspicious is crap."

"Correct. Trenton played along to further the conspiracy to get rid of the threat. He has the skills to strangle someone. Capshaw, not so much." Duncan pointed a marker at her. "Try this. Capshaw, Trenton, and Framingham run the scheme. Capshaw tags the investors to steal from. Trenton hides the money in the phony accounts. Framingham identifies properties for laundering the rest of the cash. Each man gets a cut."

"Naif finds out." McAllister traced the line. "They lure him to Winding Valley. Capshaw rents the property. Trenton does the killing, Capshaw takes Naif's car. Where does Framingham fit in?"

"He provided Capshaw with the post-homicide hideout. A place to stay out of cell range, or so he claimed, to fit the alibi. I bet Pittsburgh police get Capshaw's phone records and geo-data will show he wasn't in Frostburg."

"And Capshaw?"

Duncan leaned on the table. "My guess? He saw the police closing in and wanted to come clean, maybe in exchange for a deal. He was stupid enough to tell Trenton and Trenton got there first."

"If he was at Capshaw's. Nobody saw him far as you know." McAllister sat again. "How do you get to Pittsburgh from Dunbar if you don't drive? Not like there's a bus every thirty minutes."

"Who says he doesn't drive?" Duncan looked at her. "He has a car."

"But no license." She paused. "However, a guy guilty of double homicide and investment fraud probably doesn't worry about little things like driving without a license. He have an E-ZPass we can check?"

"No." Duncan rubbed his face. That was the hole in their theory. Nothing placed Trenton at the scene of Capshaw's murder. "We can check the video from the Turnpike toll-booths in Monroeville, but there are thousands of cars going through every day."

"Hmm." She sat on the table. "Be nice to put him at Capshaw's before he comes in this afternoon."

Duncan scowled. Yes, it would. But just how would he put Trenton in Squirrel Hill? Hopefully Polencarz had gone through the house with a fine-tooth comb. Because Duncan had nothing. And he got the feeling this would be his last crack at the piñata.

* * *

It was the most awkward sleeping position ever.

Someone had set off a hard rock drum solo in Sally's head. The low light stabbed her eyes with the force of a thou-sand-watt light bulb.

"What the hell?" she mumbled. Her voice sounded grav-elly and her throat felt parched. Where was she?

"Oh good. You're awake. I was afraid you'd never come to. It's almost noon."

She blinked in the direction of the voice. Benjamin's figure resolved from fuzziness into view. He leaned against a table, arms crossed over his chest.

"Benjamin? What are you doing here?" What was *she* doing there? The last thing she remembered was finishing up her wine, trying to be polite when all she wanted to do was go home.

Finishing it with Benjamin.

Bands of panic tightened around her chest, but she fought against them. Panic would not do her any good. Her brain still fogged, she forced herself to push through. What had happened? Obviously she'd underestimated Benjamin as a threat. Too focused on Mark, she'd pushed the shy, boyish delivery guy aside. Figuring out why might be important, but that could not be her immediate concern. She had to think.

Focusing helped with the mush in her head, but not the pounding. She took stock of her surroundings. She sat on a wooden chair. Not in any kind of apartment, but what looked like an office trailer, the kind they used at construction sites. Her arms were locked behind her. With a finger, she explored her wrists. She could barely reach, but thought she felt a piece of plastic. It felt like…

"Do you have me bound with a zip tie?" she asked. Drugged, kidnapped, and trussed like a turkey? Anger flared, doing more to burn away the residual fuzziness than any focusing exercises.

"Yes." He wrung his hands. "I had to make sure you couldn't go anywhere. Your ankles are tied too. But I'll undo them as soon as we leave."

Leave? "You drugged me. Where the hell am I and who says I'm going anywhere?" Unfortunately, he'd done a good job with the zip ties. She really couldn't move under her own power.

"I knew you'd be upset. If you just listen, you'll understand."

"Understand? What the hell is there to understand?"

"We're soul mates, Sally. We're meant for each other. If you spend some time with me you'll see."

CHAPTER THIRTY-SEVEN

Duncan glanced at the clock. Twelve-thirty. McAllister offered to bring back lunch, but he declined. Better to eat an uninspiring sandwich from the vending machine than meet a suspect with the remains of his meal spattered on his uniform. He called the public defender's office again and got the office recording. Well, it was noon. Hardly surprising.

Another bit of information had trickled in from Polencarz. The Capshaws' neighbor reported seeing a car matching Trenton's at the scene the day of Ray Capshaw's death. The neighbor could only provide a partial plate, but it was a partial that could be Trenton's.

Duncan bolted down a plastic-wrapped ham sandwich, and had just polished off a candy bar when Geoff Abercrombie from the tech division stopped at his desk. "Working through lunch. Must be serious."

"Geoff." Duncan crumpled the candy wrapper and tossed it in the trash. "I could say the same. Not often you guys make personal visits."

"I'm heading out early. Wife insisted on going away for the weekend, but I wanted to get you this first." He held up a sheaf of paper held together with a binder clip. "Results of our treasure hunt through the Naif computer."

"You found something."

"Computer and smartphone." He handed over the paper. "We recovered a rather lengthy email thread between Naif and

Ray Capshaw. It's on top."

As Duncan read, he frowned. "Definitely about financial mismanagement. But this sounds like he wasn't acting on a tip. This came from his own suspicions. He thought Capshaw and Trenton worked on it together."

"About halfway through, he mentions another name. Mark something-or-other."

"Mark Framingham." Duncan found the email that referenced the real estate attorney. Naif's speculation matched his. Capshaw stole the funds, Trenton funneled it, and Framingham cleaned it through real estate purchases. "That all?"

"Next page. There's more on the phone. Another email thread and some deleted text messages. All in the same vein."

"Naif said he was bringing in the police and SEC. No wonder Capshaw and conspirators freaked."

"We also found a file inside a password-protected folder." Abercrombie leaned over and flipped some paper. "I'm no financial genius, but this Excel sheet sure looks like he was doing some serious number crunching."

Duncan didn't understand all the details either, but he understood totals. Capshaw, Trenton, and Framingham put away a tidy sum. Money Naif threatened to take away. And send all three men to prison. "This is good. I wish there was something connecting all of them to the scene at Winding Valley."

"There is. Flip back to the emails." Abercrombie pointed "Email from Mark Framingham to Naif. Says he knows all about the scheme. He's getting cold feet and he wants Naif's opinion of how to proceed. Can he turn state's witness or something? He'll get disbarred, but at least he won't go to jail."

It wasn't Trenton who played the role of snitch, it was Framingham. "They set up a meeting at Winding Valley. How much you want to bet Naif showed up and found Trenton instead? The man is a former Army Ranger. He probably didn't ask Naif twice to shut his mouth. Hell, he might not have even asked once." He looked up. "Your timing is impeccable. Trenton is coming in for an interview at one. I could kiss you."

"I don't think my wife would understand and you're not my type. You can buy me a beer." Abercrombie grinned.

"Done. Enjoy your vacation. Tell me what those are like when we get that beer."

Abercrombie zipped up his jacket and left. Duncan glanced out the window at the swirling snow. Abercrombie better like skiing or sitting in front of a roaring fire, the only two activities appropriate for this weather. If this interview went well, he would enjoy a beer in front of his own fireplace that evening. He might ask Sally to join him. Surely he'd connect with her by then. The euphoria of closing a big case would definitely be that "right time" he'd talked about for other things, too.

❋ ❋ ❋

Not five minutes later, Trooper Kristin Freeman at the front desk buzzed Duncan's desk. "Your one o'clock interview is here." Her voice was oddly neutral. Duncan had known Freeman for ten years. Not a neutral kind of person. Which meant Trenton or his lawyer had gotten uppity and Freeman was trying her very best to remain professional. "Stick them in conference room one. They're early. Let 'em wait."

"You got it." Freeman's smile could be heard in her voice. They must have been very uppity.

Duncan waited another ten minutes. Yes, it meant his visitors would be irate. Good. If they were, it would be more likely one or both would blurt something useful. Duncan used the time to triple check everything he'd been told to date. Then he went to the conference room, giving Freeman a grin on the way past. "Sorry to keep you waiting," Duncan said as he entered. One glance told him Trenton fumed, but his attorney was moderately more composed. "I see they've gotten you coffee. Good." He sat and smoothed his tie.

Trenton's face held the contemptuous look of someone who thought the police wasted his time. Nero was curled up under the table. "This is Ralph Clearfield, my attorney. You can address your questions to him."

"Mr. Clearfield, Mr. Trenton. Thank you for coming down." Duncan pulled out his notebook and pen. "Now. Mr. Trenton—"

"Shouldn't you start with Miranda?" Trenton said, voice snappish.

"You are here for a voluntary statement," Duncan said, keeping his voice mild. "You insisted on bringing an attorney, but that's your call. You aren't in custody and you can leave any time. Right now, I'm questioning you as a potential witness. Miranda doesn't apply."

Trenton's lip curled. "But if I don't answer, you'll keep on harassing me, right?"

Clearfield held up his hand. "Mr. Trenton, please. Why don't you let me handle this?" A stocky African American, Clearfield wore a well-cut dark blue suit, but not custom. The plain silver cufflinks shone on his white shirt and a blue tie tastefully shot with red and gold threads finished the picture. "If Mr. Trenton isn't in custody what's this about? If he's only a witness, you could have questioned him at home."

A successful man, but not an ostentatious one and hard to rattle. "I tried," Duncan said. "Your client told me point blank to get out and he refused to answer any questions without you present. Totally unnecessary, but there it is. If you're telling me Mr. Trenton still won't answer questions, then you are wasting my time." Duncan closed the notebook, hoping his voice held just the right amount of warning for people who wasted the time of a state trooper.

Clearfield glanced at Trenton. "Ask your questions."

Duncan reopened his notebook. "Mr. Trenton. You claimed to have reported suspicions of financial discrepancies to Steve Naif."

"That's right." Icicles could have formed on Trenton's

words and his eyes had a disturbing lack of sparkle.

A killer's eyes. "Are you sure you didn't talk to someone else?"

"Who else would I talk to? The secretary?" Scorn dripped from Trenton's voice.

"Mr. Trenton, please." Clearfield studied Duncan. "I gather from the question that you have information that indicates otherwise."

"I'm merely suggesting that Mr. Trenton may have incorrectly remembered who he reported these discrepancies to," Duncan said, keeping his focus on Trenton.

"I stand by my earlier statement," Trenton said, voice hard, the irritated look on his face unchanged.

"All right," Duncan said. "Second. Ray Capshaw told us he rented that cabin for his partner for the purposes of an illicit romantic meeting. However, another witness statement says that isn't the case."

"That idiot lawyer—" Trenton said, snarling.

"Mr. Trenton, please." Clearfield glared at his client. "That's not a question, Trooper."

"Let me finish." Idiot lawyer. How many of those were involved in this case? Only one. "From what we've learned, Ray Capshaw rented that cabin for the purpose of meeting his partner. I was about to ask if Mr. Trenton had any insight on that."

"He does not," Clearfield said. "He's not involved in the personal lives of his employers."

"Fair enough." Duncan weighed his next move. "On the day of the fire and Steve Naif's death, were you at the Winding Valley ski resort?"

"I don't ski," Trenton said, voice hard.

"I didn't ask if you skied. I asked if you were there."

Before Trenton could reply, Clearfield jumped in. "I fail to see the purpose of that question."

"Witnesses saw a man with a Golden Retriever at Winding Valley that day." Duncan pulled out the statement, but he didn't need to look at it. "I wondered, since it was nominally his employer who rented the cabin, if it was him."

"There are lots of Golden Retrievers in the Laurel Highlands," Trenton said.

Another evasion. "Named Nero?" The questions hadn't cracked Trenton's stony exterior, but in Duncan's experience the evasions proved Trenton's story was not legit.

Trenton opened his mouth, but Clearfield stopped him from speaking. "We can't possibly know the name of every Golden Retriever in this area. Is that all?"

"No." Duncan retrieved the statement, noting neither man even glanced at it. "Ray Capshaw was murdered recently. I'm assuming you know that."

"Mr. Capshaw died in Pittsburgh," Clearfield said. "That's not a state police matter."

"True, except that he had a meeting with me the day he died," Duncan said. He spoke to Clearfield, but his gaze never left Trenton. "I suspect, although I cannot know, he intended to talk to me about Steve Naif's death."

Clearfield coughed. "Even if that's the case, it doesn't have anything to do with Mr. Trenton."

Duncan evaluated his opponent. Guilty men usually betrayed signs of nervousness, but not Trenton. His expression could have been carved from bedrock. Duncan knew this was a man used to facing danger much more serious than a prison sentence and not flinching. "Another witness saw your car, or at least a car matching the description of yours, in Capshaw's driveway. Were you in Pittsburgh that day? Perhaps visiting your boss?"

"My car is a Honda Civic, Trooper. Very common." Trenton stared at Duncan, a malicious glint in his eye.

"We have a plate number," Duncan said.

Trenton was stone cold. He didn't move, didn't flinch. But his gaze became a little too intent and the tiniest sheen of sweat appeared on his forehead.

A less experienced investigator might have missed it.

Duncan didn't. He rolled the dice. "The witness also said he saw the driver." He let the statement hang.

Trenton snorted. "Like some old coot in S—"

Clearfield turned to his client. "Bob, be quiet." He faced Duncan again. "Trooper, unless there's a charge forthcoming, this conversation is over."

Duncan paused. The Shaughnessys' statement was significant, but it put Trenton at the fire scene hours before the actual blaze, which had obscured the time of death sufficiently that Naif could have been killed hours after Trenton had been seen. Which the defense would undoubtedly argue was the case. If Duncan couldn't put the accountant at the Capshaw scene, defense would say the car had been loaned to someone. Finally, Duncan didn't feel solid enough on his motive. Something else the defense was sure to exploit. No, he could get an arrest warrant, but he didn't want to. Not yet. "I'm not charging Mr. Trenton at this time."

"Then we're done." Clearfield stood and Trenton followed suit. Nero leapt up from his place under the table. "Don't bother calling my client again unless you intend to make an arrest. Is that clear?" Clearfield motioned Trenton to precede him out of the room and both men left.

Close. Duncan gathered up his papers. Close, but not quite.

❋ ❋ ❋

After the interview, he went back to the bullpen. McAllister worked over a pile of paper. He sifted through the piles on his own desk. "We requested the records for all real estate deals conducted by Mark Framingham for Capshaw & Associates. Where are they?"

"Right here. I've been working on them all morning."

He pinched the bridge of his nose. "McAllister."

"I'm in trouble, aren't I?"

"I love your initiative and the way you're willing to help me out."

She leaned her chin on her fist. "But?"

"I don't love the way you don't tell me about it first. Knock it off, please."

"Got it, Boss."

He walked over to her. He might be irritated, but he was also sure McAllister had more patience for this type of thing than he did. "What have you found?"

"A lot and nothing." She sorted the papers. "Okay. Framingham joined his firm about four years ago."

Duncan pulled over a chair and sat. "He told Sally he'd only moved back to Pittsburgh a few months ago and we confirmed that." Sally had not called him. She might be busy, but after he was done with McAllister he'd try her cell again.

"Correct." McAllister tapped a sheet. "He worked in the firm's Arizona office for several years then relocated. He took over the C & A accounts about a month after he returned. Since then, he's run a very good shell game. All these are the properties he's bought and sold on behalf of C & A."

Duncan scanned the list. "Uh, that's a lot of property."

"Yes, it is." She handed him her handwritten notes. "I'm not an expert in real estate. But no one in their right mind buys and sells within weeks. Sometimes as long as a couple months, but no more than that."

Duncan sat back. "It is, however, an excellent way of cleaning money. It's as we thought. Trenton and Capshaw steal it, Framingham cleans it, everybody gets a piece of the pie." He rubbed his chin. "You think they recruited Framingham before he returned to the area or after?"

"Based on these, I'd say after. Before Framingham showed up, the C & A account was pretty quiet. After that..." She mimed an explosion with her hands.

"Nobody at Framingham's firm noticed?"

"I called." She reached for a bottle of Mountain Dew. "All the attorneys at the firm are more or less independent. As long as you log plenty of billable hours, you're left alone."

"I wish I had a job like that."

She rolled her eyes. "You do have a job like that. As long as the assignments get done and the paperwork turned in, even Sheffield leaves you be. How else would you get away with all this investigative shit?"

She had a point. He stood. "What about witnesses? Can we put any of the major players at these properties?"

"Not yet and believe me, I've tried. Been burning up the phone lines all morning. The places are empty. But the paper says something went on. Nobody paid attention is all." She shrugged.

"Well, we're paying attention now. I've met Mark Framingham. He'd shoot someone. I don't think he'd strangle his victim. Too personal. That leaves Trenton." He walked over to his desk to retrieve the Shaughnessys' phone number. "Get a photo of Trenton and call these people. Push them to remember. We've got to put Trenton at either scene."

"Didn't they already do that?"

He shook his head. "A man with a dog isn't good enough. But we get an ID, even a tentative one, and I'll get a warrant."

She took Trenton's photograph. "You think he's good enough to evade us?"

"No." He shook his head. "Army Ranger or not, no one is that good. We'll get him. We just need one thing to tie him to either scene and we'll get him."

CHAPTER THIRTY-EIGHT

Sally flexed her arms, as much as she could, against the ties. Soul mates? When had she ever done anything to give Benjamin that impression? She'd been nice to him. Polite, just like she'd been raised. Except…she thought of many of the other folks at the courthouse. To a lot of them, a FedEx delivery man was invisible. The guy who made sure their packages arrived. Benjamin complained more than once that they frequently used the wrong name. Except her. She'd been kind and he latched on to that like an abandoned puppy. Of course, it also wasn't as if she'd led him on. Puppy-like he might be, but he was also an adult, responsible for his own actions.

The headache receded somewhat, but her arms were on fire. She had to figure out some way to get free. But she also had to be careful. She was no mental health professional, but she'd defended enough clients with psych problems to know that if she tried head-on confrontation, it would only agitate Benjamin and put her in danger. More danger than she was already in. Fortunately, her bladder provided a perfect avenue of action. "Benjamin, I have to go to the bathroom."

He paced by the windows, but faced her, lines creasing his forehead. "Bathroom?"

"Yes. I have to pee. It's been over twenty hours, you said? That's a long time to ask a girl to hold it."

"But that means cutting you free."

"Yes, it would. But you don't want me to have an accident, would you? Or hurt myself?" If he loved her as much as he said he did, or at least obsessed enough, playing on his sympathy would get her further toward her goal.

"Well, no, but…if I let you go you might escape. Or hurt me. I know you take self-defense lessons because I've heard you talking to Doris." He walked back and forth, short nervous steps while he wrung his hands.

"I'm not going to escape." Sally tried for the voice that she used with recalcitrant clients. "First, you have my shoes. You said it's snowing. Running through snow with bare feet wouldn't be a good idea. Second, you have my coat." A medium-sized space heater ran in the trailer, the only thing between her and hypothermia. "I wouldn't hurt you. When have I ever made you think I'd do that?"

He clasped his arms around himself.

Once she started to talk about using the bathroom, she realized how badly she had to go. Her bladder screamed at her. "Please, Benjamin. I really do have to pee. I'm not going anywhere else." She'd said she wouldn't hurt him and she wouldn't. But there were a lot of things she could do to stun that wouldn't injure him. And then she could retrieve her cell phone and call for help. She smiled, hoping it was winsome and not threatening.

It worked. Benjamin picked up a knife that looked a lot like the small utility knife she carried, bent and sliced the zip ties at her ankles. Then he went behind her to release her hands. She stood and immediately dropped back into the chair.

"What's wrong? Are you okay?" Benjamin hurried in front of her and felt her forehead.

"I'm fine. Just a little dizzy, and my arms and legs are full of pins and needles." Scratch any plan to overpower him. She hadn't counted on the lack of circulation or still being woozy.

"Do you need help?"

"No, I'll be fine. But may I have my purse, please?"

He narrowed his eyes. "Why do you need your purse to

go to the bathroom?"

Damn. "I have a bit of a headache. I have some aspirin in my purse. And I'd like to freshen up a bit. You know, comb my hair, refresh my lipstick."

He stared at her long enough that Sally was sure he'd say no. But he walked over to the table that held her coat and shoes, then handed her the purse. "Okay. If you aren't out in five minutes, I'm coming in to check on you."

"Thank you. I'll be back." She plucked the purse from his hand, resisting the impulse to snatch it. Then she casually walked to the bathroom, both to avoid suspicion and because she felt like she'd just gone three rounds with her defense instructor. Five minutes was plenty of time to do what she had to do.

❊ ❊ ❊

Duncan faxed Naif's emails to Polencarz at her office. In the meantime, he called Sally and Mark Framingham. No answer for either one. If Sally didn't answer her cell, she was either in court or a meeting. As far as Framingham went, it was almost two, but if Duncan needed to make the drive to Pittsburgh he would.

His cell phone rang and showed a Pittsburgh number. Not Framingham, though.

"Trooper Duncan, Detective Polencarz."

"Detective, I wondered if I'd hear from you. I assume you got your trace evidence. You see my fax?"

"I did. On both counts." Her voice sounded grim, but triumphant. "No prints. But several hairs. Still waiting on the phone data."

"What kind of hairs?"

"Consistent with the fur of a dog. A Golden Retriever. Same kind of dog at both scenes? Too much to think they're different animals. At least for me. I believe we both have enough for warrants. Dunbar is closer to you."

"Agreed. I'll handle it. We'll figure out the details later. While I do that, you can do something for me."

"Name it."

Duncan read off Framingham's address.

"Framingham's the one who lured Naif down to Winding Valley. While I go to Dunbar for you—"

"I'll run over to Avalon and pick up Framingham. Got it." She paused. "Call if you don't get Trenton."

"Will do." He hung up. "McAllister. Want to take a ride?"

She jogged over to his desk. "Trenton?"

"You got it. Just as soon as we get the arrest warrant." He stood and pulled on his jacket. The snow really came down, making it almost impossible to see. The perfect weather for arresting a war hero.

McAllister must have felt the same, because she said, "I kind of hoped it wasn't him. Despite the evidence. Man wins a Silver Star and gets arrested for murder? That's not right."

"No, it's not. But past actions are no indication of future performance."

"Just like financial investments." She sighed.

"Yes. See if we can fast-track that warrant. I want to get to Dunbar before the sun goes down." He picked up keys and gloves. Arresting a military hero who happened to be an Army Ranger would be hard enough. He didn't want to do it in the dark.

❉ ❉ ❉

An unknown car stood in the drive when the two troopers pulled in.

"Whose is that?" McAllister asked, nodding toward the car, a maroon Chevy Malibu.

"Don't know. Maybe something Framingham laid his hands on." Be nice if he could kill two birds with one stone.

Duncan surveyed the car, which had one of those jar candle-shaped air fresheners hanging from the rearview. "Hold on." He went back to his car and ran the plate through the computer. Then he returned to where McAllister crouched behind the Malibu.

"Got it?" she asked, *sotto voce.*

"Registered to Sharon Glessner," Duncan said, also keeping his voice low.

"A hostage. Fabulous." She reached the Sig at her duty belt.

"Possibly. I'll take the front. You go in the back." Duncan removed his own gun from its holster. His hands felt damp inside his gloves. He told Sally he didn't regret his actions last fall and he didn't. But the thought of walking into another hostage situation triggered some bad memories.

McAllister glanced at him. "You okay? I can do this alone. Or we can get someone else."

"If I can't handle it, I have no business wearing a uniform. Let's go." Pushing aside his thoughts, he approached the front door. McAllister moved to the back, swift and silent as a cat.

He pounded on the door. "Bob Trenton. State police. We have a warrant for your arrest." No sound came from inside. He reached out and turned the door handle. Unlocked.

Moving as quietly as he could, gun at the ready, Duncan entered the house. He heard a dry sob from the back room. Gun up, he entered.

Turned out Bob Trenton was at home. He stood behind a middle-aged woman whose brown hair showed silver at the roots, her face ashen. Mostly because Trenton had a checked bandanna around her throat like a noose.

"Drop it and let her go." Duncan held his Sig steady. He might have a shot. He might not. Where was McAllister?

"I'd rather not," Trenton said. "Much more effective where it is."

"I said let her go." Duncan's hands felt like they shook,

but the Sig stayed rock still.

"And if I don't?" Trenton asked, voice monotone. "You won't shoot. You might hit Mrs. Glessner. My poor cleaning lady."

Glessner squeaked.

Trenton pulled the bandanna tighter, causing her to wince. "I think maybe you're the one who should stand aside. Let me go and she doesn't get hurt."

The woman sobbed. "Maybe you'd better do what he says," she said, voice choked.

"Let her go." Duncan repeated his command. Out of the corner of his eye, he saw movement and assumed McAllister had made her entrance.

"No."

"Let her go." McAllister rounded the corner, her own Sig drawn and aimed directly at Trenton. "Now. Do it!"

McAllister had proved herself a good trooper. She'd do what she had to do. But she was too young to have to deal with shooting a man. "Trenton. You're a decorated soldier. A war hero." Trenton didn't speak. No sweat dotted his forehead and his hands didn't move.

"I assume you're here because you think I murdered two men. Or was somehow involved. If I did that, why wouldn't I kill a third time?" Trenton sneered at Duncan, then glanced at McAllister. "You miss and there'll be hell to pay."

McAllister had the better shot. She'd most likely miss Glessner. Then again, stressful situation, anything could happen. "Capshaw and Naif were threats. Mrs. Glessner? Not so much. That's the difference. You're trained to take out the threat. If anyone is endangering you now, it's me and Trooper McAllister. Be the man who won that Silver Star. Let her go."

Trenton didn't move. Just as Duncan thought they'd stand there, locked in a stalemate forever, Trenton let one end of the bandanna fall, and released his hostage. He held his hands out to his sides. Glessner screamed and bolted for Duncan.

"Go in the living room, ma'am. We'll be with you in a second. McAllister. Cuff him." He held his gun steady, as McAllister pulled out her cuffs and secured Trenton's hands. Only when Duncan knew the suspect had been secured did he holster his gun with an internal sigh of relief.

CHAPTER THIRTY-NINE

Duncan sent McAllister to tend to Mrs. Glessner while he took care of Trenton. "Why'd you do it?"

"You were sure I wasn't going to hurt her," Trenton said, voice calm. "Very trusting of you."

"You're not a killer."

Trenton chuckled, a dry, mirthless sound. "Yet you're arresting me for the murders of Steve Naif and Ray Capshaw."

"I told you. They wronged you. Mrs. Glessner didn't."

McAllister returned. "She called her son and will come down later to give a formal statement. She told me she was cleaning and talking to Trenton when we pulled up. He saw the patrol cars and the next thing you know, he restrained her with the bandanna." McAllister shook her head. "How do you go from hero to murder?"

"Ask me that again when the system you pledged your life to turns its back on you." Trenton snapped, his voice unmistakably bitter.

Trenton hadn't gotten a pension upon his discharge, Duncan remembered. A discharge that hadn't been his fault. Maybe the epilepsy had been triggered by something in combat. Trenton sure thought he was entitled to something. "It doesn't give you the right to steal and commit murder."

"Oh? Tell me, did you play cops and robbers as a kid?

Duncan nodded.

"Bet all you ever wanted to do was be a cop. Me, all I wanted to be was an Army Ranger. Like my dad." Trenton's eyes flashed. "The day I put on that beret he was so damn proud. Then I got epilepsy. I couldn't continue to serve after that."

"That make you mad?" McAllister asked.

"Not nearly as mad as when they told me I didn't qualify for a pension." Trenton sneered. "Bad enough the thing I loved most was taken from me. Those insensitive bastards in Washington didn't even feel they had to compensate me for the years I'd given in the line of duty."

Because those were the rules, which Trenton knew when he signed up. Duncan doubted pointing that out would help. Like most military, Trenton served out of love of country. Feeling like he was abandoned by the powers that be would quickly turn that love into a much darker emotion. "Mark Framingham."

"What about him" Trenton asked. "He's a pussy."

"How was he involved? Something with real estate sales? Was he your money cleaner?"

Trenton only smiled, a wry, twisted gesture.

"I—" McAllister started to speak.

Duncan's phone rang and he answered it without looking at the caller ID. "Duncan."

"Trooper Duncan. Detective Polencarz."

"Detective. We just took Bob Trenton into custody."

"Good to know, but not why I'm calling. Mark Framingham."

"What about him?"

"He's gone. Neighbors say he left this morning. Car's missing. He didn't go to work."

Duncan stared at Trenton. "Thanks." He ended the call. "Where is Mark Framingham?"

Trenton's smile grew.

"Boss—" McAllister tried again.

"McAllister, get a BOLO out on Framingham and his car."

"Jim!"

Duncan looked at her, slightly surprised at her insistence. "What?"

"Trenton's car is gone. He drives a silver Civic, right? That's not what's in the garage. It's a dark gray BMW." She jerked her head at Trenton. "I ran the plate. It's Framingham's."

No wonder she'd been insistent. The switch would make Framingham harder to find. Trenton didn't have E-ZPass. No way of checking if he got on or off the Turnpike. "Put the BOLO out for Trenton's Civic."

"Already done."

Duncan took a step closer to the handcuffed accountant. "I'm going to ask you one more time. Where is Mark Framingham?"

"He came by earlier. Said he wanted to get out of town. I let him take my car if he promised to keep his trap shut." Trenton shrugged. "Like I said, he's a pussy. But where he went? I really couldn't tell you."

Duncan pushed Trenton toward the front of the house. "McAllister. Put him in the car. Then get the dog."

"What are we going to do with him?" she asked.

"I'll call the kennel from last time." It was doubtful Trenton would be allowed to take his service dog to jail, but there had to be organizations that would take the Golden.

McAllister left with the prisoner and Duncan examined the room. The bare spots without dust where the military memorabilia once stood. Had Trenton put it away because he knew his actions didn't become a Ranger? "Heaven has no rage like love to hatred turned," he said to the empty room.

Empty except for McAllister, who had returned promptly and held a leash in her hand. "Sounds pretty deep for you, Boss."

"Just a line I remembered from high school. Something about how the strength of our hate is comparable to the strength of our love, or something like that."

"Like Trenton?"

"Yup." He shook himself. "Let's go." They would stake out Framingham's vacation condo. Look for relatives in the area. Framingham was an attorney, not a survivalist. It shouldn't be that hard to track him down.

* * *

The snow continued. At least six inches had fallen since noon. Duncan got Trenton to the Uniontown booking station, where they processed him and took him to holding. There would be a territorial fight over who had the right to try him first, Fayette County or Pittsburgh. That, however, was an argument for someone above Duncan's rank and pay grade. Afterward, he and McAllister went back to the barracks. Four o'clock, way past the end of their shift. Still no sign of Framingham. They'd find him. Time for Duncan to go home and put his feet up.

McAllister finished off her paperwork and exchanged her state Ford keys for her own. She faced him. "Plenty early, Boss. What are you going to do with your night?"

It had been a while since he'd had a Friday night off. He didn't want to spend it with Rizzo. "Not sure. I thought about going home, but maybe I'll go out for dinner, or drinks. Something," he said.

McAllister grinned. "Would this dinner and drinks involve company?"

"Perhaps." Why the hell not? He'd told Sally later. Well, it was later.

"Enjoy your night. Whatever you do." McAllister winked. "I'm sure your evening will be more exciting than mine."

Duncan watched her retreating back, then grabbed his cell phone. The call to Sally's cell immediately went to voicemail. Again? The silence unnerved him. Then again, perhaps her recent absences had backed up her work and she was still at the office. He dialed the public defender's office. The secretary, Doris, answered.

"I'm looking for Sally Castle. Is she in?"

"Ms. Castle called in sick today. Migraine."

"Thanks. I'll try her at home." He hung up. Puzzling. Under usual circumstances, Sally, a workaholic like him, rarely took sick time. Recent circumstances had been anything but normal and she still hadn't missed much. It had to be one hell of a migraine. Perhaps she silenced her phone. Even if that was the case, he didn't think she'd go an entire day without checking it.

Something could be wrong with her cell, but doubtful. She lived in Uniontown, not Confluence. Nevertheless, he dialed her apartment. After half-a-dozen rings, her answering machine picked up. "Hi, this is Sally. Can't come to the phone right now, but leave a message. Thanks."

Perhaps she was sleeping or taking a bubble bath. "Sally, it's Jim. I have tonight off and wondered if you'd want to get together for a late dinner or drinks. Nothing fancy. Dex's? If you're feeling better, that is. Give me a call on my cell. Talk to you later."

She was sleeping off the migraine meds. Or she'd gone out. Or she was in the shower. Or the bath. Lots of reasons she wouldn't answer her phone. Still, better safe than sorry. He'd go in to Uniontown and check on her. If she was home and feeling better, who knew what would happen. If not…well, he didn't want to think about that scenario.

* * *

Everything about the trailer turned out to be shoddy. Even the toilet paper. But Sally didn't have time to worry about that. Stamping her feet to warm them, she rooted through her purse.

The first thing she noticed was that her cell phone was gone. Shit. Benjamin must have taken it. Second, no wonder that pocket knife he had looked familiar. It was hers. She'd taken it from the emergency kit in her car when she went into the bar. Benjamin swiped that, too.

Okay, strike Plan A. She popped two aspirin for the last of her headache. The circulation had returned to her arms and legs, but she still felt painfully weak. If Benjamin had her knife, she had a better chance of getting injured than succeeding. While she could convince him to let her use the facilities, such as they were, he probably wouldn't be as accommodating about the emergency room.

She'd return to the main room and stall while she thought of a Plan B. It had to be late in the afternoon. People would miss her. Friday night, Jim would call. As far as he knew, Sally's stalker was still out there and unknown. Jim would not let the weekend go by without checking in. Worst case scenario, she'd have to keep Benjamin talking and hope the snow continued long enough to keep them in one place until the cavalry arrived.

Back in the trailer's main space, she put her purse back by her coat. "Much better."

"I was just about to come get you." Benjamin pulled aside the cheap plastic blinds. "Why is it still snowing?"

Outside, Sally could see the solid wall of white. Local weather this morning called for flurries and perhaps an inch or two of accumulation. Judging by the snow mounded at the side of the window, they'd missed that one by a mile.

The little space heater labored mightily, keeping the air chilly but tolerable. Sally didn't want to think what would happen if they didn't have it. Where were they? The cheap trailer, furnished like a field office, argued for a construction site. She leaned against the desk. "Tell me, what's the plan? Why haven't we left already?" His answers might provide something she could use to escape.

"I wanted to." Benjamin prowled along the wall, occasionally twitching aside the blinds as though he expected the snow to cease. "After we left the bar, I had to get rid of your car. Then I had to stop at your apartment. By the time I did all that, the snow was really coming down and I was afraid to drive far. I heard a guy at the courthouse talking about this place. I figured it would be a good spot to wait until the weather cleared up, but it hasn't."

"It's the time of year for it." Her head didn't throb as much, but the details of last night were fuzzy. She remembered getting together with the others from the courthouse. She'd shooed off Glenda and agreed to stay with Benjamin. That had been a mistake. But then, nothing. Nothing specific. "By the way, have you seen my phone?"

His eyes narrowed. "Why do you want your phone?"

"I don't want to use it. But you know how much those things cost. It's not in my purse. I hope I didn't leave it at the bar." If she could get it back, maybe she could still dial 911 and they could use the phone's GPS signal to find her.

Benjamin patted his front pants pocket. "Don't worry, it's right here."

Eww. Her pick-pocket skills weren't good enough to retrieve it without notice and she had no desire to put her hand in that particular pocket anyway. "Oh good. Where are we going to go? After the snow stops, I mean."

He stopped his manic pacing. "You're awfully full of questions. Don't you want to go with me? Maybe I should chance the snow, knock you out again—"

"No, no. Nothing like that." He really had made a total break with reality. If he had been one of her clients, she would be arguing for a psychiatric evaluation. Being the hostage cut back on her sympathy, though. "I'm curious, that's all. I want to know what's ahead for us."

"You'll see. All in good time." He went back over to the blinds and pulled them aside again. "I wasn't planning on snow like this. We might have to spend another night here. I don't like it. Staying means more chance we could be found. But if we run off the road, we'll definitely be found."

Another night in the cold. On the other hand, more time for her to be missed and found. And more time to come up with Plan B. In a situation like this, every extra minute counted.

CHAPTER FORTY

Duncan worked first shift Saturday. The snow piled at least eight inches deep when he woke up. Rizzo loved it, refusing to come in until Duncan dragged him in by the collar. The forecast called for another eight inches to a foot over the course of the day. Fantastic. Duncan didn't bother with much shoveling. He'd only have to do it again later.

Sally hadn't called last night. She hadn't answered his knock when he stopped either. Sleeping? She wouldn't go out alone. Not with Framingham on the loose. Then again, her car hadn't been in its usual spot. Maybe she'd gone somewhere with a friend or family.

Saturday morning didn't bring a call either. Not even a text. Troubling. His shift stayed busy enough in the early hours he didn't have time for an unscheduled run to Union-town, but he called her around ten. "Sally, it's me. Let me know how you're doing, okay? I'm worried." He stared at his phone. It was completely unlike Sally not to return his calls. He'd make a point to stop by her apartment after he got off. Make sure she was okay. She wouldn't be driving anywhere on a day like this. He hoped.

He was on the road when his radio crackled around eleven. McAllister. "Duncan, you out there?"

He keyed the mic. "Yeah. What's up?"

"You need to come out Route 51, northbound. Half a mile past The Bar Fly. Now." Her voice seethed with tension.

"You sound worked up."

"Just get out here."

She hadn't sounded that wound up when she found Framingham's car. What was so sensitive she wouldn't put it over the air? But he trusted the younger trooper. If McAllister said to meet her, he'd go. He turned on his siren and lights, and headed out to The Bar Fly. The roads, slick with half-melted snow, foiled his desire for speed. Snow swirled, little frozen dust-devils, but he pushed it as much as he could.

As he approached, he saw McAllister's Ford parked behind a pile of snow under a leafless tree alongside the road. As he got closer, he saw that she had cleared off the sides and back of a car, but not enough to identify the make. He unconsciously went on alert. McAllister wouldn't hesitate to put a simple abandoned vehicle on the airwaves. There was only one reason to insist he come out to see it.

Sure enough, when he parked behind the car and saw the license plate, a cleared square in the sea of white, his throat seized up. Sally's.

He got out. "Status."

"Motorist called in an abandoned vehicle. It's been here since last night. I brushed off enough snow to ascertain it was empty and see the plate. When I ran the number and saw the name on the registration, I called you." Her tight voice matched the skin by her eyes. None of her usual banter, either.

"Any sign of Ms. Castle?"

"Car's empty. No purse. At first I thought out of gas or a flat. But the tank is three-quarters full and the tires are good. There's a Triple-A sticker on the bumper and they haven't been called. I checked. Keys were left in the ignition."

"Does it start?" Duncan grabbed a pair of nitrile gloves from his belt, professionalism kicking in. Someone was in a world of hurt if they'd harmed Sally. McAllister walked beside him, an expression on her face that must have matched his own.

"I started it and let it run for three minutes. I also

checked the engine compartment. Nothing seems wrong. There's more." McAllister headed for the car, her own gloves already in place.

Sally was supposed to be at home. In Uniontown. What was her car doing out here without her in it?

McAllister opened the trunk. "Her briefcase is here." She picked it up and she undid the snaps. "It's full of papers. Would Ms. Castle walk away from her car and leave her unlocked briefcase behind?"

"No." Duncan inspected the case. He didn't see any damage, every paper neatly tucked away. He pulled out his phone and dialed the barracks to get Gerrity's home number. "Mr. Gerrity," he said, when the lawyer answered. "Trooper Duncan. Your secretary told me Ms. Castle called in sick yesterday. Did you know about that?"

"Yes, I do keep on top of where my assistants are."

"Have you talked to Ms. Castle?"

"No, I left her alone. Migraines are killer. She didn't need me bothering her if her head was splitting."

"Does she get migraines often?" In over a year, Duncan hadn't known her to, but he didn't know everything.

"Not that I'm aware of. But there's a first time for everything."

"If she calls you, please let me know. And tell her to call me." He recited his cell number.

"Is there something wrong?"

"I don't know. Thanks." He snapped the phone shut.

McAllister bit her lip. "I don't think she'd have walked off without her keys. Not if it was mechanical problems. She'd have stayed put and called Triple-A."

"Agreed." He looked up and down the road, but saw nothing. "Stay and get someone to tow the car. I'll be in touch."

"Like hell," McAllister said. "I'll call someone to get the car. Then I'll go back to the barracks and check overnight accident reports. Where are you going?"

"I'm calling someone to meet me at the courthouse. Then I'm going to her apartment."

"I'll meet you there when I'm done. If she's in trouble, I want to help."

Framingham missing. Now Sally was gone, too. Duncan didn't think he'd find anything at the public defender's office, but that was the last place he knew Sally had been seen. Maybe this would be the one time in his investigative life that coincidence did exist and she was indeed at home. If so, migraine or not, she would open that door. If someone had stolen her car, Sally either didn't know or didn't report it. But if it hadn't been stolen, he wanted to know why it was out on Route 51 without her.

* * *

Weak winter sunlight leaked through the battered blinds. Sally had dozed on and off through the night. She needed to stay strong and that meant she needed sleep. But it was damned uncomfortable to sleep in the chair, and the stress and the nagging chill combined to make it impossible to sleep soundly.

Benjamin had taken her Thursday night. He said something about it being almost a day when she woke, so that had been Friday late afternoon or evening. Another night gone and now it was Saturday. Thursday evening through Saturday morning with no contact. Someone had to be looking for her.

Benjamin allowed her to scrounge some bottled water and a few energy bars from the desk, but it wasn't enough. Her stomach gnawed at her spine. She studied him as she chewed. "I know you didn't plan to be here this long. Does this throw you off? Are we going to have to stop for supplies?" If so, she would find a way to communicate her predicament. Come hell or high water.

She had recovered enough strength that she probably

could take him, except for that knife. While she doubted Benjamin knew how to use it as a weapon, that fact only made him more likely to injure her. Not less. She'd managed to keep him emotionally stable. If her attack failed, who knew what that would do to his already fragile psyche. "Are we going to be able to leave soon?" she asked. She knew the answer. The sky beyond the window stretched a sullen gray, but the snow, big thick flakes, looked like it had slowed. She was on borrowed time.

"We'll be able to leave as soon as it's dark," he said. "I don't want anyone to notice a car leaving a construction site that is supposed to be closed."

He might be psycho, but still capable of thinking. Maybe she could find a crack in his plan. She frowned, faking concern.

"What? You look worried. The roads will be clear."

"It's not that. I'm thinking what will happen when I don't show up to work on Monday. That'll be two days of unexplained absence in a row. It could ruin everything." If only another storm would roll in, but it was too much to ask Mother Nature to do Sally's work for her. But while Jim may not have been able to contact her during the week because of work, he'd call tonight or tomorrow. He had to.

He tapped the pocket carrying her phone. "You don't password protect your phone. I sent an email to your office saying you had a migraine to cover Friday. Then I sent another telling them there was an emergency with your mom and you'd be in Pittsburgh next week."

She ground her teeth. Damn it. But she never requested leave by email. Would Doris be surprised enough to mention that to someone? "But what if my mom gets suspicious? I always call her on Sunday nights. If I miss a call she'll get worried and come looking for me. You don't know how tenacious she can be."

"She's in Pittsburgh, right? By the time she gets really worked up and contacts someone down here it'll be too late."

Which might be true. She tried another tactic. "I hate to

be a Nervous Nelly, but you really don't think someone will find us?"

"Doubtful." He grinned faintly, but it disappeared in a trace. "The construction site is shut down for a long weekend because of snow. No one is going to come here until Monday. We'll be gone by then."

How many construction sites were near Uniontown? Sally could only think of one, on the edge of the city heading south on 119 past the Laurel Highlands Middle School. About a mile beyond the city limits. "But what if someone sees my car?"

"Don't you remember? Your car isn't here." Benjamin's voice, smug, yet delighted, made him sound like a small child who'd done some marvelously clever, complex trick. "I left it on the side of the road heading north. That should throw people off. You see, I've been planning this for a while."

A rock settled in Sally's stomach as she realized that the plan, while not perfect, might be good enough to deceive people for the weekend. Jim's distrust of anything unusual was her best hope.

CHAPTER FORTY-ONE

Duncan called ahead to have someone meet him at the courthouse. As it turned out, that someone was Doris.

"Mr. Gerrity said you needed to look in the office," she said. "I hope nothing is wrong."

"I don't know. Yesterday, Ms. Castle allegedly called in sick. Did you speak with her?"

"She did, but I didn't talk to her."

"Why not?"

"She sent an email. It said she had a migraine, had taken some medicine, and was crawling back to bed."

Duncan frowned. Communicating important information via email wasn't Sally's style. "She'll be in Monday?"

"Oh no," Doris said and flipped on the lights.

"Why not?"

"Later in the day I received another email saying she'll be out all next week."

"Why?"

"She said she had to go to Pittsburgh. Emergency medical issues with her mother." Doris frowned. "I hope everything is okay. I mean, the last thing Ms. Castle needs with all this stalker nonsense is problems with her mother."

A shiver that had nothing to do with the snow outside ran down Duncan's spine. "Show me her office."

Doris wrung her hands. "I can't. There are legal files in there. It would be a breach of confidentiality."

"I don't want to look at the paper. I want to see her

office."

Doris shook her head. "I can't. Not that I don't want to, of course. But I can't let you back there without a warrant or court order."

Concerned for Sally, but still keeping to the office's ethics. Sally would approve. Duncan found it beyond maddening. "Tell me, is it usual for Ms. Castle to schedule leave via email?" Was Doris irritated at being called to the office on a Saturday and that was why she proved difficult?

"Well...office policy says it's acceptable for an employee to request leave, sick or vacation, via email."

"I didn't ask if it was acceptable." He maintained a professional tone but his irritation grew. The situation felt very, very wrong. "I asked if it was Ms. Castle's usual practice to request leave via email."

Doris cracked. "No, it isn't. Sally calls, no matter how sick she is. It must be a hellacious migraine. She didn't even email from her computer. It came from her iPhone. I could tell by the signature."

"Tell me this doesn't feel wrong to you." He held her gaze. "I need to get into that office."

"I can't, I'm sorry." She looked around. "You know, they never turn the heat on for the weekend. I'm chilly. I'm going to get a cup of coffee and I'll be back." She gave him a heavy look.

In other words, she would give him an opportunity to snoop. She'd have plausible deniability if he got caught. She told him not to.

But before either of them could move, a FedEx delivery man came in the door carrying an envelope. "Hey, Doris. I figured I'd have to get someone else to sign for these. Overnight. Lucky you're here."

"Bit of an emergency," Doris said, reaching for the signature tablet. "Where's Benjamin?"

"Who the hell knows," the guy said, shaking his head. "Blew off yesterday and today. The boss is pissed as hell. I'd be surprised if old Benjy has a job come Monday."

Duncan stared at the deliveryman. "Who?"

"Benjy. Benjy Kardys. He has the courthouse delivery route."

"Benjamin," Doris said, correcting him. "He doesn't like Benjy. Ms. Castle is always telling people."

Kardys. The one he'd questioned after the flower delivery that contained the dead rodent and who later showed up at Sally's apartment. The guy Duncan dismissed after speaking to the FedEx supervisor. "What did you say?"

"Benjamin," Doris said. "Ms. Castle—"

"Not you. Him." Duncan pointed at the deliveryman. "Kardys ditched work?"

"Today and yesterday," the man said. "Not like him. He loves this route."

They assumed the flowers had been tampered with prior to reaching FedEx. Maybe not. If Kardys was always at the courthouse, he'd be placed to deliver the other notes, too. That substitute delivery route. Possible he'd volunteered for the assignment because he knew it would put him at Sally's home. The night he'd responded to the graffiti, the Uniontown officer had reported a couple had seen a delivery guy with some boxes earlier.

Now he was missing. Just like Sally and Framingham.

His phone rang. Alan Porter, another trooper. "Yeah, Porter."

"You're looking for Mark Framingham, right?"

"You got him?"

"Idiot slid off the road on Route 41 heading south. Driving too fast in a car with bald tires."

Right, Framingham had taken Trenton's car for his escape. Probably not in the best shape after sitting in a garage. "He hurt?"

"Not seriously. Bumps and bruises. Nice golf-ball on his forehead. Where do you want him?"

"By a stroke of luck I'm at the county courthouse. Bring him to the jail. He and I need to have a chat." Duncan ended the call. Then he dialed McAllister. "Run a complete background on a Benjamin Kardys. I want everything, even something as minor as spitting on the sidewalk. Bring what you find with you when you meet me." He spelled Kardys's name.

God bless McAllister, she didn't waste time asking why. "On it."

Ending the call, he turned to Doris. "Change of plans. I want you to check Ms. Castle's office. Every shred of paper. Then call me." He handed her a business card.

"What if I don't find anything?" she asked.

"Call me anyway. On my cell, not the barracks. Got it?" He didn't wait for a response. Leaving Doris and the FedEx guy, he pushed out of the office and headed toward the bridge to the jail. Benjamin Kardys. Mark Framingham. One of them knew where Sally was. And Duncan was pretty damn sure it wouldn't turn out to be her home.

❋ ❋ ❋

What time was it? Sally glanced at the clock on the wall. Noon. They wouldn't stay another night. Benjamin jittered like he'd shotgunned six cups of coffee. He wanted to be gone. She had to do something, but what? If she kept talking it might give her an idea. "I've been thinking. Everything was from you, the notes, the flowers with the rat."

"Yes. The rat sucked, but you had been a rat. I forgive you, though."

He forgave her? "I'm really sorry if I hurt you. But what did I do?"

"You went out with another guy."

Jim? "I had no idea you were so attached. What did I do to deserve it?"

"You're always nice. You always use my full name, like I want people to. You say hi, ask how I'm doing. You care." He turned, his expression confident. "Do you know why I don't like to be called Benjy?"

Sally shook her head.

"My last girlfriend called me that. It was her nickname for me. We were close. I was going to ask her to marry me." He shrugged.

"What happened?"

"She didn't get me. I tried to make her understand. I even got her an expensive present, though I couldn't afford it."

The thought came in a flash. "The chocolate."

"Her favorite, imported from France. That stuff's mega expensive, you know?"

"You stole it." The item of low value. Low monetary value, that is.

"Yes. After that, she filed a restraining order. Her brother told me that if I came around their house any more he'd hurt me. That's when I left home and came to Uniontown."

He had a history of unstable behavior. "When was that?" Sally suspected she knew.

"Oh, about three, no four, years ago."

Three or four years. The amount of time Benjamin had been in Uniontown. She'd been right. He had the mental maturity of a teenager. Unfortunately, no one had noticed it, or cared, until now. "You also graffitied my door. That was horrible."

He nodded. "I'm sorry. But I offered to go with you to that dinner and you went with another guy. I guess the jealousy made me to it. I came back later to get rid of it, but the guy chased me away." He leaned against the cheap table. "Honestly, it surprised me he wasn't more suspicious when he questioned me about the flowers."

Because Jim had no reason to be suspicious. Not at that point. Was he suspicious now? God, she hoped so. She had to keep stalling. "Okay, I get all that. But why didn't you just ask me to come with you now? Why drug and kidnap me?"

"You might have said no," Benjamin said, shrugging. "I couldn't bear that, Sally. I couldn't. But I also knew I'd never be able to force you to go with me. Not if you were conscious and able to fight. That was the mistake I made with Daphne."

"What mistake?"

"I never acted. I just talked. I wasn't going to lose you. That's why I had the drugs."

"What'd you use?"

"Rohypnol. Half a tablet in your wine. I miscalculated. You stayed unconscious longer than I planned. We should have left late Friday night. The snow wasn't as bad then, but I didn't want you to wake up on the way. You'd panic, and I wouldn't be able to explain things in a car. Make you see."

Roofies. In alcohol. No wonder she'd passed out quickly. "Why didn't you leave Uniontown immediately?"

"I had to get rid of your car. That took time, leaving it, transferring you to my car, making sure we weren't seen." He pulled out a small bag that looked like a mini medical case, set it on the table, and rummaged inside, his back to her. "Then you were out. Then the snow. I don't want to hurt you, Sally. Believe me. I love you."

"But we're done with that, right? You see you don't have to do that. You could really injure me with more drugs."

"I wish that were true. But you still might change your mind and I can't risk it. I'm afraid I'm going to have to knock you out one more time." He turned from the table. In his hand were a syringe and a bottle of something clear.

She couldn't wait for Jim. She had to do something and fast.

"I've calculated the dosage very carefully. You'll be awake in a few hours, but you won't notice when we leave."

CHAPTER FORTY-TWO

Duncan paced the interrogation room at the county jail. He paused occasionally to glance at the clock, where the hands seemed stuck at one. What could take this damn long? On one hand, Porter didn't say where on Route 41 Framingham had been apprehended. Then again, it couldn't be far if Porter could bring his prisoner to Union-town.

Damn snow. That had to be the delay. Duncan had looked out the window on his way to the jail. White powder drifted deep against the windows, the cold air pushed out from the glass. The rate of snowfall changed every fifteen minutes.

The door opened to admit Porter, who hustled in Framingham, his hands cuffed in front of him. "Sit down," Porter said. "Trooper Duncan wants to talk to you."

Framingham stopped. "Can't you take me to booking and get it over with? I've got nothing to say."

"I said sit." Porter applied pressure to Framingham's shoulder until he dropped into the chair.

"Or else you'll kick the shit out of me?" Framingham asked with a sneer.

Duncan took the seat opposite. "You've been watching too many bad movies."

Framingham touched the bandage on his forehead. "That asshole Trenton. He probably gave me the damn car expecting me to wreck it. He's trying to pin this on me, isn't he?

Asshole. Well, try again. I'm not talking."

"I don't give a damn about your dealings with Trenton. That's out of my hands." Duncan leaned forward. "I'm more interested in the location of Sally Castle. Where is she?"

"How the hell should I know?" Framingham touched the bandage again and winced. "Can I at least get some ice?"

"Focus, Framingham, focus." Duncan snapped his fingers. "Are you sure you don't know where Sally Castle is? Because if you're lying, it's not going to go well. The DA will tack a kidnapping charge on top of everything else. Now is not the time to play games."

Framingham's gaze snapped forward, wound forgotten. "Kidnapping? Whoa, whoa, whoa. Who said anything about kidnapping?"

"I did."

"I don't know anything about that. Swear to God. As your buddy here can tell you, no one else was in the car with me. Hard to hide a grown woman in a Civic."

Duncan glanced up at Porter, who solemnly shook his head. Sally hadn't been in the car and there'd been no sign of her. Porter wouldn't bury the lead like that. Duncan stood. "Then we're done here."

"Wait a damn minute." Framingham tried to follow suit, but Porter kept him in place. "You bring me here, ask me one question, and that's it?"

Duncan zipped up his jacket. No more wasting time. "I'll let the DA handle it from here. Conspiracy, theft, murder, threatening a public defender, kidnapping…I hope you're not planning on taking any vacations any time soon."

"Screw that." This time Framingham succeeded in getting to his feet. "I take it back. I'll talk about anything you want. I'll tell you all about the whole freaking scheme. I am not going down for kidnapping. And I am sure as hell not getting stuck with a murder charge." His face was red, his breaths deep and angry.

Duncan looked at Porter again. Was Framingham guilty

of the conspiracy and theft? Almost certainly. Kidnapping? Duncan was less sure of that. And growing even less so by the second. Damn it. "Trooper Porter can take your statement. I have things to do." He left the room, hoping against hope that McAllister had found something.

* * *

Duncan took the stairs to Sally's apartment two at a time. The superintendent hadn't answered the door and McAllister hadn't arrived. "Sally, it's Jim. Open up." He knocked on the door, but heard nothing from the other side. "I know if you've got a migraine you feel like shit, but open the door."

Nothing.

Footsteps on the stairs. He turned. McAllister. "She not answering?" she asked, jerking her chin at the door.

"No." Duncan knocked again, this time more of a fist pound that reverberated through the hallway. "Sally, if you're in there, say something. Even if you can't open the door." Still no answer. "You find anything?"

"Yes. You're not going to like it."

He took the paper out of her hands. Thirteen years on the job meant he had an extensive vocabulary of profanity. Most of the time he never used it. He explored the outer edges now.

"Your reaction is much milder than mine," McAllister said, unzipping her jacket. "Order of protection filed against Benjamin Kardys in Lehigh County by Daphne Burgett four and a half years ago. Burgett was his girlfriend. According to the order, he started sending disturbing notes, each one professing undying love. He has a record. Misdemeanor larceny from a high-end French chocolatier. Burgett's favorite. At his sentencing, Kardys claimed he did it out of love."

The pages crumpled as Duncan clutched them, reading. "Community service and time served. God I'm such an idiot."

"How would you connect such a penny ante charge to the current situation? Anyway, it all came to a head when he said he wanted to take Burgett away from it all. She filed the restraining order. He completed his community service for the theft and left for Fayette County."

"How did FedEx miss this on a background check?"

"They didn't. I called the FedEx facility where Kardys worked. They subcontract their checks. All they get is a pass-fail decision."

"The background company didn't consider this grounds for failure?"

"I called them, too. The conditions are different depending on the position. Applicants are asked if they have any felony convictions, not misdemeanors. Often, the mere existence of a restraining order isn't enough as long as the applicant discloses it, which he did. It was a temporary order, in a different county, and near its expiration date."

Duncan's swearing took on a sulfurous tone.

"When I was growing up, my neighbor taught me to curse in Polish," McAllister said, but there was no humor in her voice. "When you run out of English words, I can give you some Polish ones."

"Go get the building super. We need to get this damn door open."

McAllister nodded and jogged down the stairs.

He pounded again. "Sally, it's Jim. If you're in there, open up." He used his best crowd-control voice, which echoed in the empty hallway.

The door across the hall opened. "She's not there. Stop yelling." A man in a T-shirt and sweats leaned against the doorframe. The vacationing neighbors had returned.

Duncan flashed his badge. "How do you know she's not there?"

"We got back Thursday night. Didn't see her car." The guy shrugged. "We don't have assigned spots, but every tenant has a usual parking spot and hers was empty. Her car wasn't there this morning when I got home, either."

"When did you get home Thursday?"

"Late, maybe ten. I worked graveyard Friday and got home around six this morning. Come to think of it, I didn't see her car last night when I left, either." He lifted an eyebrow. "What's up?"

Duncan looked over as McAllister mounted the stairs, superintendent in tow. "Get this door open. Now."

"Hey, shouldn't you have a warrant?" the neighbor asked.

"We have reason to believe that Ms. Castle is inside and in peril," McAllister said. "I suggest you get back into your apartment, sir, and let us do our job." She unholstered her Sig and nodded to Duncan. "Right behind you."

Duncan drew his weapon as the superintendent unlocked the door and scurried away. Gun ready, Duncan pushed the door open. "Sally, you in there?" he asked.

The dark apartment had a cold, unoccupied feel. The troopers moved from room to room, weapons up. All unnecessary. No one was home.

❅ ❅ ❅

"Where'd you get the syringe?" Sally tried to keep her voice steady, but it wavered as she looked at Benjamin's hand.

"A guy I know is a vet. I stole it from him. You wouldn't believe how hard that was." Benjamin flicked the needle.

"You can't be serious. This isn't necessary."

"Yes, I am. I can tell you aren't completely convinced, Sally. I think it'll be better if you sleep through the travel period and we start fresh when we get to our destination."

A complete break with reality. The syringe changed everything. "Listen to me. You don't want to do this."

"You're right, I don't. But I want us to be together and if this is the only way then that's how it is." Benjamin set down the syringe and took a few steps toward her.

She held her ground. Don't set him off. "Where are we going? I might not have the right clothes."

He shrugged. "I took care of that, too. I stopped at your apartment. Easy, since I had your keys. Anyway, I have a place in West Virginia. We can stay there."

"West Virginia is pretty close. I'm not sure that'll work. What happens after a week? I know you said you covered that, but emails and texts won't work forever." Don't move. Keep him calm.

He shrugged. "By then there will be a lot of places we could be."

"You don't plan to stay in West Virginia?"

"Oh no." He rubbed his hands together. The adrenaline coursing through her kept her warm, but edges of Benjamin's lips looked blue. The space heater must be losing its battle, which meant the temperature outside had dropped. "We'll go someplace else by the end of the week. By the time you or I are missed, the trail will be as cold as the air in this place."

"They'll look for your car."

"It's not a Ferrari. They can't check every Nissan out there. Trust me, we'll be safe and able to be together. Unlike Daphne, you're going to see this is perfect. Deep down, you already know it or else you wouldn't have been so nice and thoughtful. You'd have treated me like all the rest. But you didn't. You're different and that's why I love you. And you love me. You only need time to realize it."

Stockholm syndrome. It had hit Patty Hearst. Why not Sally?

He reached out to her. Instinctively, she flinched and staggered back, colliding with the workbench against the wall.

His expression hardened. "Sally, you're making me angry. I've been reasonable, haven't I? We're having such a good talk. Maybe it's an act. Are you playing with me?"

She couldn't wait for Jim any more. Snow or not, bare

feet or not, she had to make a break for it and hope she saw a car along the road before she froze. But first she had to get past Benjamin, who stood between her and the door. She patted the surface behind her. There. Under a pile of paper something that felt like a length of wooden doweling. Any stick was a weapon. Her fingers closed around it.

"I'm sorry, Benjamin. I can't go with you." She stepped forward and swung the rod.

And missed.

Fully committed to the swing, her momentum carried her forward past Benjamin as he dodged. Then her toes caught in a rip in the thin trailer carpeting and she stumbled. Her knees hit the floor and her forehead banged against the metal desk, a shock of pain that momentarily stunned her, leaving her motionless.

Benjamin's weight pinned her as he knelt on her back and pried the dowel rod out of her numb fingers. "I knew it was too easy. You're just like all the others. Just like Daphne." His voice turned hard, almost brittle. Completely unlike his usual soft tones. "But I'm not giving up. Not this time." With surprising strength, he clamped her hands together and pulled her off the floor.

Through the fading haze of pain, she heard him fumble with a box. Then he forced her back into the chair. A moment later, she heard the familiar sound of another zip tie binding her hands behind her by the wrist.

She lashed out with a foot and collided with his thigh. He grunted, but being seated robbed Sally's blow of most of its force. Being barefoot didn't help, either. *You were stupid, Sally. Overconfident. Again.* Even though she thought she'd been careful this time. She fought to control her breathing. Hyperventilation wouldn't help her situation.

He grasped her ankles and used more ties to finish binding her in place. He stood. "You shouldn't have done that," he said in a voice devoid of emotion. "I had begun to think maybe the narcotics weren't necessary, but now I see they are." He seized her hair, yanking her head back. His eyes had a new, wild light in them. "I'm not letting you go, Sally. Don't you see that? Fight all you want, but it's going to happen. You and I. We're going to get away from all these distractions and build a new life. Accept it and you'll be happy."

Her eyes watered, but only partly from the pain in her head. She'd had her chance and blown it. Yet another example of poor decision making. Benjamin wasn't living in this world and nothing Sally said would bring him back. She could see it in his eyes. Her brother Jonathan once told her you always had to watch the quiet ones. Now Sally knew what he meant. She hadn't raised her voice before, hoping that staying calm would help. So much for that. "You can't do this." Where was Jim? Either he'd been taken by the ruse or he searched in vain. Either way, he'd be too late to help her. Hoping against hope someone visited the site on Saturday, she yelled with all her remaining breath. "If anyone is out there please, help me. Anyone!"

Benjamin grabbed her jaw, pinching it open hard and tears came to her eyes. "I wish you hadn't done that." He pulled a bandanna from his pocket and forced it into her mouth. He looked at the clock. "Two-thirty. It'll take eight hours to get to my cabin in this weather. No good you waking up in the car and fussing. I'll give you the drugs at four. You'll sleep for a while and by the time you wake we'll have started our life together. It'll be fantastic. I promise."

CHAPTER FORTY-THREE

Duncan holstered his Sig. "Glove up," he said. "Start searching."

"What are we looking for?" McAllister pulled on a pair of nitrile gloves.

"Anything that might tell us where she went." The living room appeared its tidy self, nothing on the floor, quilt thrown across the sofa. He went into the kitchen and opened the fridge. "Half a jug of milk, Thursday expiration. She'd get rid of that if she was leaving for a week." Every item in the fridge stood in its place, unchanged from the last time he'd looked.

McAllister flipped through the mail. "This is all from Wednesday. She didn't retrieve Thursday's or Friday's mail. She never made it home."

Duncan opened the hall closet. One empty hanger. A North Face jacket hung next to a light spring trench coat and a rain slicker.

"Which one is missing?" McAllister looked around him.

He thought. "Cashmere overcoat, the one she wears to work and for dress." He shut the door.

"Not what I'd expect her to wear on a trip to see her mother."

He bent to pull a white cord from behind the hall table. "She'd take her phone charger, though."

"Unless she has a spare." McAllister looked into the bathroom. "Shampoo and conditioner are gone, body wash is here." She opened the medicine cabinet and frowned. "Mascara here, eyeliner gone."

"Let me guess. Not what you'd expect."

She closed the cabinet door. "Mascara's a makeup essential. I don't wear a lot of makeup unless I'm going out, but I do put on mascara. Even for a shift."

He moved to the back-room office. McAllister followed. The black laptop sat on the desk. "It's password-protected, but try this." He scribbled the password on a slip of paper. "I'll look in the bedroom." He went across the hall, opened the closet, and stared.

Sally's organizational tendencies extended to her closet. The racks held blouses and skirts. His chest tightened as he recognized the red blouse and black skirt she'd worn to the Le Mont. Formal wear on the left, business attire in the center, casual clothes on the right. The orderliness extended to shoes, too. Heels in the left-hand column of cubbies, casual shoes on the right.

McAllister entered the room holding the laptop. "I'm not having much luck here. She must have changed the password. Got a guess for me?"

"Never mind. We don't have time. Look at this closet." He stepped back to give McAllister a better look.

She set the computer on the bed and scanned the closet's interior. "She's only missing business attire. Three pairs of jeans here. Blouses gone, not sweaters. Sneakers left behind, one pair of heels missing. Wrong clothes for a trip to take care of your mother."

He stepped to the dresser and yanked open the underwear drawer. No panties, but at least four bras. He tried to visualize the contents when he'd searched the night of the graffiti. The contents of the drawer seemed thin. "Does this look right to you?"

She looked in the drawer. "Not unless everything is in the wash." She looked in a wicker hamper. "Empty. She might be at the laundromat now, but..."

"Why wouldn't she answer her phone?"

McAllister looked around. "I won't ask how you knew this is where she kept her undergarments."

Duncan slammed the drawer shut.

McAllister continued. "Someone wanted clothes to be missing to support the fact that she was out of town, but he took the wrong ones." She looked at him, her eyes troubled. "Boss, take a deep breath. You're going to bust something. Now what?"

"We put out a BOLO for Kardys's car?"

"Did that as soon as I saw the background check. Nothing yet. The snow isn't helping."

"Put it out again, increased urgency. Extend it to all surrounding counties. By now, he could be in Maryland, Ohio, or West Virginia. Send it to those state agencies, too. You have Kardys's photo?"

McAllister patted her shirt pocket.

"Show it to other building residents and the super. See if someone has seen him."

"He's the stalker. Damn." McAllister's face took on a stony set.

"Sally saw a delivery man. Sweet, but harmless. I should have known. Too focused on Framingham."

"I was too, for God's sake. He had the best motive."

"When we find Kardys, stay out of my way. Get someone from the Uniontown PD to guard this door." He turned and stalked toward the living room.

"Will do," McAllister said, grabbing her radio and following. "But fair warning. If he's hurt her, I'll kill the son-of-a-bitch myself."

*　*　*

Her jaw hurt. The gag leached every bit of water from her mouth, making her simultaneously dry-mouthed and drooly. Her facial muscles had cramped hours ago. Her jaw would be stuck this way before it was all over.

Jim, where are you?

She had no idea what time it was. Heavy clouds obscured the sky. Mid-afternoon? Generally, the winter sun had completely set by the time she got home at six. It hadn't. Yet.

Across the room, Benjamin puttered with the syringe and bottle, humming tunelessly. The sound made the hair on her neck stand up. As soon as it was dark, she knew he'd jam that needle into her and make his getaway. It seemed crazy, his scheme that if they were only alone for enough time she'd come to realize she loved him. He truly believed it. Why had she not seen this? Because he'd been like a younger brother. Or that kid in high school, the one she'd thought of when Benjamin proposed taking her to the charity dinner. It was easy to overlook the fact that Benjamin was older. Physically. Mentally, a shrink would most likely say Benjamin operated about at the level of that high school kid, which led him to form irrational attachments.

She was a professional. Why hadn't she seen it? Because she'd been distracted, by Jim and by Mark.

Her stomach churned and growled, reminding her that all she'd had to eat lately were a few energy bars. Would Benjamin feed her before doping her up? Would an empty stomach mess with the drug? No, wasn't that why doctors had you fast before surgery? So you didn't get sick. Had he properly calculated the dose of whatever he intended to use? Who said the drug for an animal would work the same way for a human? Would it send her into a coma or worse?

She squeezed her eyes shut and hot tears leaked out. She needed Jim to get there. Soon.

✳ ✳ ✳

They re-issued the be-on-the-lookout for Benjamin Kardys and his Nissan to every police department within a hundred miles and the FBI, just in case they'd crossed state lines. Then they hit the highways of Fayette County. Duncan knew even with such a large number of eyeballs looking it would take time to find Kardys and Sally. He chafed at the delay. Around three o'clock, Nicols tentatively suggested he and McAllister go home and let others take care of the search. He took one look at both troopers and dropped the suggestion.

After leaving Sally's apartment, Duncan had gone to all her usual spots. Dex's. The local laundromat. The bar she liked to go to at the end of the week to hang out with her court-house friends and enjoy a glass of local wine. No Sally.

At about three-thirty, the radio crackled and Porter's voice came through. "Duncan, you copy? Sighting on that Nissan."

Duncan snatched the radio. "Where?"

"Construction site south of Uniontown. Route 119, just past the middle school. Someone who works at the site drove by. No one should be there, but he saw a car. He wanted to get home before the next belt of snow came through, so he didn't stop, but he did call. Could be your guy."

"Copy that." He thought a moment. He should take backup. He keyed the mic. "McAllister, you there?"

"I am and I heard. On my way to the site now. ETA ten minutes." A siren wailed in the background. McAllister didn't intend to waste time.

"Meet you there." Duncan replaced his radio, flipped on the lights and siren, and hung a U-turn to head south on 119. The snow had tapered off. But even if it stayed blizzard condi-tions, it wouldn't matter to him. With any luck, Kardys would be cautious and wait for dark. Again, totally irrelevant. With both Duncan and McAllister on his tail, there was no place for him to hide.

CHAPTER FORTY-FOUR

Benjamin inserted the syringe into the bottle and carefully drew a small amount of clear fluid. He cleared the air in the syringe and a few drops spurted from the needle.

This was it. She was out of options. Bound and gagged, all of her defense knowledge would be useless, any ability to talk Benjamin back to some semblance of reality long gone. She doubted Benjamin would remove the gag before jabbing her anyway.

Jim remained as her only hope and that hope was fading fast. Not his fault. He was one guy and Pennsylvania was a big state. They'd look outside Uniontown first. Assuming they looked at all.

As if in response to her thoughts, Benjamin turned. "Not long now. I don't want to give you too much. There could be complications and we don't want that right? How about some water?"

She made a *hmph* sound through the gag. It would get the cloth out of her mouth.

He came over with a bottle of water and pried the gag out, the fabric crusted with dried saliva. "I'll hold the bottle. I'd untie your hands, but you've already shown me you're not ready for that."

She gulped down some water, not caring it spilled down her front. "Benjamin, listen. Please," she said, her voice gravelly from disuse and dryness. She hated the fact she had been reduced to begging. But logic hadn't worked. Neither had force. Begging was all she had left, but in her gut she knew it was useless. "You don't want to do this."

"But I do. Oh Sally." He pushed some hair from her face. "Don't worry. It will all work out. I promise."

Stress and hunger made her too tired to nip at his fingers. "Benjamin, for the love of God, please. I don't want you to get hurt. That's what's going to happen. Maybe both of us. You don't want that, right?"

"No one's going to get hurt. I'll take you away from all the distractions. You'll realize your feelings run deeper. Everything is going to work out."

"No, it's not. You have to listen to me." She gulped and licked away the tears running down her cheeks onto her lips. "You keep saying you don't want to hurt me, but you're hurting me now." She didn't even need to fake crying. If that didn't crack Benjamin's shell of insanity, nothing would. "I'm begging you, for your sake and mine, don't do it. Just let me go."

He smiled and patted her cheek. "You're sweet, Sally. That's how I know you love me. You might not realize it now, but you will." He stood and checked his watch. "Almost time." He fetched the syringe and an alcohol swab, laying both on the table ready for use.

Sally slumped, as much as she could while held to the chair as failure stared at her. She'd failed. She would be unconscious before too much longer and there was nothing she could do about it. Jim hadn't made it.

Then her ears picked up a noise. The crunch of tires on snow. One car. Maybe two. She was sure of it.

❋ ❋ ❋

Duncan killed the engine and let his cruiser roll to a halt in the parking lot. No lights or siren. No sense alerting Kardys to his presence. Through the gloom, he made out one car in front of the warehouse. He got out and went up to it, thankful for the thick snow that muffled his steps. He brushed away the accumulation from the plate, Kardys's number burned in his memory. It matched.

They were still here. Unless they'd left in another vehicle. Duncan surveyed the lot. In the faint light, he thought he made out one set of tracks, although they were mostly filled in by now. A trailer-style office sat next to the warehouse, windows covered by plastic blinds. He swore he saw a light inside, faint but there.

McAllister rolled in and parked next to Duncan's patrol car. She'd also shut off her engine, lights, and siren. "See anything?" she asked when she joined him, voice low.

"Car's over there." He pointed. "Lights in the trailer."

"Less visibility in the warehouse."

"I think he's in the trailer."

McAllister shifted her focus to the shabby trailer. "Seems it would be less secure."

"Perhaps, but he's tried misdirection at every turn. This is the final attempt." He walked toward the trailer, breaking a path. His breath fogged before him in the afternoon dusk. A few flakes of snow swirled through the air. "Maybe Kardys thought while the attention was on the warehouse, he'd be able to sneak out." Duncan drew his Sig.

"I'm right behind you," McAllister said, drawing her own weapon. "You sure you want to go in guns out with Ms. Castle in there?"

"Yes. I don't know if he's armed."

"We going to knock?"

"That's the plan." He pounded on the door. "State police. Benjamin Kardys. We know you're in there. Open up and come out slow, hands in sight."

No response. He pounded again. "Pennsylvania state police. We have the trailer surrounded. Surrender yourself now, before this gets messy." He waited. No sound came from within the trailer.

❋ ❋ ❋

Benjamin clutched the syringe and whipped around. A few drops of liquid fell from the needle. His face scrunched, his expression between confusion and panic.

Sally's heartbeat sped up, as impossible as that seemed. Jim had made it after all, against the odds. Just like he promised he would. But he wouldn't come in pell-mell. Not if he thought she'd be in danger. For all he knew, Benjamin held a gun to her head. Jim wouldn't risk her safety.

Except Sally knew Benjamin to be unarmed. Sure, he had the syringe in his hand, and he might stick her in desperation, but it was now or never. She had to let Jim know it was okay to come in.

"State police. This is your final warning. Open the door." Jim's voice reverberated through the trailer.

Sally summoned what remained of her strength. "Jim!" She heaved herself to the side, toppling the chair.

The door exploded and Benjamin screamed.

❋ ❋ ❋

The shoddy door didn't stand a chance.

As soon as Duncan heard Sally's cry, he planted his heel on the door's handle and delivered a push kick that sent slivers of plastic flying as the door crashed inward. He charged into the trailer, McAllister behind him.

Kardys cowered against the wall, a syringe at his feet. Sally, in a toppled chair, struggled in the corner on the floor. "Hold still, Sally. I'll get there. Benjamin Kardys, you're under arrest. McAllister, cuff him." He held his gun steady.

"What about Ms. Castle?" McAllister holstered her Sig and pulled out her handcuffs.

"Not until the suspect is secure and we're sure the threat

is removed."

As soon as the metal touched his wrists, Kardys turned into a banshee, but McAllister handled him. Not all that gently, either.

Duncan holstered his gun, rushed over to Sally, and righted the chair. "You okay? Stupid question. Hang on." He fumbled a knife out of his belt.

Sally gasped, head back, her cheeks shiny with tears.

"Sally, tell them it's a mistake. Tell them. I wasn't going to hurt you." Kardys sobbed and struggled against the cuffs as McAllister herded him to the door.

"Get him the hell out of here," Duncan said, eyes on Sally. "Mind the syringe." The side of her face was red where it had struck the floor, but he couldn't see any obvious wounds. Her eyes stayed wide, face bloodless. He brushed hair off her cheek.

She tilted her head forward to look at him. "Took you long enough." Her voice quaked, but the attempted joke meant she maintained a spark of fight.

"Had some communication problems. Hold still." With a quick stroke, he cut the zip ties around her ankles and leaned over to slice the one on her wrists.

Her arms fell to her side. Then she wrapped them around herself and bent forward.

"No rush. Sit there until you're ready to move."

She sat up. "I'm not sitting in this chair one more freaking minute."

Duncan looked around and pulled the wheeled chair from behind the desk. Then he helped Sally change her seat. Her skin felt clammy and her feet had a bluish cast. He picked one up. Ice. He warmed his hands with his breath, then applied them to her skin.

"Oh, God. That's better." She hadn't unwrapped her arms, but she shook anyway. "Ow, ow."

"What?"

"It feels like my arms and legs are filled with shards of

glass."

The effects of the blood returning to normal circulation on top of the shock. He needed to get her a blanket, but there was nothing in the office. Through the windows, he saw the blue strobe lights of the ambulance he'd called. They'd be able to take care of her. "Where are your shoes?"

"Over there. With my coat." She nodded toward a workbench. On it lay the brown cashmere coat and a pair of black heeled shoes.

He picked one up and looked at it. "You wore these in this weather?"

"It wasn't snowing Thursday night when I left work. Next time I'll be sure to wear my get-kidnapped-in-the-snow shoes."

Still trying to crack jokes. He had a powerful urge to kiss her. But now was not the time for any of that. She needed care. He draped the coat over her shoulders. "Snow's pretty deep. I can carry you to the ambulance."

"Any press here?"

Duncan looked. "Can't tell. But I wouldn't be surprised to see a crew from the *Herald* if someone monitors county emergency communications. I'm sure they do. Not every day an assistant public defender gets kidnapped."

"Then I'll walk. The last thing I need is my mother seeing a picture of me being carried out of a trailer. She'll have kittens." Her hand trembled as she pushed back her hair and she smushed her feet into the shoes. "By the way, impressive entrance. You scared the shit out of Benjamin."

"Good. I meant to. It's been a long day. I will say I don't think I've ever made a suspect squeal like that before. He hurt you?" The answer better be no.

She shook her head. "Not really. Jim...I think he's deranged. Really. Something in his psyche is just broken. I'd feel sorry for him if I wasn't the target."

"Sally, don't even think—"

"No worries. He won't be able to get defense from the

public defender. At least not this office, since it would be a conflict. But if anyone isn't all there, it's Benjamin Kardys." She stood, wobbled, then fell back toward the chair.

He grabbed her arm. "Whatever. Not your problem and not mine. Let's get you to the EMTs."

"I don't need EMTs." She grabbed a handful of his jacket and clutched him as they walked to the door. "I need to go home and get warm."

"Tough shit. You're getting checked out. Don't think I won't carry you over there. And if they say hospital, you're going. Period." He led her down the rickety steps. McAllister had tucked Kardys into the backseat of her Ford and the ambulance stood off to the side, medics at the ready. The snow had picked up again, all the vehicle lights illuminating the whirling flakes of white.

Sally didn't offer much resistance, a result of relief, resignation, or exhaustion. Or maybe a combination of all three. One thing was for certain. He wasn't letting her out of his sight after the medics cleared her. Not for the rest of the night.

* * *

Once Duncan deposited Sally safely in the paramedics' care, he patted Sally's knee. "I'll be right back."

"Promise?" Worry lit her eyes as she clutched the shock blanket draped around her.

"Promise. If they don't take you to the hospital, someone has to drive you home. I won't let that someone be anyone but me or McAllister. Since she has charge of Kardys, that leaves me." He flashed a smile and headed over to McAllister. The adrenaline of crashing the trailer had faded, leaving him limp. He couldn't quit yet. He still had a job to do.

"She okay?" McAllister nodded to the ambulance.

"She will be." He looked in the backseat at Kardys. His voice barely penetrated the glass, tears streaming down his face. "Good thing you're taking him in. He'd accidentally bang his head off the top of the car if I had to do it."

"No, he wouldn't. You're better than that." She glanced at the prisoner. "I wish he would invoke his right to be silent, though. I'm tired of listening to him whine." McAllister shook her head. "Anyway, I'll run him in, then I'm clocking out. After that I'm calling Tommy-boy. I need a drink."

Duncan grinned at her.

"Shut up."

"I didn't say anything."

"Also, I radioed Nicols. He said take your time. Make sure Ms. Castle gets home safe. She can give her statement tomorrow."

"Thanks for the assist. You didn't have to, but I'm glad you did. You earned that drink and more."

"I told you. Anytime. You'll always be the boss." She got into the car and pulled out, headed toward Uniontown.

McAllister was good people. And Nicols, too. As Duncan headed back to the ambulance, a sense of gratitude and relief almost overwhelmed him.

The paramedic looked up at the sound of footsteps. "Heart rate and respiration are normal. She's slightly dehydrated and body temp is low, but not low enough for hypothermia," he said in response to the unasked question.

"Shock?" Duncan asked.

"A bit, but what she really needs is warmth, water, and rest." The medic faced Sally. "We can take you in to the hospital if you'd like."

Sally pulled her coat tighter and the blanket slid off. "No. I want to go home and sleep in my own bed. Right after I give my statement."

"The statement can wait," Duncan said. "You'll remember more if you give your brain some time to process the events."

"You either take it now or you wait until at least Monday. Because I'm going to sleep tomorrow, too. The whole damn day." She climbed down from the ambulance.

"I'll talk to Nicols and see what he says, but I don't think he'll fuss over waiting two days. I've gotta turn the Ford in, though." He held out a hand to steady her. "We'll get your stuff back to you as soon as possible. You might not care about the makeup, but you'll probably want the underwear."

"Don't tell me you've been in my drawers."

He shrugged. Probably the wrong time to tease her about the double entendre.

"Keep it. I can go shopping for new stuff."

"Okay, but I can't do it until Monday evening. I'm on duty until three." He raised an eyebrow at her puzzled frown. "I wasn't kidding. I'm not letting you out of my sight. Not any time soon."

"That'll make things interesting." She tried to laugh, but tears welled in her eyes.

He took her elbow. He eased her into the cruiser's front seat. Then he got in and fastened his seatbelt.

Sally clicked hers on. "How'd you find me?"

Duncan pulled out as he recapped the search for her. "So yes. I've been in your underwear again." He cracked a grin.

Her laugh sounded weak, but it was a laugh. "Both times in less than ideal circumstances. Let's change that for next time, shall we?"

✳ ✳ ✳

The dull gray of the day gave way to night. Sally dragged herself up her apartment stairs, Jim ready to catch her if she fell. True to his word, he had not left her side and he'd been the rock she'd leaned on ever since he'd burst through that door.

At the barracks, Nicols had talked her out of giving an immediate statement, convincing her to go home and rest. Then Jim had clocked out and driven her back to Uniontown in his Jeep. She asked about Rizzo, knowing he'd want to take care of his loyal companion, but he assured her Rizzo was in capable hands with Marge. "You're my concern right now."

Unlocking her door and entering the dark space felt like falling into a warm, comforting pool. "Cup of tea?" Jim locked the door behind him.

"Yes, ch—"

"Chamomile. No sugar. Got it."

She almost dropped the overcoat on the floor, but she hung it up. Such a nice coat, but after the last few days she wanted to burn it. In fact, she wanted to throw every stitch of clothing she was wearing into a pile, soak it with lighter fluid, and drop a match. Her mother would be horrified. Too bad. "Do I have clean clothes here or did he take everything? Or did you guys?"

"You have clothes," Jim said as he laid his hat on the front table. "Kardys didn't take everything. In fact, he took the wrong things. We didn't need to confiscate your entire wardrobe for evidence, just the things he packed. If you want to get changed, go. I'll make the tea."

She went to her room and slipped on an oversized t-shirt and her last pair of yoga pants. She must have looked like death warmed over, but she got the typical once-over response when she returned to the kitchen.

"Your tea." He handed her a mug. "I don't think you should be alone tonight. Anyone I can call for you? Your sister, maybe? A friend?"

"Would you stay? Please?" The words came out before she could stop them. Friends and family were all to the good, but she wanted Jim for company that night. Not for sex. He would make her feel safer than anyone else she knew and she desperately needed to feel safe at that moment. His day had been exhausting in its own way and he probably wanted nothing more than to go home to his dog. She didn't regret asking though. He said never to hold back what she needed.

He hesitated. "All right, but no funny business, missy. I need to go secure my gear." He paused at the door and turned.

"You know, we're making a habit of this. I should buy you a gun safe. Maybe for your birthday."

"How romantic."

"But practical." He winked. "Lock up behind me. I'll be right back."

She sipped her tea while she waited. Less than five minutes later, Jim returned and she let him in. He held a small gym bag in his hand. "What's in the bag?"

"Found a pair of sweats that aren't too filthy," he said, double-checking the locks. "The other thing I should do if we keep making this a thing. Leave some clothing at your place. I'm not that fond of sleeping in my uniform." He stroked her cheek.

Her faced heated and she knew it was bright red.

"Be right back," he said, voice soft.

After he'd changed and returned, he sat on the couch. She set her mug on the coffee table and snuggled against him. He wrapped his arm around her and she sagged into his solid warmth, feeling the last of the tension leave her. Then he pulled her favorite quilt around her and tucked in the edges. "Better?" he asked.

"Much." Her eyelids drooped. "Thanks for having my back," she whispered.

Jim's grip on her arm tightened, his voice sounding like it came through a tunnel. "Always."

THE END

ACKNOWLEDGEMENTS

I can't believe I'm writing acknowledgements
for my second book.

First off, a million thanks to my husband, Paul. You've never stopped believing in me and it means more than I can say.

Once again, a million thanks to my critique partners – Annette Dashofy, Jeff Boarts, and Tamara Girardi. You guys ask the tough questions, never let me skimp on the work, and never let me take the easy path. That in addition to finding all my reused words, overuse of "was" and all the other little stuff. You all rock.

Thanks to my technical advisors, Corporal Brian Carpenter of the Pennsylvania State Police and Chuck Van Keuren of the Allegheny County Public Defender. Also, Lee Lofland and his wonderful staff at Writer's Police Academy. WPA is where I learned about fire scene investigation. As always, any technical errors in these pages are strictly my own.

I would not be here without the support of so many wonderful people in Sisters in Crime and Pennwriters. Both organizations give access to great education and wonderful support networks. Thanks also to my blogmates at Mysteristas. Love you all!

ABOUT THE AUTHOR

Liz Milliron is the author of The Laurel Highlands Mysteries series about a Pennsylvania State Trooper and a Fayette County assistant public defender in the scenic Laurel Highlands. The first in the series, *Root of All Evil*, was released in August, 2018. Liz's short fiction has appeared in multiple anthologies, including *Murder Most Historical* and the Anthony-award-winning *Blood on the Bayou*. She is a past president of the Pittsburgh chapter of Sisters in Crime, as well as a member of Pennwriters and International Thriller Writers. She lives outside Pittsburgh with her husband, two teens, and a retired-racer greyhound.

Erin McClain Studio

LizMilliron.com